# 81
# minutes
# to
# Maddening

a novel
by
Bill Dughaille

Based on notes made in a school exercise book found on a London Underground platform at Heathrow airport.

# London Underground: Piccadilly Line

**Towards Heathrow airport**

Cockfosters
Oakwood
Southgate
Arnos Grove
Bounds Green
Wood Green
Turnpike Lane
Manor House
Finsbury Park
Arsenal
Holloway Road
Caledonian Road
King's Cross St. Pancras
Russell Square
Holborn
Covent Garden
Leicester Square
Piccadilly Circus
Green Park
Hyde Park Corner
Knightsbridge
South Kensington
Gloucester Road
Earl's Court
Barons Court
Hammersmith
Turnham Green
Acton Town

Ealing Common
North Ealing
Park Royal
Alperton
Sudbury Town
Sudbury Hill
South Harrow
Rayners Lane
Eastcote
Ruislip Manor
Ruislip
Ickenham
Hillingdon
Uxbridge

South Ealing
Northfields
Boston Manor
Osterley
Hounslow East
Hounslow Central
Hounslow West
Hatton Cross
Heathrow T 1-2-3 ⟶ Heathrow T4
Heathrow T5

# Bounds Green Tube Station, North London, 05h45

*Estimated time to Heathrow Terminal Five: 1hr 21 minutes*

*Estimated time to Wood Green tube station: 2 minutes*

Bounds Green. North London. United Kingdom. 05h45.

5.45 a.m. in the morning.

Late summer. Up there, above ground. Sun was coming up when I got here.

Friday.

So, that's where I am.

What am I?

I am a teacher.

I know many things.

I know there's a plaque on the wall of Bounds Green tube station, towards the end of the platform. It commemorates the lives of sixteen Belgians and three British civilians killed by German bombs on the 13th October 1944. I know this because I've just spent fifteen minutes reading it waiting for this tube to arrive.

No names. No ages. No occupations. No individuals. Just nationalities. And those quite possibly wrong.

So.

There are things that I don't know, but I can find out. The capital of Georgia.

There are things I will probably never know. Why we exist. Why I had to wait so long for a tube. Why it isn't going anywhere now that it's finally arrived. It's been ten minutes since it finally arrived. That old saying about a watched kettle never boiling. When you're in a hurry, everybody else slows down.

There are things I could write books on without coming to a conclusion. Such as what love is in the end. What the hell is love, anyway? What bastard invented that shite?

I am a learner. There are things I am desperate to learn, but will have to wait to find out. Such as whether Maddy really is pregnant. Or if she's just making a scene.

1

She's never made a scene before. Strange that.

And, if she is pregnant, whether or not it's mine.

Of course it's bloody mine. She's mad as a bunch of frogs, but she wouldn't cheat on me. Kill me, yes, cheat on me, no.

Which is why I'm sitting in a stationary Piccadilly Line tube. On my way to Heathrow.

Underground. Under tons of earth, rock and rubbish. In a metal tube. Along with hundreds of other people whose lives will never matter. Trying with great fortitude to restrain my temper and refrain from screaming at the tube driver to get a fucking move on. Because when the only thing left in your life is to stop the woman you love leaving you you want that life to start right away.

There's a missing comma there somewhere.

That's from When Harry met Sally, sort of. The bit about things starting straight away.

Still, plenty of time. Her flight doesn't leave for another couple of hours. 13h30, to be more precise.

Half one. P.M.

Less check in. Must get there before check in. Or is it going through security?

Going through security, of course, you can check in any time you like. Eagles, Hotel California. More or less.

How long do you have to do that before your flight? Australia. Long distance. Only place further is Kiwi-country. Then there's bag drop. Two, three hours these days? Let's say two hours. That means I've got to get there by 11h30. Plenty of time.

Teacher, learner. What else am I?

I am also a doer.

And what I am going to do is I am going to fucking kill her.

When I get there.

Why am I writing this? Writing this keeps my mind occupied. Sometimes you just have to lock on to something and ignore everything else.

When the train arrived and I got on I realised I must have been talking to myself. Reading that plaque and talking to myself. Asking those dead people what they had hoped to get out of life. Whether their girlfriends had given them so much grief. That would explain why the rest of the train is jam packed while I've got some space to myself. They must think I'm nuts. It's either that or the brace on my wrist or the bruises on my face are putting people off.

I must have sat staring into space for a few minutes, I guess, when I got on board, the way you do when you've been rushing everywhere and suddenly you're sitting down and there's nothing to do but sit and wait for someone else to drive you somewhere. Or to not drive you anywhere.

Then I realised that some arsehole was standing next to me and looking pointedly at the bag I had dropped onto the seat next to me.

I dragged it onto my lap to let them sit down and looked at it. It's my general purpose bag for carrying pretty much anything. Something sticking out from the zipper reminded me that it now contained some homework my pupils had turned in a few days before. I took a couple of the worn exercise books out. Marking them would give me something to do. Sometimes one needs a completely pointless exercise to keep you occupied. There didn't seem much else to do apart from mutter dark curses to myself. Generally scare the crap out of the other passengers, just like any normal London nutter.

I made sure I took out the exercise books which had pretty pictures on the covers. That invariably meant they belonged to the girls, which also meant there was a slight chance they might have put some effort into it. Even then I only managed three exercise books before admitting defeat.

They were all as crap as each other.

Asking bored teenagers to physically write two hundred words was pretty over-optimistic.

And I couldn't stop thinking about Maddy.

Rude things. Very rude things. She deserves it.

So, I began writing rude comments in the exercise books.

They deserve it.

Then I came across Sharon bloody Runny-nose's effort. It had a pretty picture of a broken heart on the cover. I gave that double barrels of sarcasm.

Then I decided I'd make notes of precisely what I was going to tell that bloody woman when I get my hands on her.

Maddy, not Sharon Runny-nose.

And I want to make a note of what really happened. An accurate account, not Maddy's version.

So, for whom am I writing this? For you, my unborn child, I suppose. No, I don't suppose. I am writing this for you, Danny. I'll let you read it when you reach twenty-one.

Maybe twenty-six.

When you're first thinking of getting married, maybe.

Before you start dating.

The story of what really happened between your bloody mother and I.

Why "Danny"? I don't know. I don't know if you're going to be a boy or girl. But I like the name Danny. It could be either – Danielle or Daniel.

Your grandfather's name is Daniel. My dad. Everybody calls him Danny, which is just as well. He can't fucking stand the name Daniel.

I'll presume that you are going to be a daughter. Somehow I feel sure that you will be. Otherwise I'll have to change a few things before I read this to you.

Remind me never to teach you shorthand.

Ah, doors closing, we're moving at long bloody last. 05h50. We should be at Heathrow in about an hour and a quarter. Plenty of time.

No. Cancel that. We aren't actually moving. Doors have opened again. No need to panic. Still plenty of time.

Enough time for me to stop your bloody infuriating mother flying back to Australia. And out of my life. And you out of mine.

I could fly after her, if I don't get there in time. But I'm buggered if I'm going to let her make me chase her all the way around the planet. There are limits to what love can make you do, and that's one. Australia is just a continent too far.

Besides which I just don't fancy the idea of knocking on the door of every O'Connor in Melbourne and asking, 'Do you have a daughter named Madeleine who has just returned pregnant from the UK, because I'm the father and, ooh, that is a lovely large shotgun you're holding, isn't it?'

He's a policeman, so maybe not a shotgun, maybe a revolver or pistol or machine gun or something. A howitzer. Possibly Big Bertha. Who knows. Can't see the size making a difference.

The doors are beeping, the doors are closing again, and, yes, we're on our way.

05h52.

Be there by 07h10 at the very latest. 07h30 if there are any more delays.

Fuck knows what I'm going to say when I get hold of her.

Got to think of something.

"Before you hit me again ..." might be a start.

Danny, as a teacher I have learned to moderate my language. They don't like you saying fuck every second word. Not in public, anyway. And they aren't that hot on it in the classroom.

Whatever you do, Danny, never become a teacher. The pupils are thick as bricks and their parents have the intellectual capabilities of stupid wet concrete.

And as for the so-called educational experts they send around every so often to make sure we're doing our jobs properly, well, to call them arseholes would be a compliment. Just not to arseholes, which actually do have a purpose in life. And all I can say for the minister of education is that she isn't as bad as the minister for health, but then no-one is. No one could be.

I don't know if it will still be there by the time you read this, Danny, but there's a video by a group called Fascinating Aida on the Internet which pretty well describes things in the current education industry. I must warn you, it contains the odd swearword.

I'm assuming I won't have to explain to you what the Internet is. Or by the time you read this, was.

Anyway.

Trying to avoid swearing in front of pupils and their parents does tend to make you go the other way and start using words they won't understand. In the parents' case it's to confuse them – I can be so fucking polite it's painful. My favourite word is "promising".

'Mrs Nincompoop, Tracey is a very promising pupil.'

'She is? Oh, I'm so glad to hear it, Tracey, did you hear what – Tracey! Get your fucking hands away from that boy and get over fucking here right fucking now!'

Yes, Mrs Nincompoop, Tracy is very promising.

She promised to do her homework. She couldn't be arsed.

She promised to be punctual. She's always late.

She promised to abide by the school dress code. She goes around looking like a two-dollar whore.

In fact she promises to be just another non-entity in a world of redundant replicas.

For the pupils it's supposed to introduce them to unusual aspects of the English language. Doesn't work, of course. The one day I told a class, 'There's a difference between illegal and illicit. Who knows what it is?' One of the cheeky little buggers at the back piped up with 'What does illegal mean, please sir?' Their definition of illegal is getting caught.

Probably served me bloody right for trying to be fucking clever.

Talking about moderating language, I'm not sure, judging from the looks I'm getting, whether I'm not still saying some things out loud. There's an elderly Asian woman sitting directly opposite me hugging her bag to her skinny chest, staring at me with her eyes popping out, while reciting whatever her religion considers the best prayer to murmur just before you're strangled by a crazy white man.

The others around her are either pretending to be sleeping or have their faces stuck in that free advert they call a newspaper that they give out in the mornings.

I suppose I am a bit crazed at the moment. But you'll find out as the story goes that it's not my fault. Not all my fault.

I'll start with this morning.

Oh, fucking great. We've stopped. In the middle of the tunnel.

05h54. Five yards in two minutes.

Patience. Breathe. Swear.

That's better.

That's my advice to my pupils. More or less. Or the first two, anyway.

Not that they ever listen to me. I don't blame them. That's the official me speaking, the responsible adult. The advice I want to give them is along the lines of 'Get your miserable fucking arses out of here and do something. Carpe Diem, you little shits, Carpe Diem.'

That skinny Asian woman is looking even more nervous. I wonder if I forgot to comb my hair this morning. Nope, I remember shaving, so I must have combed my hair.

I got up early, four o'clock, to mark the homework. Well, the truth is I woke up and couldn't get back to sleep. Why will become obvious later on.

I had a cup of tea, browsed the various news websites to make sure the world outside still existed and whether it made any more sense than the day before. That took all of five minutes and the answer was no.

Yes to the world still existing, no to it making any sense.

I showered, shaved, dressed. Checked my mobile phone for messages.

There it was. A voice message from your mother. It must have come through while I was in the shower.

'Mark, I know you don't really love me. You've proved that. Bloody empirically, as you would put it. So I'm going home. I would tell you not to bother trying to find me, but I know you won't, so I won't waste my breath. Oh, by the way, I'm pregnant. And yes, it is yours. Don't worry, I know what to do. I can take care of myself. I really am all grown up, you know.'

A strangled sob.

'Goodbye, Mark. I loved you, for what it's worth. It just wasn't worth enough for you.'

Your mother is an actress. She's good. But her principal failing is not knowing where to stop. She followed that up with the allegation that I was born out of wedlock. Which, considering the position she's apparently in is a bit bloody rich. Then she mentioned the flight number.

And said that nothing would stop her leaving, not even if I turned up at Heathrow and begged her on my knees to stay.

Translation: you come to Heathrow, pal, and you've got a teensy, weensy chance.

Followed by something about she'd never marry me if I was the last bloke in the world.

Translation: bring an engagement ring with you, you bastard. A big one. With lots of diamonds. Because then I'm going to make a scene which will have everyone in the airport applauding. Young lovers re-united, an engagement and a wedding to follow.

Oh, yes, she'd have them in tears. And then she'd tell me to take all their names and addresses. So that we could invite them to the wedding. A gala event with her playing the leading role. And guess which sucker will be paying the bill.

Sorry, baby, I thought, I'm a science and maths teacher. I don't do drama. Okay, history, occasionally, when Sims is off with his bad back. And English, when Miss Phillips is off on conference again. Drama never.

That was my second thought. My first was:

Oh, shit.

Actually, I think the first thing I did was to stand there gobsmacked. Me, a father? Madeleine, pregnant? How can that be? Considering our relationship that was pretty fucking obvious.

Biology is the one subject I've never been asked to cover.

I think they suspect I might start teaching the classes more than they want them to know. Why fool yourself, the little fuckers know it already.

That, my dearest Danny, is one of the things I will be editing out of this narrative before I show it to you. I'll leave the unexpurgated version in a locker for you to read when your mother and I have passed on, and you have kids of your own. I've no doubt that you'll end up thinking that your father is a boring old inconsequential fart, just as my pupils do. But then I always thought that of my parents until I stumbled across some of my own family history. Like father like son, you could say.

Religion is another subject I'm not asked to teach. Apparently you're not supposed to use the phrases hocus-pocus and mumbo jumbo. Well, tough luck, I fucking do.

Anyway. This morning.

I immediately telephoned her mobile. She didn't answer. Somehow I knew she wasn't going to. So I had to leave a message. And that was what, exactly?

'Maddy, you're being silly, now. You've got it all wrong.'

'Maddy, we can work this out. Wait for me, I'll be there.'

'Maddy, I'm coming.'

'Maddy, I love you. I love you and only you.'

Apart from mum and dad, of course, but there's a difference between clarity and accuracy.

Oh, no. I clicked into teacher mode, Mr Arse, Sir. This is the message your dickhead of a father left:

'Maddy, I am not going to go running all over London to find you. Come home and stop being silly.'

I thought, at the time, under the circumstances, that that was a very restrained, calm and reasonable message to leave on her mobile.

Then I threw my mobile at the wall. It broke into about fifty different pieces.

I threw it really, really fucking hard.

I was really, really, fucking angry.

I was having a really, really bad week.

So, now, even if I could call her, I can't.

I wouldn't though. The first words I intend to have with your bloody mother are going to be face to face. Maybe even fist to fist.

In just over an hour I'm going to learn something about myself and the woman I fell in love with. Exactly what I'm not entirely sure.

I tell you something, though, I am going to get there on time. If I have to push this fucking tube to get it going myself.

Moving again. Finally. Be at Wood Green soon. We'd better bloody be.

I think the driver tried to say something over the intercom. Something about an earlier signal failure at Arnos Grove.

It was either that or he was singing 'I'm blowing bubbles' through a bucket of soapy water while farting the Hebrew Slaves' Chorus.

You'd think in this day and age they'd be able to come up with a system where you could actually fucking hear what the bloke was trying to say. Then again, these days people deliberately use communication channels to prevent you from knowing what's going on. Try phoning a help desk these days, a robot voice will offer you ten options, none of which you want.

Bloke next to me needs a bath badly.

The point is, Danny, that's human nature. In a word, it's fucked. Perverse.

The problem with humans is, ultimately, that they're human. Which is, to say, flawed, frail, and generally complete shits. Trust me, I know. I teach teenagers and have to listen to their parents. Technology can't cure that.

Pulling into Wood Green now. Platform looks suspiciously empty.

05h57.

Five fucking minutes. It should have taken two.

I should have used my car. Right now I could be sitting in that well known car park called the M25, all five lanes of it.

Oh, yes, I remember now, it's in for a service. The car, not the M25.

Or the last rites. Bloody thing is knackered. The car and the M25.

Five and a half hours still to play with, minimum.

I telephoned a couple of taxi firms. None of them could offer anything to Heathrow for at least an hour. By then, I reckoned, I could be half-way there. For a tenth of the cost. Not that I'm a cheapskate, but I do have to survive on a teacher's salary.

So, Danny, for what it's worth, when you read this in twenty or thirty years' time, this is the way we were, your bloody mother and I, in the late second decade of the twenty-first century of our Lord. And by the time you read this I might just be getting into Heathrow. By which time you'll have been born.

Oh, Christ, I've just had a thought.

What if you're twins?

Cockfosters
Oakwood
Southgate
Arnos Grove
● Bounds Green
○ Wood Green
Turnpike Lane
Manor House
Finsbury Park
Arsenal
Holloway Road
Caledonian Road
King's Cross St. Pancras
Russell Square
Holborn
Covent Garden
Leicester Square
Piccadilly Circus
Green Park
Hyde Park Corner
Knightsbridge
South Kensington
Gloucester Road
Earl's Court
Barons Court
Hammersmith
Turnham Green
Acton Town

Ealing Common — South Ealing
North Ealing — Northfields
Park Royal — Boston Manor
Alperton — Osterley
Sudbury Town — Hounslow East
Sudbury Hill — Hounslow Central
South Harrow — Hounslow West
Rayners Lane — Hatton Cross ←
Eastcote — Heathrow T 1-2-3 → Heathrow T4
Ruislip Manor — Heathrow T5
Ruislip
Ickenham
Hillingdon
Uxbridge

## Wood Green Tube Station

*Estimated time to Heathrow Terminal Five: 1hr 19 minutes*

*Estimated time to Turnpike Lane tube station: 2 minutes*

Wood Green: famous for not quite winning the award for being the most riotous place on a Saturday night in London two years running. I think they lost out to Tottenham by two smoking high-rises.

There's also a well know Crown Court down the road. I'm told it's very popular amongst the older relatives of the pupils I teach. It has marvellous, well laid-out gardens, with shrubbery and lawn and paved areas with seating. They like it so much they go on repeat trips on a regular basis. Some of them are even on first name terms with the judges. Someone once told me it had a winding path around it. Or was that bent? 06h00.

Plenty of time. Hours and hours

A bloke got on a few seconds ago. Leaned against the door at the end of the carriage, took out a can of beer, opened it and drank it in one go. Slowly, but one go.

I mean, I enjoy a good pint myself, but at this time in the morning?

Okay, there was that one time in Greece when I spent the whole night chatting up a blonde on the beach without getting anywhere, but that was Greece, I'd been up all night, it was sunrise, it was the beach, there were still a few beers in the cooler bag, it's the sort of thing you do. In Greece on the beach at the sunrise after you've been blown out by a beautiful woman. Doesn't everybody?

The London Underground isn't quite the same thing. Drinking alcohol is streng verboten for a start, though that was brought in to stop late-night drunkenness and violence. I'm not sure it covers passive first-light-of-day end-of-shift drinking.

Driver, we can leave now, all the pretty passengers who wanted to get off have got off, and all the pretty passengers that wanted to get on have got on. We've all admired the platform and pretty ugly it is. Yellow tiles the kind of colour you get whisking stale eggs from battery-farmed anaemic old-age chickens with two-day old baby milk vomit.

12

So, can we please, please get fucking moving?

Oh for fuck's sake.

Maybe this is really the End of Days. The Underground staff have all been taken up to heaven and all that's left is their clothes and us sinners here below. We're left to experience The great Tribulation. It sure as fuck feels that way.

Except I've known a number of them as parents of the kids I teach, and while there might have been one or two rough diamonds there sure as shit weren't any angels. And I'm pretty sure people who go on strike every five minutes don't go to heaven.

Or maybe they're all aliens who have been called back to the mother ship via one of those beaming devices.

Aliens. Yeah.

The platform tannoy has just announced that there are delays on the Piccadilly Line this morning and we might like to take our custom elsewhere if we wish to get to our destinations before we hit pensionable age. London Underground tickets will be accepted on all public transport, if that's running. That explains the empty platform. Usual Underground logic: when the trains are delayed the problem isn't the delay, it's the punters, sorry, passengers. Get rid of them and you get rid of the problem.

Me, I'm keeping my seat here like the others still on board. Trying to get to Heathrow on buses or taxis from here doesn't bear thinking about. Last time I got caught on the Underground as it went into meltdown I made the mistake of trying to catch a bus. So did seven million odd other Londoners, tourists, retired Home County types coming 'into London for the day', illegal immigrants, backpackers, psychopaths, nutters and Mildred from 74a, The Privets, Bournemouth. All of us at the bus stop I was at were able to wave as every single bus going anywhere refused to stop as they were already packed to the rafters.

I remember the passengers inside were looking terrified, rammed up against the doors. I think they wanted to get out before they were pulped like so many bananas in a blender.

There was a film like that about a bloke trapped in a telephone box. A truck came along, lifted the box onto the back, took it to an underground holding place where other telephone boxes were lined up, each with an anonymous victim inside. Dead.

Imagine getting onto a tube and all the passengers are corpses, grey and covered with cobwebs, with rats scuttling between their feet. No change there, then.

Could get a taxi to Paddington and then the Heathrow Express, but by this time whatever taxis there are will be taken. Anyway, the Heathrow Express will probably have delays too. It's called a sympathetic knock-on.

See, Danny, I've just spent two minutes without mentioning your mother. Which goes to prove that I have not entirely lost my mind over her.

Fuck.

I've suddenly realised.

I need a ring.

An engagement ring.

Or am I being incredibly optimistic and naïve?

Christ knows where I'm going to get a ring from this time of the morning.

Of course I could just engineer an argument so I don't have to propose.

Engineer an argument?

Who am I kidding.

We're going to have the biggest, loudest, fuckingest fucking argument Heathrow has ever seen.

I'll still need a ring at the end of it, mind.

I wonder if the armed police are on patrol there now. If they shoot when someone says fuck I'll be dead in three yards. Fortunately I never use the c word so they can keep the hand grenades in their pockets.

Still haven't moved from Wood Green.

06h04.

For fuck's sake.

In triplicate.

I said I don't do drama, but that isn't strictly true. A few months ago I was working on a school production of Cabaret, since I'm the only teacher who can play a piano to any level, and that isn't saying much. I'll get back to Cabaret later because that's a bit of a story on its own.

And, Danny, by the time you read this you'll know your mother sings. A lot. She lives for singing.

In theory I teach maths and science, but I also get to take English and History on the odd occasion, when the normal teachers are off sick, or pretty much any subject. It happens a lot at the school I'm now at. It's what's called an inner city comprehensive, which means something just short of a jail to keep youngsters occupied until they're old enough to go work on a building site, or become a beautician or cleaning lady. Or just unemployed, unemployable and on the dole. Or go to a grown-up's jail.

In fact the exercise books I've been marking were a history assignment I gave to the year eleven bunch. I really didn't have time to spare, so I gave them some work to do to keep them busy. It's the sort of thing that is a good argument for belief in a higher power that likes playing with human fate.

"Write 200 words on any tube station on the London Underground."

Talk about making things easy. A cut and paste from the Internet with a few words changed, or actually do some research for the more adventurous. Talk about the people who use it, the shops around it, the economy of the area, history, when was it built, who first owned it, where does it fit into classic London architecture, are there any special events it's related to. Arsenal, Wembley, Charing Cross, King's Cross, I mean, take your pick for Christ's sake.

Or, in other words, go out and actually look around you at the place you've lived in all your pathetic little lives.

Two days later and I'm stuck on the London Underground going nowhere, surrounded by tattered note books most of which have directly copied something from Wikipedia's including referencing numbers without the references.

I remember the first time that happened, one of the kids left the reference numbers in. I made the mistake of asking the pupil what the number was there for. He just shrugged and said, 'Dunno'.

Dunno.

Don't care. Don't give a shit. Our little lives don't matter anymore.

Yes they fucking do. Well, they do to me. At least mine does to me.

That was from Les Mis, by the way. The our lives bit.

Most schools ask their pupils, 'What do you want to achieve in life?' My one has given up asking 'Do you want to achieve anything in life.' They threw the question mark out with the garbage. It couldn't even be recycled. Nobody else would use it.

We had a staff meeting not too long after I first joined the school. The head asked for aspirational suggestions. The other teachers had heard that one before and didn't even pretend to be interested. Me, I'd been going through the records and had noticed the high drop-out of students. But more than that, not one single pupil appeared to have applied to go on to university. Not as far as I could see. So I suggested that try to break that particular ceiling and just get one of the shits into a university. Not actually expect them to last the distance and get a degree, I knew that was pie-in-the-sky, but it would be a start.

I don't think anyone actually laughed out loud. It was more a case of pitying and amused glances. The head said something about aspirational suggestions, not bloody miracles.

Of course it's not actually my school any more. Not for the last 48 hours. Free at last!

As I sit in the carriage at the moment, waiting for the driver to finish his fag break or whatever it is holding us up now – I'm going to have a word with him shortly, I haven't got any time to run out of – there are two youngish men with straggling beards wearing those semi-skirt things with white cotton trousers which identify them as Pakistani, or at least from that part of the world. They've got two large suitcases with them. I could be mistaken, but the other passengers nearby seem to be giving them a lot of sideways looks.

Shalmar kameez, that's what they're called.

Danny, memory is a strange thing. A few years ago a lot of people were blown up on the Underground and on a bus by some young murderers. Only a few years later – possibly more than that – and you couldn't tell. Almost as if London were a huge beast and such a thing a mere pinprick in terms of time and space. Just the relatives still keeping alive the memories of those lost just because they were in the wrong place at the wrong time. And that was just one of hundreds of tragedies. The Great Fire of London. The Blitz. The Troubles. The Civil War.

So, two people falling in love in London, your mum and I, well, it probably won't register in the history books, but it was important to us.

Is important to us.

Though judging by the looks the two kids are getting, I don't think people have really forgotten. Shalmar kameez might be the smartest thing going in Islamabad, on the Piccadilly Line tube possibly not such a hit.

They should have worn old grey tracksuits.

Funny place, London. I was born in Liverpool and mostly lived there, but I did a lot of growing up in London.

The kids I teach.

They come and go and the next lot are as bad as the last lot and no-one will ever remember them apart from their own family, and most of them don't have a lot of that either. Lust and hate in buckets, huge stale fatty fried chicken buckets and a two litre Coke to go.

Love and passion, not so much.

There are many things unfair in life, my dear Danny. Turning a man into a vaguely respectable human being and then leaving him is not unfair, it's downright unforgivable. I was enjoying my shitty life before your bloody mother turned up.

Hey, we're moving again. 06h06. Fucking marvellous. At this rate I'll get to Heathrow only about two weeks late. I might as well have taken a banana boat to bloody Australia.

Where do you start the stories of different peoples' lives, Danny?

I'll start quite a while before I met your mother. With the funeral of my Aunt Marigold last October.

If you do grow up feeling slightly different to other people, Danny, I want you to know that any element of insanity you might feel you have inherited is not entirely due to your bloody mother's malfunctioning genes.

Only 99.9999 recurring percent.

Aunt Marigold, I think, was incensed with the name she had been given at birth, and spent the rest of her life trying to prove that she was no Marigold. She died in a light air-plane crash. The plane belonged to her Egyptian lover of the moment. She flew it into a mountain in Morocco. She was drunk at the time, which, apparently, was quite an achievement in Morocco – being drunk, not flying into a mountain, I'm told that's quite easy to do. You just need a plane and a mountain. The fact that she had an Egyptian lover was quite amazing. She was sixty-eight and he was thirty, my age. The fact that she had never flown a plane before probably contributed to the accident. But Aunt Marigold never let such a technicality deter her.

She left her house in North London – Muswell Hill, a place that frowns on ostentatious wealth, but where all the babies wear designer nappies – to her niece and nephew, myself and Jenny. Jenny would have been your Aunt Jenny if she hadn't died of an overdose. But that comes later in this story. If I think about it too long I start blubbing. And I don't want to do that in public. Especially not in front of –

Bloody hell, we're almost coming into Turnpike Lane. Didn't even stop in the tunnel once.

06h10.

Arnos Grove is behind us. If that's where the signal failure was, maybe we're clear from here on in. Going bloody slow though.

Come on, driver, make this thing fly. I've got an appointment I can't afford to miss.

Or can I?

No. I can't.

Definitely not.

Your bloody mother is not leaving.

And she is not going to take you away from me.

No fucking chance.
Next question.

Cockfosters
Oakwood
Southgate
Arnos Grove
● Bounds Green
● Wood Green
○ Turnpike Lane
Manor House
Finsbury Park
Arsenal
Holloway Road
Caledonian Road
King's Cross St. Pancras
Russell Square
Holborn
Covent Garden
Leicester Square
Piccadilly Circus
Green Park
Hyde Park Corner
Knightsbridge
South Kensington
Gloucester Road
Earl's Court
Barons Court
Hammersmith
Turnham Green
Acton Town

Ealing Common          South Ealing
North Ealing           Northfields
Park Royal             Boston Manor
Alperton               Osterley
Sudbury Town           Hounslow East
Sudbury Hill           Hounslow Central
South Harrow           Hounslow West
Rayners Lane           Hatton Cross  ←
Eastcote               Heathrow T 1-2-3  →  Heathrow T4
Ruislip Manor          Heathrow T5
Ruislip
Ickenham
Hillingdon
Uxbridge

# Turnpike Lane

*Estimated time to Heathrow Terminal Five: 1hr 17 minutes*

*Estimated time to Manor House tube station: 3 minutes*

Time flies like a brick.

Fruit flies like a banana.

Still haven't left Turnpike Lane.

Plenty of time.

Still no information on what the problem is.

But.

Plenty of time.

06h15.

One time Maddy and I were on the tube, we got off at Turnpike Lane for some reason. Now I'd cycled through Turnpike Lane hundreds of times, and if you asked me what was there I couldn't tell you. Pound shops, probably. Betting shops, ditto. Identikit cheap tat nobody ever needs for poor people who can't afford it.

We came out on the left side. Maddy looks back down the road and gasps in excitement. The circus has come to town. Huge garishly painted trucks parked up on Ducketts Green a couple of hundred yards away. Yank flags flying for some reason. They aren't open for business, but posters along the railings assure us they will be shortly, and what an experience that will be!!! So Maddy makes me promise I'll take her to the circus when it does open. And of course I do. Promised her, that is. I would have promised her pink elephants if I could have.

Then we resume walking the other way. Across the road towards Wood Green. And your mother takes one look and sees an Indian shop selling scarves and saris and stuff and now she's really in her element. Suddenly she loves Turnpike Lane even more, it's a beautiful place. All these beautiful colours.

Maddy, what are you doing, you only ever wear black.

Oh don't be silly, Mark, these are gorgeous. And I don't always wear black.

Right. Just now, yesterday, the day before that, every day before that.

Make sense of that if you will.

Except I know that, if ever Maddy were to wear an Indian sari, she would be more Indian than the Indians.

Put her in a kilt and she'd out-Scot a Scotsman.

I don't even want to think about Lederhosen.

Danny, your mum can sing every song from A Sound of Music better than the original. She could wear Lederhosen and sing Climb Every Mountain and it would bring tears to your eyes.

I don't believe in harbingers of fate or doom, but I did cycle through Turnpike Lane last week and noticed the Sari place had closed.

And the circus must have left town months before.

Where was I?

Aunt Marigold and her Egyptian lover.

My Aunt Marigold, your Great-Aunt, was a remarkable woman. The reason she'd gone to Egypt, and then all the other countries around there, Libya, Tunisia, Jordan, Morocco, Algeria and most of the rest, was not only her love for the cultures and cuisine, but also something called the Arab Spring. As she put it, no-one was going to have a decent revolution and not invite her. I think she felt there was still time for one more outrage in an outrageous life. After the Arab Spring largely failed to achieve anything she still spent most of her time there. I think she had a motherly urge to adopt them all, before kicking their backsides into starting a new Arab Spring. And this time making it a success.

She married four times in total, all husbands died. I've never seen the term 'sexual exhaustion' on a death certificate, but apparently she pretty much wore them all out one way or another. After the fourth passed away she declared that she would only take lovers in future. And added that she didn't need any more bloody husbands to support her children, she was wealthy enough. What she needed was someone to give her those children, since her husbands had proved incompetent in that respect. Despite all their efforts she never did have any.

Or that was what I had been led to believe.

She doted on Jenny and myself. Jenny was ten years my junior. She suffered from ill health from the start. She seemed to spend more time in hospital than at home. I can't remember all the things they took out of her over the years. Spleen, half a lung here, appendix there. But she was forever cheerful. And determined.

Danny, I hope you will have many brothers and sisters. Jenny and I – well, apart from the age difference, I was deliberately kept out of her way. I never understood – or even questioned – why I was sent to boarding school. Why I was packed off to live with Aunt Marigold in London during the summer breaks. I loved it all, though. I lost my virginity at Aunt Marigold's house. She always had all sorts staying or visiting. Penelope – god, how those names must have irritated them, I think Aunt Marigold collected them for their names – was, I think, about thirty-five. She wasn't exactly the slim and trim Barbie Dolls which appear on the telly these days – remind me to ask you whether fashions have changed. More Rubenesque, the way most men prefer their women. I guess, like most adolescent males, I ogled her breasts. They were certainly breasts to ogle. More than that I never dared dream of. So, at one of Aunt Marigold's more libidinous and alcoholic parties, I was astounded to find myself in bed with her.

Enough of that. You don't want to know about that.

Though those were some of the reasons I fell in love with London.

And ended up supporting Arsenal, sort of.

Arsenal are a football team, sort of.

'Never confuse love and sex,' Aunt Marigold told me once, when I was about twelve

'What's the difference?' I asked, not knowing about either.

'I've only been in love once, and I couldn't have him,' she replied.

So, about this sex business? Auntie?

Auntie?

Finally moving.

Well, we're sort of shuddering forward as if the train is fighting with the brakes.

What's the time – 06h25.

Good thing I left early then.

There's a time to laugh, there's a time to cry, there's a time to strangle someone and that time has almost arrived.

Maybe they've gone on strike again but forgot to tell anyone. No, I can't see that happening. They like to make sure everyone knows when they go on strike. The public get quite rude when we go on strike, and we're only teachers.

Aunt Marigold.

The folks have a picture of Aunt Marigold in their lounge. It's on a cabinet along with other photographs. There's one of me in school uniform aged about ten, looking like your traditional idiot schoolboy with knock-knees, a huge grin on his face, and maggots for brains. Jenny in a pretty dress, aged about five, beaming. Various other aunts and uncles and cousins, once, twice, three times removed.

The picture of Aunt Marigold was taken in Egypt, about ten or fifteen years ago. She's sitting on the touring motorbike she used to travel on. She's wearing lace-up leather boots to the knees, jodhpurs, a blouse, long leather coat, hair free, goggles on her forehead, with a hat hanging down her back. She looks like a combination of Easy Rider, Janis Joplin, Lawrence of Arabia and Erwin Rommel. Apparently she always had a copy of Lawrence's Seven Pillars of Wisdom in one of the panniers.

She used it to hit peasants with when they couldn't understand English.

She loved motorbikes. She told me that there were only two ways of travelling, by motorbike in the sun or by train in the snow. By train I think she meant the old sleeper carriages being drawn by a monster steam engine. Orient Express type thing.

I think the motorbike also gained her a little notoriety. The locals would have been a little put off when the woman teacher from Hells Angels cruises into town and suspects you of being a naughty little boy.

She left her house to us, and a sizeable sum to her housekeeper and another instructing all of us to 'Hold the biggest bloody wake London has ever seen, including those Irish bastards.' It was the first time I saw my father cry. Not tears of – well, the tears I was to cry later. Loss, yes. But, as the Catholic priest said at the funeral, we come not to mourn, but to celebrate a life fully lived.

For Marigold that was true. Well. Sort of.

Looking back, I suspect that she felt that she had left some things undone, not finished. And wanted someone to finish them. Like me. Or Jenny.

The funeral.

Even her Egyptian lover was there. He cried buckets. Then he got drunk and kept telling people how wonderful the English were to have such a woman. It was highly embarrassing until I got drunk enough to match his emotion.

In fact Aunt Marigold's exit from this veil of tears was largely an unassisted suicide. She had been told by her doctor that she had terminal cancer. She never revealed that to anyone, except in a last private letter to mum and dad. I think she decided to go out on a high note. She certainly chose the highest mountain she could hope to get to. After all, it would have been rather embarrassing to kill yourself flying into a traffic roundabout in Luton. And Aunt Marigold understood style.

Strange thing is that she was a practising Catholic, as is my mum. Personally I loathe the Catholic Church. When I was about fourteen and old enough not to blow the house up if left on my own I was given the choice of whether or not I wanted to continue going to Mass. The answer was definitely not. My dad only goes on special occasions when he deems it necessary. The women in the family keep the faith. Though in Aunt Marigold's case, on her rather particular terms. Had someone pointed out that suicide was a mortal sin I think her response would be, 'Mortal sin be damned. I'll have a word with the son-of-a-bitch when I get up there.'

If it was on a good day and she was feeling exceptionally polite.

About this time, something I was blissfully unaware of, your bloody mother was being hailed as the new Kylie Minogue in Australia. Which she considered an insult. She was determined on being the new Dame Nellie Melba. Better than. She was planning to move to London for her career. I'm not sure I don't wish she hadn't.

Danny, I wonder how fat she's going to get with you. Might hinder her acting career a little. Still shouldn't stop her singing.

It'll piss her off no end, which can't be a bad thing. I'll have to mention it on a regular basis.

Providing I get the chance. Perhaps from a distance. Making sure there aren't any throwable objects nearby.

Danny, your mother is fucking useless at aiming things, but she's remarkably good at hitting things.

Something I wish to stress to you, my darling Danny, is that I'm of scientific bent. I don't believe in airy-fairy notions, religions, karma or superstition. I believe that will become clear. It was pure chance that your mother's and my paths should overlap. However, considering the impact, I'm quite willing to found a religion of the benevolent god of love and lust in gratitude, no matter how bogus it might be. But only if she – it's probably a she – gets me to Heathrow on time. Considering life is such a bitch that probably won't happen. Considering I don't plan to let anyone get in my way I fully intend to make it happen.

Does that make sense?

Probably not. Since I met your bloody mother nothing much has made sense.

Now we're stuck in a tunnel. Christ in a bucket.

06h30.

They should write a song about that. I will write a song about that.

The funeral of Aunt Marigold was reasonably sombre. Mum, your grandmother, held hold of dad in a way I'd never seen before. I suspect that both of them wished that they could have lived life to the full as Aunt Marigold had. Unfortunately for them I had appeared. They had to become serious, law abiding, honest, god-fearing parents. As I have now discovered. It's an awful fate. Or choice. Children make you grow old. Or up. Or both.

After the funeral we adjourned to her local pub for a knees-up. Aunt Marigold's words. And boy, I bet there were a few king-size hangovers the next day. I certainly had one. I woke up on the floor of the conservatory of Aunt Marigold's house, my arm around an Aspidistra. It was the first time in my life when I had got thoroughly drunk and not woken up in the arms of a woman. Possibly because that was our night, our family time.

Typical of Aunt Marigold to have an Aspidistra. Your bloody mother didn't know what that meant. George Orwell, she knows about him, she'd never heard of keeping the Aspidistra flying. After I'd explained it to her she'd choose the most inopportune moments in public to strike a pose of a Roman Caesar, salute and proclaim, 'Raise high the Aspidistra' before collapsing in a fit of the giggles.

Jenny lay opposite me, on a bamboo couch. I vaguely recalled bellowing things the night before about Empire and the English spirit. Singing Jerusalem. I blame the Egyptian bloke, he started it. All very embarrassing. I'm not sure which was worst. The fact that I don't believe in that shit, as a rule. Or the presence of people like Mr and Mrs Patel from the local newsagents. And my parents, of course, who knew Aunt Marigold far better than I would ever do. Far, far better. Put quite simply, Aunt Marigold had set the bar high, and I really didn't think any of us could surpass her.

Another five minutes and we're still going nowhere. I will get there on time. I can feel Aunt Marigold up there in the sky saying, 'Do it, boy, do it, Mark, go for it. It's all you have.' She's fucking right about that. Right now it is all I have. Career's probably blown now.

Sod it. Career is blown. Well, stuff them all. What fucking career? It never was a career. Teaching as a career? Give me strength.

They say that nobody ever built a statue to a critic. Well, the planet's not exactly crawling with the ones the built to fucking teachers either, is it?

Moving again, slowly.

Hoorah. We're coming into Manor House. We're almost part of the way there.

06h35.

We'll throw a fucking party.

Danny, you know what I'm going to say to your bloody mother when I get hold of her?

No, me neither.

But I'll know by the time I get there.

I make that in just over an hour.

And the one thing I do know without doubt is how to get to Terminal 5 departures from the tube platform. It just so happens that I've done it twice in the past year. Last time was in under sixty seconds. So I've got that covered at least.

Cockfosters
Oakwood
Southgate
Arnos Grove
● Bounds Green
● Wood Green
● Turnpike Lane
○ Manor House
Finsbury Park
Arsenal
Holloway Road
Caledonian Road
King's Cross St. Pancras
Russell Square
Holborn
Covent Garden
Leicester Square
Piccadilly Circus
Green Park
Hyde Park Corner
Knightsbridge
South Kensington
Gloucester Road
Earl's Court
Barons Court
Hammersmith
Turnham Green
Acton Town

Ealing Common      South Ealing
North Ealing       Northfields
Park Royal         Boston Manor
Alperton           Osterley
Sudbury Town       Hounslow East
Sudbury Hill       Hounslow Central
South Harrow       Hounslow West
Rayners Lane       Hatton Cross  ←
Eastcote           Heathrow T 1-2-3  ⟶  Heathrow T4
Ruislip Manor      Heathrow T5
Ruislip
Ickenham
Hillingdon
Uxbridge

## Manor House

*Estimated time to Heathrow Terminal Five:1hr 14 minutes*

*Estimated time to Finsbury Park tube station: 2 minutes*

The driver has just announced that we are being held here to 'regulate the gap between us and the train behind us'. Never mind the fucking gap, woman, just drive the bloody thing. The people on the train behind us can afford to be late, I can't.

Anyway, it's their fault, they should have got up earlier.

I've just realised. We have a woman driver. Oh, fucking great. She'll probably cause the poor bastard behind us to swerve and drive into a wall. That'll delay things even further.

Me sexist? Never.

Jenny woke up and cast an amused eye upon me. Because of various ailments she's never really taken to the drink. She just needs a spritzer to feel mildly tipsy, that was always good enough for her. At one point –

That comes later.

Jenny looked at me in that amused way she had. I might have been ten years younger than her for all it mattered.

'Fancy some raw eggs and milk?' she teased. It was enough to make me gag.

'I don't feel too well,' I said.

'You Southern Softies can't take your drink,' she joked. 'Remember this?

She sang softly,

'London Pride has been handed down to us.

London Pride is a flower that's free

London Pride means our own dear town to us

And our pride it for ever will be.'

'Oh, dear god,' I seem to recall saying. 'Not Noel Coward. I didn't do Noel Coward, did I? Please, please tell me I didn't do Noel Coward.'

'Too much London Pride,' she said, 'of the liquid sort.'

'I think I'm going to die. I bloody hope I'm going to die.'

'You know, you have a lovely bass voice when you're drunk.'

30

'Please let me die.'

'I'll make you some coffee,' she said, slipped off the couch and made her sinuous way to the kitchen.

I remember it perfectly. I should have thought, 'She's a beautiful woman.' After all, I had sufficient experience in women, individually, slipping out of bed to make me coffee, looking at them and thinking, 'And after the coffee ...'

But all I saw, or should have seen, was my sister looking after her elder brother. It was he who should have been looking after her.

Aunt Marigold was in that privileged position of being a relative but not a parent in which she could tell the truth to an adolescent. Hopefully by now, Danny, you'll have got over those awful years. She said to me, when I was about seventeen, and had, I presume, muttered some hatred of my parents, as you do at that age:

'You know why you were kept away from Jenny?'

Of course I didn't. I hadn't even realised that that was the case.

'Because she had to grow into her own life. It would have been nice to have an older brother there to look after her. But she would have never developed. Her illnesses – too easy to lie back and let others do everything. She had to overcome them on her own. She had to become her own person.'

She paused before asking:

'Do you understand, Mark?'

I no more understood than I understood quantum theory or why pygmies are so named. When you're seventeen you're so wrapped up in yourself – Well, I guess you've probably more or less worked that out for yourself.

Maybe I'll let you read this when you're fifteen. A pre-emptive strike against hormones.

That's pretty much the age of my pupils, fifteen or sixteen. I might have been dense, but I'm sure I was never as dense as they are. Impossible.

So. We had the wake, the folks – your grandparents – were to return to Liverpool. Jenny was going with them, she was still at university there. The plan was that she and the folks would return in the summer and we'd go through Aunt Marigold's stuff together. Or something like that. It wasn't a time to plan. We just had vague ideas. They, the folks, had exchanged a number of glances at the idea. Then I presumed they were thinking about timetables, about whether they wanted to return to London, or whether they'd far prefer to tend to the roses. Now I'm pretty sure they were thinking, 'What if he discovers those letters? Perhaps Marigold burned them. I fucking hope she did.'

I'm guessing by the time you read this people will still know what letters and envelopes and stamps are. If not, pop along to your local museum, they'll have them there. If they still have museums. Maybe they'll have put all the museums in a museum.

'Mark,' mum said, 'we could come down earlier to help you. It's going to be a lot of work, you don't want to rush into things. Not to mention putting up with antique salesmen, some of them are – well, not that honest. There's quite a lot of Regency furniture – that writing table in the study, for example. If it's original it could fetch quite a price.'

I laughed.

'Mum, I have absolutely no time at the moment to even think about such things. I've got the classes, extra tuition, Cabaret, the football – I'm snowed under as it is. All I shall do is to live here and show a light in case the burglars have been reading the obituary columns. Apart from that I'm not going to touch a thing.'

Which was quite true. I knew personally of people whose relatives had passed on, and then discovered that their loved ones' homes had been turned over by scum who appeared to have sufficient capability to read the obituary columns, but not, apparently, sufficient moral fibre to resist the lure of adding to the general mourning by breaking into said premises. And I was also faced with the challenge of trying to educate the children of said scum into being able to add two plus two and not come out with a jail sentence.

Those two Pakistani boys have gone to sleep. Strange.

On the move again. 06h38. If there are no further delays I should be okay. Presuming she's still this side of security. If she's already through – well, there's a conundrum.

Bloody typical of your mother.

She might wait in sight so that she can immediately make me grovel when I turn up. Or she might go through to make it harder for me. She'll probably wait until she sees me, then slip through security and leave it up to me to work out how to get in.

Your mother thinks she knows how to make a dramatic entrance.

Ha!

I'll probably race in, trip and slide into the baggage carousel. Disappearing down the well with the suitcases. But at least everyone will be watching.

She is going to get such a bloody hiding when I catch up with her.

I moved into Aunt Marigold's house at about the same time your mother was, apparently, taking the outback by storm in her performance of Shaw's Saint Joan of Arc. The only difference being that Joan wanted to kill all Englishmen, whereas your mother will, it seems, settle with a specific one.

The irony being that, had my ancestors decided to stay in Ireland I would never have become a middle-class Englishman. And Scouser.

After mum and dad and Jenny returned to Liverpool.

That was when I met Stella. Late October, a couple of weeks after the funeral. I remember the weather was mild, balmy even. Stella lived three doors away. She wasn't at the funeral, which was, I've now realised, a bit of a giveaway. If she wasn't on Aunt Marigold's funeral list, there was bound to be a good reason for it.

Talking of lists, this morning when I threw my mobile at the wall. It was very satisfying. However it left me with a dent in the wall, a broken mobile phone and no access to your bloody mother's phone number.

I did grab an old one I haven't used for years. I'd put it on to charge the night before. So now I have a functioning, fully charged mobile phone.

With one small problem. All my contact numbers were on the other one. The one I smashed to smithereens.

It's part of modern life. God knows what it'll be like when you grow up, Danny.

There's a scene in Indiana Jones, The Last Crusade, where Harrison Ford as Indiana Jones demands of Sean Connery as his father why he couldn't remember something, and Connery says, 'I wrote it down so that I wouldn't have to remember it.' Same thing with digital gadgets these days. When Maddy first gave me her number, did I try to remember it?

No, of course not. That's what I had a mobile phone for. When I wanted to call her I clicked on 'Maddy' in the address book. I couldn't even tell you what the first digit is.

There was a time an address book was a physical thing.

She calls it a cell phone. Apparently everyone in the world apart from the British and the French call them cell phones. The French because they're obdurate bastards, the British because it's a mobile phone for Christ's sake. Why call it anything else?

Your bloody mother is one hundred percent Australian because that's where she was born and that's where she comes from.

She is also one hundred percent Irish because her surname's O'Connor and that's where some of her ancestors came from.

There are other bits and pieces she's picked up over the years and she's also one hundred percent them too.

But above all she's five hundred percent female.

Or, as she puts it, 'All woman'.

Just like nitro-glycerine is all explosion.

Coming into Finsbury Park now.

Finsbury Park is one of those major intersections. You can change for the Victoria Line underground, or "mainline stations" as they've just announced. You hear people say things like, 'We get the Piccadilly Line to Finsbury Park, then change to get a train to Stevenage.' Or Pooplebutt. Or Popplewhistle. Or Mars. Or wherever. It's like they have their journey all planned out, and this is a major junction, but it's one they've decided on. As I tell my pupils, it's a pity life isn't that neat. You don't know how it's going to turn out. The major junctions aren't signposted. You have to take your chances when they appear, because they will be fleeting and far between.

Like falling in love.

06h45.

An hour and a quarter. It should have taken me about twenty minutes.

06h45. Still 06h45.

I don't fucking believe it.

I've just heard Aunt Marigold say something.

'Mark, why didn't you get a bloody motorbike like I told you to?'

Aunt Marigold, I promise you I will start saving up for a decent motorbike the minute this is over. A huge, fuck-off powerful one.

I've always wanted a motorbike.

I must think. I must know what it is I'm going to say to your bloody mother when I get hold of her.

And a sidecar for your mother and you.

It'll be fun, Danny. Trust me, you're going to love it. We'll drive like the wind.

Cockfosters
Oakwood
Southgate
Arnos Grove
● Bounds Green
● Wood Green
● Turnpike Lane
● Manor House
○ Finsbury Park
Arsenal
Holloway Road
Caledonian Road
King's Cross St. Pancras
Russell Square
Holborn
Covent Garden
Leicester Square
Piccadilly Circus
Green Park
Hyde Park Corner
Knightsbridge
South Kensington
Gloucester Road
Earl's Court
Barons Court
Hammersmith
Turnham Green
Acton Town

Ealing Common — South Ealing
North Ealing — Northfields
Park Royal — Boston Manor
Alperton — Osterley
Sudbury Town — Hounslow East
Sudbury Hill — Hounslow Central
South Harrow — Hounslow West
Rayners Lane — Hatton Cross ←
Eastcote — Heathrow T 1-2-3 ⟶ Heathrow T4
Ruislip Manor — Heathrow T5
Ruislip
Ickenham
Hillingdon
Uxbridge

# Finsbury Park

*Estimated time to Heathrow Terminal Five:1 hr 12 minutes*

*Estimated time to Arsenal tube station: 1 minute*

06h48.

My watch seems to have stopped.

Old couple just got on. What in hell's name are an old couple doing up at this time on a bloody Underground train? They look as miserable as sin.

I don't blame them. They're supposed to be at home still under the duvet enjoying the golden years of their lives.

For some reason my pupils think I'm a boring stiff git who needs to get a life. Apart from Sharon Runny-Nose, one of my skinnier pupils who wants to have an affair with me. I told your bloody mother I wasn't interested in any of my pupils that way. I know what happened might have looked bad, but it wasn't my fault.

It was pretty academic, really, your mother's telephone number. I knew she wasn't going to answer hers no matter what happened. Not if she recognised my number calling. Which is why I got the old one out and recharged it. She wouldn't recognise that one. If only I'd memorised her number. Or even just written it down. But even if I could I am not about to lower myself into sending her endless voice messages or text messages to tell her how far I'm progressing on my crusade to get to Heathrow on time. And anyway, you can't use a mobile phone on the Underground at the moment, while it is underground. Not the London Underground. No doubt, by the time you read this, modern technology and the Underground will have advanced to the extent that you will be able to sit in an Underground carriage in the deepest part of the deepest tunnel and text to miners trapped miles below in some salt mine in Siberia: "R U OK?"

"No, we're trapped under tons of earth in a salt mine in Siberia. What do you think, we're having a fucking holiday in Horsham? Prick. Message ends."

Ah, Danny, my dear Danny. What will life be like in twenty years' time? What will you be like?

06h50. Moving again.

It's one of those strange things about life. I'm impatient to get to Heathrow, yet the faster I get there the less time I have to write down this note to you. If your mother is reasonable I will be around to see you grow up, and it won't matter so much. If she isn't, or something happens, I want you to know about the father you never met. I'm not given to premonitions, but I have to say that the omens do not look good.

Or perhaps it's a case of wondering whether my actions are indicative of something I don't wish to acknowledge.

Danny, if your mother refuses to have anything more to do with me, would you mind if I kidnapped you?

You know, I think I bloody will.

That missed phone call in the shower. Did I deliberately tune it out, knowing that it was only going to be your mother? Did I deliberately tune it out, knowing that it was only going to be someone I didn't want to talk to. I.e. everyone?

Hell, as Jean Paul Sartre said, is other people. And he should know, for him other people were French.

I don't know. One can theorise anything.

So, let me tell you what really happened.

There was me and Stella and the Gang of Six. And Bella's.

Manners. Culture. Mores. Do they change over time? Are some universal?

I ask this because some little prick has got on to a tube with some empty seats, decided that the best place to sit was right next to someone who was trying to get some work done, even if he had to walk down the entire fucking carriage to get here, past all those empty seats, and is now taking up the space I need, and has opened a little prayer book and is muttering little prayers to himself.

Fuck off you cunt.

Jesus, an Englishman would never do that.

Get pissed, disturb everyone with loud football chants, yes, but only after lunch, and the train would be too crowded to work in anyway, but they wouldn't have the temerity to sit next to you while mumbling incantations to themselves.

If I decide to marry your bloody mother it won't be in a bloody church. Marriage is a difficult enough relationship without starting it off with religious crap.

Your bloody mother will insist on a replay of Julie Andrews getting married in The Sound Of Music. With extra nuns.

And the driver's just announced that we'll be sitting here for a few minutes because of those signal failures in the King's Cross area. Maybe if she does that start-jerk-shunt-stop routine again I can accidentally elbow the prick in the mouth.

Wait a minute. I thought these signal failures were in Arnos Grove. Have they migrated? Did they get married and have fucking offspring? Or did they live in sin and have bastard little signal failures?

Jesus wept.

I must point out, Danny, that your mother never was one to sleep around. Much like my Aunt Marigold, she was very selective. Buggered if I know why she chose me. I suspect she might hate me. I was happy before I met her. Not exactly a pillar of rectitude, but happy.

Well, perhaps happy isn't the right word.

Now Stella and I, we had the perfect relationship. There was absolutely no chance in hell I would ever think of marrying her. As the song goes, 'Don't marry her, fuck me.'

That's a song you will not be allowed to listen to, Danny.

Stella and I first met when I was wheeling my bicycle out of the front gate on my way to school. And there you go, straight off you're into questions. What is a bicycle? What is its cultural import? What sort of person rides a bicycle? What does it say about the owner, the society, the historic situation. Well, that's what I ask, anyway.

In London at the moment it can be a method of transport, a status symbol – they can cost a small fortune – virtue signalling, or an early attempt at suicide, especially the ones racing around central London. Personally I bicycle because I enjoy it, and it gives me an excuse to avoid bringing work home most times. And I use the word "bicycle" rather than "cycle" because "cyclist" these days puts me in mind of a twat on a very expensive piece of rare metal – mined by child slaves in Africa – wearing very expensive and very tight lycra just to show the world what a wanker he is.

They even have an acronym for it. MAMIL. Middle Aged Men In Lycra.

I read somewhere that, when the very first bicycles came out, society generally considered the riders to be a bunch of wankers. Some things never change.

Penny Farthing Pricks I think they were called.

It might have changed by the time you read this Danny, but currently a very good rule is to keep well away from any man wearing Lycra or maroon trousers. They are visible outward signs that the person in question is a complete loony. And if you ever encounter a man wearing maroon trousers over Lycra, run for your life, the Apocalypse has started. The thing is, what did Stella see? An impecunious young teacher pushing an old bike, or a wealthy young eccentric with his own house? I know what I saw in her: a hedonist looking for a good time and wondering if I might be entertaining for a while. Before being dropped when the next good time came along. We could have been mirror images in that respect. I just drop faster.

She said hello and I said hello and she said we were more or less neighbours since she lived a few houses down the street and she was terribly sorry to hear of my aunt's passing away and I realised that if she knew that Aunt Marigold was my aunt then she undoubtedly knew a lot more about me than I knew about her. Not being a natural gossip I tend to forget how quickly information can pass from mouth to mouth. There's a local corner shop nearby, very pleasant Indian couple running it, the Chandras, very sociable, remember everyone's names, ages of their kids, birthdays, that sort of thing. Plenty of places in London you can live without ever knowing your neighbour's name if you so choose – "kept himself to himself" is the sort of thing you often hear when someone's found to have been dead in their flat for five years without anyone realising. But if you've got a job and a social life you just need a couple of gossips around and they'll know your whole life story. And there'll be others around quietly listening in.

Stella, for example, mentioned that she'd heard I was a keen tennis player. True enough, but I hadn't advertised the fact. Presumably someone had noticed me carrying my stuff into the house, including a couple of tennis rackets and a carton of balls.

She said she played with a club down the road, and maybe I'd like to try them out? I said that sounded an excellent idea, and we agreed to meet up the following Saturday afternoon and she'd drive us there.

Down the road turned out to be half an hour's drive away. There was at least one tennis club within walking distance which I'd noticed early on and had intended checking out, but, I thought, what the hell?

I think the driver just farted unexpectedly. Either that or she dropped the brake for a second. Train did a kangaroo jump. The bombers have woken up. They're busy rabbiting on at each other in foreign. Probably wondering where they are.

Coming into Arsenal. 06h55.

I wonder if they're playing tonight.

I wonder if I'll get to Heathrow by tonight.

What a fucking ridiculous idea.

I've got plenty of time.

But, Danny, there's just that niggling question.

Do I really want to get married?

I mean, marriage is unnatural for a man, if you think about it.

Stella used to say I over-thought things. Danny, if there is one thing you really, really want to think long and hard about doing, that is marriage. And then don't.

After all, I'll still be your dad even if I don't marry your mum, won't I?

```
┬  Cockfosters
│  Oakwood
│  Southgate
│  Arnos Grove
●  Bounds Green
●  Wood Green
●  Turnpike Lane
●  Manor House
●  Finsbury Park
○  Arsenal
   Holloway Road
   Caledonian Road
   King's Cross St. Pancras
   Russell Square
   Holborn
   Covent Garden
   Leicester Square
   Piccadilly Circus
   Green Park
   Hyde Park Corner
   Knightsbridge
   South Kensington
   Gloucester Road
   Earl's Court
   Barons Court
   Hammersmith
   Turnham Green
   Acton Town
```

| Ealing Common | South Ealing |
| North Ealing | Northfields |
| Park Royal | Boston Manor |
| Alperton | Osterley |
| Sudbury Town | Hounslow East |
| Sudbury Hill | Hounslow Central |
| South Harrow | Hounslow West |
| Rayners Lane | Hatton Cross  ← |
| Eastcote | Heathrow T 1-2-3 ──→ Heathrow T4 |
| Ruislip Manor | Heathrow T5 |
| Ruislip | |
| Ickenham | |
| Hillingdon | |
| Uxbridge | |

## Arsenal/Gillespie Road

*Estimated time to Heathrow Terminal Five: 1 hr 10 minutes*

*Estimated time to Holloway Road tube station: 2 minutes*

Platform's pretty crowded. Unusual for Arsenal.

Or Gillespie Road as some insist on calling it.

Danny, in case you've been brought up in the outback far from civilisation and a plug-point for the Internet, allow me to give you a brief potted history. "The Arsenal" are a football team based in this part of the world.

There's another football club around here called "Tottenham Hotspur". They loathe Arsenal the way a spurned wife feels for her ex-husband. I support Arsenal. The kids at school support Spurs. But there's a history behind the whole thing.

What happened is that Arsenal used to be a football team of workers from the arsenal at Woolwich in South London. They turned professional and moved up here to North London for financial reasons. The area they moved to is called Highbury. The tube station was originally known as Gillespie Road because that's the road it was built next to. Sometime after World War I they renamed it Arsenal so that fans would know where to get off. A few years ago Arsenal moved to a new stadium named The Emirates after the airline that sponsors them.

Spurs fans have always regarded them as interlopers – hence the use of the original name, Gillespie Road – and between them they developed a relationship which, if they had the weapons, would result in mutually assured destruction. Whenever they play each other the police have to turn out in force to keep the peace, or at least keep the injuries down to an acceptable level. For some reason football fans seem to keep their biggest hatreds for the club nearest them.

Football is like religion. It was invented by man so that they'd have someone to hate and go to war with.

I can see the tiles on the walls now spelling the name Gillespie Road. Dark brown tiles. Chocolate Brown.

Is it better to hate someone you once loved, or is indifference the real killer?

Your mother supports Liverpool.

Because I was born in Liverpool I am twice a traitor to my pupils; firstly for not supporting Liverpool, secondly for supporting the Arsenal.

Oh, and, Danny, it's 'The Arsenal', not 'Arsenal'. Don't ask me why. Some things just are.

Apparently your great-great-great (and maybe a few more) grandfather on your father's side began to emigrate from Ireland to the United States during the potato famine, only he only got as far as Liverpool, where he met and married a widow who owned a pub. His son or grandson decided to head for Australia around about the beginning of the First World War. So your mother decided that, if she had to support a football team, it would be Liverpool.

Liverpool, by the way, are shite.

And your mother comes from a long line of pissheads.

My ancestors emigrated for much the same reason, but stayed in Liverpool and eventually became middle-class in the post-hippy era.

I think I would have preferred them to own a pub.

06h56. Finally moving again. Not very fast, and more of a shunt than anything, but going in the right direction at least.

Plenty of time.

Let me go back to the Gang of Six, because that's what caused the problems.

There was myself, of course. Stella, Phil, Jess, Rob and Carol. They all played at the tennis club. One of those exclusive tennis clubs where you were permitted to join on an unspoken points basis, rather like the Australian immigration code, but with different rules. At least I think they are different.

First, race, or ethnic origin. Their token black quota was already taken up by a Kenyan called Keith, who drove an expensive looking black BMW and was a businessman. I rather liked Keith. He confided to me once that the only reason he belonged to the club was that he loved tennis, but otherwise he longed to shove a stick of ginger up the secretary's fanny.

Much as I sympathised with the sentiment, I have since never been able to look at a stick of ginger without a shudder.

In fact Keith disappeared after a couple of months. Afterwards a couple of plain clothes detectives came around, asked a few questions, but we never did find out what happened to him. But it did allow the members' committee the opportunity to turn down any further applications from "those people".

It was the type of club that did not, ever, expect the police to come calling. And if they absolutely had to, well, that was what the servants' entrance was for. In fact, if you were to ask me what the club felt like, the ambience as it were, I would say old-colonial chic, or maybe even cheek. It felt like you could drop it down somewhere along Agatha Christie's Nile and it would fit perfectly. They even had a little bar in the clubhouse for snifters afterwards.

So, I was Anglo-Saxon, a strong recommendation. But then came job, or career. Bankers were welcome: Stella was a "financial consultant", and Phil worked in the "banking industry". Jess was a designer of some sort, Rob an "IT consultant", which I presumed meant IT bullshitter as he didn't seem to know anything technical but could recite buzzwords with ease – he used phrases such as 'going forward' in a way that made absolutely no sense. Carol was an administrator in the NHS. She drove an expensive open-topped sports car, so I guessed her official title also included the word "consultant".

As a teacher, and especially a Science and Maths teacher, I came highly recommended to their lordships and ladyships on the membership committee. You'd be amazed at how many of them who thought it might bring free extra lessons for their little shits.

You would think money would play an important part, and it did, only not in quite the way it normally does. New members were expected to earn a certain amount, but not obviously a huge amount. Madonna would never have made it. An impecunious teacher who could be sufficiently patronised was far more their style.

I had the same problem as Keith. I love my tennis.

And both Jess and Carol, I could see at a glance, were highly intelligent women, attractive, and not overly worried about loyalty to their partners.

Slappers with brains.

Coming into Holloway Road.

07h00.

Can't believe it's taken this long to get this far.

Still, can't be more than another hour or so.

Still got four and a half hours to play with.

Thinking about it, I'm sure I've got a journey planner in my bag.

Yes, found it.

Estimated time from Holloway Road to Heathrow Terminal 5 is one hour and nine minutes.

ETA now 08h09.

Get me to the terminal on time.

That doesn't scan.

Don't worry, Danny, I'll be there in good time.

And then …

That's the bit I haven't worked out yet.

But I will.

And then …

So long as I get to push you in your pram, Danny.

I'll push it a lot faster than your mother would. You'll like that.

Cockfosters
Oakwood
Southgate
Arnos Grove
● Bounds Green
● Wood Green
● Turnpike Lane
● Manor House
● Finsbury Park
● Arsenal
○ Holloway Road
Caledonian Road
King's Cross St. Pancras
Russell Square
Holborn
Covent Garden
Leicester Square
Piccadilly Circus
Green Park
Hyde Park Corner
Knightsbridge
South Kensington
Gloucester Road
Earl's Court
Barons Court
Hammersmith
Turnham Green
Acton Town

Ealing Common          South Ealing
North Ealing           Northfields
Park Royal             Boston Manor
Alperton               Osterley
Sudbury Town           Hounslow East
Sudbury Hill           Hounslow Central
South Harrow           Hounslow West
Rayners Lane           Hatton Cross  ←
Eastcote               Heathrow T 1-2-3  →  Heathrow T4
Ruislip Manor          Heathrow T5
Ruislip
Ickenham
Hillingdon
Uxbridge

# Holloway Road

*Estimated time to Heathrow Terminal Five:1 hour 9 minutes*

*Estimated time to Caledonian Road tube station : 2 minutes*

Holloway. Used to be synonymous with the women's prison around these parts. Closed a couple of years ago, I think. Held most of the famous woman prisoners for part of their time, from mass murderers to suffragettes to suffragists. Ruth Ellis was executed there. Last woman to be executed in Britain. One way to be remembered.

Teachers invariably think of their pupils' futures. What do you want to be? What do you want to make of your life? My lot think being locked up as a serial killer would be cool. Unfortunately they currently lack the necessary intellectual wherewithal to move from the thought to the implementation, and I sure as hell ain't going to teach them that, I've got my own life to live.

07h02. Still in platform.

If I remember correctly Holloway Women's prison was closed so that it could be pulled down and replaced with housing and green space. For which read 'property development', i.e. money. The newspapers these days are full of complaints about how expensive London property is, how young families can't get on the property ladder, how nurses and teachers and such are forced to live miles out from where they work. I dare say it will be the same when you've grown up.

I read somewhere that the Mosleys were held in a cottage in the grounds of the prison during World War II. Oswald Mosley was a Fascist, leader of the Blackshirts and personal friend of Adolf Hitler. Interned for treason, his wife was sent to Holloway, he to somewhere else, Churchill decided that they should be together so he was sent to Holloway as well. The Mosleys were, of course, part of the set, or the Set. So they got better conditions. Pity the Germans didn't drop a bomb on them, that would have been karma.

Young girl has just got on. Looks about fifteen, is probably eighteen or twenty. Very small boob tube, no boobs to speak of, some sort of metal stud in her navel, tiny skirt, ridiculously high heels. Earphones. Chewing gum. Dead look in her eyes.

Don't think she's one of my pupils.

Still, a lot of them look the same.

She's sat down directly opposite prayer man next to me. He's almost quivering. Looking at her in disgust. Pity she didn't sit next to him.

At least it stopped him reciting whatever god-awful tosh it was.

People can be strange. There was an incident a year or so ago when a bomb was left in a train and went off close to an Underground station called Parsons Green. It was a dud; burst into flames which fizzled out quickly. A month later people are packed into a train going to Waterloo not far from Parsons Green when some fuckwit standing in the middle of them begins reading out loud from the Bible, presumably the Old Testament because it was all about homosexuality being a sin and how the world was doomed and the end was nigh. The other passengers freaked out, forced the doors open and jumped onto the tracks to get away, scared shitless he was about to detonate a bomb. If any of them had touched the live rail it would have killed them. As it was the track operators had to switch the power off, there were massive delays, and it turned out the bible thumper was a harmless nutter.

It does raise some interesting questions about human behaviour. Why were they so freaked out by a bloke reading from a Christian bible? And why did they jump out themselves? Why didn't they throw him out?

Apparently one of the things he kept saying was, 'death is not the end'. In the old days some thick-voiced Cockney bloke would have said, 'It will be for you if you don't stick a sock in it, mate.'

Someone else noted that the area around the idiot had become quite empty. One way to ensure your own private space, I suppose.

At least it gave the train people the opportunity to introduce their own train-speak, and announce that the passengers had 'self-evacuated' the train, cue much sniggering from news announcers who should be old enough to know better, never mind my lot of snot-nosed little brats who have minds of which the description 'puerile' would be an improvement.

Danny, every so often I read of teachers having affairs with pupils. It's something I have never understood. I have never, ever met a pupil I found in the least attractive. Skinny bags of mucous and acne which could only be attracted to members of the same species and god knows what that species is, it sure as hell ain't human.

I like telling them, you were made of mud and slime, you are mud and slime, and unto mud and slime will you return. For some reason they take it as a compliment. Starting calling themselves the mud and slime kids.

Sharon Runny-nose. Poor kid. She has the hots for me.

Poor me.

Danny, if you're like the average female, you'll have at least one crush on an older man. And he'd better not take advantage of you or I'll kill him.

Hormones. Along with the mucous and acne.

Sharon Runny-nose wanted me to take advantage of her. Those eyes of hers, not limpid pools as the poet would say, rather desperate and hurting. I love you, why can't you love me.

(A) Because I'm your teacher, and (B) because you're about as sexually attractive as frogspawn on a cold winter's day.

They've just made one of those automated announcements on the platform. Apparently there's "a good service running on all lines". I think the driver's just said "Bollocks, there is" over the intercom, but I could be wrong.

07h03.

Doors still open.

Tennis and the girls.

They all wore plunging necklines, and bent very low at the net when their partner was serving to me so that I could enjoy the view while losing my concentration. After a short while they gave it up. They realised that I was deliberately aiming the return at their cleavage. When asked why by Jess one evening in bed I explained that it was both the physical and technical challenge, and that it decided who I would choose for the post-match entertainment. Women with bruised boobs aren't much fun. The ones who can get out of the way fast enough are.

I seem to recall her response included the words 'you arrogant turd'.

Though that was after the encounter back at my flat, when Rob and Stella were away, and Jess ripped off her top and shouted, 'You bastard, look what you've done!'

Very interesting round blue and purple mark.

She didn't refuse my offer to kiss it better.

It was one day, a Saturday in late November before the frosts had started, when we were all there, waiting our chance for a court, when Phil, I think it was, murmured, 'I wonder if Mark would be interested in popping along to Bella's with us afterwards.' So typical of Phil. He was quietly requesting agreement or otherwise from his fellows. He was a complete dick, but a very polite one.

'I doubt if Mark's tastes would include Bella's,' said Stella. Which meant, 'It's bad enough I have to share him with you lot, let's not make things even worse.'

Now that might sound arrogant, but it isn't. I know that Stella, apparently my then girlfriend, shared more than her financial interests with Phil when they were away on business. You could call it a sort of merry-go-round of who's available. If Stella and Phil were away, and Carol and Rob were incommunicado, Jess and I would make up a not so lonesome twosome. If Rob was travelling and Stella on the road Carol and I would sink our sorrows in a few drinks and comfort each other afterward.

Driver has just informed us that we are being held at a red light but should be on the move shortly.

Firstly, I'm pretty sure we weren't being held at a green light.

Though, who knows, in the world of the Underground maybe they do stop at green. They seem to stop for fucking everything else. Litter on the line. Bad smells. The wrong sort of snow. Evil leaves.

Secondly, the driver hasn't got a clue in shit when we'll be on the move. Probably doesn't care. Their only destination is the end of their shift. It's not as if they're travelling to new and exciting places. Someone else's holiday isn't usually that exciting.

I remember Jess lying back the one time, commenting on the quality, and wishing that Rob would hurry up and propose to her.

'You want to get married to Rob?' I asked.

'Of course. I love him. At least, I love him about as much as I've loved anyone. He might not be much to write home about in bed, but he'll make a good husband. And he's got a decent job.'

Women can be very cutting to the man who has just made love to them. Thanks, stud, but otherwise you're pretty useless. And you don't make enough, anyway.

I was silent for a few seconds after that. Eventually she asked,

'What are you thinking?'

I pursed my lips and replied,

'I'm reviewing the situation.'

'What does that mean?'

'Can a fellow be a villain all his life?'

'Eh?'

'Better settle down and get myself a wife.'

'Stella?'

'A misery, she'd make from me ... I think I'd better think it out again.'

'What are you talking about?'

'Fagin, from Oliver, the musical.'

'Oh, dear god, not more musicals. For fucks' sake, Mark.'

I think my search for a wife started that afternoon. A wife who would look up to me, think that, for all my faults, I was God's answer to her prayers. A wife who hadn't shagged all my closest friends.

Instead, Danny, I got your mother.

I suppose one out of two wasn't that bad.

So, we went to Bella's that evening. And I discovered the old truth, that you should be more careful about your friends than your enemies.

Well fuck me sideways we're actually moving again. At least the doors have closed.

07h05.

No, doors are closed but we aren't moving.

No, we're actually moving.

No. Stopped again.

Bella's.

We arrived at Bella's as a group. The door was opened by a large black man wearing a tuxedo, a pink tutu and sunglasses. And a look on his face that announced very clearly that he didn't do humour. Stella announced us and he stood back to let us in.

'I must introduce you to Bella,' Stella said, leading me through while the others wandered off. I gathered that it was polite custom to introduce new guests to the host on the first occasion so that she could give you the once-over, thereafter you just wandered in and did your own thing, whatever that was. Being new I naturally glanced around. Stella seemed a bit feverish, anxious to get the introduction over, looking neither left nor right.

I wondered if she knew that there were half a dozen CCTV cameras in every single room and passage. They weren't obvious. You had to look up into the shadows to catch a sudden reflection of a lens to realise they were there. CCTV is so ubiquitous in London these days most of us don't notice it any more. But having it indoors at a private party marked the place as something more than just a social urbanite bash.

We're on the move again. 07h07.

Plenty of time.

Metal tummy still looking blankly in front of her. Chewing gum.

Prayer man still quivering.

Now there's an epitaph for a gravestone: Plenty of time.

We became known as the gang of six because we did things together, not because of any notorious deeds. Pubs, clubs sometimes, cinema, a play or two. The Maid of Muswell was our favourite pub, even though it meant a walk back uphill afterwards. Sometimes we'd had enough to warrant waiting for a bus. Sometimes, somewhere along the way we'd break out into "Show me the way to go home, I'm tired and I want to go to bed" repeated ad nauseam.

Admittedly I was the one who normally led that song. They joined in because they thought they should.

But in reality it was all very tame stuff to begin with. Some wag at the tennis club decided to call us the gang of six and the name stuck, partly because the middle-aged tossers at the club needed some vicarious thrill in their lives, partly because the others liked the notion.

One time it was just me and the girls, we went out to a restaurant. I was bored out of my skull. Women talk should be constrained to women.

And we're off. As in vaguely moving.

The driver has just announced that it will be slow going again.

Christ in two buckets.

Plenty of time.

Right, we're definitely on the move again thank god. 07h10. They must have cleared their little signalling problem. Caledonian Road next. According to the journey planner we'll be at Heathrow in one hour and seven minutes.

One thing is for sure. Your mother would never have tolerated the Gang of Six.

None of them sang, for a start. Not what you'd call singing.

Cockfosters
Oakwood
Southgate
Arnos Grove
● Bounds Green
● Wood Green
● Turnpike Lane
● Manor House
● Finsbury Park
● Arsenal
● Holloway Road
○ Caledonian Road
King's Cross St. Pancras
Russell Square
Holborn
Covent Garden
Leicester Square
Piccadilly Circus
Green Park
Hyde Park Corner
Knightsbridge
South Kensington
Gloucester Road
Earl's Court
Barons Court
Hammersmith
Turnham Green
Acton Town

Ealing Common        South Ealing
North Ealing         Northfields
Park Royal           Boston Manor
Alperton             Osterley
Sudbury Town         Hounslow East
Sudbury Hill         Hounslow Central
South Harrow         Hounslow West
Rayners Lane         Hatton Cross  ←
Eastcote             Heathrow T 1-2-3  →  Heathrow T4
Ruislip Manor        Heathrow T5
Ruislip
Ickenham
Hillingdon
Uxbridge

55

# Caledonian Road

*Estimated time to Heathrow Terminal Five: 1 hour 7 minutes*

*Estimated time to King's Cross St Pancras tube station: 3 minutes*

07h11

I think Pentonville prison is around here somewhere. I think maybe someone is trying to tell me something. Prisons. Crime and punishment. Stuck in a tube. There's a metaphor floating around there somewhere.

I wonder what they're doing above ground. We aren't going anywhere, that's for sure.

Maybe there's been a nuclear explosion and everything above ground has been wiped out.

Maybe the sun is shining, it's a lovely day, there are maids and chimney sweeps and bakers dancing and singing just like they do in Oliver.

Crossed with Hair, hippies in the park singing This Is The Age Of Aquarius. That'll be Oliver With A Twist, the musical just waiting to be made.

Maybe it's just another humdrum day with traffic jams and noise and going nowhere just like us here in Hades.

07h12.

Driver's just played one of those automated announcements telling us to mind the gap. I think it might be irony.

That's not something I tell my pupils, the bit about having plenty of time. I tell them that time is running out, it'll be university then a career, marriage, kids, and then they'll wonder what happened to time, so they'd better start concentrating now and use every second they've got. Well, that's what I tried to tell them once. I got as far as the university bit and was met with howls of derision. At least it was nice that for once the teachers and pupils agreed on something. Pity it was about how little future they had.

Though I think some of the laughter began with the idea of getting married. Having kids they understood. Getting married was an ambition too far.

Argue for your limitations and surely they will be yours. Thank you Richard Bach. I'm not the fucking Messiah. Just call me Brian.

At what point do you just throw up your hands and give up? Just accept that some things are meant to be and you can't change them no matter how hard you try? Let's face it, the only chance they've got of getting into university is in specimen jars. And even then they'd fail.

Maddy, on the other hand, I know she and I could make a go of it. We have to. I know we can. Just give love a chance.

Other things, well. Just well.

Just fucking well.

07h15. Finally moving again. With a whimper.

Who would think a hundred ton train could be indecisive?

There's this kid called Chris. He could make something of his life. Trouble is he's what they call of mixed parentage, with a different coloured chip on either shoulder. Or to be more accurate, he's what they call of mixed parentage and the trouble is that he has a different coloured chip on either shoulder.

White mother, single; black father disappeared, probably the same night Chris was conceived. Mother's a recovering drug addict and practising alcoholic, surviving on benefits and topping that up with occasional prostitution. Chris wants to be a rebel nigger in the hood, a streetwise fighter hating whites, especially grown-ups. Unfortunately for him he owes his upbringing to his white mother. Apparently that consisted of equal parts being screamed at, coming home to find her comatose and having to call an ambulance, and periods when she's taken the pledge and is wobbling along parallel to sanity under prescribed methadone treatment.

Story goes that she discovered him bunking off school once, when he was about ten and she was having a relatively stable period. She dragged him back to school by his ear, step by every step, screaming and shouting and calling him a little shit amongst other things. Took him to the head-teacher, told the head he had her permission to give him a good thrashing, smacked him across the head a couple of times to demonstrate how. I wish I could have been there to see that.

He now has the best attendance record in the school. He's bigger and stronger than his mother these days, but he's still scared shitless of her, and I don't blame him.

He's decided he wants to be a rap artist. If there's one thing I can't stand it's rap. But I heard him in the playground about a year ago. He had a good voice. I told him so, and suggested that he should think of proper singing. He shrugged his shoulders and said, Yeah, whatever.

What can you do?

Oh Christ we've stopped again. For fuck's sake! What's wrong with the fucking driver, has she stopped to powder her fucking nose?

Oh, great, apparently we're experiencing signalling problems in the Hammersmith area. Which gives whole new meanings to pretty much all those words, especially the "experience" one. Typical of your bloody mother to choose the same day as the Underground to throw a wobbly.

Stella.

Moving again. Coming in to King's Cross.

07h19.

Call it 07h20.

We seem to be repeating a pattern.

Arrive at station.

Go nowhere for five minutes.

Finally creep away at the speed of very, very slow.

Take five minutes to arrive at next station when it should have taken two.

Rinse.

Repeat.

Let me see, how many stops to Terminal Five? 25 or so. That makes 250 minutes in total. Four hours and ten minutes. Means we get to T5 at half one. Same time Maddy's flight leaves.

That is seriously fucking impossible.

Cockfosters
Oakwood
Southgate
Arnos Grove
● Bounds Green
● Wood Green
● Turnpike Lane
● Manor House
● Finsbury Park
● Arsenal
● Holloway Road
● Caledonian Road
○ King's Cross St. Pancras
Russell Square
Holborn
Covent Garden
Leicester Square
Piccadilly Circus
Green Park
Hyde Park Corner
Knightsbridge
South Kensington
Gloucester Road
Earl's Court
Barons Court
Hammersmith
Turnham Green
Acton Town

Ealing Common      South Ealing
North Ealing       Northfields
Park Royal         Boston Manor
Alperton           Osterley
Sudbury Town       Hounslow East
Sudbury Hill       Hounslow Central
South Harrow       Hounslow West
Rayners Lane       Hatton Cross ◄───────────┐
Eastcote           Heathrow T 1-2-3 ──► Heathrow T4
Ruislip Manor      Heathrow T5
Ruislip
Ickenham
Hillingdon
Uxbridge

# King's Cross St Pancras

*Estimated time to Heathrow Terminal Five: 1 hour 4 minutes*

*Estimated time to Russel Square tube station: 2 minutes*

07h20

King's Cross St Pancras Uncle Tom Cobbley and All. Just about every Underground Line goes through here, Piccadilly, Victoria, Circle, Metropolitan, Northern and Hammersmith and City. That's even before you get to list the destinations on mainline trains.

I can confidently list the Underground Lines because I'm sitting here in a stationary tube with the map on the bulkhead. I can confidently list some of the train stations because your mother and I came here a few months ago. I wanted to show her the Lovers' Statue in The Meeting Place at St Pancras. My way of saying I love you, I suppose.

I've been trying to remember whether I ever said those words to your mother.

I love you.

I mean, I showed her in plenty of ways that I did love her, and that's got to be better than words, hasn't it?

The Meeting Place.

It took ages to find. You'd think they would have signs to it. It's upstairs, almost in a corner. I know it's about fifty feet high, but it's dull bronze and blends in with the background. Well, that's what I pointed out after we'd spent twenty minutes searching before coming across it by accident.

As we looked up at it I mentioned Brief Encounter, which threatened to be a mistake, since she's seen it before and just had to do an over-the-top rendition of the plummy voices.

'Oh! Dahling! Dahling, I must flah!'

And then she answered herself:

'Must you, dahling? Dahling, must you just? Flah? Dahling?'

At that point the various Japanese and other tourists who had been gawping at the statue turned to gawp at us. So I took your mother firmly in my arms to stop that nonsense. And just to be sure I kissed her full on the lips. And she responded in kind. And there we were, locked in a passionate embrace, eyes closed, deaf to the sound of a thousand camera flashes going off. It was only when we came up for air, and looked into each other's eyes that we noticed that we were the centre of attention of around a thousand lenses. A quick sheepish bow to our audience and then a strategic retreat. Your mother is very fond of grande passion of a dramatic scale in public, real passion she prefers to keep private. Which is very much my own approach to the whole confusing business.

Then we wandered around the complex hand in hand. It's quite a labyrinth. It was much of a voyage of discovery for me as well as for Maddy. I've passed through plenty of times, but it must have been several years since I had been there on the upper decks, as it were. Last I remember of it it was crumbling away, ignored and forlorn, especially St Pancras, looking all dirty orange. They've redone the whole lot, quite a few years back as far as I could gather, and it's all modern and swish and shiny. Part of that was to do with Eurostar, the Channel trains, and making it international. And then of course there were the Olympics, when they decided to tart it up for the visitors and important people.

There's a story that they always spruce up things wherever the queen goes to visit, so she's grown up with the notion that everywhere in peasant-land smells of fresh paint and scaffolding is always covered with pink silk.

And then, because there's only so much modern and swish and shiny you can take, we wandered outside the station – stations, I suppose, there's King's Cross and St Pancras – and, wonder of wonders, there was some water feature they'd created which played music. It was some artistic installation there for a limited period of time. It was beautiful. Maddy fell in love with it immediately. So did I.

A thought crossed my mind that I'd like to drag my class to it, and tell them to close their eyes and just listen. Didn't take long to accept that their response would be, "What the fuck for?" and then they'd try to nick it or just break it.

I took a picture of Maddy showing off in front of it, she took one of me looking thoughtfully into the distance, then we grabbed a friendly

Japanese tourist who happily used my camera to take a shot of the two of us arm in arm. He couldn't speak a word of English, we couldn't speak a word of Japanese, but I guess the sign language for "Can you please take a picture of us we're young and in love and stupid" is universal.

And to cap it off, being a lovely sunny day, we had to find an ice-cream van and have the obligatory ice-cream. Before following the Regents Canal to Camden, which your mother loved, of course. Canals and locks and open-air food stalls with sizzling sausages and clothes shops and the occasional punk dressed in bovver boots and tartan and orange hair. Plus a couple of hundred thousand other tourists. Normally it would be my idea of hell, but if Maddy loved it I was prepared to forgive it for a season or two. Now I'm a hundred metres below sitting in a tube going nowhere and wondering why the lights have just gone off, leaving just the emergency ones glowing. Platform lights are still okay.

No, lights are back on, driver is revving up the engine. Not going anywhere, but the noise sounds promising.

If she drops the clutch suddenly we're going to fuck off at speed.

An American couple have just got on. They emerged onto the platform with half a thousand suitcases each, saw the tube waiting, rushed on with a couple of suitcases, rushed off for the next, rushed on again, off again, until the final suitcase had been piled on. The woman giggling and chattering the whole time.

Then they asked someone whether this toob was going to the airport. Unfortunately they asked someone polite. If it had been me I would have said no, waited until they had lugged all their baggage off and the doors were closing, and said, 'Only joking, mate.' Some people deserve to be found guilty just by the way they look.

He's about fifty-five, tanned, fake, carrying some spare pounds. She's forty-five-ish, been around a very large block too often, spends a lot to disguise it. Not man and wife. Mutton dressed as a kebab, as I like to call it.

Okay, maybe not half a thousand, but he's got at least two huge suitcases plus smaller bags, she's got around five of various sizes.

I can guess their story. Both over here on business, met in the hotel bar, he heard her accent. Said something like 'I recognise that accent. You're from the States, arncha?'

She replies: 'Well, yeah, I'm from Pisskillmountains in Montana, but I operate out of Noo York these days.'

'Pisskillmountains? I nearly had a brother-in-law from there once. Only he came from Shitdiggershole in Nevada.'

'Now isn't that a coincidence?'

They get together, have a few drinks, she realises that this is The One, he thinks, Hey, great, I get a shag tonight even if she looks a bit on the old side, beggars can't be choosers – or whatever phrase the Yanks use. So they end up in his or her hotel room, have it off, probably wake the neighbours, he thinks that he'll be able to tearfully regret that he has to part the next day, promises to write – or e-mail, or text, or whatever – only to find that she's on the same flight as him the next day.

A right bummer.

Never trust men, my darling Danny. The only two girlfriends I pretty much never cheated on were your mother and someone called Wendy, but as she was seven at the time and I was five I don't think that counts.

Though in my defence I must point out that your mother was the first girlfriend I ever had who wasn't likely to cheat on me. It's the way humans are made.

Why is it I can never forget Wendy?

According to one of my pupils the Underground is so named because it runs under ground. He presumably then spent five minutes trying to find the rest of two hundred words and failed. Surprised he didn't just add "Fuck it, can't be arsed." Thing is, he's wrong, quite a bit of it runs above ground, and there are other sections which run in culverts, i.e. sort of in ditches, not underground. There's being pedantic and there's being just plain bloody wrong.

Science is exact. Mathematics is exact.

And yeah whatever is not a reasonable response.

Sure as fuck isn't an acceptable one.

Unless I'm the one saying it.

The Yank woman has her hand on the Yank bloke's thigh. Yuk. Get yourselves a hotel room. And tell him that shorts do not suit his flabbiness.

Bella.

Bella had a thousand faces, all carefully botoxed and made up with industrial strength powder and fillers. She had pitch-black hair, dyed, and was wearing a full-length black dress, long sleeves to the wrist, neck covered up to the chin.

And then there were the two most important parts of a woman's body: the eyes.

Hers were pure evil. With a smile. Devoid of humour.

Behind her were two enormous black blokes, bouncer types. Dressed in tuxedos, bow ties. Dark glasses. They followed her everywhere, like two guard dogs. Later I learned that they and the bloke on the door were hired for the night. I wouldn't be surprised if they went for a pint together after their duties and said something like, 'Thank fuck that's over, that's one real weird woman.'

'Bella, darling,' said Stella, 'this is Mark. He's the most wonderful teacher I've ever met.'

Bella paused, looked at me as if wondering how much amusement I was going to be, and then held out a wrinkly hand partly covered by a lace glove for me to kiss. At least, that's what it seemed like.

'Mark, how absolutely wonderful to have you here,' she said as I gently pressed her hand in what otherwise would have been a handshake.

'Wonderful,' I think I replied. Stella squeezed my shoulder.

'He doesn't say much,' she said, 'he's like a monk at times.'

What was I supposed to say, "Delighted to be in the dope house with fruitcake woman"?

Bella raised a hand in a languid fashion. A waitress in a bunny-girl costume with a trayful of drinks appeared immediately at her side.

'A drink for Mark,' intoned Bella. 'And Stella, of course. Choose your poison, dearest.'

'I'll have the orangeade,' giggled Stella. 'Try the apple juice, Mark.'

Stella picked up a cocktail glass of some orange liquid. I politely lifted a glass of some green stuff and raised it in salute to Bella. Then I pretended to take a sip. I took in a breath.

'That's got some zing,' I said in feigned surprise. Bella clapped her hands.

'Zing! Yes, exactly. Mark, I love you. You'll fit in perfectly. Zing. Indeed. Now I must circulate. Enjoy yourselves, darlings. Zing. Yes, Zing.'

I'd picked up the word zing from some cartoon comedy about Dracula's daughter I'd half-watched on the television a few weeks before. I don't think Bella had seen it.

Stella downed her orange drink and grabbed another off the bunny-waitress before she disappeared. I looked around for useful pot plants.

We seem to be moving at last. Pretty much the same way a kangaroo does. Gaboing-gaboing-gaboing. Brakes seem to be stuck on. Train's filled up a bit. Still got some space to write this. But if we have any more delays it's going to be like the black hole of Calcutta in here.

07h30.

Plenty of time.

Calcutta isn't called that any more. Can't remember exactly what it is called. No, Kolkata, that's it. Bombay is now Mumbai for some strange reason. Beijing used to be Peking.

Bloody daft. We don't get upset at the French calling London Londres and they aren't overly bothered because we don't call Paris Paree.

'Oh, Calcutta' was a stage play which, if said in French, translated as O quel cul t'as, or Oh what a lovely arse you have. To get past the censors. Are they supposed to rename it as Oh Kolkata?

Fuck's sake.

Kolkata probably translates as Would you like some tea with bread and jam in French.

When I went to school we did the Mikado. It's a traditional school thing. Every final year class gets to do a musical. My school – the one I teach at now – hadn't done one for a while. When I suggested it there were a lot of rueful faces. Apparently the last one had been a disaster. Most of the class couldn't sing. Those that could all wanted the main roles. Parents ended up having fist fights in the playground over whether Johnny should play the leading lady. The musical they chose was Grease, which was far too close to reality to be comfortable. Drugs, thugs, knives, sex and hot cars, just lacking in the looks department.

It's a weird movie, Grease. The ultimate moral of the story appears to be that you should turn yourself into a slut to get your man, never mind the fact that he's a dead-beat. I can understand kids loving it, it's got some good tunes and probably reflects their lives more closely than Romeo and Juliet. What I can't understand is why Hollywood made it. On paper it must have sounded a complete disaster. Especially to the more righteous financiers in the United States. Mammon is good, sex is the work of the devil. Unless you're married. In which case you need to spawn as many sprogs as possible to provide cheap labour for the rich and worthy.

One of the other alternatives is, of course, West Side Story. My lot would have brought real knives.

Funny thing about humans. Grease: high school students, two a penny, irrelevant; West Side Story: no-bit gangs all of whom could disappear into Alcatraz and rot their lives away and no-one would notice. Yet it's important to them. Like Rick says, of all the gin bars in the world you walk into mine. It might only be a shitty life, but it's mine.

Coming into Russell Square.

Your mother doesn't like Grease. She says it's too shallow. Personally I think she's pissed off that they didn't wait until she was old enough to play the lead role.

07h35.

Only five thousand stations to go

I can't remember the last time I prayed. Might be a good time to try to remember some of them. In time for the airport, anyway.

'Dear God, make me on time and make Maddy be reasonable and listen to me before she clouts me again. Please.'

Cockfosters
Oakwood
Southgate
Arnos Grove
● Bounds Green
● Wood Green
● Turnpike Lane
● Manor House
● Finsbury Park
● Arsenal
● Holloway Road
● Caledonian Road
● King's Cross St. Pancras
○ Russell Square
Holborn
Covent Garden
Leicester Square
Piccadilly Circus
Green Park
Hyde Park Corner
Knightsbridge
South Kensington
Gloucester Road
Earl's Court
Barons Court
Hammersmith
Turnham Green
Acton Town

Ealing Common          South Ealing
North Ealing           Northfields
Park Royal             Boston Manor
Alperton               Osterley
Sudbury Town           Hounslow East
Sudbury Hill           Hounslow Central
South Harrow           Hounslow West
Rayners Lane           Hatton Cross  ←
Eastcote               Heathrow T 1-2-3  ──→  Heathrow T4
Ruislip Manor          Heathrow T5
Ruislip
Ickenham
Hillingdon
Uxbridge

# Russell Square

*Estimated time to Heathrow Terminal Five:1 hour 2 minutes*

*Estimated time to Holborn tube station:1 minute*

07h35

Metal tummy has just got off. Russell Square. That'll be the British Museum and several universities. She certainly didn't look like a university student. But then, who knows, maybe she's a visiting professor. Professor of Feminist Studies and related shite.

There's a park up there. Correction. There are loads of parks up there. All over the place. Makes it look untidy.

Maddy was constantly amazed by the number of parks in central London. I can't remember which one it was, the one where she expressed her amazement, St James' Park I guess. I pointed out that we were walking on the same ground the beaus in romantic fiction would have done, the women in carriages, men on horseback, or just strolling along seeing and being seen. She thought it a wonderful idea, put her hand daintily on my arm and strolled daintily along as if she had a dainty parasol in the other dainty hand. She was wearing the usual black skirt she likes, quite voluminous so it swishes as she walks if she so desires. Ahead of us there was a woman dressed in Muslim style, brown veil, brown lumpy dress down to her feet. Next to her was what I presumed was her teenage daughter, high black veil over her head and wrapped around her neck, but wearing the tightest blue jeans I have ever seen. East meets West and does my bum look big in this?

How's this for a discussion: when Metal tummy left the little praying prick gave a sigh of relief and for some reason turned to me.

'An abomination in the sight of the lord,' he said.

'Eh?' I asked, not at all impressed with a total stranger spouting nonsense at me.

'That girl-child with her nakedness and the studs in her flesh. It is not right. She tempts men into the way of the devil.'

'What,' I asked, 'that lady boy?'

'Lady boy?'

'Young bloke dressed up like a girl. That's what he was.'

'Eh?'

By this time the Yanks and the bombers had woken up and were taking notice.

'You get a lot of them around here. They sell themselves for money to older men.'

'Eh?'

'You could have got a discount, I reckon.'

He took the opportunity of the doors still not closing to scuttle off. Thank god. Now I can concentrate on this.

Bloody weirdo foreigners. Addressing a stranger without being introduced. Interrupting someone trying to write some notes down.

07h37.

Moving again.

In my previous school we had a good old discussion about what it meant to be British. Plenty of hands raised and 'Sir! Sir! Me sir!' Lots of good suggestions. Then we discussed whether any of them were exclusively British, or whether most nations or cultures aspired to them. One day I thought I'd do the same with my current lot. Then I looked at them without the rose-tinted glasses of youthful idealism and decided to give it a miss. For a start most of them weren't born in Britain, certainly their parents weren't. And those that were probably don't think of themselves as British unless they're in France or some other country, and then they'll only identify as English anyway. Mainly in opposition to being French.

You could say that it's a question of class.

Danny, if I have a hand in your education you'll know all about Keir Hardie. If it's just your mother bringing you up, god help you. Still, if that's the case, at least you'll know every female character in every Shakespeare play. Your mother plays a very strange Ophelia, and much prefers a tom-boyish Juliet. She decided early on in our relationship to call me Romeo in more intimate moments. Recently she's changed that to "You fucking bastard". But, to be honest, those weren't really that intimate moments.

I think I prefer Romeo.

The driver has just announced that we'll be slightly late because of ongoing signalling problems in the Barons Court area. Well, Hammersmith, Barons Court, more or less the same thing.

Slightly late?

07h40.

Slightly fucking late?

Should be okay once we get past Hammersmith. That's only about ten stations.

Why did we choose Cabaret instead of Romeo and Juliet, or, even worse, Macbeth?

Macbeth The Musical. Oh, god, please, please let me write that. Probably already been done, though I've never heard of it.

The point of a school musical is to show both pupils and parents that everyone can sing, given the time and effort. Those that refuse to accept that can be given jobs as scene shifters, announcers, anything. It's one of the few times everyone gets a part to play. The kids learn team work, discipline, you name it. Plus they learn proper music.

I knew that if I suggested it to the head it would become the latest silly idea Mark had thought of, so I put the thought into the music teacher's head instead. The music teacher is a lovely little woman. She's bloody useless playing music, can only play the violin, can't keep discipline in a class, but her knowledge of theory and musical history is second to none, and she has a really good ear for which voices are doing what.

The head said we could go ahead with it. I think she was confident it would be a complete disaster. We chose Cabaret. I could say that it was because of the historical significance, because it's a classic, or any number of reasons. Truth is I chose it because we could hide the ugly fuckers with loads of make-up.

Coming into Holborn.

07h43.

Not too long now. And then ...

Danny, sometimes it's better to be extemporaneous

That means procrastinating until the shit hits the fan in the hope you'll have thought up a plan by then.

Cockfosters
Oakwood
Southgate
Arnos Grove
● Bounds Green
● Wood Green
● Turnpike Lane
● Manor House
● Finsbury Park
● Arsenal
● Holloway Road
● Caledonian Road
● King's Cross St. Pancras
● Russell Square
○ Holborn
Covent Garden
Leicester Square
Piccadilly Circus
Green Park
Hyde Park Corner
Knightsbridge
South Kensington
Gloucester Road
Earl's Court
Barons Court
Hammersmith
Turnham Green
Acton Town

| | |
|---|---|
| Ealing Common | South Ealing |
| North Ealing | Northfields |
| Park Royal | Boston Manor |
| Alperton | Osterley |
| Sudbury Town | Hounslow East |
| Sudbury Hill | Hounslow Central |
| South Harrow | Hounslow West |
| Rayners Lane | Hatton Cross ← |
| Eastcote | Heathrow T 1-2-3 ⟶ Heathrow T4 |
| Ruislip Manor | Heathrow T5 |
| Ruislip | |
| Ickenham | |
| Hillingdon | |
| Uxbridge | |

# Holborn

*Estimated time to Heathrow Terminal Five:57 minutes*

*Estimated time to Covent Garden tube station: 2 minutes*

07h43

I do not believe this. A man has just got on with a carrier bag full of pies or pasties, sat down at the other end of the carriage, and is now determinedly hoovering the lot, one by one. He's got this immense paunch, if he were pregnant it would be ten of the little buggers. He's like a mechanical chomper. Chomp chomp chomp hoover hoover hoover next pie chomp chomp chomp. He's not even looking at them, never mind tasting anything.

The people around him are looking a little green. I don't blame them. It must stink to high heaven. Hot pies in an enclosed space before breakfast? Gross.

I think they're from Greggs. I can't see the name on the bag, but they're the only ones likely to be dispensing pies at this time of the day. I mean, I know they're supposed to be good, but a whole carrier bag before eight a.m.?

We seem to be upwind, thank god.

The Yanks haven't noticed. They appear to be having a snogging contest. I do hope he doesn't think there's an Underground version of the Mile High Club.

Now there's an idea. I get to Heathrow, find Maddy, and before she can get going into her "Betrayed innocent lover girl" bit, ask her what she thinks of doing it on the Underground. Chances are she'll stop, think, giggle and then say, 'Oh, come on then, where?' Though if the question arises, did the earth move, the answer might be, yes, but the bloody tube didn't. We could start a fashion. A sport. Special points for different stations. A ten for coming at Mornington Crescent.

Just don't mention the pies.

I said the last time I was at Terminal 5 it took me sixty seconds from tube to departures, and that's true enough. But that was pretty straightforward. I was going to see someone off, they were waiting for me, they were

73

straight economy class passengers, normal people. This time it sounds like enemy territory. I remember Stella and the others comparing departure lounges, which I realised were lounges reserved for premium passengers. Being economy no-frills myself I've never been in those lounges, and I doubt if they'd let me in to find your mother. Being the bloody-minded woman she is she's probably bought a first-class ticket just so that she can sit in a first-class lounge and enjoy the sight of me trying to get in.

Did I mention that your bloody mother can be a bit bloody minded, Danny, my darling?

Keir Hardie was the founding father of the Labour party in the UK. Your great grandfather was Labour, working class, and proud of it. That's your great grandfather on your decent side, i.e. your daddy's side. Your great grandfather on your mother's side was probably Jack the Ripper. Your great grandmother on your mother's side was probably also Jack the Ripper. Or Attila the Hun.

It was the Labour Party which paved the way for your grandfather to go to university. Which is where things become messy, because the Labour Party became middle class, then upper class, then establishment, then imploded. Just remember, if you work for a living then you're working class, and never trust any other class, they'll screw you soon as they get a chance.

If you're a head master or head mistress then you're a wanker.

Sorry, but there it is.

Young woman a few seats away doing her make-up. There was a time that would have been considered extremely common, if not downright prostitute-ish. These days the debate over such things is more evenly balanced. Half of women think it's lazy and sluttish, the other half think it's worth another ten or fifteen minutes in bed, men have just decided to shrug and accept it. It's not their make-up and they only get in trouble if they mention it.

The Yanks have come up for air. They seem to have realised that there's only so much snogging you can do without sex before it becomes very,

very boring. She's laid her head against her chest. He's quietly checking his watch where she can't see.

'So, honey, when are you going to take me to your ranch?'

Oh, do shut up. For Christ's sake. Fucking ranch. My fucking arse.

'Shucks, baby, that's a difficult question to answer. Like I told you last night, it's a working ranch, and right now they're rounding up the cattle for market. They know what they're doing, and I doan interfere while they busy.'

'Well, shucks, honeybunch, surely you know roughly when we can go there to be alone?'

'Won't be for a couple of weeks, baby. But definitely before the end of next month. That's when the sunrise gets real beautiful.'

'Aw, hun, that sounds just great.'

Puke.

He's got a ranch like I've got a pink Maserati.

I've never understood why people feel the need to lie to get shagged. Anyone asks me what I do I tell them I'm a high school teacher in an inner-London shithole. If nothing else it gets me the sympathy vote.

The problem with the kids is they have no class to hold onto. There was a time when you could be working class and proud of it. But the kids have no sense of being working class, nothing to hold fast to. You can start off as working class and become a billionaire or famous violinist or surgeon, or whatever, but you need something to start from. Nobody has ever claimed they started life as a chav and went on to great success.

Admittedly the working class of great-grandad's era were also sexist, male, racist, homophobic, all the nasty things we hate today. They also lived shitty short lives and died young. We live shitty lives for longer.

Shunt, screech, a sudden jump, stop, the Yanks faces mash each other up in surprise.

Make-up girl now has a lipstick mark going across her cheek. I think she may have said fuck.

Crawling into Covent Garden.

07h47.

Hell, that only took a couple of minutes.

Tell the driver to slow down, I'm getting culture shock here.
It's either that or a speed wobble.
We might even make it after all.
Of course we're going to fucking make it.
Failure is not an option.
I don't believe I just wrote that.
Boy, does love make you stupid.

Cockfosters
Oakwood
Southgate
Arnos Grove
Bounds Green
Wood Green
Turnpike Lane
Manor House
Finsbury Park
Arsenal
Holloway Road
Caledonian Road
King's Cross St. Pancras
Russell Square
Holborn
Covent Garden
Leicester Square
Piccadilly Circus
Green Park
Hyde Park Corner
Knightsbridge
South Kensington
Gloucester Road
Earl's Court
Barons Court
Hammersmith
Turnham Green
Acton Town

Ealing Common
North Ealing
Park Royal
Alperton
Sudbury Town
Sudbury Hill
South Harrow
Rayners Lane
Eastcote
Ruislip Manor
Ruislip
Ickenham
Hillingdon
Uxbridge

South Ealing
Northfields
Boston Manor
Osterley
Hounslow East
Hounslow Central
Hounslow West
Hatton Cross
Heathrow T 1-2-3 ⟶ Heathrow T4
Heathrow T5

# Covent Garden

*Estimated time to Heathrow Terminal Five:59 minutes*

*Estimated time to Leicester Square tube station: 1 minute*

07h48

Driver appears to be having another break. Lunch this time, I would imagine. Caviar and crayfish, the bastards can afford it. We're just sitting here going nowhere. Probably needs to get her breath back after the last sprint. Or do her eyebrows or something.

Young woman got on with one of those huge take-away mugs of 90 percent sugar coffee. I swear I'm putting on weight from just being in the same carriage as it. You can smell the sugar from five yards away.

Covent Garden. Speaking of which, all tourists are told that the first thing they must do if they visit Covent Garden is to walk quickly up the stairs to the top rather than take the lift, to admire the wonderful, and indeed unique, architecture and wrought iron railings. Of course the real reason is that it's one of the deepest Underground stations there is, with almost 200 steps to the top, and any tourist trying it is going to be pretty out of breath long before they realise they've been thoroughly duped, unless they're really, really fit. There's even a sign there warning people not to try it.

The gang went there the one time, to the opera, a special night out, I think one of the others had been given free tickets as part of a promotion, read bribe. Now we weren't strangers to the place, Covent Garden tube station, that is, and normally we'd have taken the lift, but on an impulse, as we passed the warning, I said suddenly, "Race you to the top" and ran to the stairs. Anyone with any sense would have replied, "You go for it, arsehole," and carried on to the lifts. But the gang had this image of being young and fit and daring and stupid, so they all promptly followed. I was completely out of breath by the time I got to the top, but by the time they caught up I had my breath back and they were utterly wrecked, almost throwing up. The girls were wearing evening frocks and high heels, so they had to take the heels off and carry them after a few steps. But their biggest problem was not pacing themselves. I was going at my

78

pace and they were trying to beat me, guaranteeing their breathing would be out of synch. By the time the first of them caught up with me at the top I had adopted an amused pose almost James Bondian in its coolness. The first one after me was actually Stella. I think the other lads had smoked too many cigars.

'What the hell did you do that for?' she asked once she had stopped heaving, by which time the others had arrived, and were standing around bent over in various attitudes of physical agony.

'Because I can,' I replied. 'Look at me, I'm fucking super-teacher.'

And then I added, 'The real question is why you fuckers were stupid enough to follow me.'

After which, once they'd recovered sufficiently to stumble, and had suitably cursed me for their stupidity, we adjourned to the nearest hostelry for a rejuvenating pint. Which just happened to be the Lamb & Flag, formerly known as the Bucket of Blood, when Covent Garden was actually a slum area. These days it seems that all of London is being gentrified. They've even fired the orphans who used to do the chimney sweeping. You can tell someone's class by asking them what they think of Covent Garden. If they reply, 'Lovely place, last time I was there there was this wonderful comedian who juggled, and we had some excellent food' they're either normal class or tourists. If they say, 'My goodness, that reminds me, I must check my opera membership is up to date' they are (a) seriously upper or upper middle class, and (b) too old or stupid to know what an email reminder or direct debit is.

Your mother is, of course, in a class of her own. She admired the performers outside, she thought the floating Jedi or whatever it was was 'ever so cute', she insisted we had to have a Spanish meal – one of the restaurants was serving Spanish food, paella on these huge circular cooking pans, about three foot wide. But what she really wanted, what she dreamed about, what she lusted after with all her soul, was to sing in the opera. What I dreamed about was being able to buy the opera, then I could have owned Maddy. Not that it would make much difference, she'd still throw pots and pans at me. But they would have been my pots and pans.

Someone alert the fucking press, the doors have closed and we are slowly on our way.

07h50.

On the move, if slowly. Goodbye, Covent Garden.

The driver's just warned us that because of signal failures in the Barons Court area trains are reversing at Earl's Court. So now it's Barons Court that's the culprit. To laugh, to die, to live, to die, to kick the door in and take over from the driver. These foolish things remind me of you.

Christ in a rising bucket.

Bella.

Bella's real name was Annabelle. Or at least that's what someone told me, Stella, or one of the others. I think. Normal people you know are, say, Kenyan, like Kevin, because they tell you. Of course, thinking about Kevin, checking their passport to confirm it might be a good idea. But Bella, well, you just came to 'know' something about her, a bit like osmosis. It might be true, maybe not, it didn't matter if it was true or not. She was Hungarian, she was Egyptian, she had psychic powers, she was descended from kings, she was an orphan gypsy, she was fifty, she was ninety-seven, someone said, someone overheard, it was rumoured.

Bella's house was the largest in Muswell Hill, I think. It might have been two houses knocked into one. You drifted from room to endless room, half lit, smoky, eternal twilight, small groups of shadowy people in shadowy places, strobe lights shifting the shadows continually. There was always some anonymous soothing music playing, nothing you could put a name to, almost like a creamy lullaby to soothe away your fears. You didn't need to take drugs to get high, you just needed to breathe in the air. The smell of weed was so ubiquitous you didn't notice it after a few seconds.

Some rooms were off limits, though it was easy to miss as the doors were hidden behind curtains. I'm pretty sure at least one was reserved for gambling, invitation only, money up front, no loans. Stella said it reminded her of Casablanca and Rick's and Humphrey Bogart. With Stella as Ilsa Lund, presumably. Fat chance. More like Yvonne, Rick's ex-girlfriend.

Your mother loves Casablanca. Even if nobody suddenly and spontaneously bursts into a song about music. No, wait a minute, they suddenly burst into the Marsellaise and Deutschland über Alles at some point. Different teams, though. In the real world there are no super-clean dives like Rick's.

Stopped again. In the middle of a tunnel. I can understand why people freak out with claustrophobia. I might well freak out. Not with claustrophobia. More like extreme fuckstration. That's fucking frustration.

Jesus fuck will you just get a bloody move on.

07h52.

To put it simply, Bella's place was a drugs den. Stella and the others had got into the habit of going there about once a month, getting zonked out of their skulls, and spending the next few weeks getting it out of their systems. I went along a few times to be polite, but it really wasn't my scene. I'm quite happy to indulge in illegal substances in my own home, I didn't trust Bella or the people around her. There used to be stories of people falling asleep in foreign places after accepting a drink from a stranger, waking up in a bath of crushed ice with a note advising them to get to a doctor double quick as one of their kidneys had been removed for sale. I think the stories were apocryphal, but if ever that sort of thing was likely to kick off Bella's, would have been a prime starting point.

I was introduced to the local drug supplier on the first night. A revolting, skinny, pasty-faced, greasy little thing in all black, with a gold chain and gold bracelets. No watch, he probably couldn't read a watch. He was, I guessed, only a few years out of school. Cocksure as they come.

'This is Ziggie,' Stella had said, 'he can get you pretty much anything.

'Know what I mean?' said Ziggie, winking one eye. I felt like punching him right there and then.

I never had need of Ziggie's services, but the number of dilated eyes floating around told me that that business was doing quite well.

One day I asked Stella why Ziggie had chosen to call himself Ziggie. She looked at me as if I was missing a few spanners.

'Ziggy Stardust?' she suggested.

'He thinks he's David Bowie?' I asked.

'No, Mark, he delivers stardust. You know.'

'Stardust? You have got to be joking. He supplies dope to crackheads. He is a dope. Do you know what the full title of that album is? The Rise and Fall of Ziggy Stardust and the Spiders from Mars, that's what. He's more of a lizard from Luton than a spider from Mars.'

She had frowned when I mentioned crackheads, after all that's what I had just called her, more or less. But she laughed at the lizard of Luton crack.

'Mark, you can really get on your high horse sometimes,' she said.

'Ziggy Stardust was one of Bowie's most brilliant inventions,' I said. 'Lowlifes like that arsehole shouldn't be polluting it.'

'Well, he does spell it Ziggie, with an i-e, rather than Ziggy with a y.'

'Thank fuck for that,' I said. 'Do we know if he can actually spell?'

'Probably not.'

'Anyway, stardust comes from the Carpenters song Close To You, 1970. It was a rework of the version by Burt Bacharach and Hal David from 1963. Stayed at number one for four weeks.'

'Jesus, Mark, can't you be normal? Be a football bore like most men, this music business is weird.'

'I am a football bore, I support Arsenal. That's why I prefer music, it's less painful. And I even know the lyrics,' I said. And I began to sing,

'On the day that you were born the angels got together

and decided to create a mare come true

so they sprinkled sawdust in your hair

and made your eyes of glue

boo

hoo'

She punched me in the arm.

'You're nuts,' she concluded.

Danny, personally I think I'm the sane one. But I'll leave you to decide, twenty odd years from now. And if she thought I was weird with my scattered musical trivia, it's a good thing she never met YBM. She has memorised the name of every female singer since mankind first left the caves, and most of the men, too.

Thinking of it, I remember Stella singing along to Manfred Mann, Do wah diddy, diddy, dum diddy do. Except her version went:

There she was just walking down the street
singing, do to me what daddy did to mummy to get you
snapping her fingers and shuffling her feet
singing, do to me what daddy did to mummy to get you.'

The rest was pretty filthy, but she didn't mess with the line 'wedding bells are gonna chime.'

Ziggie and Bella.

Later on I would have nightmares where I was floating through Bella's like a ghost, seeing all the others without them seeing me, their voices braying and shrieking with laughter as they warmed themselves with fires of fifty pound notes, and Ziggie as a kind of Emcee shouting them on, while Chris floated past me saying 'Your people, teach, your people'. And then I'd wake up in a sweat, and wonder, what the fuck was that all about. But that was nothing compared to when the nightmares about Jenny began.

We seem to be stop-starting our way to Leicester Square. Nope, now we're just stopped.

People ask me why I wanted to become a teacher. I didn't. I wanted to be a song writer and poet. Not a singer, though I did sing my own songs sufficiently well to be sure they scanned. Just a poet and song writer, any order you choose. Only thing is, like most stuff in the art world, when you make it big you earn a fortune, otherwise you don't earn enough to starve with. So I needed a job that would keep me going on the side until I did make it big enough to indulge myself and compose works of genius. I chose teaching partly on the basis that I could probably wing it and not have to spend too much time on it while following the true love of my life, and partly because I suspected that in most other jobs they expect you to at least pretend to give a fuck.

I always have a quiet laugh when I hear people bang on about the long hours teachers work. I'm the laziest teacher there is. I even get the kids to mark each other's homework every so often. I tell the other teachers that it gives the kids the experience of trying to understand how the marking system works, and what qualifies as quality. Truth is it saves me from having to do the bloody stuff.

Danny, the only thing a teacher can really teach their kids is how to use their brains properly and think for themselves. Doesn't matter if they can't recite their ten-times tables or know what the capital of Jupiter is, they can know every fact in the world, if they can't think for themselves they're fucked anyway.

Problem with humans is that they only want other humans to think for themselves as far as it benefits the first lot of humans. As soon as the second lot of humans start to think too much they become revolutionaries. Then you have to shoot them.

Stop-starting our way to Leicester Square. I'm sure I could write a song about that.

If I manage to get to your mother in time, and if I manage not to fucking strangle her, and if she agrees to – let me be part of your life, I almost said 'marry me' – I shall write a song called On My Way To Maddening, something like that.

Trouble with teaching is that it involves humans. At least, my last school did. This one it's more like vaguely sentient slime. But you can't help but end up wanting the little fuckers to succeed, somehow, anyhow. Even if it's teaching them how to be better crooks.

Couldn't even get that right.

Finally. On the move again. According to the driver it's going to be slow going, just in case we hadn't noticed.

Coming in to Leicester Square. Slugging our way into Leicester Square. As in, moving at the speed of a slug.

Now there's a name for a pub, The Slugging Lettuce.

08h00.

So now we're averaging about ten minutes between stations. Say, about twenty stops left, that's about two hundred minutes, just over three hours. That can't be right. Must have got something wrong somewhere. And me supposed to be a maths teacher.

Don't think I packed a calculator. Because my smartphone had a calculator on it. Not a very smart phone, in the end, not now it's lying on the kitchen floor in pieces.

Anyway, even then if it does take three hours, which it won't, I should have time to spare.

11h30 – it's now 08h00, that gives me three and a half hours. Depending on – pretty much everything, really.

Fuck it we've stopped again.

Half way into the platform.

No, wait, moving.

Stopped.

Moving.

Creeping forward.

Finally. Made it. And the doors open.

Fucking Hallelujah.

Danny, I've just remembered what opera we saw. At Covent Garden. Carmen. Yup, the story of an innocent young man bewitched by a gorgeous gypsy girl who drives him insane and he ends up killing her.

I think that was Fate having a little laugh at my expense. I'm beginning to think Taming of the Shrew would be more apt. Don't know if they made an opera of that though.

Danny, did you know that in real life no-one has ever managed to tame a shrew? They're vicious little buggers which will attack anything and eat anything. They go through their body weight in food every couple of hours. And it's impossible to domesticate the little buggers.

Completely impossible to tame them.

I don't like the sound of that.

Cockfosters
Oakwood
Southgate
Arnos Grove
● Bounds Green
● Wood Green
● Turnpike Lane
● Manor House
● Finsbury Park
● Arsenal
● Holloway Road
● Caledonian Road
● King's Cross St. Pancras
● Russell Square
● Holborn
● Covent Garden
○ Leicester Square
Piccadilly Circus
Green Park
Hyde Park Corner
Knightsbridge
South Kensington
Gloucester Road
Earl's Court
Barons Court
Hammersmith
Turnham Green
Acton Town

Ealing Common       South Ealing
North Ealing        Northfields
Park Royal          Boston Manor
Alperton            Osterley
Sudbury Town        Hounslow East
Sudbury Hill        Hounslow Central
South Harrow        Hounslow West
Rayners Lane        Hatton Cross ←
Eastcote            Heathrow T 1-2-3 ⟶ Heathrow T4
Ruislip Manor       Heathrow T5
Ruislip
Ickenham
Hillingdon
Uxbridge

# Leicester Square

*Estimated time to Heathrow Terminal Five: 58 minutes*

*Estimated time to Piccadilly Circus tube station: 2 minutes*

08h00

A woman's just got on with two small kids and half a battalion of suitcases. That doesn't bode well. Two bored kids on a tube that isn't going anywhere fast. There'll be tears before bedtime. Just so long as they have them somewhere else.

Leicester Square. Famous for cinemas and first nights and red carpets and celebrities and shit. So where has the woman and her two children come from? Presumably they're on their way to the airport. Must have stayed in a hotel overnight. So where's daddy? Why isn't he with them? I'm good at questions. Answers, not so much.

Danny, Sherlock Holmes used to be able to take one look at someone and know their entire history, their background, their motives, and where they were going and why. That was in Victorian times. These days I reckon he'd look for about half an hour and conclude, 'Watson, I haven't a fucking clue.'

Leicester Square tube station. All white tiling with blue piping.

Jenny came down from Liverpool during the uni holidays, just after Christmas. It was a new experience. She'd stayed with me before on holiday, but that was in my tiny old flat, find enough free floor space for a sleeping bag, remember to latch the bathroom door when you're in there, some things siblings don't need to share, that sort of thing. But now we shared a large house inherited from our aunt. Two bathrooms, one each. I'd made Jenny choose her bedroom before she'd gone back to Liverpool after the funeral. So although we did most things together, there wasn't that sense of living in each other's pockets there had been before.

I hadn't had a chance to sort out any of Aunt Marigold's stuff. Jenny was intrigued with the contents. Unlike me she hadn't spent much time in the holidays with Aunt Marigold. So we spent a morning wandering around trying to formulate a plan of where to put everything for when the folks got around to coming down. Jenny prodded and poked while I tried to pretend interest. The only thing that intrigued me was a locked chest of drawers. I suppose it's one of those male things. It's an adventure. A locked cabinet is a challenge to be overcome, by finding the secret key if you're a boy, or, if you're older, a twelve-pound hammer or circular saw. In the end we gave up. We couldn't find the key or the special knot you press and it suddenly clicks open to reveal a skull and box of precious jewels, and I wasn't about to damage a priceless heirloom if that's what it was.

There were wooden French windows in the kitchen that led onto a patio, but we couldn't seem to get them open either. It was still wet winter, too early in the year to have breakfast or dinner or whatever outside, so we deferred that until later, too.

221b Baker Street. Jenny and I went to have a look one day. We did a lot of that. Have a look at some tourist attraction, check the prices, decide not to go in. Some of the ticket prices they charge are just bloody ridiculous. You can easily tell which ones. They have a queue of extremely smartly dressed young Japanese women waiting outside. I don't know why. They seem to be happy to spend a small fortune for tat. Moving again.

08h03.

Christ.

Jenny was intrigued by the concept of 221B Baker Street. It's in the wrong place. It's a pure invention. It doesn't make any sense. Yet people buy into the illusion.

Then one Saturday, I'd skipped tennis, Stella popped in on her way home, and suggested Jenny might like going to Bella's. Well, I wasn't going to have that, but Jenny was all for it. Tell the truth, I'd hoped to keep Stella and Jenny apart. I was quite happy fucking Stella, I didn't want any of her more louche side rubbing off on Jenny. Jenny seemed intrigued by Stella. I think she guessed we were more than just friends, and wondered why I hadn't mentioned Stella before. Anyway, we ended up going, with my warnings about not actually drinking any of the poison supplied. She seemed quite happy with the notion.

I introduced her to Bella, and I can't say I liked the look Bella gave her. The wicked witch meets the innocent princess. But that was over quickly. We wandered around watering the pot plants while no-one was looking. Jenny was having trouble not giggling at some of the more exotic guests. I remember her whispering to me at one point that she felt sorry for the black doorman in the tutu. Not a point of view that had crossed my mind before, I don't tend to feel sorry for blokes over six feet tall who wear reflective sun glasses. But I dare say she may have had a point. At one stage I needed to go to the gents, trusting that Stella would look after Jen for five minutes. When I came out I found to my irritation that, not only had Stella disappeared somewhere, but Ziggie was trying to chat my sister up, and Jen seemed quite happy with the attention. She was probably just being polite, but people like Ziggie don't understand that concept. I exchanged some pleasantries as far as I could without vomiting, took Jen's arm and steered her towards the door, making noises about someone we had promised to meet at a local pub.

'God, let's get ourselves a real drink,' I said once we were safely outside.

'You don't like him much, do you?' asked Jen. 'Ziggie, I mean.'

'About as much as I like any rat,' I replied.

We dropped the conversation. At the time I presumed that Jen shared my appreciation of Ziggie's worth, i.e. nil.

We had a couple of drinks, went for a meal, chatted about things inconsequential, the state of the world, theories of the great philosophers, how Jenny's studies were going, pretty much anything and everything. It was almost as if we were going out together, strangers getting to know each other. I thoroughly enjoyed it, and, tellingly, didn't think of Stella once. The rest of the gang had also been at Bella's that night, they could look after her for a change.

Danny, time is precious. If I'd known how little of it I had left to spend with Jenny – well, I'd have taken care of her much better, I'd have wrapped her in love and told her not to go to the dark places. But I didn't know.

But I do know I can do something about your bloody mother.

The driver has just made a pronouncement.

We will shortly be arriving at Piccadilly Circus. If departing the train please mind the gap and make sure you take all your personal affects with you otherwise we might have to call in the police and have the service suspended unlike now when it's just going so slow a fucking snail could outrun it.

Piccadilly Circus.

Whoopee.

08h10.

The little brats have just started the 'Are we there yet?' routine with their mother. Her reply: 'Look, darling, count the number of stations.' Sound of two little snots counting loudly. On, two, three, ten, lots.

'No, darling, look, it's one, two, three, four, five, six, seven, eight, nine, ten, eleven, twelve, thirteen, fourteen, fifteen, sixteen, seventeen, eighteen, nineteen, twenty!'

Twenty fucking stops to Terminal Five.

She's told them they can have an ice cream when they get there.

We all have our own desires. And mine is twenty fucking stops away. And probably sitting there calmly enjoying an ice cream. She'd better bloody not be.

Cockfosters
Oakwood
Southgate
Arnos Grove
● Bounds Green
● Wood Green
● Turnpike Lane
● Manor House
● Finsbury Park
● Arsenal
● Holloway Road
● Caledonian Road
● King's Cross St. Pancras
● Russell Square
● Holborn
● Covent Garden
● Leicester Square
○ Piccadilly Circus
Green Park
Hyde Park Corner
Knightsbridge
South Kensington
Gloucester Road
Earl's Court
Barons Court
Hammersmith
Turnham Green
Acton Town

Ealing Common          South Ealing
North Ealing           Northfields
Park Royal             Boston Manor
Alperton               Osterley
Sudbury Town           Hounslow East
Sudbury Hill           Hounslow Central
South Harrow           Hounslow West
Rayners Lane           Hatton Cross    ←
Eastcote               Heathrow T 1-2-3  ⟶  Heathrow T4
Ruislip Manor          Heathrow T5
Ruislip
Ickenham
Hillingdon
Uxbridge

# Piccadilly Circus

*Estimated time to Heathrow Terminal Five: 56 minutes*

*Estimated time to Green Park tube station: 1 minute*

08h10

Danny, your mother is a Catholic. I used to be one once. Wasn't my fault, it was the way I was born.

I promise to prevent her from inflicting that shite on you. Well, if I get the chance.

How many Stations of the Cross are there? I'd forgotten about the Stations of the Cross until your mother introduced me to hell. And told me it was heaven.

That time we were at King's Cross, or King's Cross St Pancras to give it its full name, I remember I gave my camera to the Japanese bloke to take a shot of us. But I also remember Maddy giving her camera to the Japanese bloke's girlfriend to take a shot of us. You have to wonder. Why did we each need our own picture of us? Wasn't the point of going out together to share everything?

Well, almost everything.

I suppose if a couple splits up the one doesn't ask the other to hand over copies of photographs from when they were head over heels in love.

'Darling, you're a complete shit and I hate you to the point where I'd happily cut your balls off and spread them on toast with marmite, but would you mind making some copies of the photographs from the time we were deeply in love and I hadn't realised what a complete tosser you really are, you low-life piece of scum, sweetheart?'

But who thinks, 'I must get my own copy of this moment in case we split up' when they've no eyes for anyone but their one and only true love?

Maybe it's subconscious. Maybe Maddy intended to break up, sooner or later.

Wahay, we're off. 08h10.

Well, fuck me sideways, arrived here at 08h10, departed 08h10. Give that driver a fucking medal. A big one. With gold fucking stars. Goodbye Piccadilly, farewell Leicester Square, it's a long way to Tipperary, and my heart lies there. That's a song from the First World War, Danny. They named some trenches Piccadilly Circus and Leicester Square. So they were singing goodbye to the war. Except it was more in hope than anything else.

Talking of photographs. There was the day I took out my camera kit to sort out. I go through sudden bursts of using my cameras almost every day, followed by long periods of not touching any of them, and forgetting where I've left the lenses and the camera bodies and tripods and the rest.

I'd put everything on one of the kitchen sideboards, planning to pack away what I wasn't going to use and keep out what I was, as I usually do with such things. As I also usually do the whole lot is still sitting there now, weeks later.

Maddy picked up my monopod in its cover and asked what it was.

'It's a monopod,' I replied.

She gave me a look which pretty much said, 'Thank you for that completely useless bit of information, would you like me to kill you now painlessly or more slowly later?'

'What's it for?'

'It's like a tripod, but with one leg. Here,' I said, taking it out of its cover and unclipping and extending the legs. 'See, it extends to just below eye-height, you've got this screw just like a tripod, that's for your camera. It allows you a little more stability if you're taking a slow shot. It's for when you're out for a walk or something and don't want to lug a tripod around. And, by screwing on this knob instead of a camera it becomes a walking stick.'

I collapsed the leg back to its two-foot length.

'And it's handy for smacking disobedient dogs around the head,' I added, swinging it slightly to show its heft.

'It looks handy,' she said, taking it back and admiring it. 'I'll have to get myself one.'

'You can use this one,' I offered, 'I never do.'

Which was true. It was one of those 'seemed like a good idea at the time' purchases. And for many people it would have been. Just not me. But

Maddy thought it was a most excellent idea, and from then on she religiously took the monopod with whenever we went out with our cameras, which was pretty much every outing. and which meant, in reality, she carried it for all of five yards before asking me to hold it for a few minutes, which turned out to be the rest of the day. And it was never used to stabilise either of our cameras because we never took any photographs in low light. I like to think we have many talents between us, but I'm afraid as far as photography goes we're pretty much fair-weather friends.

There was however someone else who turned out to be a surprise cameraman.

I bumped into Chris and some of the others in the playground one lunch time. He was showing off a camera, a compact digital SLR. He was obviously proud of it, but the light in his eyes died as I appeared – typical teenage response.

'Nice camera,' I commented.

'Me uncle give it me, didn't he,' he replied. Translation: I didn't steal this one.

God knows what relationship his 'uncle' had to him. He has no uncles. Or aunts. Maybe one of his mother's passing clients.

'That's something a friend of mine at university ended up doing,' I said. 'Became a photo-journalist. Doesn't make a fortune, but he enjoys himself. Course you have to be fit and quick on the draw. And have quite a lot of guts, come to think of it.'

'Why's that, sir?' asked one of others on queue. Kids can be so predictable. Boys, anyway. Give them action and danger and they're yours for the rest of their lives. Talk about something needing guts and they'll believe every lie you feed them.

'Well, portrait photographers can control their subjects, everything is posed, they choose the light and background. Action photographers don't know when and how things are going to happen, they've got to try to be in the right place at the right time, but even then they have to be quick. Think of being at a riot: they're normally between the rioters and the police, they're trying to get the best shots of both while not getting a rock or a bullet in the head. Have a look at photographs in the newspapers sometime, you'll see which are posed and which are shot in a second. There's a very famous shot from the Spanish Civil War of a man being shot as he jumps up to charge the enemy. Shot dead in front of his eyes. Kapa, I think the photographer's name was, Frank Kapa. Became world-famous at the time. Anyway, must be off, I've got work to do.'

As I walked away I heard one of them making a comment about Chris being a war photographer, and Chris returning some usual insult. But I could tell I'd planted the seed of an idea in his head. Which was a good thing for a while. But not in the end.

Stopped again. Middle of a tunnel. Silence, apart from leaking music. Emergency lights only. No, not silence, we now have the sound of two brats wailing, one demanding to know why we've stopped, the other wanting to know whether or not they are 'there'. I will forever be amazed at how many children make it to adulthood without being murdered by their parents.

Their mother has suggested they play a game of I spy. That'll go down well in a crowded tube. 'I spy something beginning with a 'T'. '

'Toe?'

'No.'

'Train?'

'No.'

'I give up, what is it?'

'That fat old woman over there.'

'That doesn't start off with a T it starts off with an F.'

'No it doesn't, that starts with a T.'

It would certainly start the fat old woman off.

Danny, nothing personal, but if you're going to be like these brats I'm turning around right now and going home. Well, if I could, if you see what I mean.

Hello, lights back on, sound of engine being gunned, and – quick jump, sudden brake, everybody crushes up, then we're off at a crawl.

Driver has just apologised for the kangaroo bop. And reminded us that this train will only be going as far as Earl's Court due to signalling problems at Acton Town. Jesus Chris is there anyway on this bloody line that isn't having a collective signal failure?

08h20. Crawling into Green Park. And, oh, look, all those friendly people waiting together on the platform just ever so ever so eager beaver to join us. Or maybe not. From the looks on their faces I would say that 'seriously pissed off' is probably a better description.

Green Park. Junction with the Victoria and Jubilee Lines. And I can bet the Victoria and Jubilee lines are gaily feeding more and more bodies into the Piccadilly line.

You have to wonder whether they told them, 'Do not go there, catch a bus, walk, swim, crawl, whatever you do, do not go there.' Or the usual gaily automated announcement, 'Change here for the Piccadilly Line. There is a good service on all Underground Liars I mean Lines.'

Cockfosters
Oakwood
Southgate
Arnos Grove
● Bounds Green
● Wood Green
● Turnpike Lane
● Manor House
● Finsbury Park
● Arsenal
● Holloway Road
● Caledonian Road
● King's Cross St. Pancras
● Russell Square
● Holborn
● Covent Garden
● Leicester Square
● Piccadilly Circus
○ Green Park
Hyde Park Corner
Knightsbridge
South Kensington
Gloucester Road
Earl's Court
Barons Court
Hammersmith
Turnham Green
Acton Town

Ealing Common        South Ealing
North Ealing         Northfields
Park Royal           Boston Manor
Alperton             Osterley
Sudbury Town         Hounslow East
Sudbury Hill         Hounslow Central
South Harrow         Hounslow West
Rayners Lane         Hatton Cross  ←
Eastcote             Heathrow T 1-2-3  →  Heathrow T4
Ruislip Manor        Heathrow T5
Ruislip
Ickenham
Hillingdon
Uxbridge

# Green Park

*Estimated time to Heathrow Terminal Five: 54 minutes*

*Estimated time to Hyde Park Corner tube station: 2 minutes*

08h20

White and blue tiles like Leicester square. Mainly white.

Green Park. One of those daft names history has gifted us. What bloody park in England isn't green? Unless it's winter and covered in snow or it's one of those weird summers and there's a drought on, something that happens every fifty years. Still, it's part of our history. Probably named after Viscount Green, or Mrs Ethelbert Green what once had a shop there in the Middle ages. Sold condoms and kiss-cakes.

It will also be part of your history, Danny. If not because of history as history, then because it's one of the places your mother and I loved to go for long walks. Apparently they've never seen green grass in the Outback. And judging by your mother's intake they've never seen ice cream in cones either. When she found out she could have a chocolate flakey and toppings as well she was delirious. Either that or taking the Michael.

Which is another thing I try to pound into my pupils. For a long time the park was enclosed, reserved for royal use, mainly hunting. That's how most parks in England started. My pupils might have got a job being hunted, but that would be their limit, they wouldn't have been permitted in on any other basis. Keir Hardie would look at them and despair. They've been born to be peasants and they've wholeheartedly embraced that position.

Well, not wholeheartedly. That would suggest energy or passion or possibly a smidgeon of enthusiasm.

I asked my class that once, when I was subbing English. "What's a smidgeon?"

Voice from the back, "Dunno, sir, but whatever any geezer says I ain't done nicked it none, innit."

I swear they insert random words just to wind me up.

Incidentally, Green Park used to have two buildings at different times, the Temple of Peace and the Temple of Concord. They were both destroyed during fireworks displays, the one in 1749, the other in, I think, about 1814, a year before the Battle of Waterloo. I read that on a plaque in the park somewhere once. It's one of those conundrums: do you stop building Temples celebrating peaceful relations, or do you stop throwing fireworks around?

08h25.

Doors made the beeping sound indicating they are about to close. They closed and then opened again.

Still at Green Park. Still going nowhere. Even more people going nowhere. Now the two little brats are snuffling because they don't like the crowds.

Primrose Park. Other side of Regents Park. Your mother and I had picnics there a few times. It's a bit of a trek to the top, but worth it. Mostly young people doing the same as us, lying on the grass enjoying a picnic and the view, occasionally an older group being obnoxious by striding past everyone wearing heavy walking shoes and large day-bags strapped on and filled with sensible things, huge friendly smiles on their faces as they prove how fit they still were. You're supposed to relax and just enjoy the sunshine, you fidiots.

And Danny, I certainly hope I won't have to explain to you what a fidiot is. It's the same as an eejit progressing to the feejit stage.

It was the first time Maddy called me daddy. She lay her head in my lap. looked up at me and said, 'You will look after me, won't you, daddy?'

Well, of course I said yes. I leaned down and kissed her on the forehead. Never could work out why she called me that, but it seemed to make her happy. Now it looks like I am going to be a daddy after all. Either long distance or hands on.

I had two approaches to what name I called your mother. If everything was going perfectly and there was sunshine and laughter she was Brat. All other occasions she was everything from Maddy to sweetie-pie to darling to any other endearment I could think of.

08h27

Doors have beeped again and closed.

Nope, still not moving.

I'm going to have to come up with some killer line for when I see your bloody mother. Something that will completely knock her off balance long enough to get the first words in. Otherwise I might as well retire to a monastery and take a vow of silence. She can chew the hind leg off of a donkey in seconds once she hits her stride.

I did consider a line from Cabaret: 'Maddening, all I am asking for is ein bisschen Verständnis – a little understanding'. Unfortunately that might sound too much like suggesting she forgive my peccadilloes – even though I haven't actually done anything – and allow me to indulge in whatever seedy habits she suspects me of. Anyway, there's another movie in which someone asks for understanding, First-Sergeant Mulligan in Kelly's Heroes after he's dropped his mortars on Kelly's unit by mistake. Not quite the context I'm hoping for.

Hello, did the train move? I believe it is, indeed, slowly but surely creeping forward in the right direction.

08h30

Five hours until her flight leaves. It can't take five bloody hours to get to Heathrow, now can it?

Okay, let's see, say they have to check in two hours before departure, that still leaves three hours. No way is it going to take three hours.

Woman's just said to her brats, 'Look, we're moving again! See, we'll be there ever so quickly.'

'Ever so quickly?' What movie did you come out of, Mary fucking Poppins?

Your mother's a sucker for movies with Julie Andrews in. I swear she's watched The Sound of Music five times since I met her. Probably five hundred before that. Maybe just last year. I wouldn't mind so much, but she does go around singing the songs for days afterwards, even though she keeps on about how she has to rest her voice between rehearsals.

Stopped in a tunnel again, for fuck's sake.

I swear I just heard someone say those exact words under their breath. Certainly enough groans whenever this thing stops.

Danny, if you ever hesitate to do something in case you might be punished for it by god or the fates, don't. Go ahead and do whatever you want. You'll get punished for it even if you don't do it. Trust me, I know from personal experience.

Moving again.

I think someone just said 'Fucking yippee!'

I hope it wasn't me.

Finally, coming into Hyde Park Corner.

08h35.

19 stops to go.

I think it was me.

At least that would explain the covert looks I'm getting.

Actually there's an old biddy smiling at me as if she agrees.

Cockfosters
Oakwood
Southgate
Arnos Grove
Bounds Green
Wood Green
Turnpike Lane
Manor House
Finsbury Park
Arsenal
Holloway Road
Caledonian Road
King's Cross St. Pancras
Russell Square
Holborn
Covent Garden
Leicester Square
Piccadilly Circus
Green Park
Hyde Park Corner
Knightsbridge
South Kensington
Gloucester Road
Earl's Court
Barons Court
Hammersmith
Turnham Green
Acton Town

Ealing Common
North Ealing
Park Royal
Alperton
Sudbury Town
Sudbury Hill
South Harrow
Rayners Lane
Eastcote
Ruislip Manor
Ruislip
Ickenham
Hillingdon
Uxbridge

South Ealing
Northfields
Boston Manor
Osterley
Hounslow East
Hounslow Central
Hounslow West
Hatton Cross
Heathrow T 1-2-3 ⟶ Heathrow T4
Heathrow T5

102

# Hyde Park Corner

*Estimated time to Heathrow Terminal Five: 52 minutes*

*Estimated time to Knightsbridge tube station: 1 minute*

08h35

Well, bugger me sideways with a whoopee cushion, we didn't even stick around to admire the view. Doors open, five seconds later and they close again and we're off. The driver's break must be due and she wants to get somewhere she can hand the train over.

'Allo, luv, ere's the keys, I'm off for a cup o' char. Mind the brakes, they're sticking a bit.'

Or half a bottle of gin, considering what she's been through so far on her shift. Make it the full bottle, I'm feeling generous.

I'm feeling sympathy for a tube driver? I must be going down with something.

I see we're back to the anaemic yellow and blotched white tiles.

Jenny flew back to Liverpool mid-January. She much preferred flying to taking the train, even though there wasn't a direct flight. That time it was via Dublin. She liked the diversions and, incredibly, it was normally cheaper than the train.

Shortly afterward Stella announced that she had had a job offer from some new start-up in New York, that was in early February, I think. Excellent salary package. Large apartment in the prime of wherever the prime of New York is. I didn't follow all the details, but she seemed eager. It was one of those signs that a relationship is coming to an end, if it had ever started in the first place. A husband says, "Raymond got that promotion," his wife replies, "Who?" "You know, Raymond, I told you about the promotion." "Oh, Raymond, of course." More like "Oh, I wasn't listening. Can't be bothered any more. Who the fuck is Raymond and why should I care?"

"Haven't you ever wanted to work in somewhere like New York?" she asked. I shrugged and said something in reply, no doubt. My thoughts were more on the production of Cabaret, which wasn't going well, training the football teams, which were getting worse, and just school in general which was at the usual level of appalling.

Anyway, couple of weeks later, she's packed up everything, ready to go, then she's gone. Promised to phone, email, blah-de-blah. I wasn't expecting anything, and that's pretty much what I got – nothing. I have no doubt she felt the loss less than I did. And the only loss I felt was the lack of sexual exercise.

In case I haven't mentioned it, I also coach soccer. Football. Keeps me reasonably fit. Plus it allows me to say 'Good grief' on a regular basis. You'd think teenagers would have developed some form of motor skills by the time they've become teenagers. My lot try to kick a football and fall over. They don't kick a football, they kick at the football, which is a good way to give yourself an injury.

That's a point. Danny, You're going to be a little toddler. Little toddlers are renowned for – well, toddling. I don't have a lot of patience for toddling. I'd prefer it if you could develop into a top athlete straight away if you don't mind. I've never been able to say things like, 'My goodness, that was clever, little Mary, you managed to walk two paces towards the ball before falling over. Aren't you the clever one! You are, aren't you!'

And excuse me while I vomit. Patronising shite.

I shall have to develop a little patience, just for you, my sweet little Danny. God knows I've got little left at the moment.

To be honest I was probably rather relieved when Stella left. She wasn't what you'd call a bad person, just not one, as the saying goes, you'd want to introduce to you parents. And in the shit-storm that was coming I would, had I known it was coming, preferred to have faced it alone, or at least without Stella cluttering things up.

Coming into Knightsbridge.

08h37.

Why didn't I get a bloody cab at Bounds Green? I could have been at the airport hours ago.

Because there wasn't one for an hour and I thought I had more than enough time. Now it looks like I might have only just enough.

And cabs to Heathrow are only cheaper than cabs from Heathrow.
But don't ever tell your mother. She'll claim I didn't think her worth it.

Cockfosters
Oakwood
Southgate
Arnos Grove
● Bounds Green
● Wood Green
● Turnpike Lane
● Manor House
● Finsbury Park
● Arsenal
● Holloway Road
● Caledonian Road
● King's Cross St. Pancras
● Russell Square
● Holborn
● Covent Garden
● Leicester Square
● Piccadilly Circus
● Green Park
● Hyde Park Corner
○ Knightsbridge
South Kensington
Gloucester Road
Earl's Court
Barons Court
Hammersmith
Turnham Green
Acton Town

Ealing Common      South Ealing
North Ealing       Northfields
Park Royal         Boston Manor
Alperton           Osterley
Sudbury Town       Hounslow East
Sudbury Hill       Hounslow Central
South Harrow       Hounslow West
Rayners Lane       Hatton Cross  ←
Eastcote           Heathrow T 1-2-3 ⟶ Heathrow T4
Ruislip Manor      Heathrow T5
Ruislip
Ickenham
Hillingdon
Uxbridge

# Knightsbridge

*Estimated time to Heathrow Terminal Five: 51 minutes*

*Estimated time to South Kensington tube station: 3 minutes*

08h37

Doors open. Nothing happens. Life goes on elsewhere.

Above the crowds mock and sway in the sunlit day.

I started that as a Haiku, Danny. Never can get the bloody things right.

Tiles are the sort of speckled brown that probably looked very classy and expensive when new and clean. If you want to know how they're going to look after a month of tubes, people, smoke, dirt and grit, mix up a few hundred litres of strong tea with five parts compost, two hundred litres of used truck oil, a ton of coarse grit, and apply liberally.

Hello, doors are beeping, doors are closing, and here we go again on life's roundabout.

Only it's not a roundabout, that would be the Circle line.

08h40

Well, only two minutes on the platform, pretty good everything considered.

Knightsbridge.

Knightsbridge and YBM.

Pretty much every female tourist knows what's special about Knightsbridge: Harrods: a big mall of materialism, a cathedral of capitalism – your bloody mother loved it before she ever stepped inside. When she first dragged me there I asked what was so great about it.

'Dahling, it's Harrods!' she replied, putting about six big exclamation marks into it.

Personally I don't get it. But then I don't get shopping anyway. Your bloody mother actually got specially dressed up to go shopping in Harrods. Well, I say shopping, but it was more of a gala performance. She declared in the grocery section, she declared in electricals, she pretty much declared everywhere. She would have dragged me into the ladies to declare there too if she could.

'Oh, dahling! Isn't this lipstick to dah for!'

107

Well, no, actually, I haven't met any fucking lipstick I'd be willing to dah for.

She was dressed in black. Again. She loves black when she's doing melodrama, which is most times. She had a trailing scarf around her neck, chiffon or some light material. She'd notice something, cry 'Dahling, look,' flick the scarf over her shoulder, declare 'It's too, too divine! Isn't it!'

'Divine' came out as 'Deeveen!!!'

Each time she flicked the scarf it would float perilously towards something precious, or at least expensive. A Ming vase, a stand of crystal, a Noritake dinner set. A member of staff would edge nervously towards whatever it was in case they had to dive to save it. But somehow your mother managed to miss each time. And then it was on to the next department and the next terrified member of staff.

We bought something, some cheapish tat or other, I can't remember what. Your mother would probably kill me if I admitted that, it is no doubt now something she treasures deeply as a sign of our growing love. It had to go into a large carrier bag because the point was not to have something from Harrods, it was to wave the carrier bag around to show other idiots that you had bought some cheap tat and a big carrier bag from Harrods.

I called it a cathedral of capitalism, which is quite appropriate, because there was somewhere else Maddy likes getting dressed up in black to go to, and that's church. It gives her an excuse to wear a lace black headscarf. I remember when she asked where the local Catholic church was in Muswell Hill. It surprised me, I suppose because I gave up that nonsense so long ago I forget some people still do go to church.

But I've got ahead of myself again.

So, going back, before I met YBM.

Jenny had gone back to Liverpool.

Stella had left for New York.

I had so many things going on at the school I began to stop going to Saturday tennis. If I'm honest, Stella's leaving was a good excuse to drop out of the gang. We didn't have much in common in the first place, apart from bonking, partying and tennis, and Bella's never held much attraction for me. There were at least two tennis clubs within walking distance that looked more salubrious from my point of view, and I planned to visit them as soon as I got the chance. Cabaret was promising to be a glorious disaster, just as the head had predicted. The kids just had no self-confidence. Too many of them were so overweight putting them in a Cabaret line-up was just gross. We chose a shy black girl named Angela to play Sally Bowles, the original Lisa Minelli part. She'd need a lot of work, but had the basic voice which could be developed. In a way the fact that she was black was an added bonus, because Berlin of the 1930s must have had black female singers in night clubs, and the sort of night club Sally Bowles sings in would have loved to have stuck it to the Nazis. Her backing singers were just about on the cusp of being bloody awful, but the wrong side of the cusp. Fortunately the EmCee can be played for laughs; we had one kid who was so camp he could have formed a tribe of Scouts all on his own. He could actually sing. Unfortunately he knew it. The others couldn't, and he knew that too. I suspect that he was getting some of his own back for being teased about being limp-wristed. "What are we going to do about some of these flat chests?" he asked once, rhetorically, gazing at the rafters. You can imagine the affect that sort of thing had on girls of that age. The few boys in the cast at that stage just sniggered.

There were little things. We weren't at the costume stage, but it was in the background, and we did have some discussions. Pamela pointed out that some of the scenes would need pupils dressed up as Brownshirts. That worried her, as if the little buggers weren't already prototype fascists.

But it gave me an idea. Marching. Uniforms. We could use up some of the non-singers – plenty of those at that stage – to fill up stage space with some slick march routines. Nothing too complicated.

Jesus Christ! I don't know what this driver is doing, but the wheels are screeching like a hundred banshees out of hell. Almost everybody's got their hands over their ears, and the kids look terrified.

Couple of years ago they had major delays on the Piccadilly Line because of, and I kid you not, wet leaves. Apparently they turned to a grease-like substance, causing the trains to skid and wearing a chamfer into the bogie wheels. From the sound the wheels are making at the moment they won't just be worn down, they'll disappear altogether.

Ah, no, it's gone now, thank fuck for that.

Other passengers are smiling nervously at each other, where they can see each other as opposed to the buttocks of the person standing in front. They've taken their hands down from their ears.

Not quite Das Boot with the depth charges falling all around, but not the sound you want to hear fifty feet below ground.

South Kensington

08h45.

That wasn't too bad.

Wait a minute, it was another five minutes that should have taken two.

Five stops and it's Hammersmith. Then we're passed the signal failures and it's clear to Heathrow.

Five stops.

I'll just grin and bear it.

That'll be a rictus grin.

Open running.

Just five stops and we'll be motoring. I'll even offer to drive the fucking thing myself if they're short on drivers.

Red signal? What's that when it's at home, then? Full speed and damn the red signals.

ETA T5: 48 minutes. Call it fifty and keep the change.

Twenty to ten.

I can't believe it's taken this long.

But at least I'll be there before Maddy goes through security.

And if she's already gone through so will I.

I don't know how.

Think Michael Caine and a bus in the Alps.

It was the Alps, wasn't it?

Cockfosters
Oakwood
Southgate
Arnos Grove
● Bounds Green
● Wood Green
● Turnpike Lane
● Manor House
● Finsbury Park
● Arsenal
● Holloway Road
● Caledonian Road
● King's Cross St. Pancras
● Russell Square
● Holborn
● Covent Garden
● Leicester Square
● Piccadilly Circus
● Green Park
● Hyde Park Corner
● Knightsbridge
○ South Kensington
Gloucester Road
Earl's Court
Barons Court
Hammersmith
Turnham Green
Acton Town

| | |
|---|---|
| Ealing Common | South Ealing |
| North Ealing | Northfields |
| Park Royal | Boston Manor |
| Alperton | Osterley |
| Sudbury Town | Hounslow East |
| Sudbury Hill | Hounslow Central |
| South Harrow | Hounslow West |
| Rayners Lane | Hatton Cross ← |
| Eastcote | Heathrow T 1-2-3 → Heathrow T4 |
| Ruislip Manor | Heathrow T5 |
| Ruislip | |
| Ickenham | |
| Hillingdon | |
| Uxbridge | |

# South Kensington

*Estimated time to Heathrow Terminal Five: 48 minutes*

*Estimated time to Gloucester Road tube station: 2 minutes*

08h45

Danny, did you know there's a South Kensington railway station in Melbourne, Australia? I suppose it will depend on where you grow up. If I don't get to Heathrow in time you might well end up being brought up in Melbourne, Kangaroo-land. With your grandparents. The bastards.

I know there's a South Kensington railway station in Melbourne because your mother told me. It's one of those totally irrelevant facts young lovers exchange, 'Here's a bit of me for you'. I believe monkeys and chimpanzees do something similar, only with bananas.

The South Kensington in Boomerang-land is apparently on the same train line as somewhere called Diggers Rest, which is quite cool, and Tottenham, which bloody isn't. Not to mention Cheltenham and Chelsea. They can keep those.

But apparently there is a Kananook somewhere along the line. I could live somewhere called Kananook. Probably turn out to be either the most exclusive and expensive real estate, or the worst dump in the world.

Their train line is called the Metro. It's state of the art. Apart from that, according to Maddy, it's just as dirty and over-crowded as the London Underground, and instead of signal failures they have modern computers which crash from time to time, taking out the entire service.

And some of their passengers are weird, to say the least. So weird they had to produce a video called Dumb Ways To Die in order to explain to them that a train system is designed to get you from A to B, not turn you into mincemeat.

Speaking of which, platforms on the London Underground usually have bright yellow barriers at each end with signs in red, white and blue advising customers that this is where the platform ends and they probably don't want to go any further in case they find themselves testing the theory that a hundred-ton train can take out a 100-kilogram human quite easily. They have a sign saying "Danger, moving trains", which, everything considered, I find just a little bit optimistic.

Wait a minute, did I just feel something actually move? As in, you know, move? I did indeed. Hoorah, we're on our way. It must be a sign.

08h46

Looking much better now. Signal failures must be sorted. Panic over, everyone. Hopefully.

I'm not sure if there are any internationally famous shops or emporia around South Kensington, but I do know it's the closest tube to the Natural History Museum. Why do I know this? Because I had this fucking brilliant idea of taking the kids there to grind their faces into the rich cultural inheritance they were busy ignoring. I researched everything from all the usual things teachers have to make contingencies for – much like a major military operation combined with an intense health and safety drill – to exactly what it was we were going to be introducing the kids to so they might actually pay attention and learn something.

In my defence it was shortly after I'd started at the school, after I'd been politely asked by my last school to find other gainful employment. We have a powerful teaching union, so they don't tend to sack teachers, they just make it plain they'll be much better off somewhere else, anywhere else. Then they make sure all the other similar schools are aware, so you end up with Hobson's choice, teaching in an inner-city shithole.

Anyway, I presented my plan to the head, who actually laughed.

'Mark, you are a sweetie, but you're so naïve. These aren't little primary school toddlers, that would be bad enough. They aren't the nicely behaved students you had at your last school. They're vicious little –'

She paused, looking for a word other than "fucktards".

'Nihilists?' I suggested.

'Exactly. Exactly. Nihilists. That describes them perfectly. Adolescent nihilists. It is our job to protect places like the Natural History Museum for nice middle class people who will appreciate the benefits, not take a battalion of nasty little wreckers in and destroy hundreds of years of civilisation.'

Her name's Bogdanopoulos. She insists that everyone call her Miss Bogdanopoulos. The pupils, with their usual inventiveness, just refer to her behind her back as Bog or The Bog. I call her the bog. She doesn't merit capital letters.

The problem with her isn't that she's a woman. The problem is that she's a woman selected by a committee to be a head purely because she was a woman. She's a perfect example of the law that says people are promoted to one stop above their level of competence, only they sent her two further. The Peter Principle plus two. She was a crap teacher so they turned her into a crap head. It was she who decided to replace me with a 'professional' piano player for Cabaret. I think she hated me for two reasons. Firstly, I had taught at a proper school, and secondly, she could sense that I knew she was crap at her job. Everybody knew she was crap, I just couldn't hide it.

Still, it wasn't a wasted exercise. The Natural History Museum, that is. I took your mother there. She was deeply impressed by my knowledge and erudition. I will never forget the way she held tightly onto my arm, and the way she occasionally looked up into my eyes as if I was some sort of demi-god she had fallen in love with and was desperate to worship. At least it kept her bloody gob shut for a few minutes.

Then we found the earthquake simulator. From child-sophisticate to yippee in one easy move.

'Can we go on it, Mark? Please, can we? Can we?'

Of course, my love, for you I would go on the ride to hell.

Like I'm ever going to say no to your mother.

Stopped again.

I wonder where we are. Apart from being in the bowels of the earth.

Jules Verne would have loved the idea.

I think I am on the ride to hell.

Danny, the map of London Underground is iconic. Originally they tried to represent the lines as a cartographic match to geographic reality. Trouble was there wasn't enough space, especially as more lines were added. You'd end up with a map the size of a large dining table, most of it empty. Then a British draughtsman came up with a stroke of genius:

squash everything up together. People aren't on a hiking tour, they don't need to know exactly where everything is. They just need an idea of where things are relatively speaking. He designed it the same way a wiring diagram is done.

Train's moving again.

I explained that to the kids at school when giving them their assignment the other day. Consider: a British draughtsman – not an artist, not a designer – came up with this brilliant idea which is now used around the world. Think about it. It's not that an artist or designer couldn't have done it, in fact they should have. It's the fact that someone thought outside of the prevailing beliefs; you too can do it if you try. You are the future British geniuses of the world. Start thinking now.

They looked at me as if I were mental.

Apparently the draughtsman came up with the concept when he realised that people who are underground do not need a map that conforms to reality above ground. Or, in other words, isn't real.

Is it only me or is there, when you think about it, something rather sinister about that idea?

Yank is checking his watch and practising occupying three seats using manspreading.

Mrs Yank is playing with one of his buttons. Doesn't appear to mind the spread.

Coming into Gloucester Road.

08h48.

Four stops to Hammersmith and then we'll be past the signal failure.

And then it's open-country running.

Definitely.

Cockfosters
Oakwood
Southgate
Arnos Grove
● Bounds Green
● Wood Green
● Turnpike Lane
● Manor House
● Finsbury Park
● Arsenal
● Holloway Road
● Caledonian Road
● King's Cross St. Pancras
● Russell Square
● Holborn
● Covent Garden
● Leicester Square
● Piccadilly Circus
● Green Park
● Hyde Park Corner
● Knightsbridge
● South Kensington
○ Gloucester Road
Earl's Court
Barons Court
Hammersmith
Turnham Green
Acton Town

Ealing Common        South Ealing
North Ealing         Northfields
Park Royal           Boston Manor
Alperton             Osterley
Sudbury Town         Hounslow East
Sudbury Hill         Hounslow Central
South Harrow         Hounslow West
Rayners Lane         Hatton Cross  ←
Eastcote             Heathrow T 1-2-3  ⟶  Heathrow T4
Ruislip Manor        Heathrow T5
Ruislip
Ickenham
Hillingdon
Uxbridge

## Gloucester Road

*Estimated time to Heathrow Terminal Five: 46 minutes*

*Estimated time to Earl's Court tube station: 2 minutes*

08h48

Make-up girl has got off.

I have absolutely no idea what goes on in the area around Gloucester Road tube station, why people get on, and, even more mysteriously, why they get off.

She might have got off to change for the Circle Line. Or gone to the East-bound platform to return to South Kensington. I know she didn't want to go to Earl's Court. The reason I know these things is that we've been sitting here for two minutes listening to the announcers from our platform having a competition with the East-bound platform announcers. Our one says, "This is Gloucester Road. Change here for the Circle Line. The next station is Earl's Court. Please stand clear of the closing doors." The other one across the way announces, "This is Gloucester Road. Change here for the Circle Line. The next station is South Kensington. Please stand clear of the closing doors." Except the bloody doors aren't closing. And we aren't going any bloody where.

Jesus wept.

Well, there you go, some prayers work. The doors have beeped, closed, and we're moving.

08h51.

Danny, by the time you've grown up you will have seen any number of films showing underdog school children metamorphosing into super achievers. Including half a dozen or more where the scum from the shittiest of high schools somehow turn into brilliant singers and dancers and win the inter-school sing-off, or bake off or fuck-off or whatever they call those things. And they will all be led by some brilliant maverick teacher, or possibly just someone who isn't a real teacher, but he Has A Dream and blags his way into a teacher's place before convincing the class of snot-noses they can become real Stars. It's always a he, for some reason.

Personally all I was aiming for was a lukewarm production of Cabaret that wouldn't be a total failure. I was prepared to lie through my teeth and assure every Johnny's mother that Johnny really had been terrific, and a career in show-business was his for the taking. The trouble is that they lacked spirit, they lacked energy, they lacked enthusiasm, and, above all, they lacked discipline. I knew it, Pamela knew it and they knew it. Pamela could gush over them and gee up their enthusiasm, I could encourage them, but we lacked the hard edge that would allow us to give them what they needed, which was a good kick up the arse every so often, like every second fucking second.

And then, one day, I had a glorious epiphany. It was late afternoon after a rehearsal that had gone so-so, which was an improvement, but not much of a one, and Pamela and I were having a cup of coffee in the staff room. Or rather Pamela was washing up everyone else's discarded mugs as she always did, while I sat in a chair sucking on a cup of coffee complaining about things generally.

'We could get them to mime,' I think I was saying, 'But we'll never get them to march properly. They look more like the Keystone Kops than Nazi Brownshirts.'

'Dear, dear,' said Pamela, sniffing suspiciously at the dregs in a mug, 'poor Mr Grafton and his whisky.'

Sean Grafton was the geography teacher and resident dipsomaniac, otherwise known as the alcoholic. He's ex-military, one of those people who had an impeccable service record, came out of the army, and didn't know what to do with himself. Got used to hard drinking in the army, considers it normal. Gets a job somewhere the semi-permanent hangover won't matter too much, a school being the perfect place. The school needs teachers to make up the numbers, the government is big on ex-service people becoming teachers because they'll provide discipline, leadership, and, above all, be a shining example of bovine stupidity and following orders unthinkingly. The school gives him something to do between waking up and having the first drink of the afternoon. He's Scottish, doesn't talk much, very anti-social, the kids are terrified of him. They believe he's personally killed over twenty people, maybe a hundred, mostly Afghans during tours over there, and several with his bare hands. I hadn't really had anything to do with him apart from sharing the sports roster occasionally, not because I avoided him, but rather because he was very much a keep-to-himself sort of person. I had noticed that he sometimes had a twinkle in his eye late afternoon, but that I presumed was because (a) it was almost home time, and (b) he was pissed.

'Pamela,' I said as the bloody obvious collided with my cerebrum, 'why don't we ask Sean to give a hand? He must know about marching.'

'Oh, dear,' said Pamela, looking at me in her usual worried way, 'do you think he'd be suitable?'

Meaning, presumably, do you think he could stay sober for long enough?

'Suitable?' I asked. 'No. But we don't want suitable. We want someone who can kick arse. Someone who can turn those little brats into highly efficient goose-steppers.'

'Are you sure, Mark?' she asked. It was her polite way of saying 'You're fucking barking mad, Mark.'

'We've got nothing to lose,' I said. 'The worst that can happen is he breathes over me and I get drunk for a week.'

So the next day I caught him just after lunch. I explained the situation and asked if he had any advice. He went into a kind of brown study, as if he were remembering a better time.

"Buggers will need to learn discipline," he murmured.

'I know that,' I said. 'It's our biggest problem at the moment. The only way I can think of to instil discipline in those little brats is to put a pistol to their heads, and shoot a couple to prove you're being serious.'

He looked at me with a definite twinkle in his eye.

'You can leave shooting people up to me, laddie,' he said, 'I've been trained to do it.'

I guessed then that he knew precisely what his reputation with the kids was.

'So will you do it?' I asked. 'Teach them to march properly?'

'You mean, will I spend my spare time, after hours, with the pubs open, teaching that bunch of soft little London nancies how to put one foot in front of another?' he asked. He obviously also had a pretty fair idea of what his fellow teachers thought of him.

'We were kind of hoping they might achieve a goose-step or two,' I said. He nodded.

'I must be mad. All that sun out in the desert. Must have fried my brain. But, yes, I'll do it. I could do with a laugh.'

The following afternoon Sean turned up at rehearsals and the set was transformed. Everything was transformed. His voice could be heard from outside the school gates.

Funnily enough I can't recall anything he said – bawled – but it involved a lot of swearwords, even more threats, and descriptions of the brats that I could only marvel at.

The head developed a sudden deafness. The cast, not only the marchers, began to walk tall, their puny chests out. More and more students signed up. Angela began to lose her shyness and was developing into a right sly little minx who knew exactly how to flaunt her bits and pieces on the stage. Her backing singers picked up a bit of the vibe and started not only singing in tune but also matching Angela's steps.

Sean perked up no end. He started turning up in the mornings sober.

He found out that some pupils were turning up for school without having had breakfast. Which meant they ate too much too quickly at lunch and their whole body clocks were disoriented. He sorted that out with a few quiet words with the parents. He was, in a word, amazing.

But.

Hours of drill and being shouted at had turned them into almost models of British soldiers. Unfortunately they were supposed to by Nazi henchmen.

So one evening after a rehearsal, with Pamela, Sean and myself in the staff room, I pointed this out as politely as I could.

'I ken what you're saying, laddie,' he said, 'but what would you have me do?'

'First thing, we've got to get them hard-soled shoes, boots if possible. Those trainers they wear aren't making the right noise.'

'With you on that, laddie. Might cost a bob or two.'

'They don't need to be expensive. They aren't going to be wearing them often. Now, they come marching on and then the Golden One starts singing Tomorrow belongs to me. How about, the Golden One is on stage with them behind him, only in darkness. Then he starts singing, the light goes up on him, and they take one pace at the end of each line – crash! Foot down, goose-step leg forward, next line, crash! foot down, goose-step forward, and so on, until they're also in the light, standing just behind him. And they're wearing dark glasses.'

'We can try, laddie,' Sean said dubiously.

The next day he was a lot more positive.

'I was watching World At War on the History channel last night,' he said. 'We can do your thing with a modified slow march.'

That afternoon he took his marchers off to teach them the new drill and swear at them. By the end of an hour he pronounced them 'Shite, but tolerable shite. A start, anyway.'

And then one day he strode in wearing his army uniform, a full sergeant's outfit. Impressed the kids no end.

That's when they began to hit the stride I was hoping for.

And they knew it.

We were on a roll.

We were going to make it.

We were going to make it Big Time.

Tomorrow belonged to us.

Well, there you go. We're coming in to Earl's Court and, true to their word, this train is terminating here.

08h55.

Please make sure you take all your belongings with you. Automated announcements. Fucking marvellous.

08 hundred fucking fifty-five. Almost nine o'clock.

Surely they can't get any worse?

I think I just heard someone cackle.

# Earl's Court

*Estimated time to Heathrow Terminal Five: 44 minutes*

*Estimated time to Barons Court tube station: 3 minutes*

08h58

Am currently sitting on a bench on the west-bound Piccadilly Line platform at Earl's Court. The tube I was on has now reversed out. All I can say is that it got out a fucking lot faster than it got in. The driver, or whoever it was, closing the doors and making sure all the dopey passengers were out, was almost legging it down the train.

The reason I have space on this bench is that most of the other passengers took the advice broadcast over the tannoy: get out and catch a bus, taxi, passing seaplane. Walk, steal a bicycle, pram, scooter. Just don't bother sticking around here, you've got more chance of catching an STD than a train. In other words, usual response, get rid of the riff-raff and everything will be okay again.

Favourite seems to be catching the District Line to Acton Town. Then sitting on that platform waiting for bugger all to happen. According to one of the platform staff it only takes ten minutes to get to Acton on the District. Somehow I doubt it, but it isn't relevant anyway.

The reason I've not gone with the others is that I know this game. Sooner or later they'll get their shit in gear and the trains working again. Going out and trying to get the Heathrow from here by bus or whatever would be a joke.

There was a time when Earl's Court was basically an Australian/New Zealand/South African enclave. Still is, for all I know. I know the part of North London I used to live in before I moved to the Hill is pretty much non-British now. The local barber was from Cyprus. There were Greek shops, Turkish shops, Polish shops, Somalian, Eritrean, you name it.

Bloke has turned up on the platform. Tall, thin, young, bearded, pony tail, expensive coffee in a polystyrene cup. They're called hipsters, which is a polite way of spelling "prat".

God knows what will be the fashion when you grow up, Danny. I remember seeing photographs of my folks, your grandparents, wearing

122

flares. I think it was the final throw of a fashion which finally died in the 1980s – or maybe they were going to an ironic fashion dress party.

I say "died", but that isn't really true. Fashions are a bit like the living dead. You think you've killed them but they come back when you least expect it.

Strange place, London. Not so long ago they found evidence of remains of far Eastern people dating back to the Roman empire. Chinese or Japanese. When I was growing up we had a Chinese bloke in our class. We used to call him Fu, after Fu Manchu, a great film baddie from about a hundred years ago. They like to pretend that that wouldn't be tolerated now, any hint of racism, but the truth is the stiffs in the staff room wouldn't say anything. Teenage kids tend to do what they want rather than worrying about social convention. It's about their only redeeming feature. Apparently these days they use the word "gay" to mean something is shit. It gives middle-class liberal teachers the vapours.

After Stella left there were times when I felt at odds with everything. I can't say I missed Stella as Stella. I missed having someone to do things with on the weekend. Just at odd times, like Sunday afternoons. Rest of the time I was busy as all hell. It was almost as if, in those quiet times, I had a foreboding of something unpleasant coming our way.

They've just made an announcement over the station speakers. Apparently there are severe delays on the Piccadilly Line.

No shit Sherlock.

Some prayers don't work.

It was the Saturday morning I got the call from Dad. The middle of April. I'd been doing general domestic stuff, putting away dishes, putting the washing in the machine, the stuff I normally did before Saturday morning football if there was any, or the weekly shop if there wasn't.

I've heard many explanations of how people feel on going through tragedy. You do as a teacher.

Dad's voice – it sounded strange. First he asked if I was okay. I replied that I was fine, asked if he was okay.

Jenny's dead, he said.

I can hear the silence now as I stood there with a mouth that had stopped moving.

The police say it was an overdose, he said.

I wanted to say, no, it's a mistake, Jenny doesn't do drugs, it can't be, it just can't.

Looking back, I guess Dad knew that. Or thought he knew it. Jenny doesn't do drugs. Not Jenny, not our Jenny. I guess that's what he wanted to say when the police first came round.

'I'm afraid there's no doubt, Mark,' he said.

It took me a few more seconds to get my brain working again.

'Dad? I'll be on the next train up.'

'Okay, Mark. Give us a call when you know the arrival time. We'll pick you up.'

'Okay, Dad. Take care.'

And that was it. From then on it was movement, as fast as I could. Went online and booked the earliest practical train. Phoned a local cab firm and ordered a cab for Euston. Chucked some spare clothes in a holdall. Added a dark suit in the subconscious knowledge that I'd need it, and that any suits I'd left behind at the folks place would only fit someone younger and slimmer than I'd become. Phoned Dad to let him know the arrival time. Cab turned up. Told him to get to Euston as fast as he could. Sat in the back saying nothing, looking out the window, occasionally checking for speed limit signs and making sure the driver was going as fast as he could.

Arrived at Euston. Paid the cab off. Strode into the train station. Found the platform the train was leaving from. Got on. Train left. Sat staring into space for a couple of hours. Staring into nowhere. Pulled into Liverpool Lime Street. Got out where dad and mum were waiting.

I gave mum a hug. For the first time since I was a little boy I gave dad a hug too. They seemed to have aged terribly. I didn't remember them having grey, almost white, hair. Their faces were lined with grief.

Aunt Marigold's death had been a shock to them. It had been a shock to all of us, of course, but they had all grown up together. But at least Aunt Marigold had lived a full life, whooped it up, and had a memorable exit, probably laughing as she did. Every time you felt sad there was always an instant, "Do you remember when she ..."

Jenny was too young to go.

We went to the car. We didn't talk much. Generalities. Mum said she'd got my old room ready. She asked me whether I had any dietary requirements, or preferences. I said no. I've always had a healthy appetite. I've never had the urge to go vegetarian or vegan. Put a plate of decent grub in front of me and I'll hoover it up.

I guessed it was her way of keeping busy. She'd probably aired my old room, vacuumed it, put fresh sheets on, vacuumed the rest of the house, dusted the ceilings, cleaned and cleaned and cleaned and cleaned and hoped the pain would go away.

Dad – as far as I could tell he'd handled the necessities. Spoke to the police. Dealt with the funeral parlour. Had a word with Father Burns, a new priest at the Catholic church we'd gone to as children, and to which my mother still went, dad on special occasions like Easter and Christmas. The university residence had returned Jenny's effects. Except for certain things which the police retained, as her death had been designated a crime or whatever phrase they use. It turned out that she hadn't taken an overdose, she had been given what they called a bad batch. Apparently it had been laced with what should have been a filler, but was quite poisonous. For a normal person it would have been dangerous, for someone with health problems it was fatal.

One of the items they retained was a diary that Jenny was keeping. They weren't forthcoming, but from what dad said Jenny had started to take drugs in a mild form to cope with recurrent pain she used to have from earlier operations. The medication her doctor had prescribed wasn't quite doing the job, so she was supplementing. Just a little, now and then.

I guessed she had asked her doctor for something more, the doctor had replied that she really shouldn't take more than was absolutely necessary, Jenny would have agreed, but then found this wonderful if illegal way of keeping the pain at bay, and decided that, if no-one knew, everyone would be happy.

I spent the following week or so there. Maybe more. We had the funeral. The church was packed. When I was at university I doubt that I had more than a dozen or so people I could say I knew well. Jenny appeared to have touched hundreds of lives. Also plenty of her old school mates. Dad and mum's friends turned up in strength, for which I was grateful.

I basically tried to make myself useful. Fetching and carrying, driving mum around if dad was busy. Looking after others kept my mind busy.

When mum and dad weren't there to notice I popped into the police station and asked to see the detectives who were on the case. I suppose I had some vague notion of finding out who had supplied the bad batch and – and god knows what. They realised it, probably had seen it before. They very gently disabused me of the notion of doing anything.

I had no intention of returning to London at any time soon. But the thing is, life goes on. You have the funeral. Then the burial. Everybody retires to the church hall for tea and whatever. You discuss mundane things. Getting a headstone made. What it will say. How long it will be before the ground is settled enough again to take the weight.

I knew mum would end up taking fresh flowers there every week forever more. Dad would go too, I would imagine.

I walked. I walked and walked and walked. The folks' place was close to a farming area and there was space to walk alone. For miles and miles and miles. And it was the end of winter.

If I lived and worked in Liverpool I probably would have gone back to work sooner. But even then there comes a time when you've mourned just enough to start moving on. Or perhaps it would be more accurate to say that you realise the pain will never go away and you are just going to have to live with it.

Most humans have a built-in self-defence mechanism. When something bad happens or something goes wrong the automatic reaction is that it's always someone else's fault. It's only when we're alone in the dark hours that doubt creeps in. As time went on I couldn't help but feel part of it was my fault. I should have been there for Jenny more often. But I wasn't.

Dad and mum. I could see that they blamed themselves. Maybe it's a Catholic thing. You learn early on that everything's your fault and you're probably going to hell for it. And if it was already hell the following weeks were going to get worse. Not much worse. But worse.

And here comes a train. Is it going to reverse out?

09h05

Looks like it. The doors are opening and people are piling out and scrambling for the exits.

Do I stay or do I go?

The driver's making an announcement.

This train will be going as far as Northfields.

Northfields. That's within a bus ride of Heathrow. A long bus ride, but a bus ride anyway. So long as nothing else happens I'll make it, easy. Well, should be well before YBM goes through security.

What the hell am I going to say?

Or perhaps that's the problem.

I should have listened to Jenny. Not just to what she was saying, but to what she wasn't saying.

No, Jenny and Maddy are completely different people. Jenny was a saint with the gift of forgiveness. YBM is a devil with a flamethrower.

I lost Jenny. I should have taken more care of her.

Danny, I am not going to lose your bloody mother.

Especially not with you on board.

Cockfosters
Oakwood
Southgate
Arnos Grove
● Bounds Green
● Wood Green
● Turnpike Lane
● Manor House
● Finsbury Park
● Arsenal
● Holloway Road
● Caledonian Road
● King's Cross St. Pancras
● Russell Square
● Holborn
● Covent Garden
● Leicester Square
● Piccadilly Circus
● Green Park
● Hyde Park Corner
● Knightsbridge
● South Kensington
● Gloucester Road
○ Earl's Court
Barons Court
Hammersmith
Turnham Green
Acton Town

Ealing Common          South Ealing
North Ealing           Northfields
Park Royal             Boston Manor
Alperton               Osterley
Sudbury Town           Hounslow East
Sudbury Hill           Hounslow Central
South Harrow           Hounslow West
Rayners Lane           Hatton Cross  ←
Eastcote               Heathrow T 1-2-3  →  Heathrow T4
Ruislip Manor          Heathrow T5
Ruislip
Ickenham
Hillingdon
Uxbridge

# Leaving Earl's Court

*Estimated time to Heathrow Terminal Five: 44 minutes*

*Estimated time to Barons Court tube station: 3 minutes*

09h07

Right, I'm on board and sitting down again. Not many other passengers, and those there are, are fuming at being messed around. I don't blame them.

Train driver's just made an announcement: "For anyone who is unaware, the Piccadilly Line has experienced one or two problems this morning. We hope to go as far as Northfields, and, if we're lucky, up to Heathrow, but I can't make any promises."

Sounds like a cheerful chappie. Especially as most of the passengers will be calling him certain other names, none containing the word cheerful.

Driver, I hope you won't take his personally, but if you don't get me to Heathrow on time I am going to punch your fucking face in.

11h30 minus 09h07: two hours thirty-three minutes. We have to be able to get there in two and a half hours.

It was the week following my return to London that the police came to visit. At the house in Muswell Hill. A man and a woman. Very polite, asked if they could pop in for a chat, declined a cup of tea or coffee, accepted a seat, sat where I couldn't concentrate on both of them at the same time, though I only realised that later. Asked if I knew Bella – Annabelle Jenkins, I think her full name was. There was a bit of confusion, initially I didn't realise it was Bella they were talking about, until they suggested I might recall having gone to a party there. I have no doubt now that they knew every single time I'd been there. I'm pretty sure I recognised one of them. If I remember correctly she'd been snogging someone in the darkness, pretending to be high, but glancing around every so often with very clear eyes. At the time I presumed she didn't really fancy the bloke she was snogging and was looking around for someone hotter. Never crossed my mind she could be snogging a colleague in the line of duty.

I was asked if I had ever seen anything which might have looked like a drugs transaction – they were, I presume, being convoluted so as to not ask any leading questions. I replied that I was pretty sure that sort of thing was going on, but it wasn't my scene and I hadn't actually seen any drugs changing hand. Which, on reflection, was quite true. I knew for certain it was basically a drugs den, I could smell the stuff, I could see the effects, but since I had never bought anything nor seen a blatant transaction I wouldn't have been much use in a court trial.

Then they asked whether I had met someone calling themselves Ziggie, to which I replied that I had, once, and so much disliked him had avoided him thereafter. I didn't add that he was almost certainly the chief dealer, it was pretty obvious they knew already.

They asked questions about the gang of six – they didn't use that stupid phrase, fortunately, it would have marked us out as complete tossers – which I answered as truthfully but also as minimally as possible. Yes, I knew Stella, she had got a job in New York a few weeks back. Yes I knew the others, we played tennis together, or had done so, for one reason and another I'd been so busy with other things I hadn't gone recently.

09h10. Doors have closed. We're moving off. Be at Barons Court soon.

Whether or not they were satisfied with my answers, or whether they knew I was telling the truth, just not a lot of it, I don't know. But after about twenty minutes, maybe half an hour they stood up and thanked me for my assistance, and there was an artificial pause before one of them asked, had I heard the news about Ms Jenkins, and again there was a bit of confusion before I remembered it was Bella they were talking about. I replied that I hadn't been there for a good month or two or three, nor seen the others, so, no, I hadn't heard any news.

She's dead, said the one copper.

Took an overdose, sort of, said the other.

Bad batch, said the first. Cut it with something they oughtent.

That's the problem with these sort of things, said the second. You can't trust the quality.

After which they said, once again, ta, sorry to have been a bother, we can find our own way out.

I made bloody sure they did. They had the look of people who could accidentally lose their way in someone else's house very easily. With profuse apologies prepared in advance.

I don't know what was going on behind the scenes. Had the Liverpool police been in touch with the Met in London? Was it a pure co-incidence?

One thing I was sure of, it wasn't a co-incidence that both Jenny and Bella had died from a bad batch. I didn't know how, but Ziggie had supplied the drugs for both.

Were the police setting me up deliberately? Expecting me to go looking for Ziggie, confront him, stir things up a bit while the coppers watched for fallout? Somehow I couldn't see that happening. It would be bound to come out, and they'd have their careers handed to them on a plate.

Or maybe not. Who knows how the average detective's mind works? I've had parents praising me for my commitment and dedication and hard work and all that bollocks, and I spend most of my time avoiding exactly that. Maybe they were throwing a pebble into the lake to see what rippled around, as you could say.

Was I going to take the bait if that was the case?

I didn't honestly know. Having a middle class upbringing doesn't prepare you for going out to extract vengeance. Not when you've had Though shalt not kill drummed into you from an early age. I'm told that's why the military don't like conscription. It takes too long to train middle class snowflakes out of bad habits, such as not really wanting to kill people.

Stuck in the tunnel again. They should write a song about it. The amount of time we've been stuck in a tunnel so far you could write an entire fucking opera. With fucking cymbals. And quite possibly symbols.

Innit.

09h12.

I wanted Chris to take the part of the Hitler Youth singer, the boy who sings "Tomorrow belongs to us". Pamela looked at me in bafflement when I suggested it.

'He's got a good voice,' I pointed out. 'Untrained, I know, but that's what we're here for.'

'Yes, but, Mark, um … He's …'

'Too short?' I asked.

'No, too – not too – I mean – well, Mark …'

'Too tall?'

'No, Mark, Mark you know –'

'Eyes too close together?'

'Really, Mark –'

'Ears too big? Lots of teenagers have big ears. Can't be helped.'

'Mark.'

'We could pin them back.'

'Pin them back?'

'His ears.'

'Mark!'

'Yes?'

She leaned forward.

'He's of mixed parentage,' she whispered.

'Yes, he's a half-breed, I know. I noticed first time I saw him. So what?'

I felt just a smidgeon of regret as her face went through several convulsions at the term. But Pamela was just so uncritically politically correct I couldn't help it. Teachers are supposed to encourage their students to think, not to accept all and any bullshit going.

'But the part – well, he's supposed to be a blonde Aryan. Blue eyed, you know. The boy singing that song.'

'Yes, I know, he's a fascist. You're not telling me you have to be a white to be a fascist, are you? Anyway, I've always seen it as the song of a youth who's looking to the future and sees it to be bright. That's part of the point. The characters don't know what's coming. The boy singing it doesn't really know what it means.'

'Mark, you just want to wind the audience up.'

'Nonsense, Pam, it'll be thought provoking.'

'The parents will be confused.'

'That would be a major miracle with the kind of parents we're talking about. I doubt if any of them have ever seen Cabaret before. And to them, Churchill is just an insurance company. World War Two is a movie on the telly at Christmas time.'

'Mark, it's just wrong.'

'Tsk, tsk, Pam, you're letting your prejudices show. Anyway, if they've never seen Cabaret before what difference will it make if someone naturally tanned sings that song?'

'Stop it, Mark, I'm not taking the bait. Speak to the head if you want. If she agrees, fine, otherwise forget it.'

So, I spoke to the bog. She told me to stop being silly.

It was, as they say, academic anyway. I caught Chris on his own one day as if by accident and suggested, as if the thought had just struck me, that he might like to audition for a part.

'You're jigging me, right? That's not no my thing. I doan do that kind of shit.'

I could have cheerfully strangled him for that double negative alone. Or smashed his head against the wall while screaming "Not no is not street talk. It's syntactically incorrect even for rap." But I knew that, even if it weren't correct in street talk terms, it could well be the following day.

'Think about it,' I said, 'it's going to be a lot of hard work and we're going to need every decent voice we can find. But it'll be worth it.'

'It'll be worth it?'

'It'll be character building.'

'You think I need character building?'

'Probably not. But think about it.'

I left it at that.

09h12. On the move again, slowly.

The following day Sharon Runny-Nose auditioned. I believe that you can teach anyone to sing. Apart from Sharon Runny-Nose.

Fortunately I wasn't there that day so I didn't have to break the news to her gently.

Unfortunately I wasn't there that day to prevent Pamela from softening the blow by making Sharon Runny-Nose my personal assistant.

"Can I get you a cup of coffee, Sir?" "Can I polish your shoes with my tongue, Sir?" "Will you fuck me so I can have your babies, Sir?"

No, no and thrice no. Go wipe your nose you horrible brat.

We're getting in to Baron's Court which means we're now almost above ground. Or at least we're open to access for mobile phones. Bloody things are going off left right and centre. Great. Having to listen to a hundred fuckwits screaming 'I'M ON THE TUBE!' 'I'M GOING TO BE LATE!' Yes, you are going to be late you fucktard morons. Why don't you learn to send a text message quietly? Do you think the world really wants to listen to your irrelevant lives?

We have a digital revolution which makes the Industrial Revolution look like a blip, we live through an incredible, mind blowing change in communications, transport, economics, politics, society, pretty much everything, and what do humans produce out of it at the end of the day?

'I'M ON THE TUBE!'

As for shite like Twitter, I don't even want to think about that. Try to get the kids to read and understand concepts in a rigorously produced and peer-reviewed text book and you struggle. Send them a tweet saying the earth is flat and they'll believe it without question.

There was a panic in Oxford Circus last year in which some celebrity tweeted that he was hunkering down in Selfridges to shelter from gunshots, the next moment people are fleeing down the street. Armed police all over the place. Turned out there were no gunshots, but there might have been a bit of shoving and pushing between two young men who had bumped into each other. That's how World War Three is going to start, not with a bang but with a tweet.

I used to confiscate mobiles which went off in the classroom and hand them to the head's secretary at the end of the class for safekeeping. Then I discovered the head had ordered the secretary to just hand them back when asked, which was pretty much two seconds after I'd given them to her. So if the little shit in question had another lesson with me afterwards they'd deliberately get someone to call them so it would go off again. In the end I learned to tell the class we'd wait until whichever little turd it was to finish their phone call before carrying on. At the end of the day I think it was a combination of peer pressure and pure boredom that made them give up that game.

Oh, great, one of the wankers is talking to his office, loud enough for the entire train to hear, giving out orders as if he's the managing director or CEO or whatever they call themselves. Probably looks after the post-room judging by the cheapness of his suit. What is it in the psyche of arseholes like that? Hell, you hear that sort of boasting bullshit in a playground full of teenagers, you'd expect a grown man to behave like an adult, not a fourteen year-old.

Danny, I hope things have improved by the time you read this, but basically today humans talking to a mobile phone are worse than drivers inside cars. At least the driver is in their own world, mobile phone users just act like it. Almost as if they were high on drugs, wafting around in the clouds, while in reality they're walking into lamp-posts.

Now there's a great scene from Star Trek they missed out on. Captain Kirk flips open his communicator and shouts

'I'M ON THE TUBE! I'M GOING TO BE LATE! NO, THE FUCKING TUBE! YES, SIGNAL FAILURE!'

If the Piccadilly Line was in charge of the Mars probe it would have had signal failure before it cleared the tree-tops.

Still, looking on the bright side I am now only thirteen stops from Heathrow. I might be able to survive listening to a bunch of complete wankers.

Personally, if I absolutely have to have a conversation on one of those blasted things I keep it to the minimum. Ever since I was on a bus and received a call. Whoever it was asked me where I was. I replied, 'I'm on a bus', very loudly. That's when I realised that a mobile phone could easily also turn me into a complete fucking wanker if I let it.

Though I am tempted to get my mobile out and scream into it, 'YES, I'M GOING TO BE LATE FOR DOUBLE MATHS. I KNOW, FUCKING NUISANCE, ISN'T IT.'

Let me try phoning Maddy.

Ah, no, I can't can I, I don't have her number.

FFS.

09h15.

Piece of cake, Danny, piece of cake. We're going to make it with time to spare, no problems, as they say in Kangarooland.

Wait a minute, the driver's trying to make an announcement over the hubbub and he doesn't sound chuffed any more.

I do not believe it.

I do not fucking believe it.

It's just been announced that the train is terminating here because of a security alert.

That's it. Everyone out and leave the station as quickly as possible.

Take your personal effects with you.

They'll blow up anything left.

For fuck's sake.

09h15.

For fuck's sake.

In fucking triplicate.

I do not fucking believe this.

## Barons Court

09h40. Back at Barons Court after a long journey and almost half an hour, now sitting on a bench waiting for another train.

Danny, In the unlikely event that you find yourself kicked out of a tube at Barons Court, there's a little coffee shop there, just outside. Stop, relax, have a coffee, and wait until they re-open the station. Do not, as I did, as I was instructed to do, take a left turn out of the station, another left, and then walk to Hammersmith tube station. Because, you know what? That will also be closed. They will suggest that you take either the H91 bus to Hounslow West, or the 267 to Kew Bridge Station and then the 237 to Hounslow. Or something like that. Maybe the 666 or the 69. I can't remember which one I caught. Whichever one it was the driver wasn't in any hurry to go anywhere. At one point he refused to move until the schoolkids who had slipped in through the exit doors to avoid paying got off. And then there was the woman who got on with a pram. Only there was already a pram in the space provided for wheelchair users, so they had to negotiate space between themselves. Only the new woman with a pram hadn't applied her card to the card reader yet, and the driver wasn't going to move until she had, but she wasn't going to until she had secured her pram. And so on and so forth and for fuck's sake.

There's a scene in the film Patton, he's on a bridge where he shoots a farmer's jackass that had been holding the convoy up while German planes merrily shot them up, before telling the troops to throw it over the side into the river. I know how he felt. If I had a firearm I'd be shooting jackasses too.

And it's peak traffic jam time so it takes us about three days to trek fifty yards in a bus. Somewhere along the way someone reads out a news flash from their smartphone: a Hitachi train had crashed into some overhead power cables somewhere close to Paddington overnight, so all overland trains to Heathrow have been cancelled including the Heathrow Express, which leaves the Piccadilly Line as the only viable option in.

Which cheered us up no end for some weird reason. We might no longer be on the Piccadilly Line, but at least we were moving, they weren't.

Then we get about five stops along the way to somewhere and the bus driver announces that the tube security alert is over so anyone wanting to go to Heathrow might want to think about going back to Barons Court or Hammersmith. So a whole bunch of us sheep do so without thinking, how does the bus driver know the tube's working again? So we board another H91 or 267 or 666 or 69 going in the opposite direction and get back to Hammersmith to find it's still closed. And then we hurry back to Barons Court and it's also still closed. And the station staff outside advise us to take a left turn, another left, and then walk to Hammersmith tube station and catch either the H91 or 267 bus. Or maybe the 666 or the 69. And then while we were contemplating whether to strangle them or smash their heads into the closed gates, hallelujah, the gates open again and the Piccadilly Line is running again.

Sort of. Limping, maybe.

So here I am sitting on a London Underground bench. Waiting.

A tube's just pulled in. And it's almost empty. I don't know how they managed that. Probably reversed it at Earl's Court or somewhere. Won't stay that way for long. I'll have to write faster, I'm going to run out of elbow room soon.

Avanti.

Or something.

That Indian bloke.

Geronimo.

Cockfosters
Oakwood
Southgate
Arnos Grove
Bounds Green
Wood Green
Turnpike Lane
Manor House
Finsbury Park
Arsenal
Holloway Road
Caledonian Road
King's Cross St. Pancras
Russell Square
Holborn
Covent Garden
Leicester Square
Piccadilly Circus
Green Park
Hyde Park Corner
Knightsbridge
South Kensington
Gloucester Road
Earl's Court
Barons Court
Hammersmith
Turnham Green
Acton Town

Ealing Common
North Ealing
Park Royal
Alperton
Sudbury Town
Sudbury Hill
South Harrow
Rayners Lane
Eastcote
Ruislip Manor
Ruislip
Ickenham
Hillingdon
Uxbridge

South Ealing
Northfields
Boston Manor
Osterley
Hounslow East
Hounslow Central
Hounslow West
Hatton Cross ←
Heathrow T 1-2-3 ⟶ Heathrow T4
Heathrow T5

# Leaving Barons Court

*Estimated time to Heathrow Terminal Five: 41 minutes*

*Estimated time to Hammersmith tube station: 2 minutes*

09h48.

Right, back on the tube. It isn't going anywhere at the moment, but at least it's a tube, it's pointed in the right direction, and I'm on it.

Sharon Runny-nose turned up at the house for the first time one Thursday morning. She had some notes about the production she thought I'd want to see. Or so she said.

Rule number one of teaching: don't take work home with you.

Rule two: don't take your students home with you.

Rule three: don't let the buggers get a foot in your door.

I thanked her and told her not ever, under any circumstances, to come to the house again. She looked tearful, so I gently explained that I could get into a lot of trouble if she did. I didn't add, 'Just like last time', but I definitely thought it.

I should have belted her across the head to make sure the message went in. Because it didn't, as I was to discover later.

I sent her on to school, following half an hour later. First thing I did was arrange a meeting with my union rep, Michelle. I call her Shell. She calls herself a feminist, but I think of her more as an equalist. She's equally scathing about men and women. She organised a meeting with the head for a few days later, and I told her what had happened.

"I think you're over-reacting, Mark," the bog said, "she was just trying to be helpful. I'm sure it won't happen again."

She was pissed off that I'd told her. If anything bad happened she wouldn't be able to claim that she knew nothing and I should have come to her straight away. Which is, of course, exactly why I did it and made sure my union rep was with me. I knew it was going to happen again. I'd seen the look in Runny-nose's eyes. The only thing that was going to stop her would be my demise. And even then she'd insist on leaving roses every bloody anniversary.

In the weeks after I got back from Liverpool after Jenny's funeral I wandered through the rooms in the house in Muswell Hill. I sat on the bed in what had been so briefly Jenny's room, but couldn't sit still. Every room had ghosts of memories, from Jenny to those long off days when I would explore the house and neighbourhood in my summer school holidays. One Sunday afternoon I found myself wandering through the rooms of the house, missing Jenny more than anything else. I idly poked around the rooms where we'd stored the extraneous furniture.

I found the chest of drawers we'd tried to open. I tried pulling out the top drawer. For some reason, after a little pressure, it slid open. It hadn't been locked at all. I guess it had just been stuck, maybe some of the wood wasn't properly cured and had swollen in damp weather. Whatever the reason I found myself looking at piles of old correspondence. Personal stuff, letters upon letters. They looked like they must have been written centuries before, but that's probably because email arrived in time to save me from having to rely on the written word to ask my folks for a subsidy, so any letter which doesn't look pristine seems to have the aura of 1800.

I glanced at the top one. It was addressed to Aunt Marigold, which made sense. The postmark was blurred, but I thought I could make out nineteen-eighty something. I debated whether to open it or not, or maybe leave the lot to Mom and Dad to sort out.

The one I'd picked up seemed different. More worn. As if it had been opened and read and re-read a number of times. Eventually I decided to have a quick look and then decide who should sort the rest out. It went something like this:

"My dearest Mari"

There was a bit of waffle then:

"If only we could live in a perfect world. But, as you say, society will always lay the blame of the parents on the child. We will look after her and treat her as our very own daughter. And I don't blame you or him for anything. If only polygamy were legal. But I suppose we're too old and missed the bus on running away and starting our own commune in the

141

depths of the American wilderness. The important thing now is that you get better."

There was a bit more – a lot more. And I've probably got the tone wrong, but it was a letter from mum to Aunt Marigold. It didn't make an awful lot of sense, but I gathered that Aunt Marigold had gone, or was going through some illness, and my folks were looking after someone's baby.

Adults do that, Danny, they have conversations between them which make sense to them because they've been through the same experiences, but to anyone outside the gang they might as well be speaking gibberish.

I tossed the letter back on the pile and closed the drawer. I was in a skittish mood that day for some reason. My thoughts jumped from the school musical to football practise to classes I needed to prepare for but couldn't sit still long enough to do.

The door chimes are beeping, the doors are closing, and we're departing Barons Court. Driver isn't saying anything. I doubt he's got anything printable to say.

09h50.

Hello. Our old friend Mrs Yank is in this carriage looking severely pissed off. I think I can spot Mr Yank in the next carriage. The Two Pakistani boys are at the end. They look shattered.

Some schoolkids making a noise at the doors.

The one time, at the house in Muswell Hill, I forget what we were doing, something domestic or other. Your mother and me. Anyway, I think the radio was on, or the television, and there was a report of a school teacher who had run away with a sixteen-year-old pupil. I suppose you automatically presume it's a male teacher and a female pupil, though there's been a spate of women teachers being convicted of having sex with underage boys recently, so, who knows, maybe we're reaching equality.

Anyway, in this case it was a male teacher and sixteen-year-old girl, and they'd run away, it was believed to either the Isle of Wight or France. Right pair of idiots. Their mugshots appeared in every newspaper and on every television between Aberdeen and Berlin, and they were picked up in Paris after a few days.

Maddy looks up from whatever it was she was doing, looks me straight in the eyes and asks, have you ever slept with any of your pupils?

Now on the face of it that's a pretty silly question. Like, if I had, I'm going to say, 'Yeah, course, doesn't everyone?' I'd lie and say no, wouldn't I?

Though with her looking directly into my eyes I'd have to be a pretty good liar not to give myself away.

'Maddy,' I said, 'I'm going to introduce you to some of my bunch one day. You won't be asking if I'd slept with any of them, you'd be wondering if anybody would sleep with them. Or anything. Seriously, I'm sure their mothers love them, or at least some of them, but physically they're about as attractive as ET after an accident with a food blender.'

She looked at me in silence for a few seconds.

'I notice you didn't say no,' she said.

I sighed. YBM has to be bloody correct and right at the same time.

'Okay, Maddy, no. No, I have never slept with any of my pupils, girl, boy, mucus-lizard or any other gender. Okay?'

'I don't believe you,' she said, giving up the concentrated stare and continuing with folding up a jersey – I remember now, we were doing the laundry – 'the only male teachers who didn't try to get off with me at school were either too old or gay.'

I sighed.

'Maddy, that's because you are sexy, beautiful, lovely, intelligent and pretty much all round the perfect young woman. You turn men's brains to mush, they can't help it.'

She stuck her tongue out at me.

Then she said:

'I still don't believe you. But, so long as it's in the past and you don't do it again, I forgive you.'

Well, that was kind of your mother, wasn't it, Danny?

Coming in to Hammersmith.

The driver's just announced that we might be slow-going because of an earlier security alert. No mention of the signal failures. You might think he'd rather not mention those.

I've just realised. In theory I should still have loads of time, but it's just struck me that your bloody mother probably expects me to turn up around about an hour after I got her bloody phone call – which makes it about an hour ago. Patience isn't exactly her strong point. She'll probably give it half an hour, go through security determined to put it all behind her.

I could always buy a ticket myself, just to get through security to wherever she is. I've got my credit card with me.

Fuck.

No passport.

I'll come up with something.

The driver's making an announcement.

Okay, this is what he said:

'Ladies and gentlemen, we were having some minor problems earlier, but then the fat Controller took over and now things are really stuffed.'

So, at least someone hasn't lost his sense of humour. Not that he sounded overly amused.

09h57.

We should get into Heathrow by ten thirty if nothing else goes wrong.

Plenty of time.

Why do I feel I should be singing that hysterically while tap-dancing in a top hat?

In a mine field.

FFS.

Cockfosters
Oakwood
Southgate
Arnos Grove
● Bounds Green
● Wood Green
● Turnpike Lane
● Manor House
● Finsbury Park
● Arsenal
● Holloway Road
● Caledonian Road
● King's Cross St. Pancras
● Russell Square
● Holborn
● Covent Garden
● Leicester Square
● Piccadilly Circus
● Green Park
● Hyde Park Corner
● Knightsbridge
● South Kensington
● Gloucester Road
● Earl's Court
● Barons Court
○ Hammersmith
Turnham Green
Acton Town

Ealing Common         South Ealing
North Ealing          Northfields
Park Royal            Boston Manor
Alperton              Osterley
Sudbury Town          Hounslow East
Sudbury Hill          Hounslow Central
South Harrow          Hounslow West
Rayners Lane          Hatton Cross  ←
Eastcote              Heathrow T 1-2-3  →  Heathrow T4
Ruislip Manor         Heathrow T5
Ruislip
Ickenham
Hillingdon
Uxbridge

# Hammersmith

*Estimated time to Heathrow Terminal Five: 39 minutes*

*Estimated time to Turnham Green tube station: 4 minutes*

There are three Underground lines that use Hammersmith. The Circle, District and Hammersmith and City. That's what the map says. What looks like one of the platforms for trains going toward central London appears to be full of middle aged German tourists waving maps of the Underground while interrogating anyone looking slightly like platform staff. They're laden with cameras and surrounded by enough luggage to kit out Dr Livingstone, I presume.

Well, if the Heathrow service is fucked I presume the one going in the opposite direction must be pretty fucked too.

Other platform looks full of schoolkids and office workers. They're going to be late for school.

I am able to note these details because we've been sitting here for about five minutes going nowhere.

Schoolkids who were on have got off.

We've just been told that we're being held here to regulate the service.

At least I think that's what the bloke said. He sounded like a Nigerian with a sore throat speaking from the bottom of a wet well.

Just drive, man for Christ's sake. You can regulate later as much as you want.

Jenny and I visited pretty much ever tourist and non-tourist place we could. If ever the phrase 'bushy-tailed and bright-eyed' applied to anyone, it was Jenny.

Christ, I don't believe it. A huge, fat woman has just got on. She's got a choice of almost anywhere to sit. Which is just as well because she needs about four seats. She hasn't got an arse the size of Wales. She's got an arse that looks Wales look small.

There's a seat free next to two elderly Portuguese. They're quite small. They're sound like they're having an end-of-marriage argument, which probably means she's saying something like 'remind me not to forget

146

tomatoes, darling,' and he's replying, 'don't forget to get tomatoes, my dear.'

She could have sat next to them.

There's a group of Eastern European builders further down, two seats free there. She could have sat next to them.

A young Italian couple further down, the girl's so far down the bloke's throat it's one and a half seats free. She could have sat next to them.

The two Japanese girls and bloke. Loads of space there.

Quiet English builder, arms folded, eyes closed, seat either side free.

Three seats side by side.

So where does fat-arse sit?

Right next to the one bloke trying to write down some notes.

She's overflowing her seat, I think I might get smothered in cellulite.

Smothered or asphyxiated, one of the two.

Not so much Miss Piggy as Mrs Porker.

And she's got the regulation litre cup of over-sugary fat-laden coffee, and her little piggy eyes are staring ahead blankly as her huge fat piggy cheeks wobble as she stuffs her huge piggy snout with cookies or biscuits from a five kilogram bag.

It's not easy to concentrate while a ton of lard in vaguely human form is threatening to overwhelm you.

But I must.

I'll move seats as soon as I get a chance.

Jenny

Oh, dear.

Lard-arse has just informed me rather haughtily that other people can read shorthand as well. Now she's waddled off to find a seat as far away as possible.

Well, shouldn't be reading what other people are writing, then, should you, fuckwit?

Surprised the train didn't tilt as she moved.

Danny, one of the big stories these days is obesity. Used to be smoking, alcohol. These days it's not only horror stories of the diseases which are a result of being overweight, but also stories of people catching planes only to find they're trapped in their seat by some morbidly obese fellow traveller next to them. God knows what it will be as you grow up. Guaranteed the medical fraternity will decide that something is bad for you and the media will declare it a crisis. That's what the media exists to do.

Though what the media will be by then is anyone's guess. Do you know what? When I was born the Internet didn't exist. Well, not the modern one, I'm sure there were geeks around in darkened rooms sending each other a byte at a time. When I was a teenager I was convinced my folks, your grandparents, must have gone through the Blitz. Dad must have been a bomber pilot, gallantly risking his life to drop a load on Hitler's Berlin. But of course they weren't, they were more children of the Sixties, or Long Sixties at the most.

Which poet was it who said something along the lines of, to be alive and young in that time was pure heaven? Something like that. One of the Romantics, I think. Wordsworth, probably.

The pensioners had the war. The oldest pensioners. Then you have the Sixties, all flower-power and hippies and anti-Vietnam demonstrations. And then nothing until now and a bloke sitting in a stationary tube train going nowhere. I will certainly remember it, but I don't think it is going to define a generation.

Moving again.

10h02.

One hour twenty-eight minutes.

I think it was the Wednesday after that Sunday that the head called me into her office. Wednesday afternoon. There was some woman sitting there with a cup of tea. I wasn't offered one, but then I never had been before. The head came out with it pretty much straight away.

'Mark, this is Jane Horrorbollocks. She's a professional pianist and has agreed to take over the production of Cabaret. I'm sure you'll agree that the children have reached a stage where they need someone who can take them that one little step further. And there really are too many other things for you to do."

To say I was gobsmacked would be an understatement. I didn't know where to start. She'd deliberately denied me any support when I started the project. She'd refused to fund anything. She'd done nothing. Nothing. Pamela, the kids, Sean and myself had sweated buckets. We'd dragged ourselves up kicking and screaming. We'd done everything. And now bitch-face was handing it all over to someone who had done nothing, zilch – and by the sounds of it was being paid for it.

No discussion, no forewarning.

Above all, the kids and I knew each other. I might not be the best, but they knew my weaknesses and I knew theirs. It's like a team getting to know and support each other. How the hell were they supposed to gel with a complete stranger in a few weeks. After all, there were less than eight weeks to go. I snapped. Not in a screaming, shouty way.

I said simply, "I'll tell the kids I've been fired then,' I said, turned, walked out and closed the door very quietly. Because when you've decided on revenge the last thing you want to do is waste your energy on temper tantrums.

Not that I actually formulated or mentally verbalised it that way as I walked out. I could summarise my mental output as: Fuck you. Oh, and fuck Miss RubberButtocks as well. Not in a sexual way, though.

There comes an emotional point when we refuse to contemplate that our feelings or reactions could be wrong, or even childish. I was in that zone right then.

And I was fucking right to be.

Oh, look, we've stopped again. Middle of nowhere.

10h03

Nope, driver's not going to give us a clue.

Oh, sorry, there's a faint wheezing which sounds like the driver's trying to whisper something. Otherwise known as the tannoy system being fucked.

Ho hum.

Ho fucking hum.

It was towards the end of the afternoon. I had planned on sticking around for rehearsals. Now there wasn't any point. I met Pamela in the corridor and told her what had happened. She looked back in disbelief.

'You must have misunderstood,' she said.

'Ask her yourself,' I replied. 'I'm off home, since I'm no longer required.'

'But, Mark, what am I going to tell the children?'

'Tell them the truth. Sometimes you work your balls off to achieve something and some son of a bitch takes it away. Or a bitch of a bitch, in this case.'

'Tell them not to pay the ferryman until he gets them to the other side,' I called back over my shoulder as I walked away. 'Otherwise he'll drop you in it half way.'

That was it as far as I was concerned. If the subject came up in class I stamped on it. The kids had to get used to the new reality and the less it involved myself the better.

I encountered Chris in the corridor one day. As soon as he saw me a cynical grin split his face.

'So you got fired then, maan,' he said. 'That's what happens when you don't belong.'

'Don't worry, Chris, I won't be making that mistake again.'

Then a few days later it all became irrelevant. Because that's when the news about Jenny arrived.

Moving again. Slowly.

10h04

Piccadilly doesn't stop at Turnham Green after seven in the morning. Next stop Acton Town, then a clear run up to Heathrow Terminal Five. We'll be there by ten-forty-five. Eleven at the latest. We're pulling in now. Wait a minute, this isn't Acton Town. This is Ravenscourt Park.

The Piccadilly Line doesn't stop at Ravenscourt Park.

Seems it does now.

Cockfosters
Oakwood
Southgate
Arnos Grove
● Bounds Green
● Wood Green
● Turnpike Lane
● Manor House
● Finsbury Park
● Arsenal
● Holloway Road
● Caledonian Road
● King's Cross St. Pancras
● Russell Square
● Holborn
● Covent Garden
● Leicester Square
● Piccadilly Circus
● Green Park
● Hyde Park Corner
● Knightsbridge
● South Kensington
● Gloucester Road
● Earl's Court
● Barons Court
● Hammersmith

**Ravenscourt Park** ○ Turnham Green

Acton Town

| Ealing Common | South Ealing |
| North Ealing | Northfields |
| Park Royal | Boston Manor |
| Alperton | Osterley |
| Sudbury Town | Hounslow East |
| Sudbury Hill | Hounslow Central |
| South Harrow | Hounslow West |
| Rayners Lane | Hatton Cross ← |
| Eastcote | Heathrow T 1-2-3 → Heathrow T4 |
| Ruislip Manor | Heathrow T5 |
| Ruislip | |
| Ickenham | |
| Hillingdon | |
| Uxbridge | |

# Ravenscourt Park

10h06.

Haven't a clue how long it takes to get from Ravenscourt Park to Heathrow. According to the journey planner we don't stop here. According to the driver he doesn't either, but seeing as we are parked alongside the platform he's opened the doors to let some cool air in.

How very thoughtful of him.

It's a glorious day of sunshine and tall, slowly-scudding clouds, the sort John Constable painted, though I guess he wouldn't have included a tube station. His paintings all have a stability and serenity about them, as if they're saying, 'this is the way life is, was, and forever will be, take it easy, enjoy the scenery'. I don't believe he ever painted something called "Young man in a panic to get to his girlfriend before she flies out of his life forever."

The Saturday after I'd found the letter, the school football teams played another school, about the only school in the area with a reputation lower than ours. We got clobbered, in a couple of cases literally. Any normal ref would have handed out half a dozen red cards to the other team, but we got the one who wouldn't need glasses because he would have failed the physical in the first place, had he had one.

Failed the physical? I surprised he found the fucking football field.

Come Saturday evening I decided I'd earned myself a couple of whiskies. A couple of decent whiskies. I never drink whiskey down the pub. They serve you just enough to dirty the glass. And I don't drink alone, so I made sure I had the bottle with me.

While I was sipping the second, watching television with half an eye, planning on who and how I was going to deal with first, I noticed that someone had left a voice message on my answerphone, sometime in the afternoon, presumably. I pressed play. Turned out to be Donald.

'Hi, Mark? Long time no see. Just to let you know we're planning on going to Bella's tonight. Stella said she'll be flying back from New York in a week or so for a short while. See you later.'

Ha! I thought. Good luck with Bella's, I think you'll find it's closed. Permanently.

I was about to sit down and resume my drink when a thought struck me. Donald and the others would be much more likely than me to know that Bella was no longer with us, so perhaps there was something he hadn't mentioned?

On a whim I checked that I was suitably attired, and strolled out for a walk, coincidentally passing Bella's place. It was about six in the evening and still light. There were a number of windows open and just enough noise escaping to show that it was occupied. I stood watching for a while. A couple turned up and knocked on the door. The tutu-clad doorman opened it and allowed them in.

I stood there for a little longer, letting the whiskey and my mood get to me. I'd just go in to see what was happening. Find out where Ziggie was. Hopefully dead from his own poison.

No, fuck it, I was going to go in and find Ziggie and –

I didn't know what. By then I was on my way to the door. I knocked. Tutu-man opened it, nodded recognition, and let me in.

I took the glass the waitress gave me and headed in to do a search of the rooms. By mistake I took a sip of whatever battery acid was in the glass. If I wasn't already flying on whiskey mixed with medication I would have done a vertical take-off with that stuff.

Killed off a pot-plant with the concoction and moved on.

Nothing in the first room.

Nothing in the second.

Nor the third.

10h10.

Stamford Brook. Can't stop here, no platform for us.

Ah, we can stop here after all. We just can't get out. There's a railway track between us and the platform.

No, wait, we're moving again.

Thank god.

Bella's place.

Remainder of the gang of six in the fourth room. Ducked out before they noticed me.

Went upstairs. Into the one of the double rooms. It was pretty crowded, smoky. People were wandering to and fro.

And then, like Moses parting the waters, the crowd parted and I saw your bloody mother for the first time, about fifteen feet away. She had a cigarette holder in one hand, complete with cigarette. It wasn't lit. She never actually smoked, she valued her vocal chords too much. Sharing a smoky room was a sacrifice. Smoking was a big no-no.

She took a breath and blew out non-existent smoke in a way that said 'Oh darling, really' in about forty-two languages, including Nordic and Swahili. Then she turned to casually see if anyone had appreciated this performance.

And our eyes met.

And a millisecond later she dropped the pose and we just looked at each other.

She had the most gorgeous eyes I have ever seen.

Apart from that she was stunning, composed, confident, vulnerable, mysterious, entrancing, bewitching, ethereal, mysterious, the most beautiful girl I had ever encountered. The most beautiful woman. Girl, woman, princess, goddess, who cares. I wanted to take her in my arms and hold her and hold her and hold her, just hold her and keep her safe.

I decided in a split second that she was going to be mine. I think I thought, 'She's mine'. Perhaps it was 'She has to be mine'. For all I know it was fucking 'Gloop?'

But for a second I was besotted. I couldn't take my eyes off of hers. And she wasn't looking anywhere else either.

Then the waves of people came back together and the curtains closed and she was gone.

And sanity returned.

I was there to kill Ziggie, not to fall in love.

Having quickly scanned the room for the little shit I moved on. Into the next room.

No Ziggie.

Another room.

No Ziggie.

I tried the last room.

No Ziggie.

I came out of that room having decided to give it up as a bad job. The most I was going to do if the bastard appeared was to try to pick a fight with him and hopefully accidentally break his neck. He wouldn't retaliate unless he had about five gorillas to back him up. Whatever happened it probably wouldn't be worth it. It had to be kill or nothing.

As I came out I almost walked into someone. She skipped back a step.

Your bloody mother.

'Hello,' she said after a pause, 'I'm maddening.'

I swear she said maddening.

'I'm sure you are,' I replied, as soon as I had my breath back. 'Is it universal or personal?'

'Sorry?'

'Being maddening.'

'Madeleine! I said I'm Madeleine!'

I looked at her, trying to think of something to say. Or trying to say something to think of.

'Well?' she asked.

'I'm fine,' I replied.

Fucking idiot.

She gave a delicate little snort.

'I wasn't asking you how you are. I was asking what your name is.'

'Oh. Mark.'

'I knew that.'

I paused to take that in, and waited for Divine Inspiration.

'How did you know that?'

'I asked someone.'

Normally I would have sarcastically enquired why, if she already knew my name, she had to ask me for it. But because I was stupid and had just fallen in love I could only think, 'Wow! She actually asked someone who I was! She must be interested!'

And anyone less under the spell of stupid might have wondered, who did she ask, and what was that person likely to say of me?

'Well, hello, Mark,' she said, presumably having decided that either (a) I was a strong man of few words, or (b) I was the village idiot whose tongue needed rolling back into my head.

'Well, hello, Madeleine,' I said with the suave sophistication of a five year old with thinking problems.

After we had looked at each other for a few more seconds I took one of her dainty little hands in mine.

'This is no place for a sweet little girl like you,' I said. 'There are some nasty people who want you to take nasty substances so that they can do nasty things to you.'

She cocked her head at me.

'And you won't?'

'To be honest, I'm just too knackered. I've had the worst week of the worst month of the worst year of my life.'

I paused.

'Why don't we go for a drink in a nice quiet pub and I'll tell you all about it.'

She laughed. In a very ladylike way. It tinkled.

'That sounds like the worst offer I've had since I arrived in Pommy-land. Wait here, I'll get my coat and stuff.'

I stood and waited. I wasn't sure what had just happened. But I was going to wait on that spot until Maddening came back or hell froze over.

And then Ziggie appeared in front of me.

'Well, well, if it isn't a stranger,' he said.

I noticed that he had Bella's two gorillas just behind him. Unlike with Bella they didn't look bored. They looked like they had a new master who had given them a taste for red meat.

'I suppose you heard about the terrible accident dear Bella had,' he continued.

'No,' I replied, 'I got a message from Donald and decided to pop in. So what's happened to Bella then?'

'Dead, darling, dead. Todt. Vreckt.' He giggled, confirming my suspicions that he was close to fully off his rocker.

'Dead? How?'

I was desperately trying not to let my hands bunch up into fists. Otherwise I wouldn't be able to strangle him.

'Oh, you know, wouldn't listen to those dear to her, wouldn't take advice. It's amazing how people have accidents.'

I stared at him for a few moments. I don't think he knew exactly the words he was using.

'Well, you take care, take care, take care,' he said, and wafted along, the gorillas giving me a last look-over before following.

10h12. Just passing Chiswick Park. I don't think we'll stop here, there's another track between us and the platform again.

Nope, going through, slowly, but going through.

'Who is that little bogan?' asked Maddy as she came up alongside me, taking my arm. She was wearing a coat which had more fashionability than weatherability, a hat which had every single ounce of practicality scraped out of it and replaced with attitude, and a handbag which announced its aggressiveness by staying quiet.

'He's one of the nasty men I told you about,' I replied. 'Come on, let's get out of here and I'll tell you more.'

We slipped out more or less unseen – the party had reached the stage where people were no longer interested in anything anyone else might be thinking of doing, most of them didn't know what they were doing themselves any more.

'So who was he?' Maddy asked once we were clear and walking down the evening street.

'Calls himself Ziggie,' I said. 'He's the local drug dealer, nasty, oily little piece of shit. I was kind of planning on murdering the fucking little rat tonight. Though in his case it wouldn't be so much homicide as insecticide.'

She laughed again, that wonderful laugh.

'You sound like my dad. He's a policeman. Are you?'

'God, no. I'm a teacher.'

'A teacher? You don't sound like a teacher. You're pulling my leg. A teacher wouldn't swear the way you do.'

'That's because you've never met a teacher in their natural habitat. Imagine having to pretend to be polite and courteous and clean thinking throughout the day. What do you reckon happens when teachers get a chance to let rip?'

'I hadn't thought about it that way.'

'So what do you do, then? Apart from looking gorgeous?'

'I'm an actress. A singer actress. I'm here to get some experience. I got my degree a few years ago. Now it's full speed ahead.'

We chatted further on the way to the pub – I'd be lying if I said I could remember exactly what we said and how we said it. I'd never fallen in love before – lust, yes, plenty, love never – so I was still getting used to the feeling.

We went into the pub, I ordered a red wine for her, a double whiskey for myself, I didn't want beer on top of my earlier drinks.

We found a comfortable nook away from the main part of the pub. We sat next to each other without thinking, as if we had been going out together for years. It was a quiet Saturday night, the afternoon crowd of football supporters had left, the evening crowd seemed happy to sit chatting while nursing their drinks. The television had been turned off. There was a jukebox, but that was playing very softly.

She had to try my whiskey to confirm it tasted like unwashed old socks and sandpaper just like her dad's normal tipple – her description – and then sat back, looked at me with those gorgeous eyes of hers, and asked me why I was having the worst week of the worst month, etc. Personally I could have just sat there getting drunk on her eyes and whiskey without the whiskey, but I guessed that might have bored her.

So, I explained about Jenny, what a wonderful sister she had been, how she had died, having to go up to Liverpool for the funeral, mum and dad struggling to come to terms with everything, Aunt Marigold's funeral, all the rest. She made the right noises in the right gaps, gasped at the right junctures, squeezed my hand to show she shared my pain, shifted close to me, said 'Oh you poor thing'. When I paused for breath she said,

'Jenny sounds like a real angel. I wish I could have met her.'

Now, considering YBM normally reserves the limelight for one person, i.e. herself, that was quite an amazing performance. Strangest thing is, she meant it.

Anyway, I went on to mention the school performance of Cabaret – she clapped her hands in delight, and announced that she'd played Sally Bowles in her school production. Then I mentioned the bit about being dumped in favour of the professional piano player, and she exclaimed, "Bitch!" in such a thoroughly heart-felt way I knew she understood my feelings. Finally I brought up the football team's abject failure that day and she was restored to happy mockery, commenting something about "Yes, I can see how losing a football match after all you've been through could be the final straw. Honestly, you boys and your football!"

Then it was her turn. She was the third child of a police sergeant and a nurse, the third daughter of a family desperate for a son, though they tried to hide their disappointment at her arrival. For the first few years of her life she was a combination punch-bag and dress-up doll for her sisters, and not much at all for her parents who had seen daughters born twice already and the novelty had long wore off. By the age of five she was already plotting her escape, working out where to run away to. And then, miracle of miracles, unto them a son was given, unto them a son was born. And Maddy said it with such a combination of utter sarcasm and honest relief I half expected a heavenly choir provided by Monty Python to appear in a sunburst, humming, led by the archangel Michael Palin.

This hallowed son proved to be her salvation. From then on her sisters doted on the miracle prince, completely forgetting her existence, leaving her free to pursue her own aims, and those had been clear from very early on: she was going to be a singer, a singer stroke actor. It might have started with seeing Sound of Music on the television, but there was another model she held in highest regard, quite an unexpected one: Vera Lynn, or Dame Vera Lynn as she now is. What had happened was that her parents owned an old gramophone of some sort, a record player, which pretty much was left in its box along with the few records they had. Maddy discovered it and an LP of Vera Lynn, and she couldn't get enough of it. She was lucky enough to have her own room, and her parents, perhaps to make up for their execrable treatment of her, perhaps to save their own sanity from having to listen to We'll Meet Again for the hundredth time in a day, bought her a pair of earphones.

From there on there was no stopping her. She lived for music and musicals. Before long she was in the choir and then head singer. And largely because she was so single-minded and driven she escaped most of the problems and doubts and worries that afflict us as we grow up. She'd had a number of small parts as a child actor, done a degree, been "resting" a number of times, got the chance of a role in a soap opera at the same time as the opportunity arose to come over here to act in several disparate roles for short periods around the country. For her there was no hesitation. Her opinion on soap operas might not be literally unprintable, but I don't want you reading that sort of language whatever age you are, Danny. For her acting and singing was a combination of the classical and the Golden Age of Hollywood, and she was going to ignite a brand new Golden Age.

Ironically, and much deserved, her sisters and her mother became slaves of the Number One Son. They treated him as a little god, pandered to his every whim, and naturally he took it as his due. When he was eighteen they were still drawing his bath for him, making sure it was precisely the right temperature, that his towels were out, his soap was ready. His opinion was always sought before the dinner menu was decided upon. The only person who could decide which channel the television was switched to other than blue-eyes was his father. And though his father was a man who took a spare the rod and spoil the child attitude, he was powerless against three women. That aside he was only too willing to indulge the boy-child himself.

Maddy never suffered any problems on that score. He tried ordering her about one day as he did with her sisters. She gave him a good slap and warned him not to try it again, adding for good measure that if he went whining to any of them she'd come into his bedroom at night and strangle him. He showed early signs of intelligence by not saying a word, and never, ever again trying to treat her as his servant.

These days, having grown up, they get along a little better, but she's still somewhat contemptuous of her sisters, both of whom married young and already have families and the accompaniment, drudgery. Apparently both weddings were shotgun weddings. As far as Maddy was concerned that indicated either comprehensive stupidity in not being able to manage birth control, or far worse, deliberately getting pregnant to ensnare a man. For Maddy any woman doing that is so far beneath contempt there is no way back.

Her brother, perhaps unsurprisingly, venerates her. Possibly because she's making a name for herself, and his friends are all star-struck that she's his going-to-be-famous sister.

So she flew over here. Moved into a shared house down the road in Bounds Green the day she landed. Got invited to a crazy party by one of the other sharers. Found herself all on her own at the party when the other sharer took some tablets and started talking to an invisible meerkat. Saw me, thought, he looks trustworthy, or at least more trustworthy than the other creeps, and that was that. She said it in a teasing way that said she wasn't really serious, she knew I was trustworthy, of course, except we'd only just met and she wasn't entirely sure. Personally I was more than sure, I was sure enough for both of us. What of, I probably couldn't have articulated at that moment, but I was too comfortable to want to.

By that stage we were into about our sixth round or so and they were calling last orders. I had a look at my watch.

'Bloody hell,' I said, 'it's almost midnight. They must have a late opening license, it's normally last orders at eleven.'

I looked at her.

'What say we go back to my place and order some scran?' I suggested.

'Scran?'

'Food. It's Scouse slang. My mum would kill me if she thought I was using it. I was brought up to speak proper, I was.'

She smiled.

'They call it tucker in Australia, but only in three situations: either to be ironic, or to be patriotically Australian, or because they're bogans. Sometimes all three.'

'You don't sound Australian,' I said.

She gave another smile.

'I've been using your accent,' she said. 'It's a kind of flattened English with any variation beaten out of it. I picked up on it watching British television at home. My favourite accent is Dick van Dyke alongside Julie Andrews in Mary Poppins. She sounds so terribly, terribly English, his is so way off the scale of being terrible it comes back to being good by the back door. The thing is, if I'm going to be any good as a singer in musicals I have to be able to sing as anyone, from Porgy and Bess to Chicago to Joseph and the Technicolor Dream Coat.'

I didn't make the mistake of pointing out that Joseph is traditionally played by a male singer. I already had a feeling that such technicalities were only likely to irritate her.

'So, what about it?' I asked. 'There's a place close to Bounds Green does lovely deep-pan pizzas. They do deliveries, half an hour max.'

'I'm starving. Do they do meat pizzas?'

'Their pepperoni is world famous.'

'Strange I haven't heard about it then. Come on, let's go.'

I never thought about it at the time, but a return to a cold and empty shared house on your first Saturday in a strange city in a strange country might not appeal. Taking your chance with a man you have only just met – well, all I can say is, maybe I have a more honest face than I ever suspected.

Nah, that's impossible.

I will never forget strolling back from the pub that night. It was a gorgeous warm spring evening. It was dark apart from the street lights. Despite the hour there were plenty of people still about, people on their way home from a night out, people giving their dogs a late night stroll before beddy-byes. We nodded to each and every one and said good-evening in the best Dickens style. Maddy presumed it was quite normal. I had to explain later that it was extremely abnormal, and the reason the strangers had replied so politely was that they must have presumed that we were either (a) American tourists or (b) stark-staring mad and probably dangerous and best humoured.

Somewhere along the way I took Maddy's hand, or maybe she took mine. It just felt so right. And then we got home and I found a flyer for the pizza shop, we agreed on what we wanted and I made the order over the phone. Then I made another drink, whiskey for me, and, thank the angels, I found a bottle of red wine to Maddy's taste and she had a glass of that.

Foul stuff.

Having had that drink and finished off the pizzas I suggested she might want to sleep over in one of the spare bedrooms. I offered her a tour of the place, which ended in my bedroom.

"I'll share this one with you," she decided, putting her arms around me and kissing me.

"But no funny business, Romeo," she added.

"Your wish is my command, oh Maddening," I replied.

And so, on our first date, first night together, we slept with each other. Just that. Literally. I was knackered anyway. I hadn't realised just how much I'd been relying on the bottle as a sleeping tablet. Maddy was still exhausted from the long flight and jet lag.

It was the best kip I'd had since before Aunt Marigold's funeral. It was like coming home after rough seas.

Cockfosters
Oakwood
Southgate
Arnos Grove
● Bounds Green
● Wood Green
● Turnpike Lane
● Manor House
● Finsbury Park
● Arsenal
● Holloway Road
● Caledonian Road
● King's Cross St. Pancras
● Russell Square
● Holborn
● Covent Garden
● Leicester Square
● Piccadilly Circus
● Green Park
● Hyde Park Corner
● Knightsbridge
● South Kensington
● Gloucester Road
● Earl's Court
● Barons Court
● Hammersmith
○ Turnham Green

Acton Town

| Ealing Common | South Ealing |
| North Ealing | Northfields |
| Park Royal | Boston Manor |
| Alperton | Osterley |
| Sudbury Town | Hounslow East |
| Sudbury Hill | Hounslow Central |
| South Harrow | Hounslow West |
| Rayners Lane | Hatton Cross ◄─────────┐ |
| Eastcote | Heathrow T 1-2-3 ──► Heathrow T4 |
| Ruislip Manor | Heathrow T5 |
| Ruislip | |
| Ickenham | |
| Hillingdon | |
| Uxbridge | |

# Turnham Green

*Estimated time to Heathrow Terminal Five: 35 minutes*

*Estimated time to Acton Town tube station: 3 minutes*

10h14

Have just crept into Turnham Green like an errant husband tiptoeing his way up the stairs in the early hours of the morning hoping not to be noticed.

And it looks like we'll be stopping at Turnham Green anyway. Maybe we're doing the scenic route today. Ladies and gentlemen I give you Turnham Green. Round about this area you'll find almost chocolate box descriptions of England: green and pleasant little parks below the railway line, people walking their dogs, jogging, just strolling along. The occasional church steeple amidst the houses. Red buses in the distance. A pub on the corner. Very quiet and peaceful.

It wasn't always thus, of course. At some point in the civil war Charles I came down here with about twelve thousand troops. He found the Parliamentary army ensconced here with twenty-four thousand, and very wisely decided to bugger off back to Oxford to go into winter quarters.

Why the fuck did the silly buggers let Charles II back in? We could have been a comfortably settled republic by now. Talk about unfinished business.

It's a funny thing, history. I understand the Serbs are still a little pissed off about having lost the battle of Kosovo back in 1389. Now I've heard of holding a grudge, but isn't that pushing things a bit far? Still, not far away from London, and in the same country – technically speaking – there are people still passionate about the Battle of the Boyne, and that happened a few hundred years ago. Considering my ancestry I think I'm supposed to be one of those but I can't be arsed.

In my more naive days I asked a history class if anyone knew what the Battle of the Boyne was. There was a sea of bemused faces looking alternately at me and their follow pupils. Finally a hand went up and on more intelligent lads suggested, 'World War Two?'

'Not World War Two, no,' I replied. 'You're probably thinking of the Battle of the Bulge.'

'My mum's got that,' said one girl proudly. 'She's always going on diets.'

Madeleine reserves a special hatred for Cromwell. Not "the English", she dislikes the English as a group about as much as she dislikes any other nationality. Just Cromwell himself.

10h15.

And thus started our relationship.

Maddy was still fast when I woke up on the Sunday morning. I showered and put the kettle on, made myself a coffee, got the breakfast stuff out. I knew Maddy wasn't a vegetarian or any of that nonsense, and she had an appetite to rival mine. Whether she was into eggs, bacon and the rest I didn't know, but then we pretty much didn't know much about each other anyway. I knew she was perfect, and that was good enough for me.

She tumbled into the kitchen around nine o'clock. We kissed, I made her coffee, and we sat comfortably silent while she infused herself with caffeine. After that we had a full breakfast, she had a shower, and we were both bright-eyed, bushy-tailed and ready for our first full day together.

I suggested we walked back to her place in Bounds Green. They'd caught a taxi the previous evening, and that's a good way to forget how quickly you can get around on foot in London. She agreed on the proviso that we swapped shoes.

Good point. She was wearing high heels. Not very high heels, but not good for a few miles stroll. And she could have fitted both her tiny feet into one of my trainers.

So we caught the 299 bus to Bounds Green. On the way there was an automated announcement repeated every so often, 'Please hold on, the bus is about to move.' The problem was that it was played only once the bus had been moving for a while and was completely useless. After the third time I put an arm around Maddy and held her tight. She turned an enquiring face to me.

'Well, you heard,' I said, 'it's official, you have to hold on tight.'

'But the bus is already moving.'

'That's not why I'm holding tight.'

'I'll bet you say that to all the girls.'

'I've never said it to anyone else. Scout's honour.'

'Mmm,' she said, disbelievingly, and looked out the window. She didn't ask me to remove my arm, however. I took that as a positive sign.

They don't play that announcement any more for some reason. Pity.

When we got to her place I waited downstairs while she went upstairs to put on some fresh clothes. The place was pretty dire. It was the sort of place where people paid per room per month, or possibly even per week, some long-term students – a year max – others itinerant tourists. The kitchen sink was full to overflowing. The carpets were greasy, the walls had a sheen of dirt. It was the sort of place I had stayed in as a student, and I'd had a ball. Looking back on it we should have been permanently hospitalised with food poisoning.

Maddy came back down as I was trying to guess the age of the pots and plates in the sink by the number of grease rings. She grimaced.

'Actor's res,' she said. 'Cleaning happens on an as needed basis.'

'In that case this lot is about two years overdue,' I said.

'I've lived in worse. Listen, Mark, I've got rehearsals starting Tuesday, and I've got loads to get done before then.'

'Well, we'd better get started, then,' I replied.

She gave me a look that suggested that what she really wanted to say was 'So long and thanks for all the kip'. Then she smiled.

'Okay, Romeo. First thing is to work out where this theatre is.'

So we went into the West End and got a map which showed where all the theatres were. Hers was a tiny one down a back street which looked like the arty sort of thing where new plays were held before not going on to any sort of acclaim ever.

And, having established the location, we gave up the rest of the day to tourist delights. A long walk along the Embankment, hand in hand, lunch at an open-air café, a stroll to Westminster, Horse Guards. Tube back to Bounds Green, bus to Muswell Hill, back to my place, Order a take-away delivery, have a couple of drinks while waiting. Watch a totally forgettable movie on television while eating the take-away. Another drink, a snog on the couch, then bed, and this time not to sleep.

To think that was just a few months ago. Feels like a couple of days. Or is that a couple of daze? Bloody marvellous times.

There's some wanker on his phone speaking foreign very loudly. Bloody mobile phones again.

Maybe the rest of the world calls them cell phones because people who use them in public should be locked up in cells. I swear these days if I find myself in a bus or tube or train carriage with just one other person sitting right at the other end, it's a 99 percent chance they'll have a mobile phone and need to shout into it so loud people five miles away can hear.

In the Middle Ages people apparently went around wearing perfumed posies hanging around their necks because, basically, life stank. Open sewers stank. Rubbish stank. Unwashed people stank. Today we look back in amazement. I wonder what your generation will make of people going around shouting into little boxes.

However, Danny, another wonder of our modern age is the way people go around with earphones either in their ears or massive ones over their ears. On the one hand it's a polite way of listening to music or the radio or whatever without inflicting your odious and obnoxious lack of taste on your fellow humans – or possibly limiting the chances of someone punching your lights out because you're such an arsehole. On the other hand some people use it as a defence mechanism, of drowning out the noise of arseholes who have to leak noise pollution into the atmosphere of civilised humans. And that's what I'm going to do now. I carry a pair of what I call fuck-off large earphones, designed by the manufacturers with sound-cancelling capability to kill off external noses, and worn by me in a way that says to anyone thinking of interrupting me, "Fuck Off". I still have seven other pairs I bought before I found these ones.

Not that it works perfectly. You could wear a sign above your head that reads, "Do not disturb me, just fuck right off", and there'll be at least one moron who will ask you why you've got a sign above your head which reads "Do not disturb me, just fuck right off", and then wonder why they've just had their teeth punched in.

And then, of course, you have the creepy weirdos who deliberately interrupt people to irritate them and provoke a response. The sort of pervert who sits next to you while you're reading a book and then deliberately and obviously reads it too, almost gobbing on your shoulder, and then asks you a question about something in it, just in case you've missed the fact that you've got a pervert gobbing on your shoulder while reading your book.

Not to mention the babel of foreign voices. The Portuguese are banging away at each other, presumably discussing the state of their veruccas. The Eastern European builders are apparently exchanging dirty jokes, they're laughing loud enough. The Italian couple are having an argument. The Japanese appear to be telling each other how huge the size of a cucumber was, if their hand gestures are anything to go by. Either that or they work in a sex shop. Fat-arse is moaning to someone on her mobile. The only person not contributing to the hullabaloo is the quiet English builder trying to sleep. And he's probably Irish.

Danny, there is something called misophonia. It's a little studied affliction whereby the sufferer develops an inability to tolerate certain noises, such as someone eating crisps with their mouth open, or the sound of a branch rubbing against a window pain. A baby crying endlessly. Thing is, it can lead to all sorts of things, panic attacks, outbreaks of violence. One of the characters in the musical Chicago, Liz, tells how the sound of her boyfriend popping chewing gum drove her nuts. She warned him to stop it, but he just laughed at her and popped one last time.

"So I picked the shotgun up and fired two warning shots," I think she says, adding, "I fired them into his head."

It's those jackasses again.

The boyfriend's name was Danny. Just a coincidence.

There is one thing that can really, really drive me to murder. And that's someone yakking endlessly, and loudly, and inanely, and like a real twat, into their mobile phone. And right now he's doing it. The bloke in the cheap suit with the cheap perfume. I call it Tosser's law. Did I say 99 percent? In fact, scientific testing has proved that if there are only two of you in an entire carriage there is a 99.9 recurring percent chance that the other person will be a tosser shouting into a mobile phone. And if you are the only person in the carriage it's probably you. Or the driver.

Do I kill the tosser in the cheap suit with the cheap perfume or put on the earphones? If I kill him we'll be delayed even further.

Bugger.

Okay, fuck-off earphones on now, music player switched on, the world outside switched off, and I can relax to some decent music.

Hmm, "This is the end". That will be the sound track to Apocalypse Now. Not entirely sure that's appropriate. Certainly hope not.

Enfin. We move.

10h17.

Fingers crossed. Acton Town next, and then straight on to Heathrow. No District Line signals nonsense. We should have a clear run now. Downhill all the way.

Just over half an hour to Maddy.

Cockfosters
Oakwood
Southgate
Arnos Grove
Bounds Green
Wood Green
Turnpike Lane
Manor House
Finsbury Park
Arsenal
Holloway Road
Caledonian Road
King's Cross St. Pancras
Russell Square
Holborn
Covent Garden
Leicester Square
Piccadilly Circus
Green Park
Hyde Park Corner
Knightsbridge
South Kensington
Gloucester Road
Earl's Court
Barons Court
Hammersmith
Turnham Green
Acton Town

Ealing Common
North Ealing
Park Royal
Alperton
Sudbury Town
Sudbury Hill
South Harrow
Rayners Lane
Eastcote
Ruislip Manor
Ruislip
Ickenham
Hillingdon
Uxbridge

South Ealing
Northfields
Boston Manor
Osterley
Hounslow East
Hounslow Central
Hounslow West
Hatton Cross
Heathrow T 1-2-3 ⟶ Heathrow T4
Heathrow T5

171

# Acton Town

*Estimated time to Heathrow Terminal Five: 32 minutes*

*Estimated time to South Ealing tube station: 4 minutes*

10h17

I remember the one time Maddy went to Heathrow to meet an old school friend who was coming over from Australia. I couldn't go with her, but I explained to her that she must be sure of what train she was on when it reached Acton Town, because that's where the line diverges. The right-hand side goes towards Uxbridge, the left side goes towards Heathrow. I explained that the local yokels in Uxbridge enjoyed a game of playing 'spot the silly tourist', where they sat outside the tube station waiting for parties of travellers who had failed to listen to the announcements, getting on an Uxbridge train instead of a Heathrow one. They reach the terminus and then wander around looking for this large airport they were expecting but not finding it.

Admittedly I was largely making that up. Occasionally tourists do manage to end up in the wrong place, but I don't think any Uxbridgeans have enough spare time to wait around for them. And I don't think Maddy actually believed me anyway.

Maybe that's a sign of a maturing relationship. Your partner doesn't mind you talking shite because they know they aren't expected to believe it.

One thing they do do on the odd occasion, at Acton Town and other stations where they've got multiple tracks to pass each other on, is announce that the train shortly due in on the opposite platform will be the first to depart, which is, I reckon, what they've just done right now.

Now don't ask me how they manage this. Possibly the other train comes out of the Acton Town depot – I've certainly never seen one overtake another before. What I don't understand is how they manage to have two trains for the same destination in the same station at the same time, especially when it's normally the other way around – not having any trains for any destination for long periods of time.

172

But it's an ideal opportunity to observe your fellow human beings. Firstly there are those who listen to the barely-audible announcement and quickly jump up to cross the platform to the other train expected to arrive soon. Then there are those who either weren't listening or did not understand, who, seeing people leaving, have a noisy conversation with the others in their group before rushing across the platform after the first group, sometimes – and this is great fun to watch – forgetting suitcases, bags, or even a baby, and then rushing back to collect their goods before scrambling across again.

Even though this other train hasn't even arrived yet.

Personally I never bother. Firstly, even if this other tube does arrive and leave first, the tube you're on is going to leave about two minutes later. Secondly, the probability is that one of the two will be taken out of service, and you might as well flip a coin to decide which it's going to be. And thirdly, you're now left alone in the solitary comfort of an empty carriage. Which is nice.

They're having an international argument on the platform. Lots of gesticulating and pointing. Enjoy, chaps.

Well, now, there's a thing. Doors have beeped, closed and we're off.

10h22

And now all those funny tourists who rushed out to catch the other non-existent train because it was leaving first are jabbering away and pointing at this one because it's the one that's leaving first. Idiots.

I felt sorry for the kids doing Cabaret. They really had put so much into it, and were now being betrayed by a bloody-minded and petty-minded woman who was just playing games to spite me. I couldn't see anything to do other than to tell them they'd need to make up their own minds what to do, I couldn't get involved. Anyway, with that bunch they'd probably do the opposite of whatever you told them to do. Unless you tried reverse-psychology and told them to do what you didn't want them to do, in which case they'd do that.

Perfectly predictably they weren't going to follow the orders of an interloper like Mrs Horrorbollocks. And Pamela couldn't control them. I don't think they would have given her a hard time on her own, she was just collateral damage. Sean might have made a difference, but he was away for some reason and didn't get back until it was too late.

The first sign of trouble was, according to the kids who insisted on telling me despite my forbidding them doing so, that the boy tasked with the jewel in the crown, singing 'Tomorrow belongs to me', began to sound like a conscript under Mussolini only interested in going home to tend his dying grapevines.

Then the Emcee and Sally Bowles suddenly decided that, instead of singing Money from Cabaret they would sing Money, Money, Money from Abba. Either they were Abba fans or they'd planned it, because I hear they did it perfectly from start to finish. Mrs Horrorbollocks gave up playing the piano because they just sang over her. I might have felt a little sympathy with Horrorbollocks had it not been how she reacted to that. She replaced Angela with a white girl because the original Sally Bowles was played by a white girl. I don't think it had anything to do with race, I think Horrorbollocks was just trying to get her own back on a bunch of kids she couldn't understand.

By the end of the first week most of the Brownshirts had deserted. That wonderful piece we'd choreographed fell to pieces. In the end there were three left, and I suspect they only stayed on to screw things up. They were so out of time with each other and the Herrenvolk boy they couldn't have been better at being bad. In fact as a comedy on how to get things wrong it sounded as if it might actually work. Unfortunately you'd need to be au fait with the original to get the jokes.

I must confess to a feeling of pride in the little buggers when I heard that the three Nazi Brownshirts left suddenly began walking like ancient Egyptians. That showed initiative and creativity. Pamela could only cover her eyes with despair. Horrorbollocks apparently couldn't play the piano and keep an eye on the backing dancers at the same time. All she knew was that someone was laughing at her. So she castigated everyone. So everyone laughed at her a bit more.

After Sean's return I met him one afternoon in the corridor with a face like thunder looking for a good valley to explode in
'You look somewhat miffed,' I said

174

'Bluidy woman!' he shouted, not caring who heard.

'I got fired. You resigned, I take it?'

'You might joke, laddie. I could have killed that bluidy woman. Trying to tell me what to do. And she hasn't a bluidy clue.'

'Oh dear, that does sound terrible.'

'I told her just where she could stick her piano. And she can. It's the only thing she'll have as a show.'

'You don't think they'll go ahead.'

'What with? The kids have given up. I wouldn't trust those brats not to turn up and sit in the audience on opening night. It would serve that bluidy woman right. And the bog, it's all her fault.'

I paused as what he said struck home.

'Careful not to put ideas in their heads,' I said, smiling. He scowled back. And then he smiled.

'Of course not,' he said.

Coming in to Ealing Common.

10h24. Two minutes. That's more like it. An almost empty carriage and zipping along. Finally things are going my way.

Now to think of what I'm going to say to YBM. Haven't got much time left.

Cockfosters
Oakwood
Southgate
Arnos Grove
Bounds Green
Wood Green
Turnpike Lane
Manor House
Finsbury Park
Arsenal
Holloway Road
Caledonian Road
King's Cross St. Pancras
Russell Square
Holborn
Covent Garden
Leicester Square
Piccadilly Circus
Green Park
Hyde Park Corner
Knightsbridge
South Kensington
Gloucester Road
Earl's Court
Barons Court
Hammersmith
Turnham Green
Acton Town

Ealing Common
North Ealing
Park Royal
Alperton
Sudbury Town
Sudbury Hill
South Harrow
Rayners Lane
Eastcote
Ruislip Manor
Ruislip
Ickenham
Hillingdon
Uxbridge

South Ealing
Northfields
Boston Manor
Osterley
Hounslow East
Hounslow Central
Hounslow West
Hatton Cross
Heathrow T 1-2-3 ⟶ Heathrow T4
Heathrow T5

176

# Ealing Common

This driver means business. Stop, open doors, close doors and off again. We'll be at Heathrow by eleven. See, Danny, I told you, plenty of time.

That Monday morning I woke up full of beans. I gave Maddy a cuddle. She returned a kind of soft murmur that I interpreted as 'Do not wake me up if you value your life', so I didn't. Instead I got up and went for the early morning jog I'd stopped doing some months before. Then I showered and woke Maddy with a cup of coffee. She almost talked me into throwing a sickie for the day so we could spend it together, but somehow I didn't want our relationship to start off with a lie.

Later, maybe, would be fine.

I left a spare set of keys for her to come and go as she liked, told her I'd be back in the afternoon, gave her a kiss and went off to work. As I walked down the school corridor to the staff room I think I was humming a tune. I remember I passed Sean and bade him a fine good morning. I wasn't cheerful. Cheerful doesn't describe it. I was full of bonhomie, it was that bad.

I suspect that Sean may have concluded that I was drunk. And so I was. But in a sober fashion. I was drunk on love. Or was I drunk in love? Who cares. It felt fucking marvellous.

Coming up to North Ealing. Not even a single stop in the middle of nowhere.

10h27.

Things are looking up. We're on the downward run now, nothing can stop us.

Tomorrow belongs to me ...

Wait a moment.

Wait a fucking moment.

North Ealing?

North Ealing's on the fucking Uxbridge line.

When the fuck did they change destinations?

Oh for fuck's sake.

177

Now I've got to get off and catch a fucking train back to Acton.

No wonder this one is so fucking empty.

North fucking Ealing? Where did that come from?

Christ, that's why those idiots rushed over to the other platform. They weren't announcing that the imaginary train about to appear was going to be leaving first.

They were saying this train wasn't going to Heathrow anymore.

Buggers must have decided that long before Acton Town.

Why didn't they tell me?

Great.

Just fucking great.

Fucking earphones.

Out.

Out.

Out.

## North Ealing platform

10h30

Sitting on the platform waiting for a tube going back so I can get off at Acton Town and resume my journey to Terminal Five.

Fucking idiot.

I now have precisely one hour to get to Heathrow, presuming she needs to go through security two hours before take-off.

I know absolutely nothing about North Ealing. Must be quite a posh place, nor do any of my pupils.

What I do know is that the next train isn't going to be here for a while. No announcements. No information. Nobody else waiting.

Danny, it was bloody lucky I noticed I was on the wrong track early, otherwise I might have ended up in Ickenham. I mean, Ickenham? Can you imagine, your last, dying words, like in Citizen Kane he breathes, "Rosebud". Imagine if your dying words were, "Ickenham ..."?

Back to that week Maddy and I first met. Maddy was full of her first day rehearsing, of course. From what I could gather it was a rather over-conceptual piece of self-conscious shite, but she was happy despite that. She was treading the boards in London. There was a stage and the smell of greasepaint and she got to sing a few songs. She was on her way.

I can't say we got into a routine, our lives were too disorganised for that. But we settled into being a couple very quickly. We shared everything. What we'd seen and done, what we were going to do. What someone at work had said or done. Chatted over our plans for going out, staying in. Rued the partings and counted the seconds until we were together again. Then, a month or two later maybe, one Saturday, Maddy had rehearsals as had become almost usual. I didn't have any sports training or other extra-curricular work, so I was doing the weekly domestics, shopping, washing, general tidying up. It was about midday, just as I was contemplating lunch, that the doorbell rang. Thinking it might be Maddy back early I opened it eagerly, presuming she had mislaid her keys.

"Hello, Mark," said Stella.

Involuntarily I automatically stepped back to allow her in, just as in the days when we were fuck-buddies.

"Surprised to see me? I thought Peter had mentioned I was back in town."

"He left a message on my voice mail. Something about you coming back for a week or so."

She laughed bitterly.

I suddenly remembered my manners and offered her a tea or coffee. We went through to the kitchen. She opened the back door, stepped just outside and lit a cigarette as she used to.

"Start-up turned out to be a shut down too," she said. "They'd been doing okay so long as their guarantors were satisfied with shiny offices and Powerpoint promises. The training side was supposed to generate income until the software side began producing product."

"But it didn't?" I suggested, to confirm I was listening, even though I didn't have a clue what she was on about.

"Nada," she said. "In the good old days you could charge big companies a thousand bucks a day to teach their clerks how to switch a PC on. They're more discriminating these days."

It hadn't taken her long to pick up the American drawl. She didn't say "clerks", though. I can't remember the exact word she used.

She stubbed her cigarette out in a flowerpot and came through to the table as I brought our coffees to it.

"They're very welcoming when you've got a work permit and a job. Not so much when the company folds."

We sat down and she gave me a long look.

"Seems like you had the right idea. Stick with what you know."

"Horses for courses," I said. "Maybe next year I'll get the urge to roam."

"I doubt it." She took a sip of coffee. "You're strange. You always seem to do what you want to."

"That's strange? Why would you do what someone else wanted you to do?"

"People make compromises. Sometimes you have to share a vegetarian even if you prefer pepperoni."

"Buying pepperoni means a vegetarian won't nick any of it."

She shook her head in a kind of despair.

"So, hooked up with anyone yet?" she asked, just a little too casually. I suspected that she had decided that I was probably the best thing on offer now, just like Jess had decided Rob would do, even if he wasn't quite perfect. She'd lost the main prize and was considering a compensation one.

"Pretty much. A lot of water's gone under the bridge recently. I've moved on." I had to, I could have added.

"I thought we were pretty good together."

Could have fooled me.

"Why don't we give it a go for old time's sake?"

She actually licked her lip with the tip of her tongue. That was one thing I can't deny. She really was good in bed. And now I was being offered a freebie.

Would Maddy mind? Not if she never knew, that's for sure.

She wasn't due back until the evening.

A train's just pulled in. I'd better take it, wherever it's going.

10h38

I could have cycled fucking faster than this.

Cockfosters
Oakwood
Southgate
Arnos Grove
Bounds Green
Wood Green
Turnpike Lane
Manor House
Finsbury Park
Arsenal
Holloway Road
Caledonian Road
King's Cross St. Pancras
Russell Square
Holborn
Covent Garden
Leicester Square
Piccadilly Circus
Green Park
Hyde Park Corner
Knightsbridge
South Kensington
Gloucester Road
Earl's Court
Barons Court
Hammersmith
Turnham Green
Acton Town

Ealing Common      South Ealing
North Ealing       Northfields
Park Royal         Boston Manor
Alperton           Osterley
Sudbury Town       Hounslow East
Sudbury Hill       Hounslow Central
South Harrow       Hounslow West
Rayners Lane       Hatton Cross ←
Eastcote           Heathrow T 1-2-3 ——→ Heathrow T4
Ruislip Manor      Heathrow T5
Ruislip
Ickenham
Hillingdon
Uxbridge

# Leaving North Ealing

10h39.

Back in a tube. Back on track, heading for Ealing Common and Acton Town. This bloody diversion – how many stops is it to Heathrow? Should I have gone on to Uxbridge and caught a bus or a taxi to Heathrow? That's the problem when they start squashing maps up and playing silly buggers with them, you never know quite where you are. The map on the bulkhead shows Uxbridge quite close to Heathrow, but for all I know they could be in separate counties a hundred miles apart.

The bog has a quite expensive smartphone. Paid for by the school, of course, apparently she needs it for her duties. Whenever there's a meeting she's got it out, tapping away importantly. It's got Internet access so she can bring up maps or pictures of buildings or hard core pornography or something equally important. The reason I mention this is that, had I such a marvellous and expensive invention I could tap into the Internet to see how far Uxbridge was from Heathrow and how to get there. I could even look up the Underground's website and find out whether there are severe delays on the Piccadilly Line.

But even if everything on there was 100% accurate it would almost undoubtedly be 100% useless.

Thinking about it, Stella and the others all had expensive, state-of-the art mobile phones. I don't recall them using them much, definitely not for browsing the Internet. Strange, that.

Let's face it, if I had a mega-expensive, all-singing, all-dancing, state of the art, Internet capable smart phone, or even smartphone, I wouldn't be using it to compute distances between Uxbridge and Heathrow. It would be lying in pieces on the kitchen floor much like my ex-mobile is now.

Danny, your mother is a woman. Women are strange. One day we're talking about food. We must have been having supper, I suppose.

Many people disagree on the difference between supper, dinner and tea.

It's easy: supper is the evening meal you have at the kitchen table, all cosy and just the two of you or just your nearest and dearest. Dinner is where you're in the dining room, presuming you have a dining room, and your food is brought to you by a butler. Oh, and you have Company and speak with a funny exccent and don't know half the guests. Poirot possibly.

I've never understood why you'd want to cook in one room and then move to another to eat the stuff, unless your kitchen was too small for a table to eat at.

Tea, by the way, is a drink with jam and bread.

Anyway, Maddy asks me what my favourite dish is. I say I haven't got one. She says you have to have one. It's the law.

So I give it some thought and decide, fish and chips. And they really are my favourite. But only if they're done properly. And suddenly she's Meg Ryan and it's When Harry Met Sally all over again. How do I like them? Do they have to have salt and vinegar? Well, if they're wrapped in paper, then definitely. However, if it's a fancy restaurant, a really fancy restaurant, no, then you want tartar sauce. What kind of fish? Cod. Hake. Who cares, so long as it's flaky, white and battered. What kind of potato? Potato-shaped ones. Ones you make chips from. For Christ's sake. I can't remember different types of potato, do I look like a greengrocer?

So I say, your turn, what's your favourite dish. And she says, it's not a favourite dish. It's a vegetable. Or a squash. It's pumpkin.

A pumpkin? How a pumpkin?

It's just that every so often she has to have pumpkin. Why? She doesn't know. That's just the way it is. Maybe it's an Australian thing. I have never, ever had pumpkin. I've not even had butternut squash, which is what I understand vegetarians eat. I would be quite happy to try it, I might even like it. Since I've never come across a foodstuff I don't like it's a pretty good bet I'll like butternut squash and pumpkin. Someone just has to shove it in front of me some time.

But it's then that I decide I'm going to surprise her with a pumpkin dish sometime. I just hoped she could hold out until Halloween. Because I was pretty sure I've never seen it sold any other time.

I asked her whether she'd ever had a chip butty. I then have to explain to her what a butty is, and then what a chip butty is. A butty is a sandwich, i.e. bread with butter, a chip butty is a sandwich with a chip filling.

Adding that you can't get them in London. Liverpool, yes, London, no. Not real, serious chip butties.

She asks whether you can get fish and chip butties. Now that stopped me for a few seconds. A fish and chip butty? I decided that the next time I'm in Liverpool I'm going to find out. Someone there must have invented such a perfect dish. Have to be with tartar sauce, mind. Salt and vinegar wouldn't go with bread.

Ealing Common here we are again.

10h44

Fuck.

Count the number of stations from Acton Town to Terminal Five and add one completely fucking unnecessary one.

11h30.

That's when we'll get to Terminal 5.

We can still make it.

So long as Maddy hasn't gone through security.

If she's in the process of going through security when I get there I'll rugby tackle her before she gets through.

It'll be painful, but it'll be worth it.

Cockfosters
Oakwood
Southgate
Arnos Grove
Bounds Green
Wood Green
Turnpike Lane
Manor House
Finsbury Park
Arsenal
Holloway Road
Caledonian Road
King's Cross St. Pancras
Russell Square
Holborn
Covent Garden
Leicester Square
Piccadilly Circus
Green Park
Hyde Park Corner
Knightsbridge
South Kensington
Gloucester Road
Earl's Court
Barons Court
Hammersmith
Turnham Green
Acton Town

Ealing Common
North Ealing
Park Royal
Alperton
Sudbury Town
Sudbury Hill
South Harrow
Rayners Lane
Eastcote
Ruislip Manor
Ruislip
Ickenham
Hillingdon
Uxbridge

South Ealing
Northfields
Boston Manor
Osterley
Hounslow East
Hounslow Central
Hounslow West
Hatton Cross  ←
Heathrow T 1-2-3  ⟶  Heathrow T4
Heathrow T5

186

## Ealing Common (2)

How does that David Bowie song go, Major Tom? "Sitting on a tin can". In outer space nobody can hear your screams. Probably the same on London Underground. Not moving. Nobody else on board, apart from the driver. At least I hope there's a driver. Maybe this tube is actually parked in the marshalling yards, and I'm all alone. Nope, don't think there's a marshalling yard with a platform that big in it.

Bella's.

Bella's had that sort of air about it. A bit like Munch's Scream brought to life, but coming through noisy, thick water, so you couldn't hear a thing.

And then you wake up next to the woman you've fallen in love with and the birds are singing and the sun is shining and the nightmare has retreated.

It's lovely and sunny now. Beautiful spring-summers day.

Has the moon lost her memory?

Well, that was a bit of a jolt. We're moving again. Nearly fell over. That'll teach me to daydream. Right.

10h48.

Full speed ahead, driver, and don't spare the horses. The only drawback is that I'll be joining the Great Unwashed again at Acton Town. Pity, I was enjoying being on my own there for a moment.

Danny, the huge fatal flaw to teaching is that it involves pupils. Ideally your mother and I should find jobs where we don't need to interact with humans, where we can bring you up in peace and quiet and solitude, read poetry aloud, but not loudly, sing songs of love and passion, but softly.

That was a load of bollocks, wasn't it?

Anyway, your mother couldn't live without an audience, even if only of one. And at the moment I don't count as that one.

That first week. I think it was the Friday she asked me where the local Catholic Church is. So I told her, it's a short walk away, ten minutes at most, called Our Lady of Muswell Hill.

'But why do you want to know?' I asked.

187

'I went to Saturday evening Mass last week,' she replied. 'But it's just not the same thing, is it?

That was when I realised that there were going to be times when YBM and I weren't having the same conversation.

'Not the same thing as what?'

'Not the same thing as going to Sunday Mass.'

Now that was unarguably true. And unarguably irrelevant.

'True enough. I find not going to Sunday Mass preferable to not going to Saturday evening Mass. Not going to either is even better.'

'Very funny, Mark. Do they have a nine o'clock service?'

'I think so. Don't tell me you want to go?'

'Of course I'm going. You don't have to come if you don't want to. I know you don't like the Church.'

What?

One. I fucking loathe the Catholic Church. The only time I go anywhere close to a church is for a wedding or funeral, and even then it's under protest.

And preferably it's a funeral for a priest.

Two. I'm in love. I want to be with Maddy every second I can, within reason. How the hell can I let her go to Mass while I sit at home wondering how long she's going to be and how much complete shite they're going to bombard her with? You don't have to come? Give me a break for Christ's sake. It's pretty much a question of whether I love Maddy more than I hate all that's evil about Rome.

So in the end it's no contest. I accompany Maddy to nine o'clock Mass. And blessed be the saints, we get into the foyer or whatever it's called, she dips her finger into the holy water, makes the sign of the cross, takes a lace black headscarf out of her bag and puts it on her head. And now she's the meekest, mildest daughter of Christ ever to grace the church's pews.

I put up a half-hearted defence. I did the responses as we did as schoolboys, 'have mercy on me' became 'have mercy on me knees' and so on. Up until she gave me a good nudge in the ribs with her elbow to indicate her displeasure.

And afterwards as we came out there was the priest, beaming and cheerful and desirous of meeting his flock, especially the new exotic sheep he's obviously clocked during the service. And Maddy is ever so the composed young Catholic woman respectful of her parish priest, but in such a way as to make it quite clear that he knows the rules and she knows the rules and he is going to obey them or else.

Son of a bitch actually had the temerity to ask me how I was bearing up since my dear Aunt's "departure." He'd only met me once, at Aunt Marigold's funeral. And Maddy takes my arm as if she were my nurse and confesses that I was still suffering, but, like too many men, trying to hide it, but she was doing her best to keep an eye on me.

The worst bit of it all is that she was right, in a strange kind of a way.

Next thing I know we've left the church, the headscarf is back in its box, and we're two young lovers again, free of all propriety. But the fucking hell was I going to allow the bloody Roman Catholic Church sneak its way back into my life.

Coming into Acton Town.

Coming back into Acton Town

10h54

What the hell am I going to say to your mother.

And I will always love you?

Too cheesy. And I can't hit the high notes like Maddy can.

You're the one that I want?

Christ, no.

Time to get off.

And get back on to Heathrow.

## Acton Town (2)

10h56

Sitting on a concrete base which is holding up an overhead gantry. Surrounded by hundreds of others who appear to have either been thrown off a previous train or have just accumulated here by aliens who are going to beam them up to provide slave labour and food for their mission to conquer the universe. Hold the rubbery ones.

Next Heathrow service has just left the Arctic Circle and will be with us in around two hundred years. And then there'll be a pause while they change drivers, stop for a fag and tea break, discuss the latest football, and then charge overtime.

I've just realised. This lot must have been here quite a while. Nobody's using their mobile phone to inform the world that they're not on a tube.

Hello. I can see the Yank down the platform. Still wearing that silly hat. And there are the Pakistani boys. That means that, while I was taking a holiday excursion to Ealing Common this lot have been here all the time. Well, fuck me sideways. I don't feel such an idiot for doing that now. At least I wasn't standing on this platform looking like a total plonker.

I think.

One Sunday afternoon Maddy's away, performing, a matinee, and I remember the business about the pumpkin and how her birthday's coming up soon. So I switch my computer on and do a few searches to find out where I can find pumpkin in the middle of summer. A British summer. And would you believe it, but I'm not the only one. There's this weird discussion on this website for mothers on where to find it, going back a few years ago. And they name a few shops, Waitrose, Selfridges, Harrods, Tesco, John Lewis. So I go on to their websites and search for pumpkin. Nothing. Maybe they sold it years ago, not any more, maybe it's just some stores in certain areas, so it's not on their main listing, who knows. So I go back to the website for mothers and continue reading. One woman bought some to cure her ferret's diarrhoea, apparently it's good for that.

Well, that would chime well during a romantic dinner you've prepared for the love of your life, wouldn't it.

'Darling, are you enjoying your pumpkin?'

'Yes, darling, it's lovely.'

'I hear it's good for curing the shits in ferrets.'

I see you can order it online for delivery from some places, tinned stuff. Well, I don't want tinned, it would be like making a fruit salad out of tinned fruit, you might as well paint 'complete arsehole' on your forehead. Either that or you want your beloved to understand that you are a completely useless bachelor and she will have to do all the cooking and cleaning if you ever get married. Well, I don't want to make that impression, so I decide to go to this little greengrocer's shop I know not too far away. It's run by an Indian couple, the kind of shop that stocks all sorts of stuff, but mainly fresh vegetables. If you ever catch a television programme called Open All Hours, that was the sort of shop except with an Indian flavour and a lot more fruit and veg.

Anyway, I know the couple well enough to say hello when I go in, she, the wife, Mrs Chandra, is behind the till, he's packing stuff at the back as he always is, or he's at the back as he always is, doing something important enough to keep him away from his wife out front. I ask her how she is, she says good, how am I, how's Stella? I say I haven't seen Stella for a while, but I've met this lovely Australian girl, and she loves pumpkin and I'd like to get some for her birthday, and does Mrs Chandra know where I can get some. Fresh, not canned.

And of course that starts a to-do. And one of the things about the Chandras you have to understand is that they don't do punctuation and they do do talking over each other.

She goes 'Oh oh dear dear dear', because apparently it's hard to get fresh pumpkin at this time of year, and it's a tragedy, because her whole happiness depends on finding me some pumpkin for my pretty Australian girlfriend and she shouts to her husband, 'Where can young Bruce (she calls me Bruce for some reason, I've never understood why) get fresh pumpkin for his new girlfriend shes Australian not Stella hes not going out with her anymore I think they broke up' and he shouts back something like dont be such a silly bloody woman you know you cant get fresh pumpkin this time of the year and she shouts back I know that but Bruce wants it for his pretty new girlfriend shes Australian its her birthday hes not going out with Stella anymore. And he swears, or at least it sounds like swearing, and comes through to the front of the shop in that slow determined way that states that he would prefer to go on unpacking or playing poker or doing whatever critically important task he was carrying out in the back, but because he values you so much and has so much respect for you he will grudgingly drag his sorry arse out front to tell you, with a little punctuation because it's you and not his bloody wife:

'You can't get fresh pumpkin this time of year, not decent pumpkin, one time her cousin brought some back but it wasn't any good anyway customs probably confiscate it.'

'Okay,' says I, 'in that case is the tinned stuff any good?'

'Ah –' starts Mr Chandra, but he's beaten by Mrs Chandra.

'You know my cousin has a shop in Southall not the cousin who brought the pumpkin back on the plane another one and you know Southall there's a huge Asian community you name it and they know good pumpkin so my cousin the one with the shop in Southall she always keeps tins of really really good pumpkin so what I'll do I'll phone her tomorrow today she's at a wedding of one of her cousins so I can't call her mobile maybe I interrupt the wedding so tomorrow I call her how many tins do you need?'

And then they're standing there looking at me, almost beaming, and I'm trying to absorb this stream of consciousness which appears to have ended in a question mark.

'Well, I don't know. I was thinking of making pumpkin soup,' I said. 'How many tins would I need for that? Just for the two of us?'

'Ah, sweet' – Mrs Chandra – 'a romantic evening just for the two of you I could cry it's so sweet but now you don't want pumpkin soup if it's a surprise cause that's the first course unless you have soup for dessert which I've never heard of you want something for dessert so the last bit is a surprise though you want coffee and cheese afterwards that's what the restaurants do so what kind of desserts does she like?'

So once again I've been hooked by a marshmallow mattress of effusion with a question mark embedded in it and I'm starting to think like she speaks because the only sweet thing I know Maddy likes is ice-cream and I'm wondering how well I really know her if all I know about what she likes for dessert is ice-cream though I don't even know that because she likes ice-cream any time of the day.

'Okay,' I said, dragging myself out of the whorl, 'I'm not sure what dessert she likes. What can you make with pumpkin?'

'Pumpkin fritters best fritters you'll ever find she does them special occasion' – Mr Chandra. 'She' being Mrs Chandra.

'Or you could make cheesecake that might be easier if you're not sure fritters can be dry if you get them wrong you know what I mean?' – Mrs Chandra.

I take a deep breath.

'Okay, I think what I'll do is hunt around for recipes and then do a few experiments to see what I'm comfortable with. So – how about half a dozen tins, would that be enough?'

'For you and your girlfriend six tins should be plenty for this one six tins wouldn't be a starter,' said Mrs Chandra, laughing. I presumed from the look on Mr Chandra's face that he knew that "this one" referred to him and that he was quite in agreement that six tins would indeed be austerity rations as a starter.

The one thing I was grateful for was that Mrs Chandra's sisters and cousins weren't there to add to the debate.

Hello, is this a train I see before me?

It says Heathrow on the front

Why do I not trust that?

In for a penny in for a pound.

Cockfosters
Oakwood
Southgate
Arnos Grove
Bounds Green
Wood Green
Turnpike Lane
Manor House
Finsbury Park
Arsenal
Holloway Road
Caledonian Road
King's Cross St. Pancras
Russell Square
Holborn
Covent Garden
Leicester Square
Piccadilly Circus
Green Park
Hyde Park Corner
Knightsbridge
South Kensington
Gloucester Road
Earl's Court
Barons Court
Hammersmith
Turnham Green
Acton Town

Ealing Common     South Ealing
North Ealing      Northfields
Park Royal        Boston Manor
Alperton          Osterley
Sudbury Town      Hounslow East
Sudbury Hill      Hounslow Central
South Harrow      Hounslow West
Rayners Lane      Hatton Cross
Eastcote          Heathrow T 1-2-3  →  Heathrow T4
Ruislip Manor     Heathrow T5
Ruislip
Ickenham
Hillingdon
Uxbridge

# Leaving Acton Town

*Estimated time to Heathrow Terminal Five: 32 minutes*

*Estimated time to South Ealing tube station: 4 minutes*

11h12.

This train is actually moving. Managed to get a seat. Everybody else was standing there asking if this really was a Heathrow train. I suspect they've all eagerly jumped on board previous trains only to have to get off again because they were either terminating at Acton or going somewhere else, so now they've become wary. So am I, but not to the point where I'm going to wait until they say that a certain train is definitely not going to Heathrow and then catch that because it will almost definitely go to Heathrow.

Love and logic are mutually exclusive.

Silly thing is that the driver was all raring to go, but there were so many people waiting to get on, others standing in the doorway blocking the doors while having loud arguments about whether it was the train they wanted, some people having got on deciding to get off, blocking the ones who had decided they wanted to get on after all, mothers suddenly screaming as they realised they hadn't dragged little Johnny on board, young tourists screaming because they'd left the girlfriend and/or boyfriend and/or suitcase behind. All the while the doors are making I'm-about-to-close bleeping noises, the driver was bleeping in his own way, the doors tried to close but couldn't, and so on.

But now we're on our way.

And there's another song about that.

And there are now only ten stops to Heathrow Terminal 5.

We're going to make it.

Jesus fucking wept.

Did I mention women are strange, Danny?

That Saturday she came back from rehearsal looking a little less enthusiastic than normal. I gave her a hug and asked her what was wrong. She said it was just an acting thing, rehearsal hadn't been perfect,

195

she'd fluffed some lines. We went into the kitchen to open a bottle of wine and immediately she sniffed suspiciously.

'I thought you didn't smoke,' she said.

'I don't. That was someone who dropped in. She smoked outside.'

I got the bottle of wine, opened it and began pouring our drinks.

'She?'

'Stella. She went off to America to make her fortune. New York. Company folded, apparently.'

'So she's back here.'

'That would appear to be the case.'

'Where did you know her from?'

'We used to play tennis at the same club. Went out a couple of times. Never turned into anything serious.'

There was a speculative look, a slight silence, and then, ever so nonchalantly:

'So, how many girlfriends have you had, Mark?'

You know, some people shouldn't ask certain questions.

'Girlfriends as girlfriends, not many.'

And some people shouldn't answer those questions. Especially if they have a reputation for being pedantic bastards.

'As girlfriends?'

'You know. Where everyone thinks you're an item. On the path to matrimony, that sort of thing.'

'You mean, if you stop seeing each other, your friends call it breaking up rather than drifting apart?'

'I think that puts it rather well.'

'So how many girlfriends have you broken up with?'

'Not one. They all broke with me.'

Pause.

She took a sip of wine while looking at me as if I were an exhibit in a zoo. A naughty exhibit in a naughty zoo.

'I'll bet you made them break up with you.'

I sighed.

'I get this feeling that I'm going to be found guilty whatever I say.'

She took another sip of wine and decided the verdict was 'Not proven – yet'.

'You mind if I ask you a question?'

Now she was asking my permission?

'Anything you want, my gorgeous, my one and only.'

'Are we an item?'

I looked at her. What could I say? That when I first saw her my mind went Gloop? and that was that, game over?

'You know that type of superglue that comes as two different agents?' I asked. 'On their own they don't do anything, but mix them together and they bond solid forever. That's us, my beautiful one and only Maddening, heart of my heart, soul of my soul, life of my life. They'll be writing songs about us in times to come.'

She smiled at the thought.

'Why don't you write a song about us?'

I paused, because I was about to admit something I didn't want to admit to myself.

'Because I'm just not good enough,' I said. 'I thought I was once, but I'm not.'

She put her glass down, came and put her arms around me.

'Will you try, just for me?' she said in that little-girl way of hers.

I had to smile.

'For you, my darling one and only, I'll give it a bash.'

'And I will sing it. I can sing, you know.'

There was only one person in the entire world who had doubts about whether Maddy could sing, and that was Maddy.

'I know you can, precious.'

I stood up.

'Now, what would you like for dinner?'

'What were you thinking of?'

'We've got mince and chicken and fish. We can have curry and rice if you like.'

'I love curry and rice.'

She jumped up and put her arms around me again.

'Can I put the curry in, daddy?'

'Course you can, my sweet.'

I kissed her. She looked back up to me.

'This Stella creature, Mark?'

'Yes?'

'Next time she turns up, tell her to have her cigarette on the other side of the fish pond.'

'There isn't a fish pond, sweetness.'

'Build one. Build a fucking big one. And while you're at it, make it fucking deep too.'

I think I could guess what kind of fish she was planning to populate it with. The little ones with the big teeth.

Or possibly the big ones with the big teeth.

Sunday we did some more touristy things. I made sure I wasn't caught looking at any other woman, irrespective of how old or ugly they were.

11h14

Approaching the next station. If it's Ealing Common I am going to go ballistic. Or something. Please, please let it be South Ealing, you know, on the way to Heathrow only nine stops away.

I don't know what some of these people are saying, but judging by the way they're craning to look out the windows, even kneeling on the seats to do so, they're pretty much making the same prayer as I am.

11h15 We're pulling in now. It's ...

South Ealing.

Thank fuck.

Nine stops to go.

And fifteen minutes left.

Cockfosters
Oakwood
Southgate
Arnos Grove
Bounds Green
Wood Green
Turnpike Lane
Manor House
Finsbury Park
Arsenal
Holloway Road
Caledonian Road
King's Cross St. Pancras
Russell Square
Holborn
Covent Garden
Leicester Square
Piccadilly Circus
Green Park
Hyde Park Corner
Knightsbridge
South Kensington
Gloucester Road
Earl's Court
Barons Court
Hammersmith
Turnham Green
Acton Town

Ealing Common                     South Ealing
North Ealing                      Northfields
Park Royal                        Boston Manor
Alperton                          Osterley
Sudbury Town                      Hounslow East
Sudbury Hill                      Hounslow Central
South Harrow                      Hounslow West
Rayners Lane                      Hatton Cross  ←
Eastcote                          Heathrow T 1-2-3  ——→  Heathrow T4
Ruislip Manor                     Heathrow T5
Ruislip
Ickenham
Hillingdon
Uxbridge

## South Ealing

*Estimated time to Heathrow Terminal Five: 28 minutes*

*Estimated time to Northfields tube station: 2 minutes*

11h16

This train's destination is definitely Heathrow. I've checked the electronic display in the carriage. I've listened carefully to the driver's announcements. I've checked the map and it can definitely not go anywhere else. Its destination is definitely Heathrow Terminals 1,2,3 and 5. I won't say it's going there, because it's not going anywhere at the moment. The only good thing is that it's not completely packed. Heavily over-crowded, yes, but not sardine time with people becoming intimately acquainted with complete strangers. I've been on tubes where people had to de-synchronise their breathing to prevent being crushed. One sneeze and ...

Hooray, we're moving.

11h18. If nothing really serious happens we should be there by 12h00 at the latest. Still enough time. Just.

The distance between South Ealing and Northfields is about fifty yards. Or that's what it's always felt like whenever I catch the Piccadilly to Heathrow. You leave South Ealing, mentally switch off, think about something else, next thing the tube's slowing down, you think we aren't at another red light again, are we, next thing you know you're pulling into Northfields. And here we are. And here are a lot of other people. On the platform.

Northfields.

Where they terminate a lot of trains because it's attached to a marshalling yard or train graveyard or wherever they store these things. I guess they just terminated two or three, because, boy is that platform packed. And those people look eager to get on, they're standing way too close to the track for my liking. One of them just needs to topple and ...

Oh, Jesus, no.

The driver's just announced that we're being terminated here because of a defect on the train.

Apparently one of the wipers isn't working.

One of the wipers isn't working?

So? It's not fucking raining, is it?

I do not fucking believe it.

I

do

not

fucking

believe

it.

11h20.

Eight more bloody stops and they're terminating the bloody train.

Because of a defective wiper.

Jesus.

Fucking.

Wept.

# Northfields

11h23

I wonder how many other people on this platform are desperate to get to the airport to meet their loved ones. I doubt if any of them are expecting their loved ones to throw something at them.

I wonder why this place is called Northfields. Maybe centuries ago there were houses to the south, and they had fields to the north. Then they built more houses on the fields to the north. But carried on calling it north fields.

Isn't it nice to have so much time to sit and idly ponder such things?

Yes, Danny, it's simply fucking absolutely fucking marvellous.

Many years ago I was wandering around Europe on a student's railcard, basically a cheap way to see the continent. These days kids that age have gap years in Thailand. Or they used to, we now live in an age of austerity, or so we're told.

Anyway, we spent ages on platforms. Chilling out. Watching the world go by. No hurry. All the time in the world. Now I'm sitting on the concrete edge of a raised garden trough on a train platform doing nothing but trying not to scream. According to a sign the garden is a herb garden maintained by the people working in the marshalling yard nearby for the use of passengers. Maybe they should have trained up wiper-fixing people rather than gardeners. Or planted hash. I could do with a decent spliff right now.

Now that would be an entrance, waft into T5 high on dope and say to YBM, 'Hey, babyo, what's flying?'

Did they ever really say 'Babyo' in the Sixties?

What's the name of that bloke, The Fonz, I think it was. What was his catchphrase?

It'll come to me.

11h25.

Still, I'm not alone.

Not alone in terms of being wound up. In terms of numbers there's plenty of us.

There's a family of one mother and four young children. Plus about fourteen oversized suitcases on wheels. The one daughter, the oldest, about ten, is trying to see how close to the platform edge she can push a suitcase without it going over. Her younger brother has asked when they're going to get to the airport so often I've lost count. Can't see him living much longer. His younger brother has been insisting for five minutes that he needs the loo. Won't be long before his mother tells him to tie a knot in it, or she'll do it for him. Probably regrets not saying the same to her husband a few years ago. Youngest one in a pram has screaming fits every two or three minutes. Husband is doing a remarkably good job of reading a newspaper and not noticing a thing. All he needs is a hat and pipe to complete the image.

Two. That's the maximum sprogs Maddy and I are going to have. Any more and she can bloody look after them herself. Three at the most.

The Yanks got offloaded here at some stage. They are definitely no longer together. He's trying to remain invisible behind a newspaper, she's at the other end of the platform looking fit to explode.

I noticed the two Pakistani boys somewhere a few minutes ago, they're looking a bit frazzled. Maybe they come from a wealthy family and aren't used to having to drag heavy suitcases around on a journey that should have finished three hours ago. Those shalmar kameez are going to need a trip to the washing machine after a day on the Underground.

Just about everybody with a mobile phone is phoning everyone they know to tell them there are delays on the Piccadilly Line. Which is about everyone apart from me. It's usually 'Darling, I'm on a train.' Now instead it's 'I'm not on a fucking train, I'm gonna miss my plane.'

That's about the extent of my rhyming skills these days.

There's a saying that you don't have a problem, you have an opportunity. It's said by morons like the bog when you point out a problem and they don't want to know about it. It becomes 'your opportunity'. She tried it with Sean once. He replied, 'I've told you about it so it's now your fucking opportunity' and walked away. She didn't like that.

But I've just had this brilliant idea. Danny, I haven't quite worked out what I'm going to say to YBM, but here's the plan: I make sure she doesn't see me until the last moment; I grab her arm, make whatever brilliant declaration I've come up with – I'm beginning to think it'll have to be the opening line to 'A Song For Maddening', but still don't know what that's going to be. Anyway, once I've got her rapt attention I keep a firm grip on her and guide her to a coffee place, or somewhere we can sit down. Then I segue neatly into a long description of all the shit I've been through getting there.

Neat, huh? I hit on it while I was thinking of that first night we met, and how she listened to all my woes and troubles.

Actually, I've had an even more fuckingly brilliant idea. I grab hold of her, get her attention, guide her to a seat somewhere, drop these notes I'm making into her little hands and say, 'Here, read this while I get us some coffees.' She gives me one of her special looks indicating she thinks I'm a retarded toddler, puts her little reading glasses on the end of her pretty little nose, the ones she's too vain to use most of the time, and starts reading. But the time she's finished hopefully she'll have ein bisschen Verständnis.

Just have to remember to tear this bit out.

No, fuck it, I'll keep it in. If she loves me she has to accept me warts and all.

Though there is the distinct possibility that she will see the scars on my face, remember why she put them there, and try to add some more.

It will all depend on the delivery.

11h32

So, back in the Chandra's shop, Mrs Chandra's promised to get me the tins of pumpkin by the Friday, I thought I'd buy something to show my gratitude, I spied a small watermelon which would be ideal for two, decided to buy it for after dinner that evening. Mrs Chandra puts it in a blue plastic bag, warns me that it's very ripe I must eat it in the next two days or I'll die of something or it won't taste nice or something I promise yes I will and make my escape.

So there I am, late Sunday afternoon, strolling along past the shops, when I see Ziggie walking along rather strangely. It's his 'I'm the main man' type of walk, he thinks it makes him look mean, instead it just makes him look like he's got a large carrot shoved somewhere painful. And he turns down a side road, and purely out of curiosity I follow him. He disappears into a car park behind one of the supermarkets, so I go in after him. And there's nothing there. No cars, no Ziggie. There's a raised platform at the back of the supermarket, presumably so that the delivery trucks can just reverse up and offload, and industrial wheelie bins scattered around, but that's it. The supermarket's closed for the day so there aren't any staff or customers around. But still, also no Ziggie.

Most peculiar, I thought. I climbed the steps onto the platform and strolled along it. And all of a sudden Ziggie's in front of me, with his black shirt, black trousers, black shoes and gold medallions. And his eyes are strangely bright, and his skin's greasier than normal, though maybe that's just the reaction to being out in daylight.

And he's got a knife in his right hand.

Not a big one.

Not a Bowie knife.

Just one slim enough and sharp enough to kill someone rather efficiently.

A train's just pulled in from the marshalling yard, completely empty, bound for central London. Still no sign of anything going towards Heathrow.

Fuck it, it is a Heathrow train.

All aboard.

Me first.

Cockfosters
Oakwood
Southgate
Arnos Grove
Bounds Green
Wood Green
Turnpike Lane
Manor House
Finsbury Park
Arsenal
Holloway Road
Caledonian Road
King's Cross St. Pancras
Russell Square
Holborn
Covent Garden
Leicester Square
Piccadilly Circus
Green Park
Hyde Park Corner
Knightsbridge
South Kensington
Gloucester Road
Earl's Court
Barons Court
Hammersmith
Turnham Green
Acton Town

Ealing Common
North Ealing
Park Royal
Alperton
Sudbury Town
Sudbury Hill
South Harrow
Rayners Lane
Eastcote
Ruislip Manor
Ruislip
Ickenham
Hillingdon
Uxbridge

South Ealing
Northfields
Boston Manor
Osterley
Hounslow East
Hounslow Central
Hounslow West
Hatton Cross ←
Heathrow T 1-2-3 ⟶ Heathrow T4
Heathrow T5

206

## Leaving Northfields

*Estimated time to Heathrow Terminal Five: 26 minutes*

*Estimated time to Boston Manor tube station: 2 minutes*

11h36.

Well, that was close. I had to grab everything and jump aboard before the bloody thing left. I tell you, when you're in a hurry they hang around for ages, but when you're not ready they're suddenly raring to go. I've even managed to find a seat. I think all the other sheep were gathered in the centre of the platform, they must be crowded in like sardines. As it is I've got a huge suitcase in front of me belonging to a Japanese girl who kept saying sorry as she dragged it in, banging it against my knees and running it over my toes. Her boyfriend with an equally large suitcase was doing the same to the woman with the three kids. She'd managed to get the pram into the central reservation and the kids seated on the seats immediately adjacent.

Those bloody suitcases are made out of reinforced corrugated iron, I swear.

I think these carriages were designed in the era when, if you took luggage to the airport on public transport, you had to carry it. That limited the number of kitchen sinks you could include. Then some daft idiot put wheels on suitcases, and the only limit then was how much pulling power you had.

They could at least measure the average space between people's kneecaps on the tube and design them around that.

Though it must be pointed out that tubes are different shapes and heights and sizes on different tube lines. They were mostly built by different companies with existing shit in the way. Nobody stopped to think, well, maybe we should standardise these things.

Anyway, on the move at last.

11h36. Still.

Still time.

If she's gone through I'll get someone to page her, or whatever they do these days. Shout very loudly in the middle of everyone.

So there we are, just Ziggie and me and the knife in his hand. And he says something like, 'You should be careful who you follow, teacher-man, maybe I should teach you.'

And I look at him. And then I come up with probably the best line I ever have.

'Typical dago,' I say, 'bringing a knife to a watermelon fight.'

'Eh?' he says, which is when I know he isn't in the same world. I slowly take the watermelon out of the blue plastic bag, and his eyes follow every single move, as if he's never seen a watermelon in his life. He looked so high he was probably seeing a huge curled-up caterpillar looking at him.

'Here, catch,' I say, and lob it gently to him. And he does just what I expect. He tries to catch it. His left hand is okay, that catches it perfectly, but he's still got the knife in his right hand. That goes straight into the over-ripe watermelon.

And then I haul off and lamp him, hard as I can. Feint with the right, left fist straight into the side of his head.

After that everything seemed to go in slow motion.

His eyes rolled slowly back into his head. He swung sideways, hips pushing out, almost as if he were pirouetting. Then, slowly, slowly, he fell over sideways and off the platform. Right into one of the huge wheelie bins.

I wish I could say that it was full of other rubbish, but I think it must have been designated for recycling, it was full of cardboard and paper which broke his fall, unfortunately.

I stood there for a few seconds, looking down at his comatose body.

The bastard still had the watermelon.

Well, I wasn't going to jump in to retrieve it, he might wake up while I was still trying to get out again, so I left as quickly and quietly as possible. I thought he might collect his gorillas and come looking for revenge as soon as he woke up, but considered it unlikely. Fortunately he didn't know where any of us lived. That sort of information you didn't share at Bella's. Besides which, he was an indoors night-time creature, he'd wait for me to turn up at Bella's again, which was not something I intended to do.

And of course, true to form, I'd done something to my wrist when I punched him. It was hurting like crazy. I went home and put a bandage on it. Then I took the bandage off and rubbed some anti-inflammatory cream in before replacing the bandage. Took a couple of pain killers. A couple of hours later I surrendered to the inevitable and went to A and E.

Where I sat for four hours before being seen. Well, to be accurate, a triage nurse reviewed my condition, concluded that others were dying faster, and I'd have to wait. And, to be fair, it turns out that waiting four hours late on a Sunday is actually pretty good going. Humans seem incredibly capable at having all sorts of weird accidents on Sundays, from mishaps with the Sunday roast to amateur sports to people who take out the car for its once-a-week spin and end up doing exactly that. Not to mention alcohol-related accidents. From what I could see they were trying to process those at double speed, quite possibly just to get rid of the abusive ones.

But finally I see a doctor and she's got the x-ray they took when I wasn't quite paying attention – they are very efficient at processing human bodies. 'Ooh, look, Mr Smith, a squirrel. Right, while you were looking away we've taken seventeen x-rays, twenty-two blood samples, your blood pressure three times, half a dozen DNA samples, given you an eye test and unfortunately an unplanned operation crept in but you won't notice a thing, er, Mrs Smith.'

She asks me what happened, and I tell her I was doing some DIY, putting up some shelves, and I discovered that, for the third time, I'd sawn one too short despite measuring it perfectly twice, and I'd just got so utterly frustrated I ended up punching the wall. And she clucks and says her husband did exactly the same once, but hasn't repeated that trick again. She advises me to calm down if I'm doing that sort of thing again, or indeed anything frustrating, and just walk away. So I say, yes, certainly, by the way, did I tell you I'm a school teacher in an inner-city comprehensive? And she looks at me and says, mmm, perhaps it wasn't the DIY you were angry about to start off with.

So then she points at the x-ray and tells me I don't appear to have broken anything, there's a little hint of a cracked bone, not serious enough for a full-on cast, a strong wrist brace should suffice for the moment. I'm to avoid using the hand as far as possible, she'll give me a prescription for pain-killers a little more potent than the over-the-counter ones, no alcohol for a few days, and if it's not significantly better in a week's time to see my doctor.

Oh, and no DIY for at least a fortnight.

Yes, sir, ma'am, certainly, sir, ma'am, if I see Ziggie in the street again I won't punch him I'll deck him with a scaffolding pole.

For Maddy I invented an accident on my bicycle. Hit a pothole and came a cropper. Pulled a muscle in my wrist. The sort of breezy language designed to assure the non-cyclist that it was just the sort of minor injury that went with the territory, nothing to worry about. Anyone who knew the first thing about cycling would have looked at me very suspiciously and asked, 'So, tell me, how exactly did you get that and only that from falling off a moving bicycle? And where are the scraped bits?' Maddy fortunately believed me and fussed over me.

Not telling the doctor the truth was to avoid complicating things. Not telling Maddy was because I didn't want to alarm her. And I sure as hell didn't want even the slightest thought of that little shithole to pollute our lives.

The little kids are becoming excited because we're getting into Boston Manor, which, as their mother is pointing out, is only seven stops to Terminal 5. Just think of that, only seven stops!

11h40.

I keep thinking that, soon as my wrist has healed, I'm going to take up boxing to learn how to punch Ziggie's lights out without breaking my wrist. Then I remember that Ziggie's lights have gone out permanently and we won't be seeing them lit again in anyone's lifetimes, thank fuck.

Cockfosters
Oakwood
Southgate
Arnos Grove
● Bounds Green
● Wood Green
● Turnpike Lane
● Manor House
● Finsbury Park
● Arsenal
● Holloway Road
● Caledonian Road
● King's Cross St. Pancras
● Russell Square
● Holborn
● Covent Garden
● Leicester Square
● Piccadilly Circus
● Green Park
● Hyde Park Corner
● Knightsbridge
● South Kensington
● Gloucester Road
● Earl's Court
● Barons Court
● Hammersmith
● Turnham Green
● Acton Town
● Ealing Common          ● South Ealing
● North Ealing           ● Northfields
Park Royal               ○ Boston Manor
Alperton                 Osterley
Sudbury Town             Hounslow East
Sudbury Hill             Hounslow Central
South Harrow             Hounslow West
Rayners Lane             Hatton Cross ←————————————┐
Eastcote                 Heathrow T 1-2-3 ——→ Heathrow T4
Ruislip Manor            Heathrow T5
Ruislip
Ickenham
Hillingdon
Uxbridge

# Boston Manor

*Estimated time to Heathrow Terminal Five: 24 minutes*

*Estimated time to Osterley tube station: 4 minutes*

11h41.

I often get Boston Manor and Manor House mixed up.

No, wait, I'm confusing Manor House with Barons Court.

Or maybe Barons Manor with Boston Court.

Boston, where the tea party comes from.

Brazil, where the nuts come from.

Confusion is a sign that the mind's tired.

Concentrate.

Anyway, Boston Manor has dark wooden benches which remind me of the "great" days of British Rail. It's even got old-fashioned clocks. It's the sort of place that reminds me of black and white movies from the glory days – Brief Encounter, that sort of thing. Or Agatha Christie's 4.50 from Paddington. The days when trains ran on time because the railways were efficient and never broke down.

The irony being that I've plenty of time to appreciate the Art Deco look of Boston Manor because, yet again, we're going nowhere fast.

Not quite Art Deco. Or, rather, it was once. The adverts are too modern.

Houses behind the white paling fence look suitably suburban. I can imagine fifty years ago, hubby kissing his wife goodbye before walking to the tube to catch the 8h30 into town to be at his desk by nine.

I wonder if the tube came out this far fifty years ago.

I wonder if they broke down as often fifty years ago.

Doors are bleeping, doors are closing, we're moving, give the driver a cigar.

11h42.

Whoopee.

Seven stops.


Whenever I've passed through Boston Manor on my way to Heathrow I've always felt it quite a pleasant place. Okay, the feeling of it belonging to the golden age of Hollywood – and though Brief Encounter was definitely very, very British, not Hollywood, they all come from the Golden Era – is an illusion, a comfortable myth we've built of a better time, possibly in the hope that somehow we can once again capture those golden days, those golden hours, those golden moments, when bliss was it in that dawn to be alive, but to be young was very heaven.

But, now we're on our way, it also feels like open country, once out here. You've got allotments, all green and well kept, along with the sheds made of bits and bobs and pieces of broken glass and anything that might serve the purpose – god forbid anyone should erect a properly constructed shed bought – bought! – from Homebase or Wickes or B&Q, or, sin of sins, from a proper garden nursery. Heathens.

And now we're going over the M4 motorway, long lines of cars stretching into the distance not going anywhere in either direction.

Just as well I didn't drive or catch a taxi then. Nothing like the superior feeling you get sitting in a train whizzing past a traffic jam. It reminds me of the early days I had a car and decided driving back to the folks in Liverpool for Easter would be a good idea. Unfortunately every other idiot with a car was on their way somewhere that weekend, and the tailbacks went on for miles. Every so often you'd see a train racing along and wonder why you bothered with the car. I remember, the bloody thing overheated. It was second-hand, cheap, and not cheerful.

And now we're going over a river, the good old Thames, and into more green and pleasant land. A golf course on that side. All trees and fairways and lawns and bunkers and bastards strolling along enjoying their game. They should be at work, slaving away.

And we've stopped.

11h44.

And silence.

Weird silence.

Doesn't anyone have a mobile phone to answer?

Someone they have to call urgently to tell them there's no news?

Someone to shout at?

A baby needing a cry?

Hello?

Even the brats appear to have gone to sleep.

I think the troops are exhausted, Sergeant, tell them five minutes rest.

Hello, driver's just announced we're being regulated to even out the gaps in the service.

Look, chum, the so-called service is completely fucked, you might as well get us up to the front line if no-one else. We'll charge on our own, even if we get wiped out to a man. Or woman. Or child. Or the fat bloke over there.

The sun is shining.

It's a glorious summer's day.

Makes you want to sleep awhile, perchance to dream.

Aye, there's the rub.

Danny, wake up, let me tell you about the time I introduced YBM to my parents. It was actually a couple of weeks before I knocked the shit out of Ziggie. It was extremely stressful for both my parents and YBM, but I thoroughly enjoyed it.

What can I say, I'm a complete bastard.

It began when I phoned home to announce the visit. Mum answered. I asked her how she was.

'Oh, you know, bearing up I suppose. Your father … Your father's still … well, you know. It's still quite difficult.'

Translation: 'I only go into Jenny's room once a day and weep my eyes out now. Your father is holding it all in and pretending it doesn't hurt every second of every minute of every hour of every day. We go to the grave and keep it neat and tidy, you know.'

Strangely enough, I did know. And hopefully that was about to change.

If only by a very little bit.

'Mum,' I said, 'I'd like to bring someone up to meet you. She's going to be my wife. Only I haven't told her that yet, so you mustn't let on.'

Silence.

Complete and utter silence.

Stunned silence.

Several times.

There were echoes of echoes of absolutely nothing.

It felt like my ear was being slowly sucked into a vacuum.

'Mum? Are you there?'

'Er? Mark? Is that you?'

What?

'Of course it's me, mum. Who did you think it was, Kermit the Frog? Did you hear what I said?'

Some more silence.

'Er, it's not a very good line, Mark. What did you say?'

I sighed audibly, just as a twelve year-old might do to a well-meaning but completely clueless parent.

'Mum, I said I've met the girl I am going to marry and would like to bring her up to meet you and dad.'

Silence again.

What's with all this silence? Was it something I said?

'I thought that was what you said.'

Okay, it was something I said then.

Then why ask me again?

Honestly, Danny, mothers, who'd 'ave 'em?

To be honest I was winding her up a bit. Actually quite a lot. The thing is, mum and dad had never met Stella, but they'd met my previous paramours. All of the girls and women I'd been involved with were Stella in one form or another, and mum and dad were well aware of it. The first girl I brought home was five years older than me and covered in make-up and tattoos. I think they had given up and decided the best thing they could hope for was that I'd end up marrying a floozy rather than just living in sin with her. Hopefully she wouldn't smoke too much or drink too much gin, at least not in front of the children, not in the daytime, anyway.

Boy, were they in for a surprise when I brought Maddy up to meet them.

A very pleasant surprise, I was hoping. More than hoping, I was convinced of it.

Okay, just a niggle of a little doubt.

A very, very, very small niggle.

Small niggles are right little bastards.

'When, er, when were you thinking of, er, what did you say her name was again?'

I was tempted to reply 'Frankenstein's daughter', but decided there were limits.

'I didn't,' I said instead. 'Her name's Madeleine. We met a few weeks ago.'

Again the temptation to add something like, 'She's a virgin.' I don't know why. Only it would come out as 'She's a wirigin.' Mum would probably think it was some kind of sect.

'Madeleine,' echoed mum as if it was a name she hadn't heard of before. 'That's – unusual, isn't it?'

Madeleine is an unusual name? Since when?

I suspect she meant unusual in the sense that for once I didn't have a girlfriend named Jezebel or Harlot or Strumpet or Miss Big Plastic Tits Of The Year. Either that or her mental processes were shutting out everything I said in the defensive kind of logic that, if you haven't heard something, it hasn't happened.

'It's French,' I replied. Mum loves all things French, so long as they come out of a magazine or film. French perfume is exquisite. A French hussy, on the other hand – well, I'm pretty sure she would have preferred an English hussy. 'But Madeleine's actually Australian,' I added, to soften the blow.

There was another silence during which I think mum debated on whether this hussy was a lumberjack, or was that Canadian?

'So, er, when, when, Madeleine, when were you thinking, er, that is, er, coming up, er, to –'

'How about this weekend, mum? I haven't told her yet, I thought I'd ask you first. She's an actor, singer, that sort of thing, she's quite busy at odd times, but I know she's got this weekend free, so I thought I'd ask you to see if it's okay first.'

An even stunned silence. For mum female actors are hussies with a capital Huss. Male actors, on the other hand, are glamorous gentlemen. I gave up trying to work that out long ago.

'Er, yes, yes, this weekend. This weekend, yes, I see. This – did you say you've proposed to her?'

It took every inch of my inner strength not to sigh again, this time very fucking loudly. I mean, for fucking Christ's sake. And me in love and all, and for the first time.

'No, mum, no, I haven't proposed to her, and don't even mention anything about marriage or anything. It's just that I am going to marry her, she just doesn't know it yet.'

Another silence.

'I'm not sure I understand, Mark.'

This time a sigh did escape.

'Mum, I remember you telling me many years ago when I was little about when you and dad first met. You said you knew straight away he was the one for you. And he felt the same. You both knew from the minute you met that it was meant to be? Ring a bell?'

Mum considered that for a few moments in another black hole of silence.

'Well, yes, but, well, Mark, I've never thought of you as being ... well, I don't know, romantic, I suppose.'

'I'm not romantic, mum, I'm in love. You can cure romance. That's a scientific fact.'

Silence again.

'Well, that's okay I suppose, Mark. What, er, time, were you planning on arriving, only I must get the house ready and –'

Translation: I'll have to scrub the floors and walls and ceilings and boil every stitch of cloth-ware and make sure there's enough food to feed the fifty-five thousand and –

'She's not, ah, not, ah, not ah –' mum began again.

'Not ah? No, mum, I don't think she's ah. She can be a brazen little hussy at times, but I've never known her being ah. In what sense of ah were you thinking, mum?'

For a moment in the particular silence that followed I thought I might have pushed things just a little bit too far. It could take mum a fair few goes but eventually she would click on to the fact that she was being wound up.

'She's not, well, a vegetarian or anything, is she, Mark? Vegan. The ones who wear black clothing.'

A Goth?

Jesus wept.

Though of course black is Maddy's favourite colour. But if I mentioned that the confusion would go off scale.

'Oh, god, no, mum, she'll eat anything. Appetite of a horse. In fact you could feed her a horse and she'd be quite happy. Just take the saddle and hooves off first. Probably warm it up a bit and chuck some tomato sauce on it. Oh, and if it's dessert you're thinking about, she loves ice-cream. A couple of tons and she's normally satisfied.'

Which on the one hand was a good thing because mum wouldn't have to worry about making special meals, she could concentrate on making her meals special as she had always done. On the other hand, good girls did not have the appetite of a horse, that's what fast girls had, despite the fact that my mother has always had an excellent appetite and would never, ever consider herself fast.

One thing was for sure, the folk's house was going to be scrubbed within an inch of its life, even if my 'wife to be' was a hussy. She, my mum, would never compromise on standards, even if I was obviously going to do so. The folks had become so terribly, terribly middle-class they were frightened of patronising the Chavs.

Having sorted mum out the next step was to wind Maddy up just a tad. I waited until we'd had supper and done the dishes and everything, and were curled up on the couch about to watch a film.

'Brat,' I said, 'you are going to go on a journey.'

'I am?' she asked. 'Says who and his army?'

'Says me and my army,' I said. 'This weekend we are going ...'

She carried on watching the television for a few seconds until she realised I was waiting for a reaction. She turned to me with a look in her eyes which said that, if it were a surprise she'd be very, very happy, and she'd love me deeply and madly forever and a day, otherwise she was going to fucking kill me.

'Yes? Come on, Mark, where are we going?'

'To Liverpool ...'

'To Liverpool? Why Liverpool? I mean I've always wanted to go to Liverpool, but -'

Pause as she makes the connection.

'To meet ma and da,' I confirm. 'Just don't let on I ever called them that, mum would kill me. It's another Scouserism I'm not allowed to use. Ma and da are mum and dad.'

Her face lights up, her mouth describes a perfect O just before she covers it with her hands. And then she goes through about fifty different emotions.

'Oh! Oh!' That's wonderful!

'Oh! Oh!' Your parents? Mum and dad?

'Oh! Oh!' Will they like me?

'Oh! Oh!' Have I got anything to wear?

'Oh! Oh!' Shit! They'll hate me.

'Oh! Oh!' Just fucking oh! oh! for the hell of it.

'But, Mark ...'

'Yes, sweetie pie?'

'Well, do you think ... well, I mean ... well, they're your parents, like your mom and dad ...'

'Mum and dad,' I corrected. 'But well spotted, Brat. Very clever. Tomorrow I might let you go to grown up school.'

'But ...'

'But what?'

'Well, what if they don't like me?'

She looked so miserable I almost took pity on her. But I didn't. One has to keep up one's reputation as a complete bastard.

'Oh, don't worry, I've fixed that for you. They already hate you. I told them that you're a divorcée with three children.'

'Mark! You didn't! You mustn't have! You didn't!'

'Oh yes I did. That way when they meet you they'll be so relieved they might actually like you. Do you want to know how old your brats are, Brat? They're called Tracey, Sharon and Herpes, by the way. One's got a squint, the other two are still in nappies. They both fart continuously. The other one has a tattoo of the Spice girls on her forehead.'

'Mark! That's not funny!'

'I think it is.'

'You didn't really tell them I was divorced with three children, did you?'

'Course not, squirrel. I'm just winding you up.'

'Ooooh, you are an evil bastard. Seriously, Mark, I'm terrified.'

'I know, kitten, but don't worry, just think of them like any audience, they'll be eating out of your hand in no time. I know I do.'

That did precisely nothing to allay her anxieties, but then the only things I knew of that could do that were travel and sightseeing. And eating and shopping. And, of course, music and singing. So over the next few days I made sure she did as much of all of those as possible. And before she knew it we were on a train heading north for Liverpool, and she was enjoying the countryside flying past, sitting opposite each other at a table.

'This reminds me of Auden's Night Mail,' I said at some stage, the clicketty-clack of the wheels on the tracks getting to me, almost hypnotising me, reminding me of the last time I had made this journey.

'What's that?' she asked.

'It's a poem Auden wrote for a propaganda film about the Post Office in 1936. Only they called it a documentary. It starts,

This is the Night Mail crossing the border, Bringing the cheque and the postal order.

It was designed to echo the sound of the wheels on the tracks. The Night Mail was a mail train from London to Aberdeen. There's another line about letters of joy from girl and boy.' I paused, grimacing, I would imagine. 'I can't remember the last time I wrote a letter to someone. A personal letter. Probably when I was at boarding school and wrote to mum and dad. And then Jenny, of course.'

'You can write to me when I'm on tour,' she said.

'Or I could email you, like most people do in the modern era.'

'I'd prefer a letter, thank you very much. With a pressed flower. A different one each time. Perfumed.'

'I'm sure you would. Of course a letter would get to wherever you might be temporarily staying after you left, so it would probably be sent back to Muswell Hill. Or they might just bin it instead. I'm afraid standards have dropped pretty badly since the days when Sherlock Holmes could send a postcard from Baker Street in the morning and expect Doctor Watson to receive it on the moor in the afternoon.'

She made a face.

'Pity. Oh, well. Email it will have to be. Just don't forget. With emojis.'

She took out a piece of paper.

'You've reminded me,' she said,. 'Right, I've got to be prepared. Twenty questions. First, what's mum's favourite perfume?'

'What?'

'Mum's favourite perfume. I need to know these things.'

I think I blinked a few times.

'I'm sure you do, Maddy my sweet. What I don't understand is why you might think I would have the faintest clue.'

'You don't know what mum's favourite perfume is? How can you not?'

I thought about that for a few seconds, trying to get to grips with the concept of wishing to remember the name of a brand of perfume.

'Ignorance of such things comes naturally to me, Brat. If you're lucky I might be able to remember your favourite perfume one day, if you tell me once a week for twenty years. Would you like to know her favourite shade of lipstick?'

She gave me her 'I think you're winding me up' look.

'Okay, what is it?'

'Maddy, how the hell should I know? Do I look like a man who memorises shades of lipstick?'

'Mark, you are bloody useless, how can I get them to like me if I don't know anything about them? I mean, what's mum look like? What's dad look like?'

I considered this for a few moments.

'Mum looks like mum,' I concluded. 'And dad looks like dad. Just like they've always done. Only older now.'

Older now. Those words echoed in my mind. I looked out of the window.

Older now.

'And of course you don't have a photograph of them on you now,' demanded Maddy.

'No, I don't think I do. There must be one at Muswell Hill, I think. I'm sure there is. I'll see if I can find it when we get back.'

I think she gave me a look which included several swear words and the proposition that I was completely fucking useless and not in the least funny.

'I should have asked you the moment you mentioned meeting them.'

I looked back at her.

'Okay,' I said, 'I tell you what, to get you prepared, how about I teach you some Liverpool sayings they like to use?'

'Such as?'

'Well, whenever Liverpudlians meet someone they say, "Worra ya like?" It's a traditional greeting. Mum uses it all the time.'

'Worra ya like?'

'That's it. And the word bad means good. Just like kids today saying wicked when they mean really amazing.'

'Such as?'

'Oh, if you want to compliment someone on their clothes, you know, or something, you'd say, Eee, that's proper bad that is. Mum will probably say it about your skirt.'

'Eee, that's proper bad, that is.'

'By Jove, I think she's got it.'

'How about, doing me ed in?'

'Doing me ed in? Oh, yes, that's what you say when you find someone funny, Eee, you ain't half doing me ed in you are.'

'How about when you actually want to do someone's head in?'

'Sorry?'

She gave me a scornful look.

'Worra ya like? You expect me to believe mum uses language like that? You told me she won't even let you use words like scran or ma and da. You must think I was born yesterday.' She gave a very ladylike 'Hmmph.'

'I'll do your fucking ed in for you if you're not careful,' she muttered.

'Bugger,' I said, 'I'd forgotten I told you that. Do you remember absolutely everything?'

That met with a look that said, quite simply, Yes.

'What's this area called?' she asked, looking out the window.

'England,' I replied. 'The green bit.'

'I mean, which county?'

'I don't know, I never was good at geography.'

'You must have an idea.'

'Well, I'm pretty sure it isn't Wales or Kent. Probably not Devon or Cornwall either. We could limit it to a number of possibilities if we exclude all the impossibilities.'

'Wales isn't a county,' she pointed out.

'Staffordshire,' I said.

'What?'

'The county we're in. It's Staffordshire. I've just remembered.'

'Hmmph,' she said, pursing her lips, and went back to looking out the window. I slid down and hooked my feet behind her ankles. She kept looking out the window, but with a smile playing on her lips.

It was a strange journey. Strange compared to the last time I'd made it, going up for Jenny's funeral. I answered Maddy's further questions as best I could, though occasionally my mind would wander back to that time. Then one time I found Maddy looking at me and holding my hands in hers across the table, and I realised that she must have noticed I wasn't listening, and had decided to just sit there holding my hands and being there for me until I came back from the dark side.

'Sorry, I said, trying a feeble smile. 'I was just thinking about the last time I made this journey.'

She smiled and pressed tighter.

'I know. It's Jenny. I can feel her.'

'We'll be there soon,' I said.

'I know. I'm shitting bricks.'

You know, Danny, sometimes your mother really does go off-script.

And then we're coming into Liverpool Lime Street station and suddenly I think I'm the one shitting bricks, like the moment in a movie when someone expendable asks the one question they shouldn't: 'What if it all goes wrong?' Ten seconds later it does and they're blown up.

The hero always survives, mind.

That would have to be Maddy. She's more heroine material than me.

Besides, she looks better in black than I do.

We got off the train and there to meet us were mum and dad. As they came towards us I was reminded of the days I would return from boarding school or Aunt Marigold's and there they'd be, happy and smiling, and mum would come running up to me, arms wide open, desperate to give her little boy a hug. And dad would hold out a hand for little me to shake just like any other grown up man. Later on Jenny would also be there, when she was well enough.

But now mum and dad walked slowly, and there were no outstretched arms.

Yet.

'Mum, dad,' I said, 'this is Madeleine. Maddy, meet mum and dad.'

And mum held out a hand to shake, to be polite, even if I had brought the hussy from hell home, and she sure as hell wasn't going to comment on Maddy's appearance. And Maddy said in her little-girl voice,

'Do you mind if I call you mum and dad? Only Mark's always calling you mum and dad, and I've kinda got used to it.'

And that's it. Mum looks a bit like she's going to well up, opens her arms wide and says, 'Aaah, of course you can, darling,' and they give each other the huggiest hug this side of Moscow. And then it's dad's turn and he also gives her a hug, and now they're both looking much happier. And we get in the car to go back to the house, and mum tells me to get in the front alongside dad so that she and Maddy can sit in the back, just like god fore-ordained it should be, the men in the front discussing important issues, the women in the back chatting about clothes and generally gossiping.

It wasn't like that, of course. Dad and I didn't say much, we just listened to mum and Maddy chattering away like two old friends who hadn't seen each other for years. Listening to the healing begin.

At one point mum said she'd put Maddy in Jenny's old room, and I knew that must have cost her and dad, to have to convert their daughter's shrine into some stranger's bedroom, especially one of my tarts. And Maddy objected and said she wasn't worthy, and she didn't mind where she slept, and she knew how hard it must be for mum and dad. And mum patted her hand and said, yes, it was hard, but time moved on.

I was tempted to suggest she slept with me just like we were doing in Muswell Hill, but, Jesus, I'm not that insensitive.

Though you do have to wonder. Respectability, propriety and pretence. I'm sure the folks never suffered from those when they were young. I know I didn't.

And so a weekend which threatened to be overcast with forced politeness turned out to be sunny and bright, and the sound of laughter echoed with the singing of birds, full of spring and the promise of hope.

Maybe that sort of crap is why my song-writing career hasn't been a stellar success.

And of course we had to do all the touristy things I would have despised normally, including taking a ferry trip across the Mersey so that we could be treated to that god-awful tune. And of course it had to be the Snowdrop, that ghastly coloured tramp steamer painted by the person who did the cover for Sgt Pepper's Lonely Hearts Club Band. At one point Maddy picked up the tune of Ferry Cross The Mersey and began singing in time, unconsciously. Then she suddenly realised that the folks were looking at her and realised what she was doing and went beetroot red as far as she could.

'Sorry,' she said, 'wasn't thinking.'

'But you have a lovely voice, Madeleine,' mum said.

'You certainly do,' added dad with fervour.

And Maddy went even more beetroot red, but was chuffed as anything, because even when you know you're good it's nice to have someone say so. And the folks were chuffed that she was chuffed and I was doubly chuffed because the folks were chuffed and Maddy was chuffed and we were all so chuffed with each other under normal conditions I would have vomited. But when you're in love ...

Well, you are, and there's not much you can do about it.

Being Liverpool we couldn't escape all the other Beatle memorabilia, despite my best efforts. Much as I can't abide their music purely through being drowned in it during my formative years, I was reminded of Help if you can I'm feeling down, the second line being I do appreciate your being around, or something like that. Mum and dad definitely appreciated their daughter-in-law-to-be being around, even if she didn't know she was their daughter-in-law-to-be, though, as I was to discover, she knew it extremely well.

Well, that was the plan.

Then.

Now ...

Only a few more stations and I'll get it sorted, Danny, promise.

We even went to see the yellow submarine on Maddy's request. Which just goes to show how much I was ready to sacrifice for her. Bloody stupid song.

Still, could have been worse. Could have been, We all live in a pink and green submarine, a barf-coloured submarine. We all live in a tub of margarine. That's the song I would have written.

On the way back on the Saturday afternoon, when we were getting in the car mum again gestured for me to sit in the front with dad.

Mum gestures in the most polite way. It's only if you have time to reflect that you realise that it wasn't a request.

She got in the back with Maddy, and away they went, chatting nineteen to the dozen. Dad and I were chatting about something ourselves a while later when I suddenly realised there was a very, very strange silence from the back. Maddy and mum not saying anything to each other? That was not good.

That was really, really not good.

I glanced around idly to check, shitting bricks.

I found mum's arm holding Maddy around the shoulders, Maddy's head on her shoulder, and Maddy fast asleep. I suddenly realised that I had really put her under some unfair pressure. She was absolutely exhausted. When I say I'm dreading meeting someone it's because I'll probably want to punch them in the face. Maddy had really been dreading meeting the folks in case they didn't like her. She had put a lot of nervous energy into our visit and I hadn't exactly been helpful.

Silly sausage. How could the folks not love her?

Mum gave me an enigmatic smile as if to say, 'I really like her. We'll keep her, shall we?'

It was nice to see mum smile again.

Though then again mum's enigmatic smiles are really enigmatic. She could just as well have been saying, 'You bloody jammy dodger, Mark, you really don't deserve such a lovely girl, you're a complete shit, just like your father.'

And who could argue with that?

Alternatively, maybe she was saying, 'She's absolutely gorgeous, I love her to bits, and if you ever, ever upset her, Mark, number one son of mine or no, and only son of mine or no, I will personally hunt you down and kill you. Slowly and fucking painfully, my darling. So just don't even think about it sunshine.'

The Germans had it easy. They only had to obey the Fuhrer. We Brits have mum to deal with.

Sunday we had to go to mass, of course, if only to show mum and dad what a good little Catholic girl Maddy was, despite the fact that she knew my folks knew I avoided the church like the plague. And it had to be the cathedral, of course, though she and mum were less than well impressed by my referring to it as Paddy's Wigwam. And Maddy was wearing her mantilla. That made her go up even higher in mum's estimation, were that possible. I was willing to bet that, the next time we came up to Liverpool, mum would have her own nice black lace headscarf ready.

Though I have to confess that even I got dressed up specially. I wore clean clothes. And they were ironed. Sort of. I sat on them for a minute as kind of manual press.

And I didn't wear the t-shirt I had with just "Christ!" printed on it.

Mum had never been happy with that t-shirt.

To be honest I had worn that first when I was seventeen, and I doubted it would still fit. Looking like a complete teenage twat had nothing to do with it.

But what really got my stomach churning was when mum and Maddy sang the hymns. Dad and I were standing either side of them, doing our usual male thing of trying to look as if we could sing but had chosen not to because of a sore throat, or not wishing to embarrass others by our superior voices, or ourselves, or something. Put a woman in a church, however, and they will be convention personified. Two occasions women will happily sing out loud; drunk at a karaoke, sober in a church. Me, drunk anytime, in a church never, unless see rule one.

Had mum or dad had any doubts about the depth of my love for Maddy, the fact that I was at Mass sober would have dispelled them there and then.

The thing was, I had forgotten the quality of mum's voice. I remember her singing to me when I was a child, but those were soft lullabies. Occasionally she might do Janis Joplin or Joan Baez or just generic protest songs – I loved We Will Overcome even though I never knew what it really meant – but again, those didn't have the power you get in a cathedral or hall designed to reflect booming voices. I suppose you sing differently to a child than you would to God.

Wouldn't it be nice if God turned out to be a child. Without the tantrums.

And it's truly incredible how they could sing of 'I' and 'me' and really mean 'our menfolk':

'Amazing grace, how sweet the sound

That saved a wretch like me (him, if he takes up the offer)

I (he) once was lost, but now am (he could be) found

Was blind, but now I (he could) see (if he really wanted to)'

And then there was the martyrs' song, known as 'Lord make me an instrument of peace':

'O loving Lord may I not seek

To be understood as to understand

To be consoled as to console
Or to be loved but to love all
because with my old man that's all I can hope for
the fucking bastard'

And, of course, mum had Maddy next to her, and their voices were building on each other. And, without realising it initially, they were getting attention from people who were wondering who these powerful and enthusiastic singers were, so early on a Sunday morn. And then they got a few more looks, because they appeared as the perfect mother and strikingly different looking daughter-in-law combo, they could have appeared on a Christmas edition of The Happy Catholic Family Magazine Without Pervert Priests.

Dad and I just continued to try to look invisible.

I might have looked to the heavens on the odd occasion. Fuck knows why, I was hardly about to receive solace from that direction.

There's a poem from World War One called An Irish Airman Foresees His Death. It's by W B Yeats and considers the conflict of an Irishman dying fighting Germans in an English war. But for a brief second I had a vision of a different kind of death, a horrible twee existence of doing the right thing, going to Christmas Midnight Mass like all good families, shepherding the excited little ones along while chatting to other church-goers about mundane matters, Maddy and me and bairns and the grand-parents, discussing school, the weather, whatever, just being horribly, horribly middle class and boring as hell.

Don't worry, Danny, that ain't going to happen. Trust me, it ain't.

I'll shoot you before that happens. Promise.

I remember that Sunday morning, before breakfast, we were in the kitchen. Maddy came out of her room in her dressing gown and pyjamas, hair all over the place, looking sleepy, probably just as she would at home in Melbourne. Mum immediately jumped up to get her a coffee.

'I haven't slept so well in years,' said Maddy, sitting down at the kitchen table, yawning. 'It was so peaceful in that room. It was lovely.'

Mum put the mug of coffee in front of Maddy and stroked her hair. Maddy picked up the coffee as if it were her due and took a sip. Mum already knew exactly how Maddy liked her coffee.

'I've always thought it had something of Jenny,' said mum.

'Serenity,' said Maddy.

'Yes, serenity,' agreed mum, having now found a comb to comb Maddy's hair.

'It's funny,' Maddy continued, 'it feels almost as if I've come home. I suppose it must be the Irish in me.'

That must have chuffed mum up no end, even if she didn't quite understand it, but nary a look passed her face.

Maddy looked up at me. I think I must have had my cynical look on.

'What's up with you, vinegar face,' she asked, 'do you always get out of the wrong side of the bed?'

For once I'm lost for words. She knows exactly how I get out of bed, she's experienced it often enough. Every day I wake up next to her I want to stay in bed and cuddle her forever, wondering if this be paradise. But I can't say that in front of mum and dad and there's an evil little glint in her eyes that tells me she knows it. And mum keeps combing her hair, doing her enigmatic smile, and, I suspect, enjoying the fact that Maddy isn't afraid to have a pop at me.

All I can think of saying is, Wait till I get you back home, but since I've been thinking that ever since we were confined to celibate rooms it's probably best not to mention it. Only thing is, before I'd been thinking of the love business, now I was thinking of the teaching-you-a-lesson business.

Then, when we're walking from the car to the cathedral, Maddy and I are in front for a change. She looks up at me, gives me her special smile, and slips her hand in mine. So I smile back and squeeze. She glances back at the folks, turns back to me and whispers, 'Mum and dad are holding hands too.'

Bliss was it then to be alive.

Sunday afternoon dad drove us back to the railway station, myself in front again of course, the ladies in the back. Once we'd got our bags on board we stood in the train doorway chatting to the folks until it was time for the train to go.

'So when will you be back up here?' mum asked Maddy. 'Soon, I hope.'

'It depends on the lord and master here,' Maddy replied, her arm around my waist.

'Lord and master?' I asked in disbelief. 'Lord and master my arse.'

'Mark, really!' said mum. 'You really should show a little more respect for – for – for Madeleine.'

She only just managed not to say 'For your future wife'.

'He's awful,' said Maddy. 'I'll bet you were much more of a gentleman when you were his age, weren't you, dad?' the little hussy asked dad.

'Different times, I suppose,' said dad with a smile.

Lying sod. Well, I suppose he wasn't lying, because he hadn't actually said anything. In fact he had dodged the whole question quite brilliantly. I must learn to do that sometime.

Soon the doors closed and we waved goodbye through the window, continuing as the train picked up speed, and right up until we definitely could not see even the slightest speck of parent.

'I do like mum and dad,' Maddy said, sinking back into her seat.

'Do you?' I said. 'I don't think they liked you very much, Brat.'

'Oh! You are horrible! No, tell me seriously, do you think they liked me, Mark? A little bit? Just a little bit?'

'They loved you to pieces and you know it, Brat. They'd probably be more happy to see you turn up than me.'

She smiled. I could see she was very happy with the idea. Come to that, so was I. I smiled back. Then I noticed another little devil twinkling in her eyes.

'Mum said you were always a little autistic,' she said. 'Is that true?'

'Brat! She would have said artistic. You just misheard deliberately.'

She gave me her happy kitten face and then giggled.

'Why did you tell mum I had an Australian accent?' she asked.

'Australian accent? I never said that.'

'That's what she said you said.'

I rewound what I had said to mum about Maddy.

'Ah, I know,' I said. 'I told her you were Australian. She must have imagined the bit about the accent. She does that quite a lot. She's the human version of an out of control auto-complete.'

I could only guess at what mum had been expecting. Some huge outback Amazon cracking stubbies open with her bare teeth while yelling 'Gooday cobber, fancy a shag?'

At some point I said something about how much I'd enjoyed the weekend, but also how much I was looking forward to us being able to snuggle up together in our own bed.

'That will be nice,' Maddy agreed. 'But I think mum guessed we're sleeping together anyway. I'll bet she and dad did before they got married.'

'Nah. She thinks you're the perfect little Catholic girl who wouldn't know what sex is, and you're going to remain chaste until your wedding day.'

'Would you like me to do that?' she asked, eyes fluttering. 'I can, if you want.'

'You flirtatious wench,' I said. 'Didn't you know that sex before wedlock is a mortal sin?'

'Just for women, I suppose?'

'Just for idiots who believe in religion. I'm a fully paid-up heathen, you're the one who insists on going to Mass. I hope you've been to confession, confessed your grievous sins, and said forty thousand million billion Hail Marys with farts on.'

'As if I'm going to tell a priest anything about what we do. Anyway, it isn't a sin if it's with the man you're going to marry.'

And that was me put in my box. I've heard of women proposing to men, but never being bluntly told that their future had been settled and their opinion was irrelevant.

Not that I was complaining, mind.

And anyway, I had got there first when I told mum that I was going to marry Maddy. Maddy was just confirming it.

So there.

It was obvious that mum and dad were going to adore her as a second daughter. I've no doubt some psychologist out there would make dubious sounds before suggesting that I was sacrificing her in propitiation to my parents. I had failed to look after their daughter Jenny as I should, so I was offering them my wife-to-be in her place. Complete bollocks. I loved Maddy, I loved the folks, and I wanted them to love each other as well.

And, as it turned out, we were going back to Liverpool sooner than we expected.

The following Tuesday evening I'm pottering around making dinner and Maddy's in the lounge going through my music collection when the phone rings, the land-line in the passage. So I answer it and it's mum.

First thing I say is:

'What's wrong?'

Because I know if the folks phone up it's only bad news. But this time mum says,

'Nothing's wrong, Mark, I just thought I'd call and see how things are going. You don't mind, do you?'

I guessed there was something wrong, but mum wanted to approach it obliquely. I just don't have any small talk. But I decided to humour her. So we had an awkward chat for a few minutes. Then mum says suddenly,

'Will you be up here next weekend, Mark? And Madeleine, of course.'

'Next weekend?' I asked. 'Is there something special about next weekend I should know?'

Then we both said together, as brain-dead me suddenly realised,

'Next Saturday is dad's birthday.'

'Of course,' I said, 'I'll be up. Definitely.'

There comes a time in your life when you can't make a parent's birthday. So you call and send them a card and a present and promise them and yourself, it's just this year, next year we'll get back to normal. Then it's also an Easter, a Christmas, and before you know it it's just normal to send a card and maybe phone. But after Jenny's death I'd promised myself to make the effort and I'd meant it.

'I'll ask Maddy,' I said, 'but her schedule is pretty hectic. And performances tend to be on weekends and evenings, so that makes things difficult. But I'll be there if you can tolerate me without her.'

'She really is a singer?' asked mum. 'She has a lovely voice.'

I don't know what it is with mum. She wanted to be a professional singer herself. I'm sure Maddy must have told her a thousand times over the weekend, she's told me it every bloody day in case I'd forgotten overnight. I think mum just somehow automatically associates singers with disreputable, probably quite coarse and common little floozies who can't wait to strip their clothes off. And of course Madeleine's a gorgeous little sweetheart and couldn't possibly one of those. Ergo she can't be a singer, whatever the evidence.

Wherever mum goes she leaves behind brick walls broken by somebody else's head.

Or perhaps mum hadn't quite got to grips with the idea that I could ever go out with someone who wasn't a total trollop.

'Oh, yes, mum, she's a singer. Two hundred percent. Sometimes she never bloody stops.'

'She just seems too nice to be a singer.'

'Kylie Minogue is a singer,' I pointed out, knowing that mum had a soft spot for her.

'That's true, poor girl,' she said. 'Hasn't she just broken up with her latest boyfriend? The toy boy?'

'Mum, you don't think I follow the gossip columns looking for reports of Kylie Minogue's love life, do you?'

Silence for a moment. I was beginning to wonder whether mum hadn't taken a degree in practical silence. Or possibly a PhD.

'I had a call from the chairwoman of the Catholic women's charity on Sunday evening. She was at the Sunday service. She mentioned how pretty Madeleine is,' mum said in an off-hand manner that should have warned me that we were approaching the real reason for her call.

'I agree completely.'

'Mark, you could have given us a little warning.'

'What, about how pretty she is? I'm sure I mentioned that. I tell everyone, except for Maddy, in case she gets a big head. And her head is perfect as it is.'

'You know what I mean, Mark.'

Ah.

'You mean about the slight Oriental slant to her visage, if I can put it that way?'

'Mark! That sounds terrible.'

'Okay, I admit it, it's not slight. But she is gorgeous.'

'Well, yes, of course she's gorgeous. It's just – I felt really put out,' mum said, 'not knowing anything about – well, about Madeleine, really.'

Of course, I thought, that's what the problem is. Mum would never be fazed by such things. But I'd forgotten about all the good-deeds-people she knew and how they would demand all the gossip, especially about anyone who looked vaguely exotic or even possibly forrin. She could put them off if she knew Maddy's background. Not knowing beforehand, well, that was vexatious. I had presumed that she and Maddy would have gone through all of that nonsense and got it out of their systems during their interminable chats, but had also forgotten how mum could walk around a subject for aeons until she felt the time propitious for saying something without embarrassment on either side. Like deliberately not asking someone if they're Jewish just in case it might offend, even though they've got a kippah on their head and a Star of David hanging from a chain around their neck and they're singing l'chaim every five minutes.

'Her story is much the same as our family,' I said. 'In the ancient days they were pagan, Christianity arrived, they became Catholic, found they were living amongst barbarians, and had to flee for their lives. Only our barbarians were the Proddy bastards and theirs were Mao Tse Tung and his killers. I've come to quite hate Mayonnaise over the past few months.'

'Mark, I haven't a clue what you're talking about.'

'Her great-grand-parents on her mother's side were Catholic. That was bad enough for normal Chinese, but when Mayonnaise Tse Tung took over in 1949 they knew they had to flee, because the Commies hated all religion, but especially the Catholics. They landed up in Australia, lived peacefully amongst their own until Maddy's mother met a good Irish Catholic Australian white boy and they fell in love. Apparently both families thought their child was marrying beneath them. I keep asking her what the Chinese is for uncivilised white bastard boy, but she won't tell me. She's promised to draw me a pictogram one day, though.'

'Oh, dear.'

Now what did that mean, for Christ's sake?

I ploughed on.

'Course, that's the official story. The unofficial one is that her one Chinese great-grandfather was a Catholic, yes, but he was also a capitalist businessman and tax-collector and having a bit on the side with the wife of the local Commie head-honcho who was away fighting in the mountains. Come 1949 and the great chicken in everyone's pot revolution and he knew he had to clear out. Being a nice guy he took his family with him. They had planned to only go as far as Taiwan with Chiang Kai-shek and the rest of his friends in the Kuomintang, but he and the captain of the boat they were on got together, got pissed, and missed, and they ended up in Australia. Turned out that the captain was Korean. South Korean. They were celebrating hating the Commies.'

'You made that up, Mark.'

'Ah, but what if I didn't?'

'Poor Madeleine. All that trouble and worry and, oh, it must be awful.'

'Poor Madeleine? Mum! Maddy had a lovely middle-class Australian upbringing, she didn't go on the long march through the mountains. They had barbecues and beaches and sunshine. They even had a swimming pool. Okay, it was only one of those framed plastic things you fill up with a garden hose every summer for the kids, but at least they had that. We never even had a swimming pool as kids.'

Bad move. Mum pretends not to hear things so she can ignore them, but she doesn't miss a trick. There was a good likelihood that, on my next visit, there'd be an inflatable baby's paddling pool in the garden just for me. If she was really angry it would be in the lounge and little Markie would have to sit in it while the adults chatted.

'Poor thing. She must have been terribly bullied growing up.'

When mum is determined to feel sorry for someone she doesn't let the facts get in the way.

'Mum, she was voted most likely to succeed by her classmates. She was made queen of the ball in high school, or whatever it's called over there amongst the didgeredoos.'

I didn't know if that was true, but I would have voted for it.

Mum sighed.

'I suppose she's out in London at the moment all on her own, rehearsing.'

Mum lived in London as a young woman. She loved it and went out everywhere, at any and all times. It was the Sixties or something. Short skirts hiding nothing and great big bongs of illegal shit. Suddenly with Maddy it's now become a dangerous Sodom and Gomorrah. And I'm inconsiderately safely at home, indoors, in the warmth, even though it wasn't then cold outside, ignoring poor young innocent, pretty Madeleine's perilous plight in the dark and gloomy shades with Jack the Ripper stalking the streets along with Fagin and Bill Sikes and his bull-terrier. Lawks a fucking mercy.

'Mum, she's in the lounge going through my record collection,' I said. 'I mean, my record and cassette and CD collection. With a glass of red wine. She's in her element. And I'm making supper tonight. Irish sausage stew. With rice. And rice isn't easy, no matter what they say. It's not boil in the bag stuff, it's rice with things in. Like, real vegetables. And I'm not sure how many green peppers to add.'

'Oh, thank god for that, you must take care of her, Mark, she's a lovely girl.'

There was a pause as I thought of how to reply to that without pushing the sarcasm-meter to overload. I'm cooking and mum doesn't congratulate me? Sausage stew is not easy to make, you can end up with just mince stew very easily. That's not Irish, that's just a clumsy mishap.

'Sausage stew isn't easy to cook, mum, you know –'

'Mark, you're as bad as your father.'

'Sorry, mum.'

'Can I talk to her?'

Which is when the penny finally dropped. I was due a severe and well-deserved bollocking from mum, but she wouldn't waste a phone call doing that. She knew I'd just put the receiver on my head and make funny faces while listening for the appropriate pause to say "Yes, mum", or even just "Fishcakes!" However, as a perfectly reasonable segue to getting some background info I should have provided to start off with, but more importantly, to having a long and worthwhile girly chat with Maddy, she was prepared to waste a few seconds on me. That was when I knew beyond doubt that, if Maddy and I ever broke up, she would always still be welcome at my parents' hearth, and if that meant me shivering outside in the cold Eastern Front, Russian snow, well, tough. The Eastern Front was probably too good for heartless, cruel, unfeeling bastards like me.

I should have guessed from the start. Mum would also never have phoned just to remind me it was dad's birthday, I would have been expected to remember that all by myself. I would have forgotten, remembered a week too late, and given grovelling apologies to be met by dad with a grunt and mum with unbearable forgiveness. However it was a pretty useful excuse to call. In fact I had a bit of a suspicion that with the arrival of Maddy she had completely forgotten dad's coming birthday herself over the previous weekend, otherwise she would have innocently shoe-horned it in somewhere. That time at the station on the Sunday afternoon: 'You will be here next weekend, won't you, Mark?'

Apparently innocent questions carrying a payload of regret.

'Just a minute, mum, I'll call the Brat and you can ask her yourself.'

Then I hold the phone to my shoulder and shout to the lounge, making sure mum can also hear:

'Oi! Brat! Mum wants to say hello.'

Then I put the phone back to my ear and say,

'She's coming, mum.'

And she sighs and says something about not using words like brat because Madeleine is such a lovely girl and it's such a lovely name. But I don't have a chance to reply because the lovely girl with the lovely name in question has rushed down the passage and grabbed the phone from me, giving me a hearty slap on my backside to say thank-you and to indicate that I was now surplus to requirements, and could make myself useful by making some tea or mowing the lawn in the dark or something.

And then Maddy and mum spend about half an hour nattering away, and I don't bother to ask what about afterwards, because I know the answer will be 'Oh, this and that'. I have never been good at small talk myself, and I have never understood what women find to talk about, and the last time I tried to listen in I fell asleep. But Maddy's happy and mum's happy so I'm happy.

And, let's be honest, some of that private natter is going to be about me, and if any bloke out there thinks they want to know what their girlfriend and their mother are saying to each about you, trust me, you don't.

Sooner or later those baby photos are going to come out.

'Oooh, wasn't he such a cute little baby! Look at his little thing, so sweet!'

Retch.

And it becomes a bit of a ritual. Maddy would phone mum or mum would phone Maddy once a week for a good natter. And initially I couldn't work out how Maddy knew immediately that it was mum calling and would rush out into the passage to answer the phone. Until I finally ask her, and she looks at me in pity and asks,

'Haven't you heard of text messaging?'

I had, I wasn't aware mum had. Turns out the folks are quite happy using modern technology when it suits them, it's just they aren't chained to it like today's younger generation. Either mum or Maddy would send a one or two word text message to see if it were a good time, and if it was one of the phones would ring.

Why they had to use a land-line instead of their mobiles I'm not quite sure. I suppose it made the call just that extra little bit special, curling up in a chair and having a good girl to girl natter. We had a beanbag type thing and I know the folks had always had an old comfy chair next to their telephone table. It had always seemed out of place in their otherwise middle class neatness and order. I think it might have been the last of a second-hand set they had bought when first married, and too poor to buy some brand-new pieces of junk.

Then again, maybe their mobile signals were just crap.

Back then, after their first conference call I asked Maddy whether mum had mentioned dad's birthday, and she said, no, which I took to mean that mum was being careful not to tread on toes. Why, I don't know, I walk on toes with gay abandon whenever I get the chance. I can only presume I got it from dad. Except I don't seem to have inherited the good manners that make it acceptable, as he does.

On the other hand, maybe, just maybe, she had also completely forgotten about the excuse she had used to call.

'It's this weekend, Brat. I'm going up, call of duty. You coming?'

And her face forms that excited look, followed rapidly by the crushed one.

'I've got a rehearsal Saturday,' she says in her "I'm sorry" little voice.

'We could go up after,' I say. 'Get there in the evening.'

'It's Saturday evening,' she says.

'Ah,' I say.

So I tell her not to worry, I'll go by myself, we'll go up together again first free weekend we get. That doesn't really mollify her, but there's nothing to be done so we'll have to make the best of it.

The next evening she gets home and proudly announces the rehearsal has been postponed till the Monday, so we're on for the weekend in Liverpool.

I never did find out what happened with that rehearsal. I wouldn't be surprised if Maddy bullied them into postponing it. You wouldn't think she could be capable of bullying, but it would be like a little kitten purring and head-butting and cuddling you until you give up and do what it wants. In the end it isn't really painful, but you know and the kitten knows who's boss.

We went up to Liverpool on the Saturday morning with Maddy both excited and strangely edgy. The folks met us at the train station and this time it definitely was arms wide open from mum, and they were wide open for Maddy who pretty much flew into them. Dad and I were very kindly allowed to follow them as they walked arm in arm to the car, dad and I having been graciously permitted the role of bag carriers in chief. Then, off home to drop off luggage and refresh ourselves after our highly taxing train journey.

After that, lunch at one of dad's favourite pubs, followed by a long walk along a section of the Canal, something mum and dad had done as a weekend afternoon treat way back in the days of innocence and poverty.

That evening we went to one of the folks' old haunts, a kind of jamming pub. It was a long, thin sort of a room with the bar at one end and a small stage at the other for musicians of any level to demonstrate their talents, or just jam or pretty much what they felt like. There was certain element of order, but not much. I think there was a chap who said who could play and when, but he didn't interrupt if others joined in unless they were creating a problem. There were stage lights, but they had the appearance of having a label attached, 'Only to be used for very, very special occasions, if we can remember how. And if they still actually work somehow.' They needed dusting rather badly.

Mum let slip to Maddy that she and dad had once played there almost every Saturday.

'That was years ago, of course,' said mum. 'You could still smoke indoors then, sometimes it was like playing in a fog.'

'What did you play?' asked Maddy.

'Oh, not much different to today. Jazz, blues, country. We didn't really separate things into genres.'

'Then I came along and they had to pretend to be respectable grown up folk,' I said. Mum and dad smiled, but they didn't deny it.

At one point, in the middle of some song or other, Maddy whispered to me that she was going to the ladies. I nodded without paying too much attention. I noticed – and ignored – the look of concern on mum's face as Maddy slipped away. It should have been glaringly obvious to anyone but a blind cretin like me. Girls always go to the ladies together. Maddy might go alone if it was just me and her out for a drink, but with mum there, they'd exchange some feminine signals beyond the reach of the male eye and announce that they were going to powder their noses. Mum knew that and was worried about Maddy not doing so.

The song ended and I started to get worried after a few minutes. Maybe I had noticed something subconsciously, maybe Maddy was just out of my sight for too long for my liking. I had left Jenny in the unprecious care of Stella, only to find her chatting to that shithole Ziggie. Now my Maddy was nowhere to be seen.

I didn't quite notice that, for the first time, they had brought down all the lights on the stage.

'And now, ladies and gentlemen,' said a voice from the darkness, while I impatiently scanned all entrances and exits for Maddy, getting more and more irritated and more and more unsettled, 'a special song for a special dad who is celebrating his birthday today.'

That's nice, I thought, someone's daddy is having a birthday, I'm fucking happy for them, now where the fuck has Maddy got too?

Danny, I can be quite obtuse at times. I'm sure you've noticed.

All went silent. Then someone began singing in the darkness, very softly.

'Oh, Danny boy, the pipes, the pipes are calling

From glen to glen, and down the mountain side

The summer's gone, and all the roses falling

It's you, it's you must go, and I must bide ...'

I turned, the hairs on my neck standing up. The house lights were coming down, and a stage spotlight was being undimmed and shone on a young woman, hands clasped together holding a microphone. She was looking straight at our table.

Maddy.

Mum and dad gasped.

She was looking straight at dad. Some trick when you've got stage-lights in your face. She must have memorised the ceiling overhead and worked out where to look and where to focus.

'But come ye back when summer's in the meadow

Or when the valley's hushed and white with snow
And I'll be here in sunshine or in shadow
Oh Danny boy, oh Danny boy, I love you so ...'
The audience were mesmerised. Dad and mum were enchanted. I was gobsmacked. I had heard Maddy sing to herself or to me, but this was giving it full whack. It was a full voice, soft but powerful, and the pitch was controlled to the smallest demi semi quaver.

It was fucking beautiful, if you don't mind me saying.

And if you do mind me saying, it was still fucking beautiful.

'But when ye come, and all the flowers are dying
And I am dead, as dead I well may be
Ye'll come and find the place where I am lying
And kneel and say an Ave there for me ...'
I think most of the audience were just enjoying a beautiful and mournful song being sung beautifully, but some might have wondered why a young woman would sing to her dad asking him to visit her grave. But if you saw it from our viewpoint, it wasn't Maddy. It was Jenny, singing through Maddy.

That's the problem with having a Catholic Irish past. Centuries later and you still can't get rid of the fucking superstition.

I hate fucking priests.

And then she got to the end:

'And I shall hear, though soft you tread above me
And all my grave will warmer, sweeter be'
And as she got to the penultimate line her left hand spread out and towards dad, and the lights slowly dimmed, the stage went black, and the final lines seemed to whisper in the air.

'For you will bend and tell me that you love me
and I shall sleep in peace until you come to me ...'
And there was a deafening silence
And then thunderous applause.

After what seemed like a few minutes but was probably ten or twenty seconds the stage and house lights went up again. The stage was empty. People looked at each other.

I'm sure Maddy would have loved to have a standing ovation, and she would have got one had she stayed on stage. But it was her birthday gift to dad, and milking it for herself would have lessened the gift.

Mum looked at dad. Dad was looking at the stage and pretending he had something in his eye. And then, from nowhere, Maddy slipped back into her chair next to me.

Christ but YBM has learnt some weird tricks about moving in the dark, Danny. She must give cats the shits.

I was about to say, 'Brat! I am going to kill you!' when dad and mum intervened by kissing her and fawning all over her. She was marvellous! Et fucking cetera.

Excuse me, what about your son, who has almost had several heart attacks worrying about where this little hussy had got to?

'Madeleine, that was so brave of you!' – mum.

Brave? Brave? Bollocks. Maddy's loved the stage-lights since she was two months old and played the infant Jesus at a nativity concert. She stole the show. Probably sang the socks off the fucking chorus.

'That was lovely, thank you, Maddy' – dad, blowing his nose.

Eventually, satiated on the gore of their adoration, she turned to me, batted her eyelids, and asked in her little girl voice whether I had liked it.

'You know I loved it, Brat. It was bloody perfect from start to finish. Fading in from the dark and fading out to the dark was genius. How long did you spend practising that?'

'I just told the lighting engineer what I wanted and he did the rest. Remember my hand coming out on the second last line? That was the signal to fade out.'

'They have a lighting engineer?'

'His name's Jimmy. It's the same person that looks after the order of playing. I think he does everything.'

'And Danny Boy? Don't tell me you've been singing it since you could talk.'

'It's been around since forever, but, yes, I did have to practise that a bit. I was terrified of my voice cracking or sneezing or something. But then I always am.'

'That used to terrify me too,' said mum. 'No matter how often I sang something there was always the fear that something would go wrong.' She gave one of her enigmatic smiles. 'You always remember the girl who sneezed at the wrong moment, don't you?'

'Oh, that is so true,' agreed Maddy. 'I remember Elaine. She discovered she was allergic to feathers on stage. Someone gave her a feather boa just before she went on. Though it could have been stage dust too.'

Okay, I decided, maybe it was kind of brave of Maddy to sing solo in a pub she'd never visited before to people few of whom she knew. It would never have worried me though. I would have been pissed when I walked on stage. Maddy hadn't even touched her drink. Very brave, you might even say. But she still could have warned me first.

'I would have told you first, she said, looking up at me for forgiveness, 'but I didn't know if I'd be brave enough to go through with it.'

That earned her another little 'Aah!' from mum.

'I'll forgive you this time, Brat,' I said, putting my arm around her. 'So long as you don't scare me shitless again. I didn't know where you'd disappeared to, you had me worried.'

I think mum was about to rebuke me for my choice of language, but Maddy smiled, kissed me, and snuggled up to me. It was then I felt her trembling slightly and realised she really had been suffering from stage fright.

Mum gave me The Look which I only just managed to ignore. Maddy gave me her under-the-eyelashes-forgive-me? look.

'I borrowed your Seekers CD to listen to it. It's got Danny Boy on it. You don't mind, do you?'

'My Seekers CD?' I asked. 'I've been looking all over for that. I thought I'd lost it somewhere.'

'You have a Seekers CD?' asked mum, stressing the "you" as if the combination was akin to coal wrapped in silk.

'Yes, I do have a Seekers CD, mum,' I replied as haughtily as a son can to his mother who might well have heard them live. 'I found it in a second-hand place off the Tottenham Court Road. I happen to like the Seekers.'

'Judith Durham,' said dad in a reverie. 'We all fell in love with her voice when we were young. You can keep your Beatles and the rest. Judith and the Seekers, they were the best.'

Mum squeezed his shoulder. He smiled, placed his hand over hers and seemed to wake up from somewhere.

'You must come up during the football season,' he said to Maddy. 'We'll go to see a Liverpool game. It's quite family friendly these days. And there's nothing quite like the feeling you get when they sing You'll Never Walk Alone. There's nothing like the sound of thousands of voices in harmony. Or sometimes not in harmony. Or not quite. But there's nothing quite like it.'

Maddy gasped and sat up.

'Oh, that's such a sad song,' she said. 'I always cry when I hear it.'

We all looked at her as if she were mad. The idea of thirty thousand Scouse thugs bellowing out 'such a sad song' was a bit beyond our imagination.

'When Julie Jordan tries to sing it and she can't,' Maddy said. 'Because her husband Billy Bigelow has committed suicide after his failed robbery, and Nettie Fowler has to take over.'

If Stella had thought my knowledge of popular music was over the top she would have been gobsmacked at Maddy's knowledge of musicals.

'Oh, of course,' said mum, 'Carousel. My goodness, I don't think I've seen that in years.'

'The song football supporters sing came from the version done by Gerry and the Pacemakers in the Sixties,' dad said. 'I doubt many of them will have seen Carousel.'

'Now I really want to see Carousel again,' said mum.

If mum wished to watch Carousel, I decided, she and Maddy could bloody watch it together and leave me out of it. I have a broad musical palate, but I draw the line at anything overly weepy. Even Cabaret only just makes it in. The ending is about as sad as they come. The characters don't know what's coming, but you do, and it isn't going to turn out fine again.

Bloody hell, we're moving again. It's been so long I'd forgotten the sensation.

11h47

No comment.

I think it was about this time that we started making our 'things to do list', or, more accurately, 'things to do and places to see' list. It was at the same time that we tidied up the kitchen and found the wooden French windows did actually open, with a bit of a push, and a lot of oil applied to the hinges and locks. It was probably also the weather drying out and turning to spring. They led onto a small patio surrounded by lawn and a walkway to a locked side gate which led on to the front gate. Once we had found the key to the side gate and convinced that to open it became our natural way of coming into the house rather than using the front door. I don't remember Aunt Marigold ever using the side gate. I suspect that it was still seen by her generation as being associated with the tradesmen's or servants' entrance, and to be avoided. Maddy and I just saw it as being not only more practical, but somehow part of us, our secret entrance and exit.

The patio had been added after my school holiday stays ended, so it was a novelty to me. It was a regular sun trap. Maddy and I would have our meals out there once the days grew long enough and the weather permitted. At other times we might sit in deckchairs absorbing vitamin D while Maddy read a book or the newspapers and I marked pupils' homework. A couple of the neighbours' cats even adopted us. I don't know if they were from the same neighbour or regarded the space as neutral territory, but there was a ginger one happy to sprawl in the sun so long as we were there, and a black and white one who took the first opportunity to curl up on Maddy's lap and purr away.

It must have been a Sunday morning when Maddy mentioned that she'd like to go to Amsterdam someday. She'd been reading one of the Sunday supplements and there'd been an article on short breaks on the continent – I guess that meant it was probably the Times or Observer. I said I had been, ages ago, and wouldn't mind going again, adding that we really, really must spend at least a weekend in Paris during the summer.

Maddy thinks that's a wonderful idea, so we get out a piece of paper and start noting things down. And it's not long before I say we should put the list on the computer because it's getting a bit silly – Berlin, Barcelona, Madrid, Rome – the Eternal City, of course! – Greece, Norway, Finland, Egypt, the Pyramids, Morocco, Jerusalem – Dublin! Of course, Dublin, but, I mean, the whole of Ireland, Cork, Kerry, the Blarney Stone, that place where they make fine linens, and where is it they do glass blowing? No need to visit the place they do bullshitting, she's already met me.

Thank you, Brat. That is the Blarney Stone.

Besides which Maddy wants to research her family tree, the Irish side. I don't make the obvious point that she could have done that in Melbourne using the Internet.

She's also dead set against putting our list on the computer, she wants a piece of paper – multiple pieces of paper – we can keep and cherish and take out and look at and remember the times we were able to put a date and a tick next to the ones we'd achieved.

'And you can't press flowers in a computer,' she said, which flummoxed me for a moment, as (a) I hadn't been planning on pressing flowers in anything, and (b) technically speaking you probably can press flowers in a computer, you just won't be able to see them and the computer probably won't work too well afterwards.

The truth is that we put about ten new places on a week, and ticked about one off, and that's just because we added places in London which we did have a chance of fulfilling in the near future.

Maddy, naturally, wanted to see New York, New York. So did I. And Chicago and Philadelphia and Delhi and Singapore and Cape Town and Timbuctoo, but it was going to be a tight squeeze what with rather liking evenings in together, just the two of us. But one day we were going to have them all ticked off.

One of the burning questions both Maddy and mum – and, I'm pretty sure dad also asked – was, when were we going back up to Liverpool for another weekend, or, perhaps, a whole week? The trouble was that other things always seemed to get in the way. Either I was busy or Maddy was.

Maddy's work was erratic at best, she was still building her career and she couldn't really decline a part that might suddenly become available.

This meeting up thing. Danny, men aren't bothered if they don't meet each other for years. When they do it's a manly handshake and an acceptance that nothing will have changed and there's no need to go on about anything. Enjoy a pint together, mention the weather, maybe the football.

Women.

If women haven't spoken for three seconds they have life-stories to tell.

And then I had one of those occasional brainwaves that make me so famous, or, as mum and Maddy put it, occasionally useful. Providing Maddy had no engagements for Christmas we'd spend it up in Liverpool, and bugger any unexpected roles suddenly coming available. But the real brainwave was that we'd get the house cleaned up, or at least part of it de-cluttered, so that the folks could come down and stay for a week in early December. That would give us enough time to actually do something about the chaos and confusion in the house, and mum and Maddy could go Christmas shopping – mum adores Oxford Street at Christmas time – and dad and I could trail after them as bag carriers before finally ending up in a decent pub with a good pint where dad could indulge in his hobby of listing all the reasons Liverpool was such a better place to live than The Smoke, starting off with the price of a pint. It was one oddity of dad's: normally he is the least critical of anything, but London seems to be a personal enemy of his.

Plus mum and dad could go through Aunt Marigold's effects. It was something we'd blanked out of our minds. But it had to be done sooner or later.

And, of course, we'd have to take in a show, at least one. Almost undoubtedly a musical. It would be up to mum and dad to choose, which pretty much meant it would be whatever Maddy wanted. Even bloody Carousel if it were on and I had a revolver pointed against my head.

And thus it was settled.

Or it was up until a few days ago. Now it looks like I'm going to be a pariah of pretty much everyone. Mum and dad will never forgive me if

Maddy disappears off to Australia. The fact that I won't forgive myself either isn't much solace. And it wasn't my bloody fault.

Problem is, thinking about it, even then mum will insist on forgiving me. Catholic forgiveness is a terrible thing, Danny. It gave Jean Valjean religion. Poor bastard.

Now there's a thought. If Maddy has any sense she'll phone mum for a shoulder to cry on. Mum will say, 'Oh, you poor thing, don't worry, Madeleine, I'm sure it's just a misunderstanding, Mark is forever upsetting people over nothing. Listen, why don't you come to stay with us for a few weeks while we get it sorted out?'

And Maddy will object just long enough to be respectable and then cave in and go stay with the folks where she'll be cosseted and stroked and treated like a little princess. That'll give me time to get the nonsense sorted out.

Except, Danny, that your mother isn't bloody sensible. She'll see it as charity, and she's too proud to accept that. Worse than that, it would be too much like My Fair Lady, and that's a musical she's never been comfortable with. If she played Elisa Doolittle the show wouldn't finish with her saying, 'I washed me hands and face I did' as she surrenders and returns to chez Professor Higgins, it would be her walking in with one of those old-fashioned copper bed-warmers with the long handle looking to beat the crap out of Higgins. And if it were a live stage performance the actor playing Higgins would look up, see the fire in her eyes, think 'Oh shit', and get the hell on out of there. Exeunt left, pursued by a mad Irish-Australian-Chinese-and-assorted-additions woman. And the curtain would come down with the sounds of props being knocked over as she chased him up and down and quite possibly over the gantries. And the players would take a bow with Professor Higgins wearing a bandage, and quite possible a hasty explanation that they were exploring alternative endings to the wonderful musical based on George Bernard Shaw's original play, and surely the great Irishman would approve, begorrah, to be sure.

No, let's face it, Danny, it's up to me to get to Heathrow in time, there's no other option.

Coming into Osterley.

11h49

Six stops to go.

It's going to be bloody close, Danny.

One hour forty one minutes to take-off.

One hour forty one minutes to goodbye.

Not if I can bloody help it.

Cockfosters
Oakwood
Southgate
Arnos Grove
Bounds Green
Wood Green
Turnpike Lane
Manor House
Finsbury Park
Arsenal
Holloway Road
Caledonian Road
King's Cross St. Pancras
Russell Square
Holborn
Covent Garden
Leicester Square
Piccadilly Circus
Green Park
Hyde Park Corner
Knightsbridge
South Kensington
Gloucester Road
Earl's Court
Barons Court
Hammersmith
Turnham Green
Acton Town

Ealing Common        South Ealing
North Ealing         Northfields
Park Royal           Boston Manor
Alperton             Osterley
Sudbury Town         Hounslow East
Sudbury Hill         Hounslow Central
South Harrow         Hounslow West
Rayners Lane         Hatton Cross  ←
Eastcote             Heathrow T 1-2-3 ——→ Heathrow T4
Ruislip Manor        Heathrow T5
Ruislip
Ickenham
Hillingdon
Uxbridge

## Osterley

*Estimated time to Heathrow Terminal Five: 20 minutes*

*Estimated time to Hounslow East tube station: 2 minutes*

11h49

I've always found Osterley a bit oppressive. It's in a deep culvert, and the sides are always covered in green, grass or climbers or creepers of some sort. It should be a pleasant, summery feel, but to my mind it's more like the threat of being buried alive by a malevolent nature. I dare say the people who get off here to work, or who live here would find that strange. But even when the sun is shining down on it as it is now it feels damp and oppressive. More like a jungle scene during the Vietnam War than cosy little London.

Doors are closing and we're off

11h51

We'll be there by 12h30 at the very, very latest. Should just about make it. One hour to get Maddy paged and have our lovers' tiff. And I warn her, if she slaps me, I slap back.

Probably.

Last time she caught me off guard.

Okay, probably not.

Definitely not, in fact.

In fact, if I see her looking as if she's about to clout me I'll lift a finger and say, 'Maddy I'm warning you …'

And she'll say,

'Oh, yes, Mark, and what are you warning me?'

'I'm warning you that I won't hit back. I can't.' Because I couldn't.

Danny, on your mother's birthday she gets pumpkin. Every birthday. I don't know how, but that's just the way it's going to have to be. In memory of her first birthday we spent together. Though there is part of that story we will leave quietly buried forever, quite literally so.

When the time came I popped back to the Chandras' for my special tins of pumpkin all the way from the foothills of Southall. There were a couple of people in front of me so I waited for them to get served before greeting Mrs Chandras. The first thing she saw was the support on my wrist.

'My goodness Bruce what you been doing you injured yourself you being playing squash again you boys always so energetic and of course the pumpkin we didn't forget my cousin sent six tins straight away just a minute while I call my husband MR CHANDRAS COME HERE A MOMENT IT'S BRUCE FOR HIS PUMPKIN is it sore?'

'No, Mrs Chandras, just a little accident while doing some DIY, it just needs resting bit.'

'Oh well that's okay at least it isn't serious you know my cousin does that all the time MR CHANDRAS ARE YOU COMING BEFORE I DIE OF OLD AGE he broke a bone and had to have a pin put in you know a steel pin you can see it on the x-rays.'

I say something about being lucky it wasn't worse, and Mr Chandras appears with a box.

'Why you need to shout woman I can hear you fine hello Bruce I've got your pumpkin here the woman's cousin remembered after I'd reminded her a few times.'

'How can you say that Mr Chandras she didn't need reminding she would have sent it straightaway she was busy with her sister's second son she thought had the measles only it was a cold let me put these in a bag for you Bruce.'

While she's concentrating on the bag and the tins and the cash register Mr Chandras looks at me.

'You know that sicki boy?' he asks.

I run through a list of my pupils to remember who's thrown a sickie recently or who was regularly sick. Alternatively which Sikh lad Mr Chandra might be talking about.

'Ziggie,' says Mrs Chandras. She stops packing and looks at me wide eyed. 'The one who looks pale white like he lives in the dark wears black and gold chains the cheap sort you get down the market you hear what happened to him they found him in a dumper truck crushed flat dead flat dead.'

She paused for effect.

'What?' I asked. Mr Chandras nodded.

'Went to sleep in one of those big wheelie bins behind the supermarket the dumper truck comes to collect they pick it up with those mechanical grabs they have empty it into the truck start compressing it they hear someone screaming far away they think only it's Sicki screaming as he gets crushed poor boy screaming as he's being crushed to death flat.'

'Crushed to death screaming his last breath poor boy though I always thought there was something not quite right about him but you don't want to speak evil of the dead do you only I think he used to do drugs his eyes never looked quite right thank you Bruce.' Mrs Chandras.

The last was because I had handed over some money for the pumpkin.

'Oh he was on drugs alright you can tell I'm pretty sure he was a dealer you know the one time the police came in asking about him they knew what they were doing I can tell you they don't ask questions unless they know the answers.' Mr Chandras.

'My goodness,' I said. 'Fancy that.'

After another few minutes of detailed and gory descriptions of Ziggie being crushed alive, and slowly, and dead flat, another customer came in and I was able to escape while they began to tell her all about Sikki's last moments on earth.

I have to admit that the only feeling I had about Ziggie's demise was relief that I wouldn't have to worry about watching my back. The idea that Ziggie might have endured a slow and painful death didn't worry me in the slightest. In fact if anything I felt that it was too fast compared to the misery experienced by people he supplied drugs to. Admittedly that makes me sound every so pompously moral, which I'm not. Not moral, anyway. So for the record, even if the tit hadn't been a drug dealer his end was thoroughly deserved purely because he was such a tit.

Of course I should have been able to work out that they would have CCTV at the back of the supermarket. And that they would share it with the police when the police came knocking, as they would after someone had been crushed to death in a dumper truck. It just didn't cross my mind at the time. So I wasn't prepared for it when it did.

Hounslow East here we are.

11h54.

Definitely on the home stretch now. Hounslow East, Hounslow Central, Hounslow West, Hatton Cross, Terminals 123 and then Terminal 5. That's a total of six stations. Five if you don't count T5. Sixteen minutes to Maddening.

ETA 12h30. Probably 12h15, with a backing wind.

I've got to do it.

For the ashes of our fathers and the children of our sons.

And daughters, of course, Danny.

Dannielle.

It sounds like a proper name.

Dannielle, my daughter, tonight you won't be travelling on a plane. Not if I have anything to do with it.

And nor will YBM.

She has to learn to take orders.

At least one, anyway.

For Christ's sake, just one.

Please? Pretty please?

Cockfosters
Oakwood
Southgate
Arnos Grove
Bounds Green
Wood Green
Turnpike Lane
Manor House
Finsbury Park
Arsenal
Holloway Road
Caledonian Road
King's Cross St. Pancras
Russell Square
Holborn
Covent Garden
Leicester Square
Piccadilly Circus
Green Park
Hyde Park Corner
Knightsbridge
South Kensington
Gloucester Road
Earl's Court
Barons Court
Hammersmith
Turnham Green
Acton Town

Ealing Common
North Ealing
Park Royal
Alperton
Sudbury Town
Sudbury Hill
South Harrow
Rayners Lane
Eastcote
Ruislip Manor
Ruislip
Ickenham
Hillingdon
Uxbridge

South Ealing
Northfields
Boston Manor
Osterley
Hounslow East
Hounslow Central
Hounslow West
Hatton Cross
Heathrow T 1-2-3 ⟶ Heathrow T4
Heathrow T5

# Hounslow East

*Estimated time to Heathrow Terminal Five: 18 minutes*

*Estimated time to Hounslow Central tube station: 2 minute*

11h54

Danny, in many ways YBM reminded me of an inquisitive but also mischievous cat or kitten which had just moved into somewhere new, and was curiously investigating every nook and cranny. Aunt Marigold's place was like Santa's fairy tale grotto to her, on an extended scale, crossed with Aladdin's cave. For a woman who had never been much into possessions Aunt Marigold had bought a surprising amount of tat. She seemed to have visited every flea-market and souk around the Mediterranean and bought at least one thing each time. I suspect she didn't buy it because she wanted it, she bought it because the little shopkeepers and their families would starve if they couldn't sell it. She was your typical brow-beating imperialistic mother who really did care for her adopted children. I'd like to think the love was reciprocated.

A few times Maddy and I went through it together, or started, anyway. Some of the stuff was theoretically easy to dispose of – mounds of local newspapers for example – but even then we'd pause as an article took our eye to wonder whether Mrs Jones of Woodland Rise had, in the end, resolved her dispute with her neighbour over the leylandii, or whether Mr and Mrs Smith, having celebrated their golden wedding anniversary (pictured) were still going strong.

Initially we came up with the bright idea of storing everything we weren't going to immediately give away or throw away in the garage, but that also turned out to be full of the types of object you didn't quite want to get rid of just in case it turned out to be quite useful, or could have been one of Aunt Marigold's most treasured birthday gifts, or something else, so it wasn't so much a case of two steps forward and one back as just no steps at all.

There was a car in the garage, not much used. No sign of a motorbike. I guess that stayed in North Africa.

The one day I found Maddy reading the same letter I had opened months before. She gave a guilty start as I entered the room.

'Do you think she'd mind me reading this?' she asked.

'Nope,' I said, 'I am quite sure Aunt Marigold would thoroughly approve of you, you little wench. And she wouldn't give a fig for what anyone thought of her or anything she might have written. Anyway, it's not Aunt Marigold's letter to someone else, it's one of mum's to her, so it's really mum you should be asking.'

'Oh,' she said, looking even more guilty. 'It's just that, well, Aunt Marigold sounds as if she was ill. You know, where mum writes things like, "When you get better". Was she ill, do you know?'

'I don't remember her ever being ill. I suppose she must have had the occasional cold or flu. She always seemed to be in permanent good health to me, robust is the word. Even better, to say she was in constant rude health covers both bases. I can't imagine her slowly wasting away with cancer. That's probably why she flew the plane into the mountain.'

She read out the date on the letter and looked up at me.

'Where were you then?' she asked. I shrugged.

'That was about the time Jenny was born. I was at boarding school. First term, if I remember correctly.'

She carried on looking at me, mouth open.

'Are my flies undone?' I asked 'Or are you just stunned by my natural beauty?'

'Mark –'

'Yes, wench?'

'Mark –'

'Maddy, if you carry on like that I'll buy an aquarium and put you in it. You can make gloop sounds every so often.'

She closed her mouth and scowled at me for a while.

'It's Jenny,' she finally said.

'What's Jenny?'

'Mark, I think she was Aunt Marigold's daughter.'

Now it was my turn to look at her bug-eyed. If it had been Stella I would have said, 'You fucking what?'

'Aunt Marigold's daughter? What on earth brought you to that conclusion?'

'Look,' she came over to me with the letter, 'see here, mum says "we'll look after her until you're better." Aunt Marigold was recovering from something, it could have been giving birth.'

'Maddy, it could have been any number of things.'

'Yes, but Jenny was born a couple of weeks before this letter. Mum doesn't mention her once. Unless the "her" she talks about is Jenny.'

I shook my head sadly.

'I see. So mum pretends to be pregnant and then suddenly Aunt Marigold gives birth and I never noticed a thing?'

'Well, you were ten years old. Would you have noticed if mum was pregnant or not? Or Aunt Marigold? You said you were away at boarding school.'

'Yes, but not for nine months.'

'And at ten years old you would know a pregnancy lasts nine months and you'd be able to tell if a woman was pregnant or not?'

Well, she had me there. I suspect I still believed the stork brought babies when I was ten years old. I mean, a ten year old boy having the slightest interest in pregnancy? Certainly not me, that's for sure.

'Seriously, Maddy, you can't expect me to believe that mum and dad lied about Jen?'

'What would you expect them to say?'

'Well – the truth, whatever that was. That Aunt Marigold had had a baby and she was poorly and they were looking after it until she got better.'

'What if she wasn't married at the time?'

That stopped me. Aunt Marigold had been married so often it seemed she must have been married forever. Yet I couldn't recall ever meeting one of her husbands, they had all died before I was old enough to remember them. Which would mean that, when I was ten, Aunt Marigold certainly wasn't married to anyone.

'What difference would that make?' I asked. 'We're not talking about the Sixties and Cathy Come Home. Aunt Marigold wouldn't have given a fig for what anyone thought. She always wanted a child of her own, there's no way in hell she would have given Jenny away if she was her daughter.'

'Mark, you remember Aunt Marigold as a strong willed woman, but if she was seriously ill, well ... Children always think of adults as, I don't know, unbreakable. Eternal. Maybe there was a reason she wanted mum and dad to look after Jenny. Maybe she only got stronger, later, because of it. Maybe she went on about wanting a child to make sure no-one would suspect Jenny was hers.'

'A reason. Such as what?'

She looked at me for a few moments before answering.

'Maybe dad was Jenny's father?'

I don't often gawp but I did then.

'What?'

'Maybe dad and Aunt Marigold ... well, you know.'

I looked at her in stunned silence for a while.

'Impossible,' I finally concluded.

'Why impossible?'

'You're saying dad had an affair with Aunt Marigold.'

'She was your mother's sister, not your father's. Things like that happen. Look, here mum says: "If only we could live in a perfect world. But, as you say, society will always lay the blame of the parents on the child. We will look after her and treat her as our very own daughter – after all, for Danny that is the case. And I don't blame you or him for anything. If only polygamy were legal. But I suppose we're too old and missed the bus on running away and starting our own commune in the depths of the American wilderness. When she's old enough we can tell her who her real mother is, but let's worry about that in future. The important thing now is that you get better." See, she says, after all, for Danny that is the case. Who could Danny be but your father?'

I hadn't got to that bit when I had started reading it a few months before. I held out my hand. She handed it over and I read through it slowly. After a second reading I concluded that it was as logical as much as it was completely impossible.

'Maddy,' I said, 'they were probably discussing a play they were writing, or a musical they were thinking of, or something they'd seen on television. They did at one stage, you know.'

She didn't say anything in a way that spoke volumes.

'Maddy, imagine if I had an affair with your sister, and she got pregnant and had my daughter. Would you forgive me? Or her?'

She stopped to think.

'I'd forgive her, help her look after the baby, and kill you,' she concluded finally.

'Exactly.'

'But mum's different. She's much more forgiving than I am.'

Now that is certainly true. Then again, so are Ghengis Khan and Vlad The Impaler put together.

'Presuming, just presuming, this is true, how do you plan to prove it?' I asked.

'Why would I want to prove it? It's their business, not ours. Every generation has its own secrets.'

So, having come up with a theory that was likely to give me sleepless nights she promptly dropped it. She held out her hand and I returned the letter. She put it back in the cabinet.

'Mum and dad can go through these when they come down for Christmas,' she said. 'As far as we're concerned we've never seen them.'

Danny, I don't think there is any behaviour your mother will not happily believe men capable of. I know that from painful experience. But she's still bloody wrong.

This tube has finally dragged its sorry arse into Hounslow Central.

11h58.

Almost there. I can even smell the aviation fuel seeping from the skies.

The driver's making an announcement.

I do not believe it.

I do not fucking believe it.

This train terminates here. It's going to be reversed towards central London.

Fuck.

Fuck.

Fuck.

Oh dear Jesus what do I do now?

# Hounslow Central

*Estimated time to Heathrow Terminal Five: 16 minutes*

*Estimated time to Hounslow West tube station: 3 minutes*

12h00.

Hounslow Central is on one of those elevated sections of the Underground, above the trees and houses. I'm sitting on the platform and can see the country for miles around. If you're not careful the phrase 'on top of the earth' comes to mind, and the next thing you know you can't get that Carpenters' song out of your mind, "and the only explanation I can find/ is the love that I've found ever since you've been around", and you spend the rest of the day going around like a grinning idiot.

The problem with me being, of course, that I was in love, totally and completely, and would happily have swapped places with the village idiot to stay so.

There's a Zen thing where you never aim at your target but just achieve your aim indirectly. So let me, my dear Danny, for a few moments, pretend that I am not fucking desperate to get to Terminal 5 and YBM.

Let me return to the story about the pumpkin.

Maddy's birthday was on the Sunday, and Saturday evening was going to be her birthday dinner and pumpkin surprise. And if I ever call you pumpkin, sweetie pie, it's because I want to eat you.

So, YBM's birthday is approaching and I have six tins of pumpkin. I scour the Internet for recipes, and in the end I whittle it down to pumpkin fritters, highly recommended by Mr Chandras, but only via his wife's special recipe, or cheesecake, highly recommended by a few people on the Internet who I've never met, but is apparently very easy to make, and, having made an edible cheesecake once before, I'm more than ready to believe them. There's also pumpkin pie which sounds like something American housewives do as a matter of form without breaking sweat, every Thanksgiving, every year, and everybody loves it, and I'm not stupid enough to think I'm going to suddenly turn out to be an American housewife in disguise.

Alternatively there's pumpkin soup, but that's the real coward's choice. Boil the shit out of the pumpkin, add cornmeal to stiffen, salt to make edible, pepper to add taste and give it a more pleasant appearance, namely that of baby puke with pepper thrown in. Bung some cream in to give it a swirl that would add twenty quid in a restaurant. Ultimately it's irrelevant. As Mrs Chandras said, the pumpkin is the tour de force, the great surprise, it has to come last, either as dessert or cheese and biscuits, and cheese and biscuits does not contain the word pumpkin, therefore dessert it has to be.

But.

This is the first time Maddy and I will be together on her birthday. Special doesn't even begin to describe it.

On the day you were born the angels got together

and the devil was inside there somewhere too

too

too

The only day more special will be the anniversary of when we met, and, believe me, I've got that date ringed for the next hundred years. Two hundred just to be on the safe side.

But.

Do I make dinner myself, including the critical pumpkin part, or do I book a restaurant and insist on a pumpkin finale? Can I insist on a pumpkin finale? I'm not too sure what the rules are on that one. My experience of restaurants is, I walk in, they give me a menu, I say I'll have that, that and that, and that's it.

A new tube driver has turned up to drive the train back to central London. Walking – strolling along as if nothing was the matter, cheerfully asking the pissed off if they're heading for central London when it's obvious they're desperate to get to Heathrow. Gets in the driver's cab, checks everything slowly, twice. Finally fucks off.

Thing is, the next Heathrow train can't get here until he's completely fucked off. Hounslow Central only has two platforms. One for trains going to Heathrow, the other for trains going the other way. Block the one and everyone else has to wait.

I can, however, report that, apart from my desire to throttle every single person working for tfl, it is a lovely, sunny day.

So was Pearl fucking Harbour.

Maddy's birthday.

Do I make it ultra-special by preparing and cooking it with my own fair hands, risking a burnt sacrifice, or do I get a proper chef to make it properly, but demean it by making it something paid for, not much better than grabbing some arbitrary perfume off the shelf without any thought attached?

Well, this is where that old military saying comes in, PPPPPP:

Prior Planning Prevents Piss-Poor Performance.

Or, in simple English, think about what it is you're going to do before you do it.

It was Sean who explained PPPPPP to me, and I believed him, since he'd been taught it in the army where lack of planning tends to end up getting you killed.

So first of all I find all the recipes for pumpkin fritters I can and identify the common elements. Then I go to the Chandras' shop, wait until Mr Chandra is definitely out of the way, buy something, and casually ask Mrs C what her secret is. And she names all these herbs and spices which I write down carefully, what type of flour to use, and finally she leans over and whispers, 'But not too much water be sure of that not too much water make it just right.'

Then I go home, open the first can, and practice, using half. Two hours later I have something representing a blob of wet, baked pumpkin porridge with added spices. But I have worked out that one and a half cans should be about right for the two of us.

The following day I repeat the process with the other half. Two hours later I have something not unlike a fritter tasting of pumpkin and the texture of sawdust. Not as spicy. Dust with Demerara sugar. Have a taste. Throw away. Not even the local feral cats would touch it. They'd probably jump on it and kill it out of a sense of self-defence.

Oh, look, a train has just pulled in. Even better, it's a Terminal 5 train. Not the one that goes to Terminals 123 and Four and confuses the merry shit out of everyone, but a genuine Terminal 5 train.

Most of the survivors have buggered off to find a taxi, bus, or walk.

More fool them, I'm getting on this train. Still just time to make it.

Cockfosters
Oakwood
Southgate
Arnos Grove
Bounds Green
Wood Green
Turnpike Lane
Manor House
Finsbury Park
Arsenal
Holloway Road
Caledonian Road
King's Cross St. Pancras
Russell Square
Holborn
Covent Garden
Leicester Square
Piccadilly Circus
Green Park
Hyde Park Corner
Knightsbridge
South Kensington
Gloucester Road
Earl's Court
Barons Court
Hammersmith
Turnham Green
Acton Town

Ealing Common       South Ealing
North Ealing        Northfields
Park Royal          Boston Manor
Alperton            Osterley
Sudbury Town        Hounslow East
Sudbury Hill        Hounslow Central
South Harrow        Hounslow West
Rayners Lane        Hatton Cross ←
Eastcote            Heathrow T 1-2-3 ⟶ Heathrow T4
Ruislip Manor       Heathrow T5
Ruislip
Ickenham
Hillingdon
Uxbridge

# Leaving Hounslow Central

*Estimated time to Heathrow Terminal Five: 16 minutes*

*Estimated time to Hounslow West tube station: 3 minutes*

Right, here I am, seat, space, I can continue.

12h07.

T5 in 13 minutes. Be there by 12h20.

Keep breathing

Where was I?

YBM's birthday. It was going to be on a Sunday. I wanted her special dinner to be on the Saturday evening before so that we could enjoy the Sunday doing nothing much.

I've tried making pumpkin fritters and proved conclusively that I was going to need a lot more practice and time that I didn't have to get them just about acceptable.

So the following day I phone a local restaurant to enquire about booking a table. Turns out the waiting time is six months. But she takes my number in the unprecedented chance there's a late cancellation.

Six fucking months? Who the fuck books a restaurant table six fucking months in advance? They're fucking lucky if I wander in off the street a minute before, no booking required. I'll bet the French don't do that sort of nonsense. In Britain they bend over for vegetarians, vegans, that sort. The French just curl their lips and say, 'Zis is ze menu, you don't like, you fuck. Off.'

I point out that that pretty much takes it up to Christmas, and she says, oh, yes, thank for reminding me, that means we're actually booked up for seven months.

Seven fucking months? You have to be joking.

But.

PPPPPP.

They might not be willing to let me book a table in a couple of weeks' time, but they can supply that most precious of things, knowledge. So I ask them if they do pumpkin desserts.

There's a silence as if I had said something particularly rude or personal. And they ask me to hold while they get the head chef on duty.

So the head chef finally gets there and asks me what I want, much in the tone of voice that says 'Why are you wasting my time? I'll be polite, but only because I don't know you, and you might be rich. If you aren't I'm going to punch you in the nose. And if I really don't like you I'll shove a cucumber down your earhole.'

So I ask him, does he do, or does the restaurant do, pumpkin desserts? And there's another pause, once again like I've broken some or other omerta.

'Pumpkin desserts?' he asks.

'Yes, pumpkin desserts.'

There's another silence, and then:

'Why?'

So I explain that I've fallen in love with this Australian, the one thing she craves from her homeland, or somewhere, is pumpkin. It's her birthday coming up, I'm determined to surprise here with pumpkin something or other, it has to be dessert otherwise it won't work. Then I explain about the fritters, and how I've been experimenting, describe the results, but say I think I could get it right in a couple of years but don't have the time right now.

Adding that, as there was a six month wait, sorry seven month wait, it was purely academic, but I'd be interested in his professional feelings about such things, so I'd know what to expect when I did find a restaurant that didn't have over half a year advance booking period.

The first thing he says, once he'd finished having a good laugh at my description of my efforts, is to point out that any restaurant that doesn't have a long waiting list isn't worth eating in, and by the sounds of it I'd be better off cooking at home rather than paying good money to eat badly cooked food when I was obviously capable of bad cooking myself. Besides which, they don't ever do pumpkin, not unless it's Halloween or something, and even then the English palate doesn't like it. But good luck with the home cooking, anyway.

So I say thank-you very much, and start calling the other restaurants on my list. And the shorter the waiting time the curter the response is.

'We have a set menu, and we don't do pumpkin.'

Actually that was the polite response. Most of them just put the phone down on me, as if I were some sort of a weirdo. For fuck's sake, of course I'm some sort of a weirdo, I'm in love.

Okay, for me that was weird.

I even considered calling the local McDonalds and Burger King, but I had a horrible feeling they might say yes. With all the good will in the world, there was no fucking way my Maddy was going to celebrate her first birthday with me in a fast food outlet.

Which proved how agonisingly middle class I had become. I remember my folks reminiscing about how they had celebrated successes by going for a sit-down meal in the local chippy.

I called the local chippy but the Chinese bloke running it didn't know what I was talking about.

A few days later Maddy announced that she had a matinee on the Saturday afternoon before her birthday, which was a bit of a pisser because she wasn't likely to fancy a night out afterwards, not with the amount of energy and concentration she puts into her performances. So I gave up on that idea and began planning a simple night in. Something like pea soup to start off with, from a tin unfortunately, but it's full bodied and there's no way I'm going to start making pea soup from fresh at this stage of the game.

Or I could get some of that freshly made stuff from the supermarket, Covent Garden or whatever it's called. Maybe really splash out and buy something from Waitrose, the essential collection: creamy Coriander and baby artichoke heart tenderly killed by strangulation with newly washed virgin hands or something.

The main: fillet steak, roast potatoes, carrots, that sort of thing. Maybe make barrel potatoes, i.e. roast potatoes cut to look like barrels just to prove you're an arsehole who likes wasting your time. And potatoes.

Dessert. Well, there wasn't much time left, but I wasn't going to give up just yet. At the same time, PPPPP: I'd have a Black Forest gateau sitting in the fridge, fresh from the baker's, with ice-cream in the freezer, and a large dustbin outside for the remnants of the pumpkin whatevers if they failed, which I was confident they would.

I really did not want to hear those words, 'Darling, at least you tried,' but they were vastly preferable to 'That was quite nice' which translates as 'Didn't put any thought into it, did you, tosser?'

Then a few days before I get a call from the first restaurant, and this young girl's voice tells me there'd been a sudden cancellation for the Saturday in question and we could have the table if we still wanted it. So I think for a couple of seconds, sigh, admit defeat, and say, yes, that would be great, I'll take it. It might not involve the pumpkin surprise I'd planned, I'd have to think of doing that some other time. But the way things were going the pumpkin surprise was likely to end up in the same category as the Russians invading Poland, yes, a surprise, but not one you'd like to experience. And we'd have a decent meal without any rushing around or burnt bits.

Then this young girl's voice says, 'I hear you were asking about pumpkin desserts.'

'I was, yes,' I say, 'but I hear you don't do them.'

There was a bit of a snort, and then she said:

'I'm head chef on Saturday so I decide what we bloody do or don't do.'

Well, that took me a couple of seconds to process. I thought I'd been talking to some young receptionist or other, it never struck me that she might be the head chef, or that a head chef would waste their time phoning up someone to find out if they were still interested in booking a table. But, of course it wasn't the table she was interested in, it was the pumpkin.

'I'm a Kiwi,' she said, 'I grew up watching my mom and gran making pumpkin, all kinds. Squashes. For me it's the flavour of home. I've worked in different parts of the world. It's only here in Pommy land you guys have a problem with the stuff. I hear you tried some and screwed up. How were you making it?'

So I explained how I had tried making it, and the dire results. Unlike the other head chef she didn't even sound like laughing.

'Yeah,' she said when I had finished, 'sounds like a bit of a mare. You were trying to make different recipes at the same time. One sounds like a Punjabi dish, thing is that's a really spicy dish, it's definitely not what I'd call a dessert. And between the two of us, you want to be careful what you call a dessert over here. Most Pommies say dessert when they mean pudding.'

Now there was a distinction I could admire.

Then she says, 'I hear you're in love, that's what's behind it.'

So I go through the story again, and this time she laughs.

'Tried love once, gave me indigestion,' she says. 'Only time I ever had it. Indigestion, I mean. Love, too, come to think about it. Okay, listen up now, we have a number of options. There's the traditional American pumpkin pie, normally with cream or ice-cream. Some Australians and Kiwis make something similar, but better. But there's something I reckon is much better. It's called pumpkin cookies, it's a South African recipe.'

'Pumpkin cookies?' I asked.

'No,' she said, 'pumpoen cookies. With a k. And the u is pronounced like an a. It's Afrikaans, I wouldn't try pronouncing it if I were you, you'll pull a muscle. Took me about six months to get it right when I was over there. They're basically fritters, usually served with a caramel sauce. How does that sound?'

'It sounds perfect,' I drooled, 'absolutely brilliant. It's very kind of you.'

She snorted again.

'It's what I do,' she said, 'I'm a head chef. And I reckon I'm good at it.'

Well, you can't say fairer than that, can you?

And so it went. I announced to Maddy that we'd be going for dinner on the Saturday evening for her birthday. I could see she wasn't overly chuffed at the idea, but I pointed out that Sunday was her birthday, we'd go for a quiet meal to celebrate on the Saturday evening, and the Sunday we'd have a relaxing day, start off with a full English breakfast, maybe go for a stroll at Oakwood or Cockfosters, have lunch at a pub somewhere. She reluctantly accepted that.

Saturday evening she got back from the matinee exhausted as I expected. We went to the restaurant for a quiet dinner where she revived over soup and the main meal. And a couple of glasses of red wine didn't do any damage. The service was very polite but carefully anonymous, and the grub was good. Then, suitably watered and rested, she perks up and starts looking forward to dessert, wondering when they're going to bring the pudding menu, which is when I tell her I've already ordered dessert, it's a surprise, thinking to myself that I hoped to fuck the head chef knew what she was doing, because Maddy wasn't looking very happy at the idea that she wasn't going to be allowed to drool over the dessert menu for half an hour before choosing.

And up came two waitresses with dessert, pumpkin fritters, or pampoon kookies, however they pronounce it, ice-cream and caramel sauce. And Maddy is ever so chuffed, not so much because it's her favourite and tastes absolutely gorgeous – that's her opinion, who am I to disagree? – but that I remembered.

It's that listening thing again.

And it tasted fucking gorgeous too.

So, we enjoy our desserts, and then I bring out a little present I'd bought for her, saying I was going to give it to her on her actual birthday but now was a good a time as any. And she's even more chuffed and excited, wondering what it could be as she rips the wrapping into oblivion.

Well, it was a little necklace and pendant to hold a photograph. Not original. Not expensive. But perfect for Maddy. And she kisses me and is all teary eyed and tells me she loves me. And then the head chef and a couple of waitresses come up with champagne to ask us how we enjoyed the meal, to toast Maddy's birthday, and then to actually sing happy birthday to her.

Me, I would have been crawling under the table in embarrassment. Maddy loves it. She's wide-eyed and obviously thoroughly enjoying herself, and they can see it so they love her a little more and she loves them a little more and I'm determined to keep down the lovely dinner I've just had and enjoyed and paid for.

The head chef was a bit of a surprise. I'd been expecting some huge Kiwi lass built out of a brick mountain, but she seemed perfectly normal, apart from being a Kiwi and having a 'don't mess with me' look in her eye.

Actually, it might have got lost in translation, but I read it as 'Don't fucking think about it sunshine.'

Nice girl.

Afterwards Maddy and I wander home in the clear night sky, hand in hand, Maddy fingering the necklace around her neck as if it were her most important possession.

And the following day we went for a long walk in the sunshine, holding hands, not saying much. Your mother still fingering the necklace.

Actually Danny, thinking about it, that Saturday night was probably the night you were conceived.

Going back into a tunnel now.

Hounslow West.

Last stretch, the run up to Heathrow. Hounslow West, Hatton Cross, Heathrow 1 2 3 and then Terminal 5. Three stations.

12h16.

We'll make it by 12h30.

We're going to make it, Danny.

I'm coming for you and YBM, I promise.

Cockfosters
Oakwood
Southgate
Arnos Grove
Bounds Green
Wood Green
Turnpike Lane
Manor House
Finsbury Park
Arsenal
Holloway Road
Caledonian Road
King's Cross St. Pancras
Russell Square
Holborn
Covent Garden
Leicester Square
Piccadilly Circus
Green Park
Hyde Park Corner
Knightsbridge
South Kensington
Gloucester Road
Earl's Court
Barons Court
Hammersmith
Turnham Green
Acton Town

Ealing Common          South Ealing
North Ealing           Northfields
Park Royal             Boston Manor
Alperton               Osterley
Sudbury Town           Hounslow East
Sudbury Hill           Hounslow Central
South Harrow           Hounslow West
Rayners Lane           Hatton Cross  ←
Eastcote               Heathrow T 1-2-3  ⟶  Heathrow T4
Ruislip Manor          Heathrow T5
Ruislip
Ickenham
Hillingdon
Uxbridge

## Hounslow West

12h16.

Deep dark underground again. There is an upside to that. All the mobile phone users are going to lose their signal very shortly. Some of them already have. Their faces are quite hilarious. They look like spoilt children who have just had their sweeties taken out of their grubby little hands.

Here we go, off again, and, yes, they've all lost their signals. Poor little ducklings.

Your bloody mother once told me, 'Mark, your problem is you don't have empathy.'

To which I replied: 'I have loads of empathy. I have empathy coming out of my fucking ears.'

Pausing before adding:

'It's fucking sympathy I've run out of.'

Hounslow West used to be more famous as Hounslow Heath. I know this courtesy of Shell, my union rep. We were in the staff room talking some shite or other – or discussing important matters of the day, whichever description you prefer. Someone, Sean, possibly – he'd come out of his shell with the progress of Cabaret – was winding up Michelle about her feminist stuff, probably about the role of women in the army, and she came up with Mary Frith, who, once again, was either the very image of a free and independent woman, or completely barking mad.

The Heath was apparently used by royalty for hunting – where have we seen that before – and also used by the military for camping on while threatening the citizens of London. But it was most popular as the haunt of highwaymen, footpads and generally the sort of person who prefers to dance in the dark to avoid being strung up in the light. They were also popular with the majority of Londoners who weren't at risk of being robbed as they didn't have anything worth stealing, but did enjoy a good yarn at the expense of the high-falutin. So you had stories of Gentleman

Highwaymen dancing with ladies they were robbing, or gallantly kissing their hands at the same time as removing their rings. The official record shows that they all ended up swinging from the gallows despite their gallantry, so history was written by the victors after all.

Mary Frith became a legend as a highway woman, though how much was true and how much invention is debatable. The legend goes that she was a Royalist, and became a highway woman during the Civil War, holding up General Thomas Fairfax on Hounslow Heath before shooting him in the arm and killing a couple of horses to discourage pursuit. It didn't work, as she was captured at Turnham Green, sent to Newgate, tried and sentenced to death, but got out of it by paying a bribe before a spell in Bethlehem Hospital where she was apparently cured of insanity. Whatever the truth of that, she was obviously an exceptional woman. She was certainly involved in criminality as defined by the authorities, though sometimes it took the form of negotiating a fee for the return of stolen property, saving the courts and what passed as police in those days quite some time. I think she had a play or two written about her. It appears that her biggest crime was in wearing men's breeches. Shell was most taken by the story.

These days the heath is covered almost entirely by urban sprawl housing Heathrow workers and families. Maybe every so often whatever's on their televisions is interrupted by the sound of ghostly hoof-beats as Mary Frith or her fellow highway people relive their earthly pursuits.

Speaking of pursuits, it's now 12h17.

12h17.

Right.

It was the following Saturday the police called again, the same ones that came around after Jenny died, a man and a woman. Maddy was home and we sat on the couch together as the copper asked most of the questions while the woman made notes in a little book.

Danny, I can't tell you how much I wanted to say to your mother, darling, go count the pigeons, go do your scales, please, for me, don't be with me now, I want to spare you this. Because I had this vague premonition it would have to do with a past I didn't want Maddy to be sullied with.

The first question was:

'Can you remember the last time you encountered Ziggie?'

Actually they didn't call him Ziggie, they used his real name and then had to explain who they meant. And that's when I suddenly realised: CCTV. The shops must have cameras watching the delivery bays at least, if not the entire car park. They weren't looking for information, they knew precisely what had happened. Unless the cameras weren't working. Unlikely.

So I decided to tell it as it happened. As I did I could feel Maddy's hand creep into mine.

I get to the end where I've left Ziggie in the wheelie bin, and the woman closes her notebook and they stand up.

'Thanks for that,' the bloke says, 'that's what we thought had happened. I hope we haven't taken up too much of your time.'

'But –' I start and they pause.

'If you have any questions, feel free to ask,' says the bloke.

'But Ziggie – he was killed in the crusher, wasn't he?'

They look at each other.

'What makes you say that?'

'Mrs Chandra – well, that's what they said at the greengrocer's down the road.'

They sit down again, fascinated.

'What did they say, exactly?'

So I repeated Mrs Chandra's description, including Ziggie's screams as he was crushed. By that stage Maddy is squeezing my hand for dear life and the coppers are almost laughing.

'Amazing what rubbish people will come up with, if you'll excuse the pun,' says the bloke. 'I'm afraid it didn't happen that way. Ziggie was already dead when they found him. He'd been taking some of his own medicine. He was probably dying when you thumped him. He was an addict himself, otherwise he wouldn't have taken the chance, not after he knew others had died. Or perhaps he'd got a new batch and thought it was clean. Or maybe he misread the label. He was completely illiterate, you know. Couldn't read a word.'

'I didn't, no.'

'They checked the wheelie bin before emptying it,' said the woman. 'The people collecting it. If there's anything in it not recyclable they leave it alone, otherwise they can get fined for – what did they call it? Impurities? So if they're recycling cardboard and paper, and some plastic gets into the process they have to throw it all away. So the people who collect it are careful of what they collect, there's no way they'd just empty the wheelie bin straight in. They could lose money.'

'They found Ziggie's body, called an ambulance,' the bloke continues. 'The ambulance people found Ziggie was dead, called us. He was taken away for pathology, and they found the drug in his stomach. They reckon he must have taken it about an hour before he died.'

'So, when I – well, it wasn't – I mean -'

They gave me a couple of pitying little smiles and stood up again.

'If you mean, did you kill him, no, sorry. You could tell your greengrocers what really happened. But I don't think they'll thank you for it. Their version is more ... entertaining, I reckon the word is.'

After they had left Maddy hugged me and hugged me and held me tight.

'You must have been worried sick,' she said. Why did you tell me it was a bicycle accident? Why didn't you tell me the truth? Were you trying to protect me? Trying not to make me worry?'

'It's true that I didn't want you to be worried,' I said. 'But I wasn't worried myself. I completely forgot about the CCTV. I never expected the police to come calling.'

I smiled, bent down and kissed her.

'Just call me an idiot I said.'

She smiled back.

'Okay, idiot,' she said.

Oh, fucking excellent. We're pulling into Hatton Cross and the driver's announced that this train will be reversing due to late running.

12h20.

Three fucking stops.

Three fucking stops and you have to reverse the service due to late running?
I don't have the energy anymore.
I can't even be arsed to swear.
I think I've just run out of time.
Three
fucking
stops.

# Hatton Cross

12h22

I'm now sitting on Hatton Cross platform number something, wondering whether to catch a bus to Terminal Five or not. We've been strongly advised to use "other methods of transport", but I think that might translate as "please go have your problems somewhere else, we've got enough of our own".

On the other hand they might just be terminating trains here and leaving it to the local bus services to pick up the remnants. If that's the case I'd better get moving.

On the other other hand, if there's going to be a tube to T5 in the next five minutes it would be better to stay.

I'll give it a few minutes.

I'm not saying that tfl staff don't do their best. But if I'm confronted by someone rather upset who demands, 'Which, please, fucking bus, please, Heathrow, please?' I tend to point to the first one going in the direction of away and say 'Hurry.' I'd be doing it to get rid of them, not help them on their way.

Half of the other passengers have taken the advice and left to catch a bus or a taxi or a something. Rickshaw, perhaps. Good luck in finding any of those.

Shanks pony. Good when you know where you're going. Or, to be more accurate, good when you know how to get to where you're going.

It was about a fortnight ago that YBM announced that she was off to Cardiff for a few weeks. She heard the news of a singing part on the Tuesday, she'd be leaving the following Sunday. It was one of those things I had successfully managed to avoid thinking about: if she was going to have a successful career in musicals and the like, she would be on the road or otherwise away for quite long periods. I dare say some couples have managed to maintain a relationship like that, but I'm pretty sure it's wrecked more than have survived. Actors and actresses are famous for getting married and divorced and married and divorced and so on. Richard Burton and Elisabeth Taylor made a full-time hobby of it.

The saying, "distance makes the heart grow fonder" has lost the extra bit which helps it make sense, i.e. "of someone closer by". The thought of losing Maddy to someone better looking, younger, richer and more successful than me was painful, to say the least.

Though the probability would be that he'd really be older, richer and more suave than I am, but that wasn't exactly helpful either.

Yeats' An Irish Airman Foresees His Death was published along with the main poem of the book, The Wild Swans at Coole. It ends with Yeats wondering who the swans will

'delight men's eyes

when I awake some day

to find they have flown away?'

It doesn't bear thinking about it, it really doesn't. Life without Maddy would be meaningless.

Ironically that weekend was one of the happiest we had, amongst all the other happy ones. Mum and dad had come down from Liverpool for a few hours with four tickets for a Liverpool-Arsenal game at the Emirates. It was a completely transparent excuse to see Maddy, and we all thoroughly enjoyed ourselves. If I get a chance I'll tell you about that day. Suffice to say for the moment that in late afternoon we stood on a platform at Euston waving goodbye to the folks, extremely tired and happy, completely oblivious to what was waiting for us around the corner. On the Sunday I went with Maddy to Paddington to see her off on her trip to Cardiff. We stood on the platform holding each other like the desperate star-crossed lovers we were.

'Promise me you'll call me at least once a day,' I said.

'And why do I have to call you? Why can't you call me?'

'Because if I interrupt one of your live performances you'll want to kill me, but if you interrupt one of my classes I won't give a shit.'

She giggled.

'Oh, okay then. But you can text me, can't you?'

'Brat. You know how much I loathe texting and every other form of social media. But since it's you I suppose I shall have to humble and humiliate myself and agree to use the shite. But no naked photographs. I have to draw the line somewhere. I have to retain some dignity.'

She paused and looked at me with a serious face.

'You've never asked me for a photograph of me without clothes on. Why not?'

I looked back at her.

'Maddy, why on earth would I want a photograph of you without any clothes on?'

'I thought all men did. Not of me, before you sarcasm me, of their girlfriend, or wife, or whatever. And the girlfriend or wife or whatever gave them a photograph to remind them of what they were missing if they were apart.'

'Maddy, I don't need a photograph to remind me of what I'm missing, my heart is already breaking just at the thought of you leaving. Actually, that happens even when you leave the room.'

'Oh, Mark, you are a sweetie.'

'Anyway, if I kept a photograph of you in your birthday suit I'd be permanently worried about losing it and some old lech finding it. It would be on the Internet and going round the world in seconds.'

She smiled.

'What about a photograph of me with my clothes on?' she asked.

I disentangled her arms, took my wallet out, and extracted a print of her from King's Cross.

'Already taken care of, Brat,' I said, showing her it. She smiled again, took out her mobile phone, and pulled a picture from inside the cover.

'Snap,' she said, showing me a shot of me when we were at King's Cross. She giggled. 'I would have put it in my locket but your head is too big.'

Then we put our respective pictures away and hugged some more.

'You know what I think, Brat?' I asked, checking the time.

'What, Romeo?'

'I think, the next chance we get, we get into one of those photo booths and have some shots of both of us taken, for mum and dad. There isn't enough time now,' I added quickly, knowing she would want to skip away immediately to do so, and almost definitely end up missing her train, 'but next time. When you get back. We could even go away somewhere just to have an excuse to be on a station platform and do so.'

'Ooh, let's,' she said. 'Mum and dad will love that.'

12h30.

Would you Adam and Eve it, I do believe there's a train pulling in.

And it's a Terminal 5 train.

Well fuck me sideways with a corncob ukulele.

12h30.

One hour.

Just enough time.

Cockfosters
Oakwood
Southgate
Arnos Grove
Bounds Green
Wood Green
Turnpike Lane
Manor House
Finsbury Park
Arsenal
Holloway Road
Caledonian Road
King's Cross St. Pancras
Russell Square
Holborn
Covent Garden
Leicester Square
Piccadilly Circus
Green Park
Hyde Park Corner
Knightsbridge
South Kensington
Gloucester Road
Earl's Court
Barons Court
Hammersmith
Turnham Green
Acton Town

Ealing Common          South Ealing
North Ealing           Northfields
Park Royal             Boston Manor
Alperton               Osterley
Sudbury Town           Hounslow East
Sudbury Hill           Hounslow Central
South Harrow           Hounslow West
Rayners Lane           Hatton Cross  ←
Eastcote               Heathrow T 1-2-3  ——→  Heathrow T4
Ruislip Manor          Heathrow T5
Ruislip
Ickenham
Hillingdon
Uxbridge

# Leaving Hatton Cross

*Estimated time to Heathrow Terminal Five: 8 minutes*

*Estimated time to Heathrow Terminals 1-2-3: 4 minutes*

12h31.

Wonders will never cease. A Terminal Five train. Straight there. Instead of going to terminal 4, that is. Because when they built T5 they decided to keep the existing line through terminals 1, 2 and 3 to terminal 4 and then back to terminal 1, 2 and 3 and Hatton Cross, but create a new spur which would go through terminals 1, 2 and 3 and on to T5.

I get confused just thinking about it.

And I'm on and it's on its way. Looks like the service has recovered.

So on the Sunday Maddy went up to Cardiff for a couple of weeks, planning to return on the Friday afternoon twelve days from then, and that weekend was going to be reserved for just us. On the Wednesday morning I was packing my stuff together for school, listening to the rain drum down outside, when I heard the front door bell go. When I opened it who should I find standing there, soaked to the skin? Sharon bloody Runny-nose, that's who.

'What the hell are you doing here I asked?'

She held up a limp exercise book as if it were a votive offering to an angry god.

'I just wanted to drop it off cause I wasn't in yesterday,' she sniffed miserably.

I sighed. If only it hadn't been raining I could have sent her off with a clip around the ear, if only a metaphorical one.

'Come on in,' I said and lead her down the passage, indicating the bathroom at the end. 'Get in there and dry yourself off as best as you can. Then I'll take you home to get some dry clothes.'

I went back to packing, briefly wondering whether it would be easier to dry her clothes in the dryer and send her on to school, but decided the sooner she was packed off the better, wet clothes or not. Let her bloody mother look after her.

Which is when Maddy turned up. The French Windows opened and the love of my life stood there, driving, I thought, all the rain away.

'Maddy,' I said, 'I thought you weren't going to be back until next Friday.'

Looking back on it that was not the best way to phrase things.

'So I see,' she said, looking over my shoulder.

I turned around. Runny-nose had come out of the bathroom wearing nothing but a towel.

'For god's sake!' I think I shouted. 'What the bloody hell are you playing at? Get back in there and get dressed you horrible little brat.'

Her mouth quivered and the waterworks started.

'Oh, for crying in a –' I turned around to Maddy hoping she might be able to supply a bit of support, or a female smack around Runny-nose's head and shoulders.

I think she said something like 'You fucking bastard, I knew it,' but what kept all my attention was the monopod she was swinging straight at my head. The next thing I knew was my head had exploded and the world had gone all blurry.

I don't know if I collapsed. I vaguely remember being on my knees holding on to a chair. I dragged myself upright and saw a figure outside the French windows. For a brief second I imagined it was Maddy. I tried to call her, I tried to say 'Maddy', but the words didn't come out. Anyway it wasn't her. She was already gone. Instead it turned into Chris happily taking pictures of me with blood pouring down my shirt and Runny-nose behind me in the altogether. I vaguely registered that she must have dropped the towel.

'Fuck you,' I said to Chris, I think. I turned around and pushed Runny-nose towards the bathroom, giving Chris a chance of snapping a shot of me apparently standing behind a naked girl holding her by the shoulders and about to provide her with more than standard education.

Then I phoned Michelle.

'Shell, it's Mark,' I said. 'I've got blood pouring down my shirt and Sharon Runny-nose is naked in my bathroom. Could you come around, please.'

I had to repeat that a few times, I think I wasn't speaking coherently.

When I finally made myself clear she said, 'I'll be there in ten minutes.'

She was as good as her word. While waiting I tried to clean up the blood. The reason it was pouring down so freely was that the monopod was compressed when Maddy hit me, with the locking studs close together. She had caught me with both the heft of the monopod and the edge of the studs, right on the side of the forehead.

Then Shell arrived, asked me to repeat in brief what had happened, which I did. She then went to the bathroom, knocked on the door and asked Runny-nose if she were there, to which she got a tearful yes. She told Runny-nose in no uncertain terms to get fucking dressed and be out in five minutes and she didn't give a toss how wet her clothes were. And if she weren't out in five minutes Michelle was going to break the door down and come in and get her. And she could spend the next bit of her journey naked.

Then she came back into the kitchen, sat me down, cleaned my head properly, and bandaged it up, saying that she didn't think it would need stitches, but it was going to go a very pretty purple, and I'd probably have a rather bad headache in the short term. She was wrong about that. I already had an extremely painful headache and it was getting worse.

Coming in to Terminals 123.

12h34.

She'll definitely have gone through security by now.

When do they board long haul? Half an hour?

Gives me just enough time.

I'll get them to page her.

Or maybe I'll just run through the terminal shouting.

What will I say when she appears?

'I love you, don't go?'

Jesus.

Just so long as she's still there. I'll figure out the words later.

Cockfosters
Oakwood
Southgate
Arnos Grove
Bounds Green
Wood Green
Turnpike Lane
Manor House
Finsbury Park
Arsenal
Holloway Road
Caledonian Road
King's Cross St. Pancras
Russell Square
Holborn
Covent Garden
Leicester Square
Piccadilly Circus
Green Park
Hyde Park Corner
Knightsbridge
South Kensington
Gloucester Road
Earl's Court
Barons Court
Hammersmith
Turnham Green

Ealing Common          Acton Town
North Ealing           South Ealing
Park Royal             Northfields
Alperton               Boston Manor
Sudbury Town           Osterley
Sudbury Hill           Hounslow East
South Harrow           Hounslow Central
Rayners Lane           Hounslow West
Eastcote               Hatton Cross ←
Ruislip Manor          Heathrow T 1-2-3 ——→ Heathrow T4
Ruislip                Heathrow T5
Ickenham
Hillingdon
Uxbridge

# Heathrow Terminals 1-2-3

*Estimated time to Heathrow Terminal Five: 4 minutes*

12h34

Now we really are smoking. Arrive 12h34, depart 12h34. If only you'd done this earlier, Piccadilly Line.

I shall have just enough time to finish this, Danny. So here goes.

We dropped Sharon Runny-nose off at her parents' place. Her parents had gone out to work but she had a key. Shell told her to go in, get changed and catch the bus to school. Shell then drove me to the school. When we got to there I was informed that the bog wanted to see me immediately. Shell and I went into her secretary's office and waited until we were graciously permitted to enter the main office. The bog took one look at Shell and said,

'This is a private meeting.'

We both sat down.

'Really?' asked Shell, making it quite clear that she wasn't leaving.

The bog shrugged and held up a sheath of glossy A4 pages.

'We've received these anonymously,' she said.

'From that little –' I began. Shell, sitting right next to me, gripped my wrist in a wordless invitation to shut the fuck up. She relaxes by squeezing squash balls. I shut the fuck up. Fortunately it was my right hand. The left would have been agony.

'I'm putting you on suspension until further notice,' the bog said. Shell said she wanted that in writing, plus the reasons why. The bog said she'd send it later. Michelle said we weren't leaving without them. The bog looks at her for a few seconds, then gives in, calls her secretary in to take down a letter. I can't remember the exact wording, something like "you have been suspended on suspicion of fucking one of your female pupils". I remember the female bit. It just seemed somewhat surreal that it needed mentioning, and the idea of it applying to Runny-nose, well, I suppose she is female, just. Thing is, to a teacher a pupil should be a pupil, they have no gender or sex or whatever it's called these days. That's why, when I refer to any of my pupils I use the word "it".

So we waited while the secretary went back to her desk to type it into a word-processor, print two copies on official headed paper, bring them back to the bog to sign, she signs them, puts one in an envelope and hands it over to me, or would have done if I could be arsed to stand up and take it, Shell does that instead. Then we walk out without saying goodbye.

Then Shell takes me to North Middlesex A and E and leaves me there, I get triaged by an unsympathetic nurse who doesn't seem impressed by the wound, tells me to take a seat until I'm called. So I do, and immediately do what I've always scorned at in other people: I take out my mobile phone to check for messages. There aren't any. So, like so many other arseholes I immediately phone someone, in this case Maddy, of course. And of course she doesn't answer. So I give that up for five minutes and then call her again. Same result. So I give it ten minutes. Same result. In the end I settle for half-hourly attempts. With the same result. Nothing.

I think it took them about six hours to get around to treating me, which, considering the earliness of the hour was surprising, especially on a weekday. Turned out to be the same doctor who treated my wrist.

'Let me guess,' she said, 'this time you decided to hit your head against a brick wall.'

'No,' I replied, 'this time my girlfriend decided to belt me with a monopod.'

'A monopod? Keen photographer, is she?' she asked, unwinding the bandages.

'Not so as you'd notice. I think it was handy, close by, and the nearest thing to an iron bar she could find in the split second she decided to try to kill me.'

'And what did you do to deserve that?' She looked closely at my head. 'Bloody good shot. She got you with the studs. Last time I saw that sort of thing was on a rugby player's head. I would say someone stood on his head in a loose maul, but that would suggest an accident. It was more like someone scraped their boot across his head several times. It was almost artistic.'

'I didn't do anything to deserve it. She found me with one of my pupils who was just wearing a towel. That is, until she dropped it. Then she was naked. Maddy – the girlfriend – didn't give me a chance to explain.'

'You were having an affair with this pupil? You're going to need a few stitches, just to be on the safe side. Don't go anywhere.'

'No I fucking wasn't,' I called after he as she disappeared off to get the stitching gear.

'Wasn't fucking, or fucking wasn't?' came the response.

I lay back and thought of sweet Jesus.

'So how did this girl – I presume it was a girl – end up naked in your kitchen?' she asked when she returned. 'Hold still, I'm just going to numb your forehead a bit. Clinically rather than with an iron bar.'

'She turned up at the front door soaking wet, claimed she was delivering some home-work she should have handed in the day before. I told her to go into the bathroom to dry off. I forgot to specifically tell her not to take her clothes off.'

'Sounds like she planned it all. Right, that's it, five stitches, should be plenty. I'll just put on a clean dressing and bandage. I'd wear a hat for the next few days if I were you. Keep it out of the nasty London air. But even if she planned it I reckon you're going to have a tough time proving it.'

'Thanks for the moral support,' I said.

'Oh, I believe you, I've seen what terrors so-called innocent little girls can be when they want to get their claws into a man. But your problem is what other people will want to believe, or what it benefits them to claim they believe.'

And as that meant the bog, I had no illusions there.

So I caught the 102 back to Muswell Hill, calling Maddy's number only once. With the same result. I could only presume that she saw my number calling and decided to punish me. So the answer was to use a different phone. When I got home I took my old little mobile out. The battery was completely lifeless, so I spent half an hour hunting out the charging cable before plugging it in to charge. Then I began self-medicating with a king size whisky for my king size headache. After a couple of those I fell asleep on the sofa.

I woke up in the early evening, took a shower to clear my head, which was thudding, made a coffee, put a new bandage on, and picked up my old mobile to phone Maddy.

I'd forgotten to switch the fucking charger on.

So I did that, sat down with another whisky and switched the television on for something to keep my eyes occupied while the whisky stopped my brain from doing too much work. Around ten in the evening I ordered a huge pizza, shoved that down my gob, looked at the now charged little phone, told it 'Fuck you', and collapsed onto my bed fully clothed. And woke up really, really early the next morning, which is where I first came in.

12h40.

Coming into T5.

I've made it.

I've finally bloody made it.

Sixty seconds, Danny, I've done it to departures in sixty seconds before, I can do it again.

Wish me luck, Danny.

Wish me fucking luck. I'm going to need it.

# Heathrow Terminal Five

12h42

Fuck.

Fuck.

Fuck.

Australia.

Qantas. It's a Qantas flight.

Qantas leaves from Terminal 3.

How the hell did I get that one wrong?

Why did I presume it was Terminal 5?

You'd think they'd have posters up telling people where flights are leaving from. I'm sure they used to.

Platform six. Platform five is the one I got off five minutes ago. I shot out of the tube and almost ran over a station attendant.

'You're in a hurry, love,' she said in the friendly tone of someone with all the time in the world.

'I am,' I replied, looking at the queue for the ticket barriers in front of me and trying to work out how to bypass them. 'Excuse me.'

'What airline, love?' she asked just as casually.

'Qantas,' I said.

'Wrong station, love. Go to platform six and catch a Cockfosters train going back to London,' she said. 'Get off at T123. That's where Qantas fly from, Terminal 3.'

Oh for fuck's sake, I didn't say.

I think I stared at her in horror for a few minutes until the ghastly truth sank in.

'Platform six?' I finally asked. 'Where's that?'

How could they have a platform six? I could only see two.

'Over there, love,' she said. 'The one you got off is platform five.'

Apparently platforms one to four are hidden out of sight, used by the Heathrow Express or NASA or Santa Claus or something.

So now I'm sitting on the floor next to platform six, keeping an eye on platform five just in case, trying to get this finished and praying that there's a train within the next thirty seconds.

Departure Boards are saying the next train is to Hyde Park. No indication of when it's leaving. Number two train is for Northfields. No indication of when that's leaving either.

When I sat down the platform was empty. Now it's about five deep and growing. Doesn't matter, I'm only going one station.

Maybe I should catch a bus.

Like it'll only take me about two hours to find out which bus to catch, where it leaves from, when the next one is due, how to recognise the right place to get off.

Et bloody cetera.

Taxi. I could take a taxi.

Just like all the other people I've noticed turning up, taking one look, turning around and leaving here. Taxis will be like gold dust.

Danny, Heathrow is a massive place. Huge. Absolutely huge. There are thousands and thousands of people working here, thousands of people flying in and out. You know something? A lot of the people who work here will never meet the people who fly in and out. They might not ever meet thousands of the other thousands who work here each day. And here's the surprising thing about that.

Danny, I ask myself, if it had been the other way around, if your mother had been the teacher at home, and I'd turned up unexpectedly and found her in the kitchen with a seventeen-year old boy wearing nothing but a towel, would I have belted her?

If I'm being really, really honest?

Okay.

I probably would have picked up the first heavy object in sight and crowned the kid. Then I would have strangled your mother.

Okay, maybe not.

I don't know.

Danny, the surprising thing about Heathrow is that it only became an airport toward the end of World War II, and even then I suspect it was still called an airfield. It was supposed to be used by either the RAF or US air force, but the war ended before they could get it operational. It was turned into a civilian airport with a second-hand military tent as a terminal. I know this because I had to wait for someone's delayed flight to land once, and when I'm bored I'll read anything. And sometimes you want to think about anything other than what you are thinking about. Such as when the next train to Terminal 3 is going to turn up.

Thing is, going back to YBM and the monopod and that morning, she had just got back from Cardiff, first thing in the morning, probably got a lift back or something, don't think the trains would have left that early for her to get in, she's probably hoping to get back before I leave for school, surprise me, she's thinking of grabbing me and giving me a kiss, we've been separated for ages, days is ages when you're in love, she walks into the kitchen and finds me with a naked pupil. You can see how she might jump to the wrong conclusion, I suppose.

Now I'm making excuses for her?

I must be nuts.

I'm in love.

Ergo I'm nuts.

I wonder if she knew then she was pregnant.

Departure board now shows the first train is for Cockfosters and leaves in 48 minutes.

The second leaves in 17.

17 what it doesn't say. Days, presumably.

The Wright brothers made the first recognised powered flight in 1903 at Kittyhawk. How long did it take humans to realise aircraft were ideal for killing their fellow man? Well, I haven't read of any being used to bomb some arbitrary natives before World War One – plenty afterward – so I guess they got seriously into the habit about 1915, the second year of the war.

Twelve years, Danny. It took them just twelve years to turn a crude ramshackle device built in a shed using bicycle tools into a lethal killing machine. Yeats' poem An Irish Airman Foresees His Death was written in 1918 and published in 1919 once the war was over, apparently to avoid charges of trying to undermine the war effort.

Then again, give your mother a monopod and she'll turn it into an offensive weapon in much less time.

If she knew then she was pregnant her emotions would have been all over the shop.

Women are like that, Danny.

A train's just arrived on platform five, heaving. I think the passengers getting off might be in a hurry. Most of them are running. One rather overweight gentleman in a suit, dragging a suitcase along, has just elbowed a woman out of the way. Another similar gent was waddling along, but his suitcase got a speed-wobble and turned over, taking him with it. Young Japanese couple racing along, the girl giggling as if it were huge fun. There's another bug-eyed, middle-aged, overweight suit-wearer trying to run with his suitcase clasped to his chest. Or maybe his paunch. Weird people.

If she knew she was pregnant she would have spent the whole journey from Cardiff wondering how she was going to break it to me.

I have the luxury of being able to sit here on the floor making these notes for the moment. As soon as the first train appears it's going to be elbow time to get on. I'm not taking any prisoners. And then once it gets to Terminal 123 I'm going to be first off no matter anyone else's preference in the matter. And then I'll be running like fuck for Terminal 3 departures, just like the bunch currently doing the fatty Olympics here now.

Maybe running up the steps at Covent Garden was some sort of practice.

Pace yourself.

Don't let yourself get winded by the bag you're carrying flapping around.

Don't shout unnecessarily.

The look on your scarred face should tell anyone in the way all they need to know.

The train on platform five is pulling out.

Bloke has just announced that it will be our next train back towards central London.

It will be here in six minutes.

Okay, Danny, I'm signing off for the moment. I'm going to find a place right at the end of the platform where the crowd is thinnest.

And hopefully it will be closest to the exit at Terminals one, two and three.

Cockfosters
Oakwood
Southgate
Arnos Grove
Bounds Green
Wood Green
Turnpike Lane
Manor House
Finsbury Park
Arsenal
Holloway Road
Caledonian Road
King's Cross St. Pancras
Russell Square
Holborn
Covent Garden
Leicester Square
Piccadilly Circus
Green Park
Hyde Park Corner
Knightsbridge
South Kensington
Gloucester Road
Earl's Court
Barons Court
Hammersmith
Turnham Green

Ealing Common          Acton Town
North Ealing           South Ealing
Park Royal             Northfields
Alperton               Boston Manor
Sudbury Town           Osterley
Sudbury Hill           Hounslow East
South Harrow           Hounslow Central
Rayners Lane           Hounslow West
Eastcote               Hatton Cross
Ruislip Manor          Heathrow T 1-2-3 ⟶ Heathrow T4
Ruislip                Heathrow T5
Ickenham
Hillingdon
Uxbridge

# Leaving Terminal Five

*Estimated time to Underground station Heathrow Terminal 123: 4 minutes*

13h15.

Hallelujah. Am now in a tube bound for central London. It's just leaving T5. I got on the minute it arrived. The platform announcer announced, "This train is ready to depart." And fuck me if the driver didn't get out his cab and go to the loo. I wanted to scream, "Where the fuck are you going", but I couldn't believe my eyes. But at least he made it back in a couple of minutes.

They aren't guaranteeing it will get to central London, it's current destination is Northfields, but personally I don't give a fuck about that. I'm only going as far as Terminals 123, or to be more precise, Terminal 3. So just a few minutes more. The good bit about Terminal 5 being the start of the Line is that, even though the platform was packed to the rafters, you can usually get on. Later down the Line, well, no chance. To be honest, I don't really fucking care. Just get me to Terminal Three on time.

At the moment I'm writing this on top of someone's huge suitcase. They're too polite or scared to object. I haven't told them that they either get the suitcase out of the way when we get to T3 or it gets thrown out of the way, onto the platform if that's easiest.

So, Danny, what the future will hold? Hopefully YBM will still be there when I get there, hopefully I will be able to talk her out of her madness, hopefully you'll grow up with me looking after you. Hopefully I'll get to see her walk down the aisle to me.

Up the aisle?

Up or down, who cares, so long as it's toward me and she says yes.

In Liverpool Cathedral.

Paddy's Wigwam.

It has to be.

By the time you read this you'll be all grown up, and will know the answer.

301

I still don't know what magic phrase I'm going to use.

Danny, whatever happens, remember: you'll never walk alone.

I'll have to wrap this up now and put it away. T123 can't be far away.

The pipes, the pipes are calling.

Oh, Danny, I love your mother so.

Author's note

This story was based on notes in a school exercise book found at Heathrow tube station Terminals 123 where the teacher Mark presumably dropped them.

All attempts to identify the teacher have so far proved unsuccessful.

Until now.

# Maddening:

# the Home Run

Based on notes supplied by a teacher in Muswell Hill, North London

# London Underground: Piccadilly Line

**Towards Cockfosters**

Cockfosters
Oakwood
Southgate
Arnos Grove
Bounds Green
Wood Green
Turnpike Lane
Manor House
Finsbury Park
Arsenal
Holloway Road
Caledonian Road
King's Cross St. Pancras
Russell Square
Holborn
Covent Garden
Leicester Square
Piccadilly Circus
Green Park
Hyde Park Corner
Knightsbridge
South Kensington
Gloucester Road
Earl's Court
Barons Court
Hammersmith
Turnham Green
Acton Town

Ealing Common
North Ealing
Park Royal
Alperton
Sudbury Town
Sudbury Hill
South Harrow
Rayners Lane
Eastcote
Ruislip Manor
Ruislip
Ickenham
Hillingdon
Uxbridge

South Ealing
Northfields
Boston Manor
Osterley
Hounslow East
Hounslow Central
Hounslow West
Hatton Cross ←
Heathrow T 1-2-3 ⟶ Heathrow T4
Heathrow T5

# Heathrow Terminals 1-2-3 Tube Station

*Estimated time to Hatton Cross tube station 2 minutes*

*Estimated time to Bounds Green tube station 1 hour 15 minutes*

15h00

Three o'clock, p.m. Post matin. In the afternoon.

Danny, I have a little secret to tell you.

Just between the two of us.

Me and you.

It's about your mother and I, and you before you were born. In fact, at the time I'm writing this, I expect you will be born in about six months.

You are going to be a lovely baby.

Trust me, I know.

What I don't know is when, if ever, you will get to read these notes. For what they are worth it's a true account of what happened between myself and your mum. No matter what your mother might have told you to the contrary.

But first I must put things into context.

I'm in a London Underground tube.

It's on the Piccadilly Line. It has just left Terminals One, Two and Three. Heathrow Terminals One Two and Three, that is. Or T123, as they call it. Heathrow Central as others call it.

The train is en route to Cockfosters allegedly. Slowly.

Very, very slowly. The Piccadilly Line is having what they describe as "minor delays due to an earlier incident". This translates as, "If you think this is bad, you should have been here earlier. Nothing was moving then."

I know, I was there when it didn't happen.

Cockfosters is at the other end of the Piccadilly Line, about a hundred thousand miles away as the flow cries. Well, at the speed this thing is going it might as well be.

Context.

That's the thing, context.

Danny, there comes a time when it's all over for the day. You've pretty much done all you're going to do, you've pretty much done all you can do, and it doesn't matter what you might think of doing next, it won't make any difference whatsoever.

Not a fucking bit.

You'll have to excuse my swearing.

I do.

Anyway.

Maybe you've won, maybe you've not won, maybe you've lost, maybe it's even stevens. What's happened has happened and that's all that's going to happen for today.

If you really wanted to be positive, to look on the bright side of life, to keep a happy hope in your heart, you could think of it as a chance to get your breath back before climbing the next mountain tomorrow.

No need to carry on rushing around, just relax, chill out, have a drink or fifteen, you might as well. I no longer give a shit how long it's going to take this tube to move, to get to Hatton Cross, whether or not it will make it to King's Cross, Cockfosters, Galway Bay, or the Outer Hebrides. Or outer fucking Mongolia for that matter.

I wouldn't mind if it ended up in New York, New York. I've never been there.

But for the moment it no longer matters.

It just doesn't matter now.

Possibly because, amongst all the other shit I have been through recently, I have had a couple of drinks.

Not too long ago.

About an hour ago.

And they've gone right to my head.

I know a song about that.

Drinks.

I needed them.

And by then there didn't seem any point in not having them.

Maybe this tube will make it to Cockfosters as it's supposed to. It might even, given luck, make it as far as Bounds Green, my departure point so many hours ago, and my target for now. So many aeons ago.

Aeons.

I like that word.

Aeons.

How many stations is that to go?

Lots.

I have been through so many different ways of being delayed and pissed off today I doubt London Underground could find anything new to amaze me with.

Cancel that. I'm sure that this bunch can find screw-up number one hundred and two just for me.

There's that saying, couldn't organise a piss-up in a brewery. The problem is, that's the one thing that most people accused of not being able to do so are extremely adept at. Not so much anything else.

Is that a bit convoluted?

Who cares.

I bet you I could organise a piss-up in a brewery. Just need a Swiss Army knife to help me open things.

Like doors.

Bottles.

Beer kegs.

A sledgehammer will do if the Swiss Army knife is unavailable for any reason.

Danny, this train hasn't actually stopped yet, but if it went any slower it'd be in reverse.

Then again, am I bovvered? It can go as slow as it wants, nice little train. Good boy. Carry on. As you were. If you can. So long as you get there in the end. Today, preferably.

It's a very pretty train, Danny. It's got wheels and walls and windows and doors and all sorts of stuff like that. And the wheels go round and round.

It's even got doors that open and close without being told.

Passengers. It's got passengers all over the place. More than you can shake a stick at.

Where does that saying come from? Why would you want to shake a stick at them?

I've just had a better look at some of them. I think I might know why. In fact waving a stick might be considered polite. Unfortunately it's so crowded there isn't enough space to wave a stick.

There's a couple of lads at the other end with bicycle boxes. The things they put bicycles into when they're flying out to bicycle somewhere. Bloody huge, they are. The other passengers crammed in next to them don't look impressed. Why don't they just ride wherever it is they're going to? Or coming from? Or both?

The train probably also has a driver, though he or she hasn't introduced him or herself yet. Probably heard what a fucked-up day the Piccadilly Line is having and doesn't want anyone to notice that he or she's doing the driving.

You know, there was a long automated announcement just before we left Terminals 123:

"This is a Cockfosters train, calling at all stations to central London and then on to Cockfosters. Passengers for Heathrow Terminal 4 should change at Hatton Cross, cross over to the other platform, and catch a Heathrow Terminals four and one-two-three train. Passengers for Terminal 5 should get off here and wait for a Terminal 5 train. The doors are closing. Please stand well clear of the closing doors."

Then the doors closed. There was a pause of about five seconds, and then another automated announcement:

"Mind the gap."

And then we left.

Mind the gap? The doors are fucking closed, idiot. Nobody can get on or off. There isn't technically speaking, a gap to mind.

I think that may be what passes for irony on the Piccadilly Line. I hear driving a tube is pretty boring. Continual signal failures interrupted by a good service every so often.

When they go on strike they achieve a perfect service. You can't catch a train, but at least there aren't any signal failures. Or if there are, they don't matter.

Waiting for this tube on the platform at T123 to go back to Bounds Green kind of summed up the day, except that earlier I had been full of hope, whereas by that time I was too drained to give a damn.

The departure boards on the platform for trains going to Cockfosters showed the next train in four minutes, destination Northfields. Sort of in the right direction, going East, but only going about a tenth of the way, maybe five or six stops.

The departure boards on the platform for trains for Terminal 5, i.e. going West, showed the next train in twelve minutes going to Cockfosters, i.e. East.

The Piccadilly Line actually goes more North and West than East and West but they like to keep it simple.

The people waiting to go anywhere were very confused.

Eventually the first train for Northfields (going East) arrives on the platform for Cockfosters-bound (going East) trains. People jump up and rush towards it.

Platform announcer tells them it's not in service.

It carries on. Empty. Dark. Abandoned. Apart from, presumably, the driver.

People sit down again.

Platform announcer tells people going to Cockfosters (going East) to wait on the platform for Terminal five trains (going West).

Because the next train from Cockfosters (coming from the East) to here is going to reverse back out towards Cockfosters (going back East).

Anyone going to Terminal Five (West), well, tough shit.

So some people go to the Terminal 5 (going West) platform to wait for the Cockfosters (going East) train.

Others, the ones who don't understand English too well, or just don't understand too well, or are under a strange delusion that the London Underground is run on logical lines, stand in the middle looking around as if trying to work out just what the fuck is going on.

Tube arrives on the platform for Terminal 5-bound trains (going West).

Platform announcer repeats announcement that this train is for Cockfosters (going East).

Get on.

Watch people get on, they ask whether this is a Terminal 5 train, I tell them no. They say thank-you very much, apologise and get off.

People are weird. They can be very polite like that at times. Other times you assume they're descended from aliens, because you've never met animals that behave so badly.

Other people get on, they ask if this train is for central London. I tell them, yes, this is a train to central London and Cockfosters.

They say thank you very much, apologise and get off.

What?

Why?

WTF?

I can only presume that, when the train left towards Central London they had a conversation along the lines of, 'That bastard told us that train was going to Central London and it has, can you believe it? .... Wait a minute ...'

Some things, like war and pestilence, give you religion. London Underground gives you philosophy. Unfortunately it's all and only from the weirder books of Kafka. Kafka with only one arm, one leg, and on a trip. Personally I go for war and pestilence every time, hold the religion.

Danny, I was trying to find a text book I'd been writing in earlier, notes I was making for when you've grown up, but I think it must be mixed up somewhere with all the others. I'm so knackered now I can't be arsked to look for it. So I've started afresh in this one. If I repeat myself at any point, well, blame the drink, I do.

No, really, I do.

Speaking of which, today's been a bit of a blur. I seem to recall running, or at least hurrying, or trying to hurry right from the moment I woke up, and that was at some ungodly hour.

If you've read the first lot of notes I made you'll know that I was on my way to stop Madeleine, aka Maddy, aka Maddening, the love of my life, my reason for being, my girlfriend, the woman I will love to the end of time, the woman I was determined to marry, the woman who is your mother, will be your mother, flying out of my life back to Australia with you on board.

As in, that morning I had learned that (a) she was pregnant with you, and (b) she had decided that I was a complete, utter and total shit, she never, ever wanted to see me again, and, not only that, but she didn't love me any more.

Or rather, that she loved me, deeply, or had, but I had obviously never loved her.

Ever.

Typical. It had to be my fault.

So I raced to Heathrow to stop her leaving.

Trust me, Danny, I did everything I could to get there on time. Everything a man made of flesh and bone and blood could do. But Fate was against me from the start. If there was a signal that could fail, it failed. If there was a security alert, that could alert, it alerted. If there was a train that could break down, it broke down.

You will have read of Murphy's law: if it can go wrong, it will. Today it was O'Toole's law: Murphy was an optimist.

I wouldn't say absolutely everything went wrong. There's a scene in the film The Battle of Britain where a German bomber crashes into the tracks in a London Underground culvert. That didn't happen today.

Either Fate hadn't seen that scene or couldn't find a German bomber in time. Or maybe it hit the wrong Underground line by mistake.

Now ... And now, well ... I'm exhausted. Shattered. Knackered.

You know, since I had a few spare minutes once it was all over I bought myself a take-away coffee, one of those revolting over-sugared lattes or whatever they're called.

Actually I know what this one is called, it's a Caffe Latte Massimo. I had to ask the bloke behind the counter to repeat it three times.

I now know what it's called, but not what that means. I think it's Italian for big massively overly expensive froth in a bucket. With added sugar.

And while I was searching for that text book in my bag I found a bottle of whiskey that I'd put in it a few weeks ago for some reason. Tullamore Dew.

Buggered if I can remember why. I can remember putting it in, but for the life of me not why. But most welcome. Most, most welcome.

Maybe I was facing a really bad day at school.

Nah. I'd never take a bottle of whisky to school. The kids would nick it within seconds.

And you know, Danny, it's illegal to drink alcohol on London Underground. I can even see a warning alongside the adverts on the bulkhead above the window. It shows a bottle and a can in a red circle with a red line drawn through them, and the diktat, "Drinking alcohol or carrying opened containers of alcohol is prohibited".

Verboten is the word. The jackboot has spoken.

So I'm drinking diluted latte instead. It must be said it tastes a lot better diluted.

I can't reveal what it's diluted with. But the bottle of Tullamore Dew isn't as full as it was before I broke the seal and uncapped it.

Sshhh, Danny. Don't tell anyone.

One of the passengers is asleep. I've always envied people who can fall asleep on public transport. It seems to be such a trusting sort of thing to do.

Danny, one day I will sing you lullabies. I promise. Lullabies to go to sleep by. I might just have to sing very, very loudly to be heard. When I do that people pay me money to stop.

There's something I must stay awake to do. When we get to Bounds Green. If we get to Bounds Green.

We will get to Bounds Green.

One day I will write a song about it.

Diluted coffee is good for staying awake.

I'm sure we'll get to Bounds Green.

Maybe not this century, but I'm sure we'll get there.

Must stay awake.

Maybe pin a note to my jacket, 'Please wake before Bounds Green tube station.'

You know, Danny, women can get little badges with the Underground circle on and the words, 'Baby on board'. It's so that other people can give up their seats for them without presuming that they are just naturally overweight. I think they should issue badges saying 'No, I'm not pregnant, I'm just normally fat'. But I won't say so in public because I'm not that suicidal yet.

Danny, in the other notes I wrote that when I got to Terminal 123 I was going to hit the ground running. I almost did.

Before I get to our little secret, here's the story of the final bit of that race. The last mile. From Terminal 5 tube station to Terminals 123 tube station, and then the run to Terminal 3 check-in. Check in or security. Whatever it's called these days. The bit where passengers go through and you can't follow them any more. The bit where lovers have to say goodbye.

You know, where the man is about to walk away to catch his flight, and he turns back and says to the woman he's leaving behind,

"Promise you'll write every day, darling."

And she replies,

"What's wrong with fucking email?"

Danny, in Jane Austen's Pride and Prejudice Jane Bennet writes a letter to her sister Elizabeth who is on a walking holiday at Lambton, close to Darcy's Pemberley, to tell her of the awful news that Lydia has eloped with the scoundrel Mr. Wickham. These days you'd send a text message if you could be arsed. People don't elope any more, they just shack up. As the singers ask in the musical Chicago, What ever happened to class? Then they rhyme class with arse.

Go figure.

And, along the way, if I have time, and the Piccadilly Line often gives you a lot of time, I'll tell you about another journey. A metaphorical journey. I would say it's the story of how your mother and I fell in love, but that wasn't a journey, that was instantaneous. We saw each other and that was it, bang, kaboom, in love, game over. The story I'm going to tell is more the story of the little things that happened to make that love work.

Well, it did work, up to a point. Up to the point your mother found me in the kitchen with a naked pupil and whacked me with the equivalent of an iron bar.

In retrospect it was a beautiful shot, she caught me full on the side of the temple just where the bar had some clips which grazed back across my forehead. At the time my aesthetic capabilities were temporarily suspended so I wasn't immediately able to appreciate the artistic element of the blow.

I was going to wait until I was old to wear purple, but my forehead has beaten me to it.

I'm told baboons find it attractive. Humans not so much.

The driver has just announced that there are some slight delays on the Piccadilly Line due to earlier signal failures, but those have all been cleared up and we should, fingers crossed, have a clear run to Cockfosters.

'A home run, ladies and gentleman,' he said.

I'll drink to that. It's what I had earlier. The home run. To stop your mum leaving. Sort of.

Danny, a home run is a baseball term for getting round in one go, without stopping on any of the bases.

Home base in this case was the check-in and security counter for Qantas at Terminal 3 departures, Heathrow airport. I almost made it to home base.

The new home base that is my target is now the house where I live, in Muswell Hill, North London, via Bounds Green Underground tube station.

It's important to note that a home run does not necessarily involve doing it quickly, nor does it mean going in the right direction the whole time, it just means not getting bowled out while you're doing it, if I can put it that way.

Because I didn't.

But I reckon I still qualify for a home run.

Purists might disagree.

I invite them heartily to fuck right off.

Or even to fuck right off heartily.

Danny, there's a film called The Longest Day, about the Normandy invasion, during World War II, 6th June 1944. Apparently Rommel said that the Allied invasion, wherever it came, and whenever it came, would be the longest day for both the Axis and the Allies. Well, the run I did from the tube at platform T123 to Terminal 3 departures was for me the longest run of my life. And trust me, I've run up the stairs at Covent Garden, I know.

The strange thing is that it didn't take long but it took forever.

Maybe that only makes sense in my mind. But it does make sense in my mind.

Was it worth it?

It had to be done.

I'd run out of everything.

There was no time left.

There was no hope left.

But it had to be done.

It's not just a macho thing, Danny. Macho things I can take or leave any day of the year.

It's love. Love for your woman. Love for your unborn child.

You can't just switch that off.

Life is a right bastard that way.

There's another reason I had to do my utmost.

If I failed the next option was flying out to Australia to find her and convince her to come back, and that would be a story that would take more than a school text book to fill. I didn't have her address there for a start, apart from the fact that she was from Melbourne.

And her mother's an Australian Chinese nurse and her father's an Australian Irish police sergeant, and you don't want to fuck with those kind of people.

So.

First, the tube journey from London Underground station Terminal 5 to London Underground station Terminals 123.

The fact that it's called Terminals 123 will give you a hint that it's not exactly right next to the terminals.

In fact it's about twenty-six miles away. The length of a marathon. And I was playing the part of the original marathon runner, Pheidippides.

I exaggerate a little.

Unfortunately, as everyone knows, he died after finishing his run.

I don't exaggerate about that.

He got to the end, announced that the Greeks had won the battle of Marathon, and keeled over.

Bollocks to that, I prefer staying alive to hobble another day.

It was 13h15, a quarter past one.

Your mother's flight was due to depart at 13h30. One thirty p.m. Mathematically that gave me fifteen minutes. In reality she was bound to be beyond security, in the plane, possibly even pushed back and the plane on the runway waiting for clearance to take off. All I could hope for was that the flight had been delayed for some reason. In my desperation I vaguely considered making a 999 call to claim there was a bomb on board, but fortunately I hadn't completely taken leave of my senses.

Well, not to that extent.

Danny, they do not have a sense of humour about that sort of thing these days. Just say the word "bomb" in an airport and fifteen over-sized coppers will suddenly drop on you, handcuff your arms, handcuff your legs, beat seventeen types of crap out of you, and then lock you up until your trial date in fifteen years' time. In Guantanamo Bay.

Danny, read your history. If I have anything to do with your education you will. Back in the year 2000 almost no-one outside of the US military knew what or where Guantanamo Bay was. Now it's a symbol of – well, many things, I suppose.

Chap called Obama said that he'd close it if he became President of the United States. He became Mr President. Twice. It's still open.

But this is really the story of your mother and I, so I suppose Guantanamo Bay will probably sound to you the same way Checkpoint Charlie of my parents' generation sounded to me and my generation. Apparently it was a good place to get cheap Turkish coffee or shot. They used to say that even the cats were bugged.

Checkpoint Charlie, not Guantanamo Bay.

Maybe Gitmo too.

Danny, I know you're still young yet, but you're never too young to think of your future. What you want to be when you grow up. Never accept limitations. You will be able to be anything you want to be. You will be able to do anything you want to do.

So long as you don't want to become the President of the United States of America. You won't, though.

It's a crap job.

President of the United States of Love, well, that's different.

But no matter what happens, somehow I will be there with you every step of the way, whispering into your ear, "Go on, Danny, my love, you can do it."

Your mother's going to be the best singer of all time. So can you. Though don't forget other cool options, like knife-thrower, or seriously top jobs like being scrum-half for Ireland in the Six Nations. Hell, Danny, there's an idea: you could be the first knife-throwing singing Ireland Six Nations scrum-half. I mean, who's going to ever top that?

We could start you off small with little wooden knives. I'll buy some tomorrow.

Anyway, your mum and me.

Your mother and I.

Your nan, my mother, has very definite views on the correct usage of the English language. She would beat me to a pulp if she heard me using slang.

Well, she would frown deeply, which, with mothers, is kind of the same thing.

Anyway. My search for your bloody mother (YBM). The hunt for YBM.

I'd got all the way to Heathrow Terminal 5 only to discover that the airline your mother was booked on, Qantas, departed from Terminal 3. So I had to catch another tube going back. When I got on that tube I'd made sure I was right in the front of the train, right at the start of the carriage. In my experience, taking things on average, the probability is that the entrance and exit to any given tube or train station will be either at the back or front. I needed every single second I could claw back from Time. I chose the front as a gamble.

As I waited more and more people were arriving at Heathrow planning on getting the Piccadilly Line into Central London, and by the time the first train appeared the platform was about ten deep and deepening. By the time everyone got on who could get on the tube was packed. Absolutely jammed. You couldn't have slipped another sardine in. Not even space for a cigarette paper.

Anyway, there's this group of young Japanese in my way. Typical of travellers these days, they've got these huge reinforced corrugated iron suitcases on wheels adding to the squashedness. Almost as tall as themselves and five times as wide. And they weren't on the short side.

What the fuck do they load those things with? You could live in the fucking things. Pile one on top of the other, bingo, you've got a two-story containerised house, ideal for the modern world. Room for two bedrooms, a bathroom, a kitchen and three large-sized reception areas. When I was travelling as a youngster all you needed was soap, deodorant, a towel and a good chat-up line.

Anyway, on my way up to Heathrow I'd had my knees bashed by other young Japanese with reinforced corrugated iron suitcases. For some reason they feel they have to wheel the blasted things down the carriage, treading on toes and taking out kneecaps. Very polite, they were, and very cheerful. Kept giggling and saying sorry. Charming young things. Apart from the physical carnage.

So we were coming into T123 and I'd decided I was going to leave that tube like a bullet to go find your mum before she could fly away to boinga-boinga-land.

You know, where the kangaroos come from.

But there's this Japanese kid with a suitcase blocking my way. And I don't know how they made the new section of tube line between T5 and T123, but as the train is going along it's loud as all hell and I can't get the kid to understand what I'm shouting at him, which is something like 'I'm getting out at the next stop, are you going to get out of the way or be flung out of the way?'

And he smiles and nods and he's full of white teeth and happiness but not a lot of understanding.

So I try to mime, 'Next stop I gettee offee, you fuck offee out of way, yes?'

And he mimes back, 'Yes, London wonderful place, I go see Queen in Buckingham Place tomorrow.' Or something like that.

And the doors start to open and he and his fuck-off suitcase are still in the way. I checked my watch.

13h19.

So I said 'Sorry', giggled in his face and shoved him and his suitcase out the door. Then I jumped out, landed on his suitcase which was on top of him, said sorry again and ran like fuck. Straight into a wall of other fuckers who were also in a hurry but didn't know where they were going. But they were coming my way.

And the other fuckers waiting to get on the tube to get on with their delayed journeys. Everybody looked really fucked off. And ready to start throwing punches.

We're coming up to Hatton Cross.

Bloody hell.

This is Formula One compared to this morning.

Danny, this diluted latte is so delicious I've come to a decision.

You know how countries have things like national plants and animals and costumes and that?

I've decided every London Underground tube station should have its own drink. A stational drink. The more diluted the better. Diluted with more alcohol. To numb the pain.

And to celebrate. I want to celebrate. Alcohol is good for celebrating. Especially when all you've got to celebrate is alcohol itself.

So, what can we come up with for Hatton Cross?

What did Rick drink? Rick in Casablanca.

The eternal love story. Doomed love. Where the bad guy could have been the good guy through the love of a good woman but her husband turns up and the bad guy ends up being the bad guy twice over. And the women love him.

Good old Humphrey Bogart.

'Whatever happens, Ilsa, we'll always have Paris.'

That was one of his lines.

Well, Danny, whatever happens your mum and I will always have London and Liverpool.

So take that, Bogie. We win, two-one.

At least we won something.

While I remember, here's a map. I'm at the bottom right.

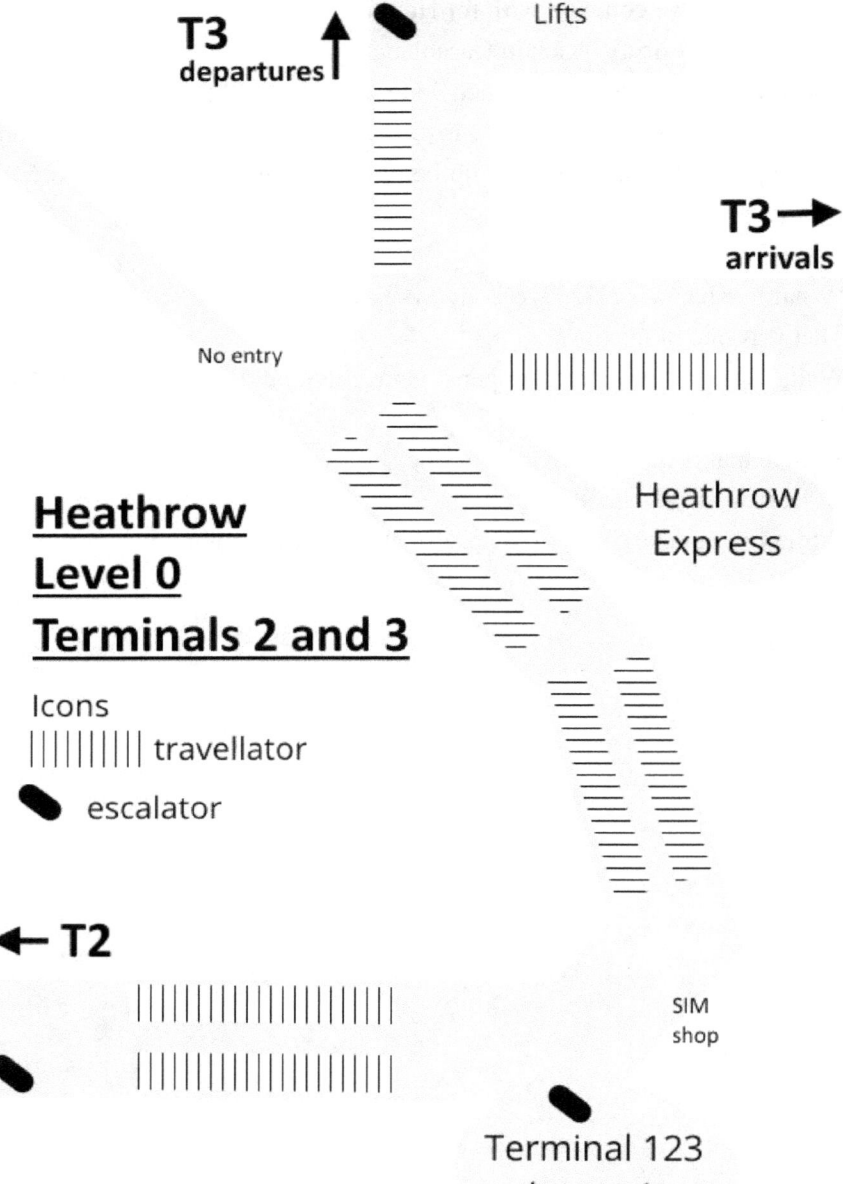

**T3**
departures

Lifts

**T3→**

**arrivals**

No entry

Heathrow
Express

# Heathrow
# Level 0
# Terminals 2 and 3

Icons

|||||||||| travellator

escalator

**← T2**

SIM
shop

Terminal 123
tube station

Cockfosters
Oakwood
Southgate
Arnos Grove
Bounds Green
Wood Green
Turnpike Lane
Manor House
Finsbury Park
Arsenal
Holloway Road
Caledonian Road
King's Cross St. Pancras
Russell Square
Holborn
Covent Garden
Leicester Square
Piccadilly Circus
Green Park
Hyde Park Corner
Knightsbridge
South Kensington
Gloucester Road
Earl's Court
Barons Court
Hammersmith
Turnham Green
Acton Town

Ealing Common          South Ealing
North Ealing           Northfields
Park Royal             Boston Manor
Alperton               Osterley
Sudbury Town           Hounslow East
Sudbury Hill           Hounslow Central
South Harrow           Hounslow West
Rayners Lane        ○  Hatton Cross  ←────────┐
Eastcote            ●  Heathrow T 1-2-3 ──→ Heathrow T4
Ruislip Manor       ┴  Heathrow T5
Ruislip
Ickenham
Hillingdon
Uxbridge

## Hatton Cross

*Estimated time to Hounslow West 4 minutes*

*Estimated time to Bounds Green 1 hour 13 minutes*

15h05

One hour and thirteen minutes to Bounds Green. I make that an ETA of 16h08. Just short of ten past four, p.m.

And then all will be revealed, Danny.

This latte is lovely.

Lovely latte.

As the song goes, Whack for my daddy-o, there's whiskey in the jar.

Don't tell anyone.

Danny, let me tell you another little story.

And the train doors are beeping and the train doors are closing and we're off. Yip-fucking-ee.

I'm sure there's supposed to be a Kee-yai in there somewhere.

Danny, let me tell you why I've named you Danny.

Whatever YBM calls you, you will always be Danny to me.

It's after my dad, Danny. He lives in Liverpool with your nan, my mum.

Your grandmother. She has a thing about people speaking proper. She'll probably allow you to call her granny, nan, never.

I think I just told you that.

Trust me, if you want to live, I can't tell you that enough times.

If you're a boy you'll officially be Daniel, if you're a girl you'll be Dannielle.

But to me you'll always be Danny.

But before we come to the secret. Hatton Cross and a stational drink like a national flower.

Have to come up with a special drink for Hatton Cross.

Dunno.

Too many stations with the word cross in the name to make a difference.

Maybe I should name it after your mother.

Cross.

That really isn't fair, Danny. Your mother isn't usually cross.

But it's funny, so we'll keep it in.

Don't tell her. It'll be our secret.

Hatton. Hatton Cross.

It's a lovely sunny summer's day above ground.

The sun has got its hat on.

Hip, hip, hip hooray.

Hat on.

Sunny.

Yellow.

Tequila sunrise.

There you go, Danny, in a future law, if I become Prime Minister or general dictator, anyone going through Hatton Cross will have to enjoy a Tequila sunrise whether they want to or not. That was easy, wasn't it?

Cheers.

If they're Jehovah's Witnesses they have to have a double.

Just in case you never get to know me properly, Danny, there's something you should be aware of.

I fucking hate religion.

Your mother is a good little Catholic.

Come to think of it – actually, I was about to say that your gran is also a good little Catholic, but I just realised, your mother is actually a naughty, naughty little Catholic girl. Very, very naughty. If she were a good little Catholic she wouldn't have a bun in the oven, would she? Not without being married. The pope will be horrified.

Or will he? Becoming pregnant is supposed to be a good Catholic habit.

Bollocks to that.

Japanese suitcases.

Hello, we're going through a culvert, open to the sky, to the birds and the bees and the glories of god that live there. It's all light and sunshine again.

There's a road alongside. Drivers whizzing along in their little cars and huge lorries.

Glorious.

Oh, Christ, and now we're open to fucking mobile phone signals.

Sounds like absolutely everyone in this carriage has got a mobile phone and they're all going off together.

Not so glorious.

There's a middle-aged woman looking at hers as if trying to remember what it is and how it works.

Just answer it madam, for fuck's sakes.

No, madam, it is not a dildo.

The ring tone is that of a doorbell. Fucking annoying sound.

Old Asian woman has answered hers. From the sounds of it it's her daughter-in-law who she's never thought worthy of her son. I think her daughter-in-law managed to say "Hello" and that was the end of her speaking part.

An old bloke holding his up above his head and peering over his glasses at it. He's slowly pushed a button.

Holds it to his ear.

Says 'Yes?'

'Yes?'

'Yes.'

Pushes another button.

Puts it back in his jacket and resumes his perusal of the Times.

Oh, joy of joys, some wanker has just shouted 'I'M ON THE TUBE'.

Someone's got theirs on vibrate, so there's at least one person left with manners.

Vibrate?

Bloody hell, that's mine.

I'd be bloody worried if I could feel someone else's mobile vibrating.

Though the young lady next to me is very close. These tube seats are ridiculous. I think they're designed for starving peasants.

At least the young lady next to me isn't an overweight builder just off site. You don't want to get stuck next to one of those on the Underground on a summer's day.

Damn. Going back into tunnel.

Vibration has stopped.

Phone vibration has stopped.

Must have lost the signal.

Train vibration still vibrating, otherwise we would have been stopped.

And this old mobile doesn't have show missed call functionality. It's out of the ark.

But at least the other mobiles have all gone dead now. For a moment I thought I was going to be drowned in a Tsunami of sound. More noise than sound.

The looks on some of the faces is quite hilarious. They thought they were about to get their mobile fix and then it was snatched from them. Petulant is the word. Adult petals.

Danny, ten years ago, maybe fifteen, the only people with mobile phones were important people and wankers. Now everybody has one. They haven't turned everyone into important people, so I'll leave you to draw your own conclusions.

Amongst the things I hate are religion and mobile phones.

Danny, I don't know what marvels you will have to look forward to. When I was growing up we were promised space travel and flying cars and jet packs and all sorts of thing. Instead we got the Internet and bloody mobile phones. Personally I'd swap all the mobile phones in the world for a jet pack. Your mum and nan would disagree, but hey, it's my jet pack.

I think we wuz robbed.

Danny, maybe someday in the future you and me get to ride the Piccadilly Line. We'll play a game. First one who sees someone with a mobile phone shouts "Mobhole!" and they score a point. Someone talking on a mobile is a "Shouty mobhole", and that earns two points if the person's speaking normally, four for a loud, obnoxious git. Spot someone with two mobiles in their hands and that's a "Double mobhole!" and earns five points. Each further mobile adds another five points, but you have to get the shout right, so someone shouting into a mobile in one hand while holding two in the other is a "Shouty triple mobhole". And if they're wearing tattoos it's "with tats!" And if they're wearing a cheap new suit it's "Shouty suity triple mobhole!"

Where was I?

Danny, if they invent jet packs in the next thirty years I'm having one before you. Sorry, but that's the way it works.

Terminals 123. London Underground station. That's right. I was about to race for the escalator.

Tell you what, Danny, that run is seared on my brain. Run for escalator, run up escalator, blocked by suitcase and arse, get past, tempted to jump ticket barrier, watch the signs for Terminal 3, swing left, do the travelator tap-dance, come back, go thirty yards, jink to the right, thirty yards, jink to the right again, sign towards Terminal 3, jink to the left, suddenly hit another travelator, now that was an experience, about two hundred yards, skid onto walkway, another travelator, another experience, going up an incline, right jink, left jink, take turn towards T3 arrivals, reverse direction, come to short travelator, and I can see the final hurdle, the stairs leading up to the sunlight and Terminal 3. I am that close to your mother, I can feel it.

The only woman I have ever loved in my life. Put a lead-lined, x-ray-proof barrier between us, sandwiched with ten-foot thick nuclear-proof concrete walls, and I would still feel her close to me.

And that's when the coppers stopped me.

That's when the coppers tried to stop me.

After all, I had more important things to do than assist the busies.

Coppers. Bobbies. Filth. Thick blue line. Those ones. Big buggers. Our brave boys in blue.

Well, the bloke was built like a brick shithouse.

The WPC didn't look big, not in comparison, but she had a certain air about her that told you you weren't about to get past her.

Coming in to Hounslow West.

I'm not sure it's legal for these tubes to go this fast. I'm sure there's a law dating back to eighteen-flibley-floor stating that they must be preceded by a man in a top hat waving a red flag, and must go no faster than five yards an hour.

Danny, I can see my reflection in the opposite window. It looks rather weird. I think my hair needs combing. Why do reflections always look strange?

I can see everyone's reflection, and they all look weird. There's this bloke about four seats away, looks like a right gay drama queen, broad-brimmed hat, cravat, extended hands resting daintily on exquisite walking stick, camel-hair coat.

Whoops.

I've just taken a sneaky peek to check.

It's actually an older woman dressed in said hat, camel-hair coat and scarf. With dainty exquisite walking stick. Sorry, ma'am. Like the hat, very fetching.

Oh well.

Hounslow West. Stational drink.

Now what shall we make that?

Cheers.

There's a song I can't quite remember which goes something like 'Lately I've been feeling something something something.'

Well, latterly I've been feeling better and better.

Ahahahaha.

Your mum and nan wouldn't get that one. Well, they wouldn't appreciate the quality.

Danny, did you know you could probably saunter from the platform at London Underground station Terminals 123 to the check-in desks at Terminal 3 in about fifteen minutes? It took me about half an hour to run it, and I never quite made it in the end anyway.

But I tell you what, Danny, it was bloody close.

Bloody close.

So, let me begin at the beginning.

Oh, by the way, Terminal 1 no longer exists. It wasn't anything to do with me. But I think it might have been a portent.

Cockfosters
Oakwood
Southgate
Arnos Grove
Bounds Green
Wood Green
Turnpike Lane
Manor House
Finsbury Park
Arsenal
Holloway Road
Caledonian Road
King's Cross St. Pancras
Russell Square
Holborn
Covent Garden
Leicester Square
Piccadilly Circus
Green Park
Hyde Park Corner
Knightsbridge
South Kensington
Gloucester Road
Earl's Court
Barons Court
Hammersmith
Turnham Green

Ealing Common          Acton Town
North Ealing           South Ealing
Park Royal             Northfields
Alperton               Boston Manor
Sudbury Town           Osterley
Sudbury Hill           Hounslow East
South Harrow           Hounslow Central
Rayners Lane        ○  Hounslow West
Eastcote            ●  Hatton Cross  ◄─────────┐
Ruislip Manor       ●  Heathrow T 1-2-3  ──────►  Heathrow T4
Ruislip                Heathrow T5
Ickenham
Hillingdon
Uxbridge

332

# Hounslow West

*Estimated time to Hounslow Central 3 minutes*

*Estimated time to Bounds Green 1 hour 9 minutes*

15h10

Some tourist's wheelie case has just gone run-about. Tube driver applied the brakes and the little monster went skittering across the doorway trying to escape. Silly owner ran after it, apologising to all its victims.

Put it down, mate.

No, not on its wheels.

Silly bugger.

Danny, top tip, latte tastes even better when there's almost none of it left. And it's been replaced with a decent drink.

But now we've got to come up with a stational drink for Hounslow West. And I know what you're thinking, Danny, you're thinking it's not going to be that easy.

Musha ring dumb a do dumb a da.

There's whiskey in the jar.

Well, Danny, Hounslow West was originally more famous as Hounslow Heath, where the highwaymen and footpads lurked, including that famous early feminist, Mary Frith, who was a Royalist and became a highway-person during the Civil War. What would she drink?

Why do they call them civil wars? Bloody people are trying to kill each other, that's hardly civil.

15h11.

Train doors have beeped, closed and we're sailing forward.

Regally.

Fuckling slowly.

Just coming above ground, passing a cemetery.

You know, I think it would be better if the doors burped before closing. Sound much better. Actually, Danny, if I were in charge I'd have them make a farting sound. Just think, the driver says, 'Please mind the doors, they are about to close,' and then you hear this loud farting noise, well, people would bloody mind the doors then, wouldn't they? Most people hear the beeping noise and decide they've still got time to jump on. Silly buggers block the closing doors, piss off the driver and fellow passengers, then act like they've done something clever.

And boy some of the drivers can get annoyed.

And sarcastic.

Mary Frith.

Mary Frith, also known as Moll Cutpurse, because Moll was a nickname for Mary and for prostitutes – see Moll Flanders written by Daniel Defoe – and because she was a pickpocket and general thief who stole purses by cutting the strings and legging it with the purse before the owner realised anything was wrong.

What would she drink? She smoked, which women weren't supposed to do. Allegedly. She graced many a tavern with her presence. She wore men's clothing. Women in women's clothing weren't permitted in taverns unless they were serving wenches. Women in men's clothes weren't permitted.

Sack. That's it. Mary Frith was once made to do penance in public for her evil behaviour, and much was made of her weeping and wailing in true and unalloyed regret in doing so, until they discovered she had consumed three quarters of sack, and was drunk and taking the piss.

Sack as in porter.

Grog. Something like that. Falling-down juice. I seem to have a vague recollection it was a type of fortified wine.

So, here's to Hounslow West, haunt of highway people, Let everyone who passes through quaff a glass of sack in memory of Molly.

Or to forget. Or take the piss. Cheers.

Some more diluted latte, Jeeves.

Don't mind if I do.

Did you know, Danny, Charles II tried to ban coffee? Sixteen Seventy Something. Coffee houses had become very popular in London by then. They were called Penny Universities because it cost a penny for a coffee and once you were in you could read the latest newspapers and discuss all the important issues of the day with other men, high and low. Very democratic it was. Women only allowed behind the serving counter, so very democratic in the ancient Greek sense. There was a Women's Petition to close down the coffee houses at about the same time, claiming that coffee was undermining men's performance in the bedroom, but apparently that was written by one of the Daily Mail's male writers as a piss-take.

We're passing a circus in the fields, Danny. You'd love circuses. Beaches, it says.

Where was I?

London Underground station Terminals 1-2-3. T123. About to chase after your mother.

Your mother is a singer. You'll know that by the time you read this. She'll have sung you to sleep with lullabies, just like my mother did with me. I remember her singing

Hush, little baby, don't say a word

mama's gonna buy you a mockingbird

and if that mockingbird won't sing

mama's gonna buy you a diamond ring.

I dream of a future in which I also sing you to sleep. But I use the naughty versions, like my dad used to. And we'll giggle conspiratorially, because we both know it's naughty and we aren't going to tell mummy, are we?

T123.

By then it was 13h20. Twenty past one in old money. Ten minutes to get to her before she disappeared out of my life forever. With you.

Oh Danny, boy or girl.

Well, by that stage, if you add in the time you need to get in and clear security and god knows what else it was really about minus an hour and ten minutes, but I wasn't about to give up just because of bloody technicalities.

I'd pushed the nice young Japanese kid and his six foot reinforced-corrugated-iron wheeled tank cum suitcase out of the door and belted it up the platform. Straight into a wall of other fuckers who were also in a hurry but didn't know where they were going. But they were coming my way.

One of them asked me, 'Where lift?' so I pointed him in the opposite direction of the escalator I was headed for, and said, 'La!' hoping he'd just bugger off and leave me with a clear run to the escalators.

Well, it's French, and he looked foreign, so, close enough.

He buggered off in that direction and the others followed. To my amazement there was actually a set of lifts there. The last I noticed of the fuckers was that they were standing in front of the lifts with a sign above that read, 'Enter the lifts from the other side'.

And then I was running and dodging like a premiership footballer ducking live rounds. I hurdled a particularly virulent purple suitcase. Just managed not to run over a little three-year-old. Almost fell into an open pram. Knocked the mobile phone out of a hipster's hand. That wasn't an accident. I had to jump a yard sideways to get the bastard. It was worth it.

These days, Danny, a hipster is a wanker with a beard, a pony-tail and a mobile phone. By the time you read this the wankers will have invented a new fashion. But they'll still be wankers.

Couple of nuns parted just in time. I could have sworn they said 'Bless you my son' as they did.

How the fuck could I be their son?

Please don't answer that one, Danny. Not even when you're fifty.

Hello, now darkness is giving way to light. Yes, Danny, we're emerging above ground again. Which means we'll be shortly arriving at Hounslow Central. Either this train is going faster than I expected or I'm drinking faster than I should.

No, plenty of dilution left for latte.

15h17.

Well, we are going slowly, but I don't think we've actually stopped anywhere we shouldn't so far.

Give it time. If this morning's journey into the hell that is Heathrow is anything to go by we've still got reversing out at Hounslow Central because of old age, termination because of a defect at Northfields, a security alert at Barons Court, termination at Earl's Court because of signal failure, and complete failure due to whooping cough at Ickenham.

Here we are, sunlight and Hounslow Central. And fucking mobile phones going off. Again.

What drink do you think we should give Hounslow Central, Danny, apart from strychnine?

Danny, never give up hope. Never. It's not over till the fat lady sings.

I don't mind the fat lady singing, it's when she sits next to me on the tube and smothers me that I get quite pissed off. Fortunately that isn't the case at the moment.

Back then, as I started my run, the fat lady hadn't begun to sing yet.

She'd only started warming up with her scales.

And she was standing in my way.

Cockfosters
Oakwood
Southgate
Arnos Grove
Bounds Green
Wood Green
Turnpike Lane
Manor House
Finsbury Park
Arsenal
Holloway Road
Caledonian Road
King's Cross St. Pancras
Russell Square
Holborn
Covent Garden
Leicester Square
Piccadilly Circus
Green Park
Hyde Park Corner
Knightsbridge
South Kensington
Gloucester Road
Earl's Court
Barons Court
Hammersmith
Turnham Green
Acton Town

Ealing Common        South Ealing
North Ealing         Northfields
Park Royal           Boston Manor
Alperton             Osterley
Sudbury Town         Hounslow East
Sudbury Hill         Hounslow Central
South Harrow         Hounslow West
Rayners Lane         Hatton Cross  ←
Eastcote             Heathrow T 1-2-3 ⟶ Heathrow T4
Ruislip Manor        Heathrow T5
Ruislip
Ickenham
Hillingdon
Uxbridge

# Hounslow Central

*Estimated time to Hounslow East 2 minutes*

*Estimated time to Bounds Green 1 hour 6 minutes*

15h20

Danny, do you know how they pronounce Magdalen College in Oxford?

They pronounce it Maudlin.

And I, Danny, must take care not to become maudlin.

Have some more latte. For the cold.

Don't mind if I do.

That's better.

It's working. Now that I've had some more diluted latte it's a lovely summer's day, warm and sunny, just how I like them.

But Magdalen Road in East Oxford?

That's pronounced Maudlin Road.

Now, how about Magdalen Street in central Oxford?

Ha! That's where they catch you. It's pronounced Mag-da-len street.

There's a reason for that.

Buggered if I know what it is.

Your mother's name, Madeleine, that's a version of Magdalen. Apparently Magdalen was a saint, but a little spin and propaganda by the early church turned her into a reformed prostitute. Amazing what people will believe.

Your mother is a little devil.

I have this awful feeling that maybe that's why I fell in love with her. She is a lovely, lovely little devil.

Doors are beeping, doors are closing, and off we go, sailing serene and fucking slowly.

Nope, a fart would definitely be better than a beep.

I can see the roofs of houses from here, Danny, miles and miles and miles of little houses.

Or should that be rooves?

Good thing I only teach English as a stand-in for when the English teacher is off.

339

I can see a pub. Pubs sell beer. Ales.

Wait a minute.

Rooves. Roof. Fiddler on the roof. Which is based in Russia. There's a cocktail called Crazy Ivan.

So, there you go, Danny, anyone passing through Hounslow Central has to consume a Crazy Ivan in homage to roofs.

Rooves?

Hooves?

Roofs.

House-top thingies.

Anyway. Back to the chase.

So I finally get to the escalators at Terminals 1-2-3 tube station. It took about fifteen seconds, felt like minutes. They're towards the middle of the platform just where I hadn't expected them. Two of them, side by side, both going up. Or should be. One's closed off with a tape across it saying 'Fuck off, closed.'

I think it actually said, 'Danger, no entry', but the meaning was the same, as I keep telling my pupils.

It's one of the shortest escalators I've ever seen. It's also the narrowest I've seen. And there's this young lady standing on it in front of me. And the only thing bigger than her suitcase is her arse. I try to dodge her on the left. No good, drop a mouse into the gap, she leans a bit and it'll be squashed thinner than a pancake.

I say, 'Excuse me, could I get past?'

Complete waste of breath. Everything about her is large, including the headphones she's wearing to blot out the sound of anyone who might be trying to get past her.

The escalator is going up. I could shoulder-charge her out of the way if it were going down, going up, no chance. If she fell back on me I'd be crushed to death.

Danny, on normal London Underground escalators you stand on the right and walk up or down on the left. It's one of those ways you can distinguish between people who are new in town or just plain rude. Never, ever block an escalator in London. It's just not done. If you're lucky someone will come up behind you and politely ask you to move. If you're unlucky they'll just plough through you. If you're really, really unlucky they'll stand behind you and cough softly.

That didn't quite work at T123, not then.

Oh, and if you're standing it's best to keep at least one free step between you and the person in front, people don't like getting up close and personal. Unless you're in love as your mother and I were. Then you stand as close as possible, holding each other. Going down I was in front, going up I was behind, both ways with my arms wrapped tight around her.

That's how it was.

Correction, Danny: That should have been, "Unless you're in love as your mother and I are." Because, no matter what, I still am.

Of course, open displays of affection are frowned on in Britain. I used to get severely irritated with young Italian couples who hadn't got the memo.

So I made sure your mum and I made up for that by spending every second on an escalator in a clinch. Especially if there were young Italian couples anywhere near. Bastards deserve it.

Back on that narrow escalator.

Check watch.

13h20.

No way I was going to make it. But no-one is going to be able to say I didn't give my last breath to get to my Maddening. So I climbed onto the space separating the two escalators and begin clambering up.

Flipping hell, we're pulling into Hounslow East already.

15h22.

Well, Danny, when I was on that escalator blocked by Ms Rump I was reminded of what Napoleon said when his generals complained about the mud before the battle of Waterloo.

'The mud is the same for the English is it not?'

'Yes, sire.'

'Well, then, you will just have to march faster.'

So I would have to run faster.

A lot fucking faster.

Napoleon never said that.

Napoleon had it easy.

Thinking back on it, as I wasn't thinking at the time, the question was, was I heading for my own Waterloo? And if so, was I Napoleon or Wellington?

Well, that's all part of the secret, Danny. But I can tell you that Bluecher did turn up.

Not the way I expected.

Not the way he expected either, I imagine.

Cockfosters
Oakwood
Southgate
Arnos Grove
Bounds Green
Wood Green
Turnpike Lane
Manor House
Finsbury Park
Arsenal
Holloway Road
Caledonian Road
King's Cross St. Pancras
Russell Square
Holborn
Covent Garden
Leicester Square
Piccadilly Circus
Green Park
Hyde Park Corner
Knightsbridge
South Kensington
Gloucester Road
Earl's Court
Barons Court
Hammersmith
Turnham Green
Acton Town

Ealing Common
North Ealing
Park Royal
Alperton
Sudbury Town
Sudbury Hill
South Harrow
Rayners Lane
Eastcote
Ruislip Manor
Ruislip
Ickenham
Hillingdon
Uxbridge

South Ealing
Northfields
Boston Manor
Osterley
Hounslow East
Hounslow Central
Hounslow West
Hatton Cross ←
Heathrow T 1-2-3 → Heathrow T4
Heathrow T5

# Hounslow East

*Estimated time to Osterley 2 minutes*

*Estimated time to Bounds Green 1 hour 4 minutes*

15h22

Nice looking place, Hounslow East. White picket railings, very pretty. Bit of greenery to keep things looking civilised.

What do you call latte with attitude?

Lattitude.

Cheers.

Girl opposite is reading a book by Donna someone or other. Her finger is covering the surname. Looks like W – something – something d –l -e.

Now that would be a brilliant name for a writer. Donner Widdle.

Enough of that. Stop being childish.

A drink for Hounslow East.

East.

The Orient.

Stella once accused me of being a right sarky git.

Stella was, well, Danny, let's just say she was an old flame of mine. It's almost the truth. Not so much lovers as lusters. She had a lovely pair of – well, you don't want to know anything about that.

Buttocks. A lovely pair of buttocks.

She often called me sarky. As in being sarcastic.

So, that's what we'll give Hounslow East.

East.

Sake. From the Orient.

We're off again.

Cheers, Hounslow East.

Back then at Terminals 1-2-3.

So I'm on the steel bit between the escalators trying to scrabble past fat-arse and not making much way because that steel is bloody smooth, the incline is too steep, and there are some irritating bits of gear sticking out of it. Like a sign saying 'Hold onto the handrail'. Another one saying 'Stand on the right'. 'Take extra care of your luggage.'

What fucking luggage?

Another a big red thing for stopping the escalator. I didn't want to stop the escalator, I was more concerned about how the big red thing was right in the path of the more tender parts of my anatomy. They could have labelled it ball crusher.

So I drop into the other escalator, the one that's switched off and start crawling up that on all fours as fast as I can. Which is when I notice the Underground bloke at the top with the 'Do not enter' tape in one hand, a radio in the other, and his mouth open as he sees me. And that's when his mate at the bottom switched the escalator back on. I guess they'd checked everything was all clear before having a two-minute natter and then switching it back on again without checking for stray teachers on all fours.

And suddenly I'm moving a lot faster than Fat-Arse and a lot faster than I expected. Those escalators don't move that fast, but when they start moving and you've been trying to run up a stationary one, you tend to shift pretty quickly. And suddenly the Tube bloke at the top gets out of the way sharpish as I come flying through. And twenty yards away are the ticket turn-styles.

After that it's wide open, no more barriers. Or so my instinct told me. Or my hopes.

Actually, every turn, every end of every travelator I prayed was the final bit before Terminal 3. In the end none of them were.

And it didn't immediately strike me that the number of people who pass through Heathrow with their luggage could create barricades faster and more formidably than Les Mis on speed.

Coming up to Osterley.

At that stage the only thing I could see were quite a few dozy tourists queued up to go through the ticket barriers. Blocking them.

Shmucks. They were in the way and I was coming through. Anything standing between me and Maddy was history.

Coming into Osterley.

Twenty six stops left, I make it.

And then, Danny, I will reveal that secret.

345

Okay, I know, you can't wait that long.

I'll drop a clue now and again. Then I'll start to reveal all at Finsbury Park.

That's only a few stops away. Twenty or so.

Cockfosters
Oakwood
Southgate
Arnos Grove
Bounds Green
Wood Green
Turnpike Lane
Manor House
Finsbury Park
Arsenal
Holloway Road
Caledonian Road
King's Cross St. Pancras
Russell Square
Holborn
Covent Garden
Leicester Square
Piccadilly Circus
Green Park
Hyde Park Corner
Knightsbridge
South Kensington
Gloucester Road
Earl's Court
Barons Court
Hammersmith
Turnham Green
Acton Town

Ealing Common        South Ealing
North Ealing         Northfields
Park Royal           Boston Manor
Alperton             Osterley
Sudbury Town         Hounslow East
Sudbury Hill         Hounslow Central
South Harrow         Hounslow West
Rayners Lane         Hatton Cross  ←
Eastcote             Heathrow T 1-2-3  ⟶  Heathrow T4
Ruislip Manor        Heathrow T5
Ruislip
Ickenham
Hillingdon
Uxbridge

# Osterley

*Estimated time to Boston Manor 4 minutes*

*Estimated time to Bounds Green 1 hour 2 minutes*

15h27

A French couple have just got on with a young child, a little girl with her thumb in her mouth. I can't tell what mummy and dad are talking about. I speak good English French, but they're talking in French French.

How does it go?

Frère Jacques, Frère Jacques

Dormez-vous? Dormez-vous?

Sonnez les matines! Sonnez les matines

Ding, dang, dong. Ding, dang, dong.

Dad taught me that. I think mum wasn't too happy with the last line.

The little girl is looking up at me with that peculiar innocent interest that children often have. She's a sweet little thing.

Osterley doesn't look too bad in the summer sunshine. But I'm sorry, it still reminds me of a Vietnam movie and I keep thinking of that line from Apocalypse Now, 'I love the smell of napalm in the morning.'

Danny, we'll have to give it an extra-special stational drink to make up for it. Something with a bit of a bang. Jager Bomb. That's it. Can't remember when I last had one of those. Bloody potent things. It was at a party somewhere, long before I met your mum. I don't remember much about that party. Nor did anyone else for that matter. I remember one of the blokes asking me, "Did we go to a party about a week ago?"

I wonder where they all are now.

Concentrate.

It's been a long day, Danny, you'll have to have patience.

Train driver's had enough of Osterley. Moving off like a duchess with arthritis.

You know, that whole run at Terminal 3, it reminded me of that bit in Hair where the farm boy visiting New York before joining the draft has taken a tablet of something and is tripping through fantastic, dreamlike scenes, floating, tumbling, flying in silence, with other noises only vaguely coming through at times. Then suddenly you're back in real life, running like hell. The again, just as suddenly, you're floating, flying through a mist of silence.

And everyone's face looks like The Scream.

So I'm off the escalator and flying towards the ticket barriers, too fast to stop, but there's this queue of tourists and travellers and general people getting in the way for no good reason. And a couple of station staff standing looking at me pop out of the escalator like a cork from a champagne bottle, open-mouthed.

And I think, fucket, I'll vault the ticket barrier.

And the ticket barrier looks back and says, fucket you will.

And it does look a little too high for my vaulting skills. About five feet too high.

Then as I come through the queues and get to the barriers I weave through the crowd to the ticket barrier and find this group of Chinese, I think they were. There's a little gap between them and the ticket barrier they're blocking. I can't understand what they're saying, but I reckon they're playing the good old family game of 'I thought you had the tickets,' 'No I gave them to you,' 'I thought you gave them to Sue', 'Yes, but Sue gave them to Joe', 'Where's Joe?' 'I don't know, where is Joe?', 'Joe's got the tickets,' 'I know, but where is Joe?' 'Fuck Joe, where are the tickets?' 'With Joe' and so on.

So I do a right-turn, left-turn, right into the small gap in front of them, slap card on yellow card reader, gates open and I'm through.

Actually the gates opened a lot faster than they normally do. I think they realised that that would be a good idea under the circumstances. Seeing as, I'd legally paid for the journey and was coming through as fast as I could and they were scrap iron if they tried to slow me down.

Somewhere behind me I hear this voice shouting, 'Hey, Joe! Hey, Joe!'

They must have thought I was someone quite different.

As I ran I checked my watch.

13h21.

Nine minutes left.

Hello, we're out into open country again. A line of trees in front of us. There's a golf course, I remember that from our journey in this morning. Lovely open grassland for miles, and some lucky buggers wasting it by playing golf along it. I won't say it's packed but it looks pretty full for a golf course on a Friday afternoon. Don't the buggers have any work to do?

Behind us there's a ginormous modern windmill on a building about half a mile away. Blades are circling slowly. Must supply them with electricity or something.

Going over the Thames. A bridge with the spars rattling past. Now crossing over the motorway. Looks like they've sorted the traffic jams they were having this morning.

Be at Boston Manor soon.

No, we're stopped. The driver appears to have decided to take a few minutes to admire the view. Can see for miles. Miles and miles of greenery. Looks like school playing fields down below. They've got the football and rugby posts in position, so that's the end of the cricket season.

Golf is a game I have never understood. I have a suspicion that it's just an excuse to get away from the wife and kids. If you were to say, 'I'm going for a stroll' they might want to come with. Saying that you're going to play a round of golf gives it a bit of fake gravitas and an excuse to leave the family behind.

Which reminds me.

Your mum and I used to love going for long walks together. We called it getting away from the madding crowd, though there were plenty of others doing the same. I suppose it was a case of getting away from the madding crowds in Oxford Street and Covent Garden and the hundreds and thousands of identikit coffee shops and burger bars to the madding crowds in the parks.

Just next to Muswell Hill, where we stayed in what had been Aunt Marigold's house, there's a parkland known as Alexandra Palace, or Ally Pally to locals. It has huge parks and plenty of walks, and a glorious view of central London. I remember the one Saturday early on in our relationship when I introduced Maddy to Ally Pally. As is usual for the season a warm burst of spring had been followed by a cold snap of spring. We'd already been weekly shopping early in the morning, dressed up in winter clothing, muffled to the eyes. Since it was still early morning, sunny, bright and crisp, the sun just up, after offloading the shopping at the house I suggested we take a stroll into the park, up to the palace. It was gloriously quiet, with only the occasional early morning jogger or dog walker around. I expect most normal people were still tucked up in bed. Certainly most sensible people.

I think it must have rained the previous night. Normally there's a haze that blurs the view of central London – it can be quite deceptive, I read somewhere that it confused the Luftwaffe during the Battle of Britain. But that day it was as clear as a bell, and Maddy fell in love with the sight. We stood on steps leading down from the Palace to the park, Maddy in front, myself behind with my arms wrapped around her waist.

'I feel like Dick Whittington,' she said. 'I can hear London calling me.'

'I think I can hear London snoring,' I said.

'Philistine. Is that the London Eye?'

'Indeed. And there's that building shaped like a pointy sausage. Old Dick Whittington wouldn't have seen those. They were built long after his time.'

'What would he have seen? The Tower of London? Where people had their head chopped off?'

'I don't know. I don't know if you can see the Tower from here. I think it might be a bit small. Though I expect people thought it was quite tall when they were rowed across to traitor's gate to have a severe haircut.'

'Traitor's gate?'

'The entrance through which condemned prisoners were taken into the Tower.'

'Where is it, roughly? The Tower, I mean. Down there.'

Well, that had me stumped.

'To the left, I would imagine.'

'You don't know? You're a useless teacher, aren't you?'

Your mother could be very hard to please sometimes.

Sometimes?

To be fair she did keep her gloved hands on my arms around her waist, and didn't object when I nibbled her neck.

There is actually a golf course at Ally Pally. Not a real one, not full size. Pitch-and-putt, it's called. Or crazy golf or something. Sounds like tautology to me.

Seeing the golf course out of the window just now reminded me of another day at Ally Pally, later on. It was a summer's Sunday by then, gloriously warm and clear and we were definitely a settled couple. We'd been to Mass and had decided to take a stroll in the park afterwards, Maddy to luxuriate in the warmth of feeling holy, myself to try to find something sinful to rub the feeling off, like coveting the ass of my neighbour. We walked past the course. It looked as if it had just opened.

'It looks lonely,' said Maddy. 'Shall we have a game and keep it company until someone else turns up?'

'Okay,' I said, 'but I'm not very good at it. A moving ball, yes, no problem. Something sitting there innocent and still, not so much.'

She looked at me.

'I don't think you've got the hang of this patriarchy business, Mark. You're supposed to explain to the good little woman how to do it properly.'

'And as soon as I find a good little woman I might do just that thing,'

She punched me in the arm.

'Bastard. Right, I'm going to make you pay for that.'

Your mother certainly has her own unique approach to sporting matters. She went first on the first hole. I watched her address the ball carefully. Then she looked up to where the hole was. Addressed the ball again. Wiggled her feet and bum to make sure her stance was correct. Checked to make sure no-one had moved the hole. Looked back down at the ball. Took a breath.

And then walloped it.

We watched it fly off and score a hole in one. In the second hole.

I suggested she take it again without penalty, this time with a little more nuance and a little less of the "belt the shit out of it" approach.

'I know what I'm doing,' she said, 'these balls are just lighter than the ones I'm used to.'

'Hokay,' I said.

We looked at the second hole. She looked at me.

'Well?' she asked.

'Well, what?'

'Aren't you going to fetch it for your little woman?'

I sighed and walked over to the second hole, retrieved the ball, and walked back. I handed it to her.

She placed it back on the tee before repeating the process of addressing the ball, wiggling her bum, checking the hole was still there, and then gave it a firm whack. It flew up, hit a tree, and came flying back straight at me. I just managed to duck in time.

Danny, Your mum can hit anything, any time, without trying. That is something that I am sure, by the time you read this, if you survive to read this, you will have personal experience of, in one way or another. Especially if you've been naughty. Even if you haven't been naughty, as I later discovered to my cost.

'That was a practice shot,' she decided.

'Yes, Bwana,' I said, and went to retrieve it again, this time from some bushes.

Your mother takes a lot of practice shots. She actually only needed three shots to complete the first hole after she'd had two dozen practice shots. I got the hole in five.

The rest of the course followed much the same process. Maddy would have a few dozen practice shots before getting it right in three, then I'd have a go and use up one or two more than her. In the end she completely beat me at the little golf thing. I think we finished with her about fifty shots ahead of me. The game had taken us about an hour, the practice shots another two or three

'I am the champion, I am the champion,' she chanted. 'You're useless, useless.'

'There's a pub at the end of the palace,' I said. 'It'll be open by now. Fancy a drink?'

'Okay, not so useless. Come on then.'

So we wandered over to the pub at the end of the Palace, the Phoenix. Rather than sit indoors we got our drinks and went down and lay on the steps looking out over London, as others were doing. Or I sat on one of the steps and Maddy lay back between my legs with her head on my chest, looking out over London.

'It's beautiful,' she said.

'Yes, you are,' I replied.

'Silly,' she said, slapping my leg playfully.

'You are. No use hitting me, it's not my fault.'

'Stop it. Tell me the history of this place.'

'Ally Pally?'

'Yes. Who built it. Who lived in it.'

'I don't think anyone lived in it. It was built for public use.'

'No prince or princess?'

'Nope. It did burn down about two weeks after opening, though, if that makes it sound more interesting.'

'What happened?'

'Sherlock Holmes and Moriarty had a fight on the dome. Moriarty dropped a cigarette and the whole lot went up.'

'Silly. Seriously, what happened?'

'Seriously? I don't know. They rebuilt it. Then in 1980 it was partially destroyed by another fire.'

'Again? Sounds like it was jinxed.'

'Not especially. Crystal Palace was built for the 1850 World Fair. Completely burnt down in 1936. Windsor Castle caught fire in 1992. I suspect the problem with palaces and castles is that there are a lot of places people don't go into very often but which still need heating and electrics. So when a fire does start it gets a good chance to take hold. Plus you have all the brocade and curtains and tapestries and furniture just waiting to go up in flames.'

'I wonder what it looked like from down there.'

'The poor downtrodden Londoners looking up at a beacon on a hill?'

'Something like that.'

'Must have been pissing themselves laughing, I reckon. When I said it was built for public use I meant the middle classes, not the chavs in the slums along the Thames.'

'Were there still slums along the Thames then? The docks? And castles and mansions upriver?'

'Oh, yes, all of life was out there. Still is, today. The Good, the Bad, the Pugly and the Fugly.'

'That sounds like a children's television programme. The Pugly and the Fugly. What does it stand for?'

'Well, if I told you Pugly stands for Pig-Ugly, can you guess what Fugly stands for?'

She turned her head sufficiently to give me an evil look.

'Mark, you really do come across as feeling superior, sometimes.'

'I am superior. I'm not as good looking as you, but I am superior. It's about the only thing I have going for me.'

'Silly.'

'That too.'

She turned back again.

'I wonder what they're doing down there.'

'I can see a couple having sex.'

'Don't be silly, Mark, you can't even see the Tower of London.'

'No, I'm wrong, it's actually a threesome. Or two dogs with six legs.'

'Idiot.'

'True.'

We sat in what I believe is normally called companionable silence for a few minutes, the sun and drinks warming us up nicely. I could have quite happily stayed there all day.

'Pugly and Fugly,' I murmured, nuzzling Maddy's ear. 'Maybe I'll write a song about them.' She sighed in contentment. And also because she was asleep.

'Twas bliss, then to be alive.

Yes, Danny, whatever happens, your mum and I will always have London.

Hello, we're moving again. Driver's obviously had enough of the view. And we sail serenely into Boston Manor.

Too late, but very serenely.

Danny, if you ever get the chance to lie back and enjoy the sunshine with a loved one, grab the chance with both hands, to coin a phrase. Life is too short to do otherwise.

And, just between us, I let her win that stupid golf thing.

Cockfosters
Oakwood
Southgate
Arnos Grove
Bounds Green
Wood Green
Turnpike Lane
Manor House
Finsbury Park
Arsenal
Holloway Road
Caledonian Road
King's Cross St. Pancras
Russell Square
Holborn
Covent Garden
Leicester Square
Piccadilly Circus
Green Park
Hyde Park Corner
Knightsbridge
South Kensington
Gloucester Road
Earl's Court
Barons Court
Hammersmith
Turnham Green
Acton Town

Ealing Common
North Ealing
Park Royal
Alperton
Sudbury Town
Sudbury Hill
South Harrow
Rayners Lane
Eastcote
Ruislip Manor
Ruislip
Ickenham
Hillingdon
Uxbridge

South Ealing
Northfields
Boston Manor
Osterley
Hounslow East
Hounslow Central
Hounslow West
Hatton Cross
Heathrow T 1-2-3 ⟶ Heathrow T4
Heathrow T5

# Boston Manor

*Estimated time to Northfields 3 minutes*

*Estimated time to Bounds Green 58 minutes*

15h34

I don't know why, but Boston Manor reminds me of Brief Encounter. It has a sort of olde-worldliness about it. Plus it's deserted right now. Not even a suggestion of someone waiting for anything. You can almost imagine the ghosts. Streets of houses behind the station. Slumbering in the afternoon sun, net curtains looking sparkling clean and laundered.

So, Brief Encounter. Another world. A world stuck in the past. What stational drink should we celebrate Boston Manor with?

Sherry. It has to be sherry. Old fashioned middle-class maiden-aunt drink. Fucking awful stuff. Way too sweet. But there you go, you don't have to have more than one glass.

I'll have a whiskey and call it sherry. I'm doing the naming so I'm allowed.

Let me get back to the race for Terminal 3 departures and your mother.

Danny, I came flying out of the ticket area at T123 like a bloody sprinter.

Thing about sprinters is, though, one, they are normally on an athletics track without the interesting addition of dim-witted tourists wandering around looking for god knows what, stopping and starting without warning, altering course with absolutely no idea of where it is they're going but determined to get in your way on their way there.

Secondly, sprinters normally have a defined course. They're on a track. They can see the finishing line. They don't have to continually look around for signs indicating the correct path to Terminal 3.

Thirdly, they don't have to suddenly jump over errant luggage floating in and out of their way. At most they have hurdles at pre-defined distances which they could run around if they thought about it long enough.

Now that would be perfect training for a world-class rugby or football team. You've got to get the ball to T3 departures without touching any of the other people around you, plus you don't know where T3 departures is, so you have to be able to know exactly where the ball is, where the non-players are, where your fellow players are, and keep an eye out for signs to T3 departures. And hurdle suitcases and sundry bags the whole way. After that the Chelsea defence are a doddle.

And I, of course, had an extra constraint: I had to keep scanning the crowds for Maddy on the off-chance that she hadn't yet reached Terminal 3 for some reason. The flight might have been delayed or cancelled and she could be wandering around. Okay, the chances were pretty slim, but the chances of getting to her in time to prevent her from flying all the way back to Australia were already pretty minimal.

Non-existent, if I were being honest.

Anyway, I come out from the ticket barriers, turn right, the signs are all pointing that way for the terminals, and there are all these people milling about, wandering about, looking around to see where they're going. At the back I notice what appears to be two happy grandparents beaming down at their little grand-daughter, about six years old, beaming back with shining little white teeth, holding balloons on long strings with the greeting, "Welcome little Syracuse". They look as if they came from a Norman Rockwell painting or one of those noir films where they suddenly turn out to be zombies and start eating people.

While I'm looking around for signs to Terminal 3 suddenly there's this young bloke in front of me, blocking me, holding onto a wheelie bag.

'Are you Michael?' he asks me.

'What?'

'Are you Michael?'

'No, I'm not Michael.'

'Oh.'

Turns to next man he sees.

'Are you Michael?'

WTF?

Just behind the girl's balloon I see a sign for T3 pointing to my left and I'm off. And within about ten yards I've left almost everyone behind me. But in front there's a little boy holding a balloon almost to the ceiling, and it's also got "Welcome little Syracuse" on it. It's in front of a sign reading 'Terminal' with an arrow confirming the direction I'm headed in. He doesn't look happy.

So, presumably some advertising stunt, but I haven't got time to worry about that because then there's a sudden flood of people coming towards me, and I'm weaving through trolleys and suitcases, and then just as suddenly I'm passed them and it's gone quiet again.

I come into an open section with a low ceiling and two long travelators either side, about a hundred and fifty yards long or so, the left-hand one going towards the terminal, the right-hand one coming towards me, an aisle in the middle about twenty yards wide for walkers. And just as suddenly as it went quiet it becomes manic again. The left-hand travelator is full of people heading away, the right-hand travelator is full of people rushing toward me, and the central aisle is funnelling a battalion of arbitrarily dressed tourists in my direction, all with varying amounts of luggage, mostly sufficient to require one or two trolleys.

I didn't hesitate. Straight onto the left-hand travelator and running like the wind. Not the wisest of moves. It was going a lot faster than I expected. That saying about hitting the ground running – it doesn't work too well when the ground itself is moving. I had to do a fair bit of arm flailing to keep my balance.

There was a little girl in front of me, fingers in mouth, staring at me, her mother facing the other way.

'Mummy, he's trying to fly,' the little girl exclaimed, tugging on mummy's skirt.

'Yes, darling,' said her mum, not taking any notice.

'He is, mummy, he is, he's trying to fly,' insisted the girl.

By then I'd regained my balance and managed to jog past them.

'Yes, darling,' said the woman. She looked at me as I passed and smiled, raising her eyebrows as if to say, 'Kids and their imaginations, eh?' I briefly smiled back as if to say, 'You don't know the half of it.'

I turned back to concentrate on the way ahead. The good thing about the travelator was that it was wide enough to take two people at a time relatively easily, so passing should have been a doddle. The bad thing was that there seemed to be no rules about it. Completely bloody disorganised. So, although there was the occasional person standing and letting the travelator take the strain, everyone else was walking, but they were walking at different speeds, some walked on the left, some on the right, some with wheelie bags behind, some had their bags alongside. And, of course, they didn't walk at a consistent speed. So it was a case of a step to the left to pass the mother and child, dodge to the right, past the old vicar on the left wandering along lost in thought. Hurry up to the woman dragging a wheelie-case while reading her mobile phone or an e-book or something, wandering from left to right like someone having been giving extreme drugs in a laboratory experiment.

The problem with people like this is that they always get in your way. It's like someone on a mobile phone coming towards you. If you move to get out of their way they'll alter course towards you. It's almost as if there were some magnetic pull around you they can't resist. This woman didn't realise I was trying to get past, she just kept wandering into my path. So I go left as she veers right, suddenly she veers left; I veer to the right as she veers left, I dummy to the left and try to shoot up the right-hand side, no good, she hasn't bought the dummy. Dummy left, dummy right, this one she falls for and veers to the right, I gallop past on her left hand side.

She still hasn't consciously noticed me.

And that's when I saw the first pair of coppers, a bloke and a woman. They were in the central aisle strolling towards where I had come from, looking directly at me as I did an imitation of some wild pecking-bird trying to pass mobile-phone woman. They wore baseball-style police caps, black boots, combat style trousers and shirts, bullet-proof vests, automatic rifles across their chests, and pistols strapped to their legs. Along with other police paraphernalia, handcuffs, presumably, radios that could reach Atlantis, depth charges, grenade launchers, usual sort of thing. The woman looked like the one in charge; she had that undefinable air of someone who gave orders. Madame Firepower, the sort of woman you call 'Miss', prefixed with 'Sorry'. The bloke looked like a very young Clint Eastwood with a huge Adam's apple. He didn't look the sort to say 'Do you feel lucky, punk?', more the sort to ask, 'Can I pump him full of lead now, please Boss?'

But what they seemed interested in was me for some reason. The woman said something to the bloke while they both looked at me. They'd stopped and slowly turned as I dodged a roaming bright shiny purple wheelie-case on the right, swung around a stationary old woman with a walking stick on her left, and nipped in-between two young women leaning against either side of the travelator while having a natter. The whole time I could see the coppers out of the corner of my eye. They had the relaxed look of cats which have just found a mouse to have some fun with, and are still deciding how.

Then, after I had passed them, they turned and began strolling in the same direction I was going in.

I forgot about them after navigating a small young woman carrying a backpack three times her size – it struck me that when I started roaming around the world back-packs were still the choice of luggage for youngsters. After all, have you ever tried using a steel wheelie-case as a pillow on the beach?

Then there was the stewardess carrying a hatbox – what idiot of an airline issues staff with hats that need a box? Completely unnecessary extra space and weight. She was holding it very daintily with the handle in the crook of her elbow, hand and fingers outstretched, very elegant, they nearly took my eye out.

Finally I was getting to the end of the travelator. I could hear the warnings. 'You are about to come off a very rapidly moving travelator and will mush your face into mash if you aren't careful.' I paraphrase, of course. But what they should have said is, 'You are about to pass an old granny quietly knitting. Do not be surprised or you might go – oh, you already have.'

I mean, for Christ's sake, that thing was doing about twenty miles an hour and she stood there calmly fucking knitting?

Fortunately I managed to collect myself in time to leap off the travelator and into a new section.

I could see a wall about a hundred yards away, with a door labelled emergency exit. The ceiling was still pretty low. A sign saying Terminal 2 via lift. An escalator to the left, coming down. I guessed that Terminal 3 check-in had to be there somewhere. There were hardly any travellers with luggage, so that was a bonus.

What I didn't like was the row of stewardesses with linked arms in front of the wall. They were standing shoulder to shoulder, three deep, each holding a balloon on a piece of string. And they looked like they were about to come straight at me. And someone with a loud hailer called, 'Okay ladies, one more time, remember we only need three seconds, and on the count – ready? And then an Adagio began playing. Albinoni, I think. And loud-hailer bloke called, 'Five, four, three, two, one, go!' And that's when everything seemed to go into slow motion. The stewardesses stepped out very smartish, right leg first, perfectly in time, perfectly in line. And my brain of perfectly logical deductions came up with the perfectly logical but irrelevant deduction that these probably weren't real stewardesses, they were dancers or models, highly choreographed, highly efficient and highly coming straight at me with linked arms. And I was headed at high speed towards them. And right then I was in line to bypass a litter bin attached to the right wall before ploughing into a string of them, and if they kept their arms linked I would take out about five, maybe eight. And while stewardesses are trained to take care of people this lot looked like they were trained to take out people.

I could see the whites of their eyes. Their lipstick was smiling, but their faces had that grim look of people who have something to do, and they are determined to do it, come hell, the Light Brigade, or me.

As we approached each other on a collision course I noticed a cameraman on the left, and beyond him some lifts. And then just as the line passed the lifts the lift doors opened and a flood of passengers emerged. passengers pulling wheelie bags, passengers pushing trolleys, passengers carrying daypacks, all charging into the flank of the stewardess line. And loudhailer man cried 'Cut! Cut!', and the line disintegrated into a bunch of individuals throwing their hands up, crying 'Not again!'

And a few freed balloons labelled "Welcome little Syracuse" ascended towards the ceiling. I then noticed that it was mainly false: panels with wide open gaps vaguely masking machinery such as ventilator pipes. And quite a few balloons presumably released in earlier runs. And so I ran into a melee of the rabble of a surrendered line and passengers heading past me in a hurry.

I looked at the lifts.

The lifts which had "Terminal 2 Departures" above them.

Plus, "The Queen's Terminal".

What, a terminal just for her?

I paused while I put my hands on my knees and tried to get my breath back.

I read it three or four times.

It still said "Terminal 2".

"The Queen's Terminal".

I looked for the sign that would say, "Terminal 3 Departures."

There wasn't one.

I looked for the sign that would say, "Terminal 3 Anything."

There wasn't one.

Being of a scientific bent and relying on the facts before me I reluctantly concluded that I had just run about two hundred yards in the wrong direction. Into some idiots filming a commercial.

I've heard of verisimilitude, but Christ sakes, couldn't they film it somewhere else?

Three of the young women I had just been about to run into looked at me companionably. We had almost gone to war, but that was over now.

'Terminal 3?' I asked, slightly breathlessly, just in case there was something I had missed. They shook their heads.

'I've been here three hours, love,' said one, 'and it's been Terminal 2 the whole time.'

'They could have swapped signs for the filming,' suggested the second.

'Nah,' said the third, 'I was there last Saturday to pick up me nan. Terminal 3 is down there, the way you came, mate.'

I took a deep breath and looked at my watch.

13h22.

There was still time. Only just. Only if I got my arse into gear and moved, fast.

I got my arse into gear and started moving, back the way I had come.

Coming into Acton Town now. Just paused at a red signal to admire the marshalling yards. Miles and miles of chain link fence. A blue and white building.

There's a train waiting on a down slope, waiting to go into Acton Town, I guess. I can see the driver leaning slightly forward in a pose that suggests he's not in any hurry to go anywhere.

As a teacher I have trained myself to remain calm and collected in all situations. The pupils might be screaming and shouting and hysterical, I was cooler than a cucumber and colder than ice, and smiling with it. And then this morning, running through the terminals, I blew that image to shreds.

My kids would've loved me for that.

They would have pissed themselves laughing at me too. How many times can you go the wrong way in fifteen minutes?

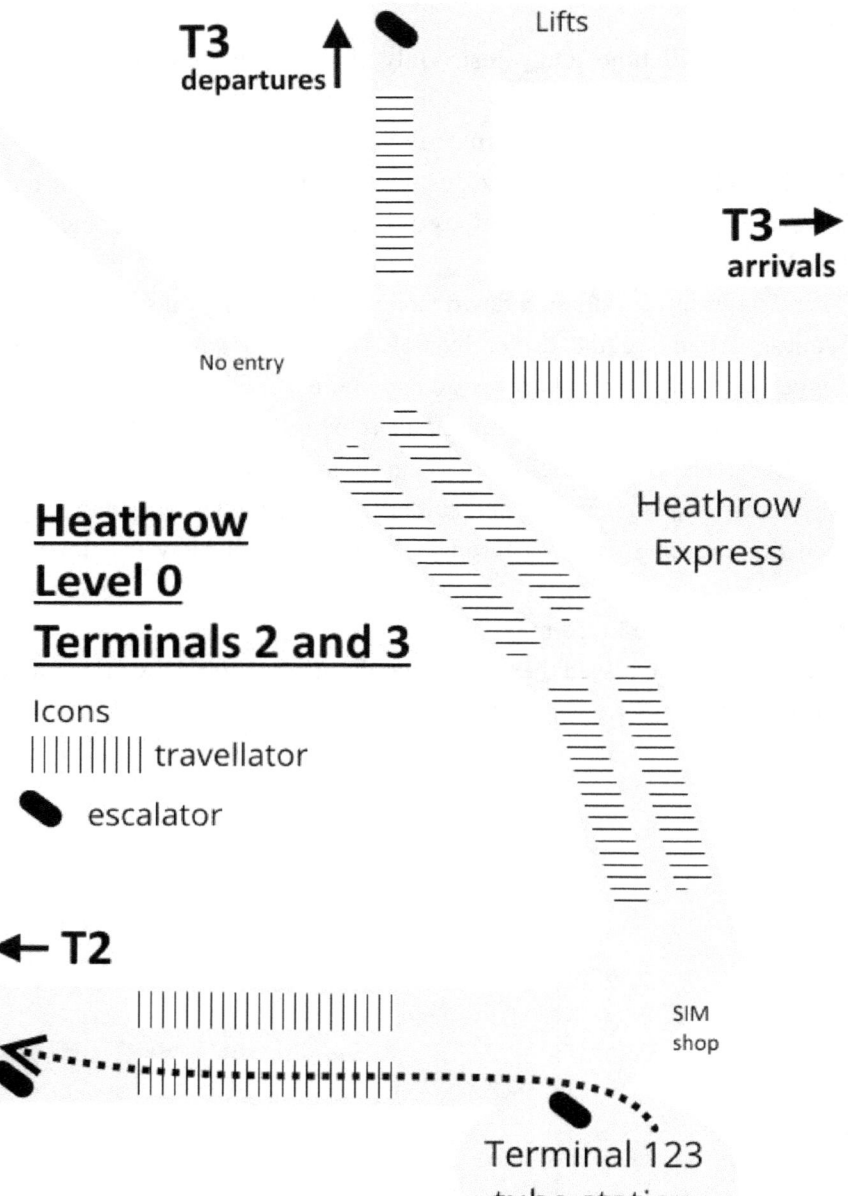

**T3**
departures

Lifts

**T3 →**
arrivals

No entry

# Heathrow
# Level 0
# Terminals 2 and 3

Heathrow
Express

Icons
|||||||||| travellator

escalator

**← T2**

SIM
shop

Terminal 123
tube station

Cockfosters
Oakwood
Southgate
Arnos Grove
Bounds Green
Wood Green
Turnpike Lane
Manor House
Finsbury Park
Arsenal
Holloway Road
Caledonian Road
King's Cross St. Pancras
Russell Square
Holborn
Covent Garden
Leicester Square
Piccadilly Circus
Green Park
Hyde Park Corner
Knightsbridge
South Kensington
Gloucester Road
Earl's Court
Barons Court
Hammersmith
Turnham Green
Acton Town

Ealing Common
North Ealing        South Ealing
Park Royal          Northfields
Alperton            Boston Manor
Sudbury Town        Osterley
Sudbury Hill        Hounslow East
South Harrow        Hounslow Central
Rayners Lane        Hounslow West
Eastcote            Hatton Cross     ◄────────┐
Ruislip Manor       Heathrow T 1-2-3 ────► Heathrow T4
Ruislip             Heathrow T5
Ickenham
Hillingdon
Uxbridge

367

# Northfields

*Estimated time to South Ealing 1 minutes*

*Estimated time to Bounds Green 55 minutes*

15h38

A train has just pulled in alongside, going the other way, towards Heathrow. I think I must have either had a sixth sense or seen a reflection somewhere, because I suddenly had this feeling of someone just behind me, watching me, which, in a tube, would be a difficult trick. I looked around to see a young girl in one of the windows of the other train, staring at us. She must be kneeling on the seat. She looks as if she wants to ask, 'Who are all of you strange people, and where are you going to, and why?'

Danny, for some reason I've just had this image of you as a grown-up, maybe twenty-one or twenty-two, sitting on a tube headed towards Central London, reading just what I'm writing now. It's a comfortable delusion, so let's pretend it's true, and you can hear a ghostly me reading these words.

In which case, first another slug of diluted latte for the throat, thank you very much, and a stational drink for Northfields to celebrate.

North. Fields.

Sure and that's an easy one, Danny.

Fields.

Fields of Athenry.

The lament of a young Irishman and a young Irish woman, separated by a prison wall, he being sentenced to Botany Bay for stealing Trevelyn's corn during the famine to feed his family, she to be left behind to look after their child somehow. The good old Irish Diaspora.

Christ knows what was good about it. Millions died. Millions forced to emigrate never to see their families again. English landlords screwing the pennies out of Irish peasants. The Catholic church screwing them by outlawing birth control, ensuring huge families, poverty and early death.

Well, Danny, one little consequence of all that is that two of the descendants of those hundreds of years ago happened to meet up and fall in love for a while in today's London: your mother and I.

So, Northfields, your stational drink will have to be a glass of the black stuff.

Guinness.

I'll drink a latte to that.

The driver's just announced that there will be a small delay while they change crew.

While they do that, back to the chase.

At the lifts to Terminal 2.

I took a deep breath. There was no chance I could get to Terminal 3 in time. I took another deep breath. Checked my watch.

13h22.

Eight minutes left.

Then I started running back the way I had come.

Pace yourself, I thought. Pace yourself. I didn't know how far it was to Terminal 3, so I had to pace myself for a small marathon. Not too fast, hold something back for the last hundred yards, when you see the finish line.

And then I hit the travelator going the opposite direction to the one I had just come, now going the same way as me. And suddenly I was flying again, arms going like the clappers to keep balance. And now there was someone on the travelator, in front of me, suitcase sitting at their side, blocking the travelator And the travelator was about four foot wide, so that wasn't easy. I came up too fast. So I vaulted the suitcase and kept running. Fortunately it was one of the smaller ones. Otherwise I could have tripped on it and slid down the metal grid of the travelator on my palms and nose.

Just then the two coppers I had seen earlier came walking back down, looking at me, their faces inscrutable. They stopped as I went past. Madame Firepower lifted a radio to her mouth and said something. I didn't wait around to listen. But I could feel them turning back in the direction I was going. I just knew they'd be sauntering after me. Or maybe I'm remembering it after the fact. Because we were to meet again. The end of the travelator was coming up. There were two more people ahead of me. An old man walking along slowly but determinedly, and a young woman just behind him. And there was this continual bored announcement from the ceiling, "You are nearing the end of the conveyor, please do not block the exit well". I have never heard an automated recording sounding like it desperately wanted to suddenly shout, 'LOOK OUT YOU STUPID ARSE!!' And just then the old man slowed as if to prepare for the imminent end of the travelator, and the woman, seeing him slow down, stepped out to overtake. No indicators, no looking in the rear view mirror, oh, no, fuck all, just step out in front of me as I was about to make a huge step for man. The old man stepped off, the young woman stepped off and they stopped and smiled at each other. Which gave me a five inch gap to jump through between them. I have this vague memory of two surprised faces looking up at me. I think I might have wiped their noses for them as I went through. And then I was past them and clear. But beyond that, about thirty yards beyond, were the crowds. And I knew I didn't have the brakes to stop in time. Anyway, they were between me and Terminal 3.

Hello, we're slowing down again. There's a bit of an embankment, and then houses, all painted a sort of creamy-yellow. Weird.

Now we're pulling into South Ealing. South Ealing already, that was quick. This train is going so fast it might get to the end before I do.

I'll just have to drink faster.

Let's hope I don't break out into song. Danny, I might not be as good as your mum, but when I sing some of the classics from the operas it brings tears to people's eyes. But we wouldn't want to get thrown off the train before we get to the end, would we?

Not this time.

Cockfosters
Oakwood
Southgate
Arnos Grove
Bounds Green
Wood Green
Turnpike Lane
Manor House
Finsbury Park
Arsenal
Holloway Road
Caledonian Road
King's Cross St. Pancras
Russell Square
Holborn
Covent Garden
Leicester Square
Piccadilly Circus
Green Park
Hyde Park Corner
Knightsbridge
South Kensington
Gloucester Road
Earl's Court
Barons Court
Hammersmith
Turnham Green
Acton Town

Ealing Common          South Ealing
North Ealing           Northfields
Park Royal             Boston Manor
Alperton               Osterley
Sudbury Town           Hounslow East
Sudbury Hill           Hounslow Central
South Harrow           Hounslow West
Rayners Lane           Hatton Cross  ◄────────┐
Eastcote               Heathrow T 1-2-3 ────► Heathrow T4
Ruislip Manor          Heathrow T5
Ruislip
Ickenham
Hillingdon
Uxbridge

371

## South Ealing

*Estimated time to Acton Town 4 minutes*

*Estimated time to Bounds Green 54 minutes*

15h41

South Ealing.

Mouldy concrete walls, a green embankment, and silver-painted steel bars.

A stational drink for South Ealing. Do we go for the South, the Ealing, or both? Let's go for the Ealing.

The Ealing comedies, that other golden era of British film. Passport to Pimlico.

Comedy.

Comedy is funny.

Something that is funny could be peculiar.

Which makes it rum.

So, Danny, South Ealing stational drink is rum. Whichever you prefer, black, white, gold.

And rum rhymes with bum, isn't that useful? We could make a song out of that.

Just a minute, Danny, my vibrator is phoning.

15h45

Well, that was an interesting call. It was Sean, the ex-army geography teacher at the inner-city comprehensive I teach at.

Or taught at.

Or maybe both.

Danny, a quick summary: Many months ago I'd talked the music teacher into a production of Cabaret with the final-year class. The head, Ms Bogdanopoulos, aka the bog, gave permission in the belief that it would be a complete failure. And it almost was. The kids were awful. Most of them only turned up for a laugh. They had no confidence. But our biggest problem was trying to instil some sense of discipline into the little buggers. And then I had this brilliant idea of inviting Sean on board. He'd been an army sergeant, and part of our production was going to involve some of the kids as goose-stepping Nazis. So we asked him to drill them. He had a reputation of being a reserved and morose alcoholic who had killed people in Afghanistan with his bare hands, so the teachers and kids tended to steer clear of him. To my amazement he agreed to my invitation with a look in his eyes which boded badly for the kids.

He was the spark we needed. I think his introductory instruction to his first group of runty Nazis was along the lines of, 'When I say jump you don't stop to ask how fucking high, got it? That wasn't a fucking question now JUMP!' It wasn't what you might call the traditional academic approach, but for a stage production by kids it was perfect. The storm-troopers learnt to march like perfectly matching robots with dark glasses. They began to take pride in their ability, and I think being bawled out by Sean without flinching acquired a certain cachet. That spread to the others in the cast. They put some verve into their singing. It looked like we were going to make it, or at least not look too godawful. We were chuffed to bits. Proud as peaches in cream.

And then one day the bog announced that she had hired a professional piano player and choreographer to take over the production to do the kids proud, and that my services were no longer required. To say that I was livid was an understatement. My revenge was simple: I told the kids I'd been replaced by Fatty-Knickers – a name I'd invented for the professional – and that they would have to make up their own minds about the situation.

Did I call her Fatty-Knickers or HorrorBollocks?

Can't remember now.

Anyway.

Fatty HorrorBollocks Knickers didn't stand a chance. She might have been good with professionals who wanted to be there, she hadn't a clue how to handle the pupils from hell who regarded her as an interloper.

Then the bog received some anonymous photographs of me in my kitchen with one of my pupils, Sharon Runny-nose, naked.

She was naked, not me.

And your mother arrived back early from a tour and surprised us. Which is when she smashed my face in with a metal pole and left me. And the bog suspended me for suspected sexual deviation. Well, for suspected of having sex with Sharon Runny-nose, which would have been sexual deviation, or at least having sex with a non-human species, i.e. a pupil.

Anyway, the very same day OFSTED had decided to drop into the school and have a snap inspection.

Quick note for clarification, Danny: OFSTED is an acronym for 'Office for Standards in Education, Children's Services and Skills'. Acronyms are so tedious and ubiquitous these days they've invented an acronym for them. OFSTED are so tedious and ubiquitous in teaching life they are their own swearword. Their real acronym should be IBS: Interfering BusybodieS. Imagine you're sitting on your own in a desert hundreds of miles from anywhere doing nothing and every five minutes an arsehole of either or no sex suddenly materialises, tells you you're doing it wrong, re-arranges the landscape, orders you to think of it in cerise, gives you a thousand item check box list to fill in triplicate then disappears, and that's OFSTED. They are to teaching what Herod was to infant boys.

Usually snap inspections are known about for six months in advance at the very least. The unusual thing about this one was that it was a snap inspection nobody was expecting. And the kids didn't raise the alarm as they normally would as soon as they saw a stranger with 'OFSTED Inspector' tattooed onto their foreheads. Sean thinks the older ones were looking forward to doing Cabaret until the bog had foisted Miss Fatty Knickers HorrorBollocks on them and ruined everything, so not raising a warning was their way of getting back at the bog.

So the bog's flustered and welcomes them into her office without thinking, and the photographs are still on her desk in plain sight for any passing visitor to see. And the inspectors take a dim view of that. So they ask her what the hell is going on. And the bog tells them that I've been caught having an affair with one of my students, so she's immediately suspended me.

But for some reason the inspectors aren't quite satisfied. They ask where I am, the bog says she doesn't know, they ask where Sharon Runny-nose is, bog says in class. So they get Sharon Runny-nose in and ask her some questions, which they probably technically shouldn't have. But Sharon

Runny-nose admits she had gone round to my place against orders, and she had taken her wet clothes off in my bathroom, and I hadn't done anything, and, and she was terribly, terribly sorry about causing a fuss. Which is when the inspectors ask the bog whether she had interviewed Miss Runny-nose before suspending me. Which she hadn't.

Then the inspectors ask her who had taken the photographs, and she admits that she suspects it was Chris, a lad I had tried to convince should audition for Cabaret without success. I had also encouraged him to follow his hobby of photography, something I had regretted when he took pictures of me with blood pouring from my head and a hysterical and naked Sharon Runny-nose behind me. So they hauled him in and gave him the third degree. And he confessed that he had taken the photographs and left them on the bog's desk while she wasn't there. But he claimed that he had done it to prove that I wasn't having an affair with Sharon Runny-nose. I don't know how he worked out that the photographs would exonerate me of that charge, but then he's a teenager, and most of the time such creatures mean well, but seem to lack the logical ability to connect the dots.

Danny, some people believe that luck plays a role in everyday life. If the inspectors had been in a good mood they might have agreed that the bog needed to do something immediately, and my suspension was understandable, if unfortunate. If they had been tired after a long day they might have shrugged and decided it was none of their business. Instead they decided to immediately suspend the bog and bring in an acting head until further notice. Personally I think the bog had just pissed off so many people the word had got around and someone was going to let the trapdoor swing sooner or later.

Sean was ecstatic. Apparently Mrs HorrorBollocks Fatty-knickers has also quit so he reckons we can restart Cabaret. I'm not so sure. As the song goes, someone left the cake out in the rain. I don't think I want to bake it again.

I asked Sean where he'd got my number. Turns out I gave it to him a couple of years back when I'd agreed to be available if he couldn't make a football match he was supposed to ref. In the end he'd made it and I'd completely forgotten about it, but he hadn't.

Strange things, humans.

It's my old phone which had been lying in a drawer. If I hadn't accidentally broken the one I normally use it would still be in the drawer and Sean would never have got through.

Okay, Danny, I admit that I accidentally broke it by hurling it against a wall. I was a tad irritated with your mother. She'd left a message on it saying something like, 'I'm pregnant, goodbye.'

That is what you could call unfinished business. But don't worry, Danny, I'm going to do something about it.

I'll work out what before Bounds Green.

Coming up to Northfields. 25 stops and 50 minutes.

I think I'll order a pizza delivery instead of making tea tonight. That run towards T3 completely knackered me. I don't have any energy left to cook supper.

Time to dilute some more latte.

I need something to keep me going.

We're coming into Acton Town. I think we must have stopped somewhere.

Well, Danny, it's all downhill from now on in. In a manner of speaking.

It wasn't then, but there you go.

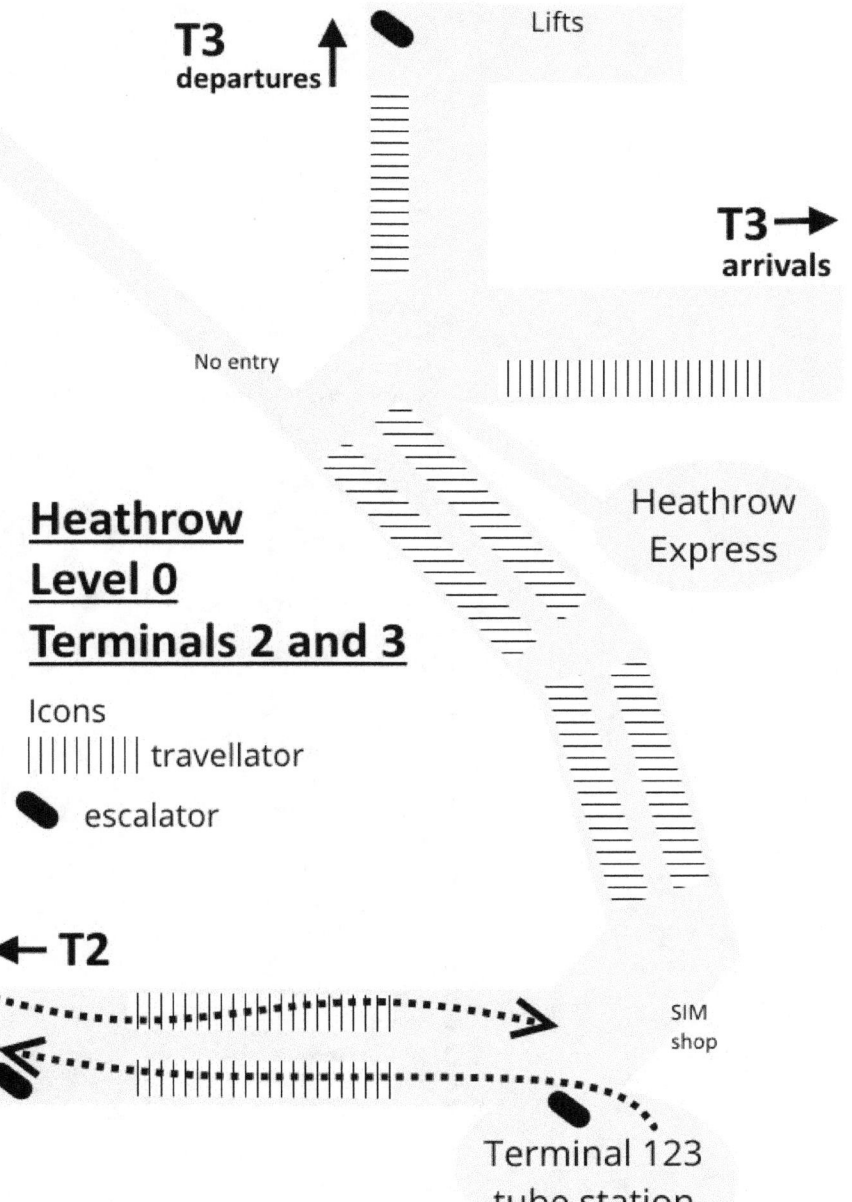

**T3**
departures

Lifts

**T3 →**
arrivals

No entry

# Heathrow
# Level 0
# Terminals 2 and 3

Heathrow
Express

Icons
|||||||||| travellator

escalator

← **T2**

SIM
shop

Terminal 123
tube station

Cockfosters
Oakwood
Southgate
Arnos Grove
Bounds Green
Wood Green
Turnpike Lane
Manor House
Finsbury Park
Arsenal
Holloway Road
Caledonian Road
King's Cross St. Pancras
Russell Square
Holborn
Covent Garden
Leicester Square
Piccadilly Circus
Green Park
Hyde Park Corner
Knightsbridge
South Kensington
Gloucester Road
Earl's Court
Barons Court
Hammersmith
Turnham Green
Acton Town

Ealing Common      South Ealing
North Ealing       Northfields
Park Royal         Boston Manor
Alperton           Osterley
Sudbury Town       Hounslow East
Sudbury Hill       Hounslow Central
South Harrow       Hounslow West
Rayners Lane       Hatton Cross ◄
Eastcote           Heathrow T 1-2-3 ──► Heathrow T4
Ruislip Manor      Heathrow T5
Ruislip
Ickenham
Hillingdon
Uxbridge

## Acton Town

*Estimated time to Hammersmith 7 minutes*

*Estimated time to Bounds Green 50 minutes*

15h52

Good old Acton Town. Last time I was here, this morning about five hours and three hundred years ago, I was going in the opposite direction and managed to end up speeding towards Ickenham instead of Heathrow. Well, the train was going to Uxbridge, but Ickenham is on the route, and I think Ickenham sounds way more interesting than Uxbridge.

Then again, this train is going towards Cockfosters. Some young tourists find that quite hilarious. Wait till they find out the names of some other British oddities.

At least I can be confident I'm not on the wrong line now. Trains from Heathrow only go in one direction. That is an incontrovertible fact. At least it was this morning. I'll check the next station, just to be sure. Wouldn't want to end up in the depot by mistake.

Acton Town. What can we say about Acton Town?

I'm sure people get off here to go home, and regard it as a welcome sight.

To me it's a changeover station. People get off trains to get on other trains to go somewhere else. It's surround by marshalling yards and wire fences.

I'm sure its mother loves it.

A stational drink for Acton Town. As the doors close and we move off. Past tall fences and low warehouses.

Simple.

It's got Town in the name. It's in London. That makes London Town. Londoners are proud of being Londoners. Therefore the stational drink for Acton Town has to be Fullers London Pride. A lovely beverage, Danny, just don't consume too much of it like I did the last time it was on offer.

Best not. Too many memories about that stuff. Not very good ones. And I'm not talking about the hangover.

We're coming up to Chiswick Park. Won't be stopping here though, it's a District line station. Unless, as per this morning, we hit a red signal. Or signal failure. Or a bump in the tracks. Or Christmas.

And, Danny, it's pronounced Chissik Park. A bit like Eisenhower, when he stayed in England before the invasion of Normandy, stayed in Southwick House, pronounced Suthik.

Thinking about it, I kind of like the idea of pronouncing them Chis-wick Park and South-wick House.

Too late, we've passed good old Chis-wick Park now. They seem to have got all the demons out of the system. Apart from the speed that is, they seem to be taking things real slow. Still, they're good at go-slows. Just don't tell them I ever said that.

Greenwich. I think we should pronounce that Green Witch. Are we on British Summer Time, or Green Witch Time? Danny, I'll have to come up with a lullaby for you about Green Witch Time.

She came sailing over the trees on her broomstick, cackling like a good un, that Green Witch in time.

Talking about your mother, how long does it take to fly to Australia these days? By Concorde? Via Hong Kong? Sloop? The old days, months, a long sea voyage to Botany Bay? I read somewhere they were planning a flight non-stop from Australia to the UK, now that they've got the capacity to do so.

Concorde. I've just realised. Concorde probably won't mean much to you, Danny. First commercial aircraft to break the sound barrier. A joint effort between France and Britain. Imagine that, the Brits and Frogs working together. In a time when everything else seemed American, Concorde stood out. People would go to airports just to see it land and take off. The word iconic doesn't come close to describing it. It was the flying version of one of the twelve wonders of the world. Then one caught fire after a fuel tank was punctured by an arbitrary piece of debris lying on the runway as it took off. It crashed and killed everyone on board. So they decommissioned the lot.

Truth was, as far as I understand, that they were too expensive to run and commercially unviable. Some people can put a price on anything.

Philistines.

Bastards retired it before I could get to have a go on it.

I wonder what the weather is like over there now. In Bong-bong land. Winter, I suppose. Dry, brown, desert, dead, miles and miles of flatness. Or maybe it's spring with dry, brown, desert, dead, miles and miles of flatness. Not to mention some of the deadliest animals and insects the planet contains. Enough about their women.

Some of the blokes are just as bad.

I hear the beaches are nice, mind. If you don't mind sharing with sharks. And Australians.

I'll worry about that later. Right now my latte is getting lonely.

And it needs topping up.

I mean diluting.

Cheers.

I remember looking at my watch as I came back towards the hordes of tourists and travellers. It was 13h23.

Seven minutes left. It had taken me less than a minute to cover two hundred yards of obstacle course. Of course I didn't have seven minutes left. But by then I was completely fixated on that golden time: 13h30.

Why is it that, you're out of time, the game's over, that's it, but you still consult your watch even though your eyes should be on the poor buggers you're about to plough into?

Debouched. Now there's a word. The area I was headed into was where three or four flows debouched into each other, a confluence of arrivals from Terminal 2 and Terminal 3 all heading towards the famous London Underground which was busy feeding in the thousands to head for departures at Terminal 2 and Terminal 3, not to mention people arriving by tube, car or bus to head for departures. Or possibly arrivals, who knows, many of them didn't.

And when that happens they all tend to pause and have loud discussion in foreign regarding which way they should be going. I was trying to keep my eyes on directions to Terminal 3 while dodging sheep and suitcases. And luggage trolleys. As I came back into the area I saw a sign saying "Terminal 3", and an arrow pointing in the direction I was going in. I looked left quickly and saw a sign saying "Terminal 2", with an arrow pointing towards where I had just come from. Why the fuck had I read it as "Terminal 3" just a few minutes before?

Then I noticed the little girl with the zombie grandparents and the balloon as I passed them about twenty yards away, and it fell into place. The balloon was hovering about ten feet above the girl, covering the bottom half of the "2". My brain, in its feverish rush to get to Terminal 3, had converted the bit it couldn't see into the bottom half of a "3". Too often we see what we want to see. I hate people who do that.

I'd slowed down to confirm my suspicions, and just then this young bloke stepped in front of me. The same young bloke as before.

'Are you Michael?' he asked.

'No, I'm not fucking Michael,' I said and pushed past.

'I didn't ask what you were doing, I asked if you were Michael,' he called after me.

'Still not fucking Michael,' I called back.

I heard him ask someone else if they were Michael.

Why not? I guess a few hundred thousand people go through the area every day, if not every hour, one of them will be called Michael. Princess Michael, perhaps.

On I went. Teenage couple with spots, thick glasses, backpacks and Adam's apples. One of them opened their mouth and their braces said something to me. No time to stop and chat. Smiled inanely. Waved. Carried on. Dodged one of those children's suitcases on wheels, the ones designed to look like animals, rejected by Dragons Den or whatever shite it was, went on to make the creator a fortune and keep countless parents happy, not to mention their kids. Shot between two Orthodox Jews pushing trolleys having some important chat about supermarket shelves covered in leopard-skin print. What? No time to wonder what the fuck that was about. Jink right to evade little old woman with fierce scowl carrying an even fiercer little Chihuahua which tried to bite me. Who the hell allowed a Chihuahua into the airport? Did she claim it was a guide dog? A guide rat? One of those comfort pets for flying? Jink to the right has driven me towards a booth cum shop selling sim cards for mobile phones. The sort of fold-out shop that collapses into a shutter-front when closed. Something about local prices versus international rip-off. There's a young salesman dressed in black waving a mobile phone and extolling the product to two young Japanese wearing thick glasses and staring at him with open mouths. He looked like a right Jack-the-lad. They looked like they only stopped for directions to the London Underground. I'm now headed directly between them. Grab the phone out of the salesman's hand as I come running through, toss it back over my head for him to catch again, didn't stop to see where it landed, had an image of exactly the same Jack-the-lad a hundred years before selling postcards to tourists just coming off the boat. "The latest technology, mister and missus, this will get to your loved ones before you even thinking of going home, yes, sir, yes, madam, and all for the price of five pence for the postcard and one pence for a stamp from the local Post Office."

'Hunderground?'

'By sea, sir, the finest ocean-going vessels in the British merchant marine.'

'Hunderground?'

Tell myself to stop dreaming and concentrate on the signs to T3. Check watch.

13h24.

Six minutes left.

Now, where are the signs for Terminal 3?

Hello, we've stopped again. About a couple of hundred yards short of Turnham Green. We're parked at rooftop level. Below us I can see a quintessentially English scene. A park, walkways to stroll along, green, green grass to have picnics on or smoke. This section has quite a few of those. You normally glimpse them as the train rushes past, little islands of peace and quiet. There are actually some couples having picnics down there. Well, it's Friday afternoon, it's a lovely day, why not?

There's a church, red buses trundling along a road beyond the park. Trees, of course. Houses which look like they were dragged up all higgledy-piggledy over the years, different times and styles.

Danny, I like higgledy-piggledy. I like the way it sounds. I like the concept. If I get the chance it'll be the first words I teach you.

Actually, Danny, the first words I think I'd teach you in an ideal world would be 'Tullamore Dew' and 'fetch'. But there you go.

Whatever happens, I will find a secret way to communicate with you over the miles and years.

We'll invent a magic telephone, what say, Danny? Just for the two of us.

The Piccadilly Line doesn't stop at Turnham Green on weekdays during normal running hours. According to the map above the window it doesn't stop there after 06h50 Mondays to Saturdays. Sundays it stops up until 07h45; in the evenings it stops after 22h30. So we won't get to stop and wish Turnham Green a stational drink, poor thing.

Be a right bummer if you turned up at 06h51.

I suppose it's a bit like playing the game of 'what if'. What if I do get to bring you up? Would you like to live somewhere like Turnham Green? What if, just by chance, in the middle of a summer's day, the train actually stopped at Turnham Green? Would you like to get off and wander along the little parks? Would it be like Dorothy or Alice? Or am I daydreaming about an illusion, an impossible illusion?

I think I'm getting a bit maudlin.

Would I look like one of the modern tedious first-time dads pushing a pram as if they were the first man to ever procreate, and were both eager to show you off but also terrified their darling might catch a cold from strangers?

Yes, I think is the answer to that.

Just to make sure I don't turn out like the pram-pushing-arsehole-from-hell, if I ever do get to push you around in your pram, me little Danny, I shall take a rugby ball along, on top of the pram hood, and every time we come to a little park I'll throw it for you to fetch. It'll take you a few goes to get used to the idea, but we'll get there eventually.

A little more latte, I think.

That tastes better and better each time. I must have more of it more often until it ends up tasting perfect.

So, Turnham Green. Hell, let's go for it. Danny, we will give it a stational drink. Even if we are a hundred yards short of the station.

Danny, there's really only one stational drink we can award it. A very, very English drink.

Cider.

Good old English cider.

Oh, I know purists will argue that it should be a Pimms, and not only a Pimms, but a Pimms No 7 with a mint sprig.

Ultra-purists would insist that mint is for chavs, it should be borage.

Well, Danny, you know what I have to say to those people?

Borage in buckets.

So there.

Turnham Green deserves a real honest English drink, not some Hooray-Henry Islington shite.

If you're going to play rugby we'll have to get you doing press-ups as soon as you're old enough.

We're on the move again. Bye-bye little park close to Turnham Green. Enjoy your picnics.

And now we're slowly sliding through Turnham Green station, lying serene and still in the sun, no passengers to disturb it. A District Line train has just gone past us in the other directions. You're going the wrong way, arseholes.

They're silly people, aren't they, Danny? Very silly people.

Anyway. Back to my mission impossible. Terminal 3 and the sim booth cum shop and the thousands of surplus tourists and travellers.

In many ways that area outside the sim booth cum shop and just beyond were only slightly less hazardous than the crowd outside the entrance to the Underground. I was desperately looking for signs to Terminal 3, determined not to repeat the trick of mentally auto-completing directions. Others headed in the same direction were doing something similar, searching for Terminal 3 or the Heathrow Express, or maybe the meaning of life. Others coming towards us were looking for the Underground, Terminal 2, Terminal 1, or they were just basically lost. And if they were looking for Terminal 1, good luck with that.

Most of them had the sort of dopy, jet-lagged look you get after a sleepless night flight from somewhere far away. It was as if we were all having some slow-motion waltz with ghosts. The difference being that I knew exactly where I wanted to be but not where it was, whereas I couldn't help but feel that many of them weren't even sure of where they wanted to be nor why they wanted to be there, which meant that they were wafting hither and thither with seriously solid suitcases getting in my way.

And then suddenly the chaos was mostly resolved as I entered the next section of travelators. Again two of them, the left hand one going my way, the right hand one coming towards us. A broad middle section for anyone not disposed to risk a moving floor. Unwisely I checked my watch as I leapt on to the travelator.

It was still 13h24.

Still six minutes left.

Now we're just passing through Stamford Brook, gliding through, like a regal ocean-going liner in calm seas. More little chocolate-box parks.

Ah, knew it was too good to be true. We've stopped. I can just see the edge of a platform ahead. Must be Ravenscourt Park.

The driver has just announced that we're being held by a red signal. We should be on the move shortly. Bloody liar. He doesn't know whether we'll be on the move shortly or when hell freezes over. But I think I am now reconciled to the whole going-slow, not-going-anywhere business.

We're just below tree-top level. The sun is throwing dappled colours around amongst the leaves. Light, translucent green, dark green, even purple. There's a certain calmness to it. Or resignation, perhaps. Some of the other passengers have the look of old soldiers who have been through it all before. They've heard the order to halt for a few minutes, so now they've metaphorically stacked their rifles, dropped their haversacks onto the grass to use as pillows, and are lying in the sun getting a tan and a kip until the next idiot order from the next idiot officer.

So why should I suddenly be thinking of Soho and Zoots?

It must have been the park we walked through after we'd been to the pub in Soho the one Sunday. That was also dappled and rippling in the afternoon sun, though that was in the spring.

What had happened was that Maddy and I had bumped into an old friend of mine who I hadn't seen for years. Shirley, her name was. At one time, long before I met your mother, we were part of a jamming group, singers, song-writers, musicians, who agreed to meet in a friendly pub and have a jamming session every so often. I'd lost touch with them because of school commitments and life generally, as you do – and the feeling that my song-writing career had stalled permanently.

Maddy and I had been strolling around Camden Town when up popped Shirley, dressed as she always had been, like a refugee from a superior Oxfam charity shop. Except now she had two lovely little boys with her, one either side. We made the usual exclamations about how long it had been since we had last seen it other, she introduced her two sweet little sons who tried to hide behind her skirts, giggling and peeking out at us. I introduced Maddy, then we said something about catching up on what had happened since whenever we last met, not expecting anything to come of it, when she said:

'Why don't we meet up on Sunday? I'm going to a sesh with the others. Soho, the old place.'

'A jamming session?' I asked, having lost the language.

'Of course, there's another type?'

I looked at Maddy.

'Fancy going to a jamming session on Sunday?' I asked.

'Is the Pope?' she responded.

I turned back to Shirley.

'Maddy's the only person I've ever known who is addicted to singing,' I said. 'She's a professional.'

'Well, then, it's a date. See you Sunday. Start around two.'

And off we went on our respective ways until the Sunday. I think Maddy was quite impressed that I had once been a devotee of jamming sessions. It was, as it were, a confirmation of our shared loves. She could never have lived without music, and I don't think she could have gone out with anyone who didn't have a similar bug.

Come the Sunday we turned up at the pub, got a red wine for Maddy and a pint for me, and sat down next to each other, my arm around her shoulders. We sat watching the usual setup: there was a small open area at one end. Two young men with beards trying to put up a microphone and get it to work. The pub was quite full, mostly young people of the earnest type, students, naïve idealists, middle class children who wanted to do good. The boys wore longish hair, quite a few beards, jeans and white t-shirts, the girls a mixture from jeans and t-shirts to men's lumberjack shirts to highly coloured dumpy or flowing items that must have been rescued from the recycling bin where they had gone to die. Some were musicians, some were in love with musicians. There were a couple of older men who had never grown out of the music scene, but none I recognised.

'I've just realised,' I said softly to Maddy, 'we stick out like sore thumbs. We look respectable. I wish I'd worn jeans at least.'

As a teacher I'd got used to buying the sort of casual-yet-acceptable-in-a-classroom clothes that could also be worn to school, to church, to social dinners, in evenings, at weekends, pretty much any time without comment. That didn't include jeans or t-shirts. Maddy mostly wore black, including flowing skirts which carried an understated kind of menacing chic. The other people in the pub were mostly dreamers, Maddy had a Dream, and the intention of making it come true. There was a palpable difference. The dreamers' clothes sang, 'I'd like to be a sailor on the Cotton Blossom number one'. Maddy's clothes sneered back and stated, 'I'm the fucking captain. The plank is over there.'

'Where's Shirley?' she asked.

'Don't know. Doesn't look like she's come. Maybe one of the kids is sick.'

Which was a problem, because Shirley was to be our bridge to the others. Without her we could only introduce ourselves as (a) a teacher who used to write songs for jamming sessions many years ago, and (b) a professional singer who could sing theirs socks off without even trying, which might be accurate but hardly polite.

The two young men got the microphone going with the obligatory 'Testing 1 – 2 – 3, testing 1 – 2 – 3' and eventually a young man with a guitar stepped up to give us his take on a Bob Dylan song. I can't remember which. Then a young woman with another guitar played Janis Joplin. She was followed by a young man who announced that he was going to perform his own song, Let Me Count The Ways.

'Pretty good stuff,' I said when he had finished, and there was a pause between the next act. 'I'm always amazed at the sheer talent you find in ordinary people.'

'Not bad,' said Maddy. 'But they put too much emotion into it. Technical control is more important. When you've got control of your voice you can control the emotion in the audience.'

By now, Danny, you will have realised that your mother is a perfectionist as far as music goes.

'Not bored are you?' I asked.

'No, no, not at all. It's just not the sort of stuff I normally sing.'

Which I think explained the slightly miffed look on her face. There was a stage of sorts, there was music of sorts, and it didn't look like she was going to get a chance to sing.

'Do you miss it?' she asked suddenly.

'Miss what?'

'This.'

'The music scene? I suppose you could say that it's a country I once lived in, but left,' I said, having given it a little thought. 'I recognise the types and scenes. But they seem to belong to a different age.'

She squeezed my hand.

'Fancy another one, or do you want to go?' I asked.

She sighed.

'Oh, go on, a little one. It's enjoyable enough, and everyone seems to be having fun.'

So I ordered another pint for myself and a small glass of red wine to accompany the glass Maddy had so far only half finished. When I sat down I put my arm around Maddy again and she snuggled into my shoulder to enjoy the acts even if she wasn't likely to get a shot at singing. We had just got nicely comfortable when an emaciated old hobo stopped in front of us.

'Mark! It is you! How's it going, mate?'

I hesitated for a second or so before I remembered him.

'Zoots!' I said, standing up to shake his hand. 'How are things? You look the same as ever.'

Which he did. I think he began growing a straggly beard as soon as he was able to, but it had never developed into anything and never would. He had always worn skinny jeans and a blue plaid shirt which seemed to hang off him. He lived off beer and cigarettes. But I'd never seen him drunk. Or eat anything.

'Good, good,' he replied. 'How's the song-writing going? Made your fortune yet?'

I laughed, regretfully, and very middle-classfully.

'I haven't written anything for ages. Listen, let me get you a pint and we'll talk about the old days.'

'Sorry, Mark, I've got the wife and in-laws over there. She gets the hump if I disappear to drink with someone else. Listen, pop in next Sunday, we'll do it then, okay? She's taking the kids back up to Newcastle.'

Kids? Newcastle? Was this really Zoots? Our Zoots?

'I'll try. Can't guarantee anything.'

'I'm in pretty much every Sunday. Listen, you remember Peter, the guitarist? You taught him the Flobblelobble Song? He's still doing that for kids' parties.'

'You're joking. I'd completely forgotten that.'

'Serious. Listen, I'll see you around, the wife, you know?'

We shook hands again and he ambled off.

'Well, there you go,' I said as I sat down next to Maddy. 'Zoots. Married. I can't believe it.'

'Who is he?'

'Clarinettist. Really good. I think he teaches, or used to do. But, married? Zoots? I don't remember him ever having a girlfriend. I always thought of him as a permanent bachelor.'

'So while you were still jamming Shirley was single and so was Zoots. As soon as you disappear Shirley starts a family and Zoots settles down into happily married life, has kids and presumably in-laws who live in Newcastle.'

'What are you trying to say, Maddy, that I'm an enemy of family life?'

'You don't think it's more than just a coincidence?'

'Course not.'

She gave me the thoughtful look that I was more used to getting from my mother.

'Okay, who were you going out with then? Back in those old days?'

I paused to think. I could have said, 'Well, there was Sharon, I remember her, and Mary, and Lulu, she was a guitarist, and Daisy, she was sort of a camp follower, oh, and Peggy and …' Followed by another ten or twenty names as I remembered each of them. Which would have been true to a certain extent, though firstly some of the relationships were of very brief duration, and secondly ticking their names off against my fingers to the woman I had decided was going to be my wife sounded like an extremely stupid thing to do.

'I don't think I went out seriously with anyone then,' I said instead. 'We were all there for the music. There were some girls who got crushes on a few of the blokes, but that never happened to me, thank god.'

She made a ladylike sound which summed up what she thought of that, and it wasn't much. It sounded as if it translated as "I don't believe you, you lying son of a bitch, and it's your fault for making me swear like that, too."

'Tell me about the Flobblelobble Song,' she said.

'Oh, that was just a bit of nonsense we came up with one Sunday after a few pints. Peter used to play the guitar at children's parties and he was looking for something different. Someone knocked over a glass and I said flobble. You know, instead of, well, you know. Peter looked and me and asked, flobble? So I nodded and said, lobble. And he asked, flobblelobble? And it just went from there. It's just a silly little thing that kids find funny. Nonsense words with repetition. We managed to turn it into a kind of song for guitar over quite a few pints.'

'Well, there you go, you have written something memorable.'

She smiled.

'Flobblelobble,' she said, and laid her head in my shoulder again.

'You are my flobblelobble, my only flobblelobble,' I thought to myself, 'you make me happy, when things are sad ...'

Nope, that was another song altogether.

After we finished that round we left and wandered slowly towards Russell Square, taking a detour through the park. We found the obligatory ice-cream van, bought a couple of 99s, and sat down close to the fountains to eat them and watch the world go by. I think it was the fountains, and possibly reflections from some windows that caused the leaves above us to seemingly dance in dappled light. Which is why I was reminded of it by the trees here now.

Having finished her ice-cream your mother decided that it was an ideal time to have a nap, using me as a pillow. As usual. And as usual I certainly wasn't complaining. I could have stayed there forever.

Hello, we're on the move again. The driver's just announced that we've got a green light. I'm not sure anyone is listening. Most are either asleep or sitting with eyes closed. There's one playing a game on his mobile, but there's always one of those.

Passing Ravenscourt Park on the port side. And on the starboard side.

Now we're definitely getting into London. High-rise buildings of flats, flats and more flats. We're at the bottom of them, you can look up and see the uniform dirty walls, doors and windows, with the occasional flutter of a piece of trapped clothing or something. And into the tunnels. Tunnels and tunnels and tunnels, the harbinger of the true Underground and Hades.

Do not go gentle into that good night.

Well, I tried my best, Danny. One day you'll be proud of me.

Sit-ups. As well as press-ups. You're never too young to start a proper exercise regime.

Here we are at Hammersmith. Just gone four o'clock. There's still light coming down from the open skies, surrounded by buildings stretching to the heavens above.

Amazing how the Piccadilly Line is behaving itself now that I'm no longer in a hurry.

Lovely summer's day.

Be going completely underground soon, just after Barons Court. And then it's just a few more stations.

I think my muscles are going to be a bit stiff tomorrow.

I've definitely earned a lie-in.

Cockfosters
Oakwood
Southgate
Arnos Grove
Bounds Green
Wood Green
Turnpike Lane
Manor House
Finsbury Park
Arsenal
Holloway Road
Caledonian Road
King's Cross St. Pancras
Russell Square
Holborn
Covent Garden
Leicester Square
Piccadilly Circus
Green Park
Hyde Park Corner
Knightsbridge
South Kensington
Gloucester Road
Earl's Court
Barons Court
Hammersmith
Turnham Green
Acton Town

Ealing Common
North Ealing
Park Royal
Alperton
Sudbury Town
Sudbury Hill
South Harrow
Rayners Lane
Eastcote
Ruislip Manor
Ruislip
Ickenham
Hillingdon
Uxbridge

South Ealing
Northfields
Boston Manor
Osterley
Hounslow East
Hounslow Central
Hounslow West
Hatton Cross
Heathrow T 1-2-3  ⟶  Heathrow T4
Heathrow T5

# Hammersmith

*Estimated time to Barons Court 2 minutes*

*Estimated time to Bounds Green 43 minutes*

16h01

You can tell we're getting into central London. All the various tube lines start meeting up. Here you can change from the Piccadilly to the District, the Circle, or the Hammersmith and City lines. One of them, as far as I remember, you have to go up some stairs, out of the station, across a busy road, and into another station. The Hammersmith and City, I think. That sort of thing is the result of trying to build a modern public transport system into a city that's already built up. Plus the fact that the individual Underground lines were originally owned by different private companies, so co-operation was not a given.

Maddy loved the quirks of London. Apparently where she grew up everything had been carefully planned and laid out.

'And they all lived in boxes, little boxes, all the same,' she sang, concluding, 'bloody awful.'

And then there was that most famous of pre-planned cities, Canberra.

'If you ever go to Canberra on a Sunday – actually, any day, really – you know what you must take with you?' she asked.

'A twenty-four-pack of stubbies?' I asked.

'No, a revolver, to shoot yourself with.'

'That bad?'

'Worse. We went on a school trip there one weekend when I was about fifteen. It's the sort of place that drives teetotallers to drink. I don't think many of us had drunk alcohol before that, but most of us returned as alcoholics without touching a drop. It's like living in a vast emptiness of carefully and precisely laid out empty houses full of polite zombies who don't try to attack you.'

'I really must send my pupils there, then,' I remember saying. I'd parachute the little bastards in. One parachute between five of the little shits.

Hammersmith.

Above this station is a huge shopping mall, very popular in the afternoon with schoolkids. They can meet up in McDonalds or Burger King or other sizzling hells and stuff themselves with lethal fast food while exchanging gossip, winding each other up, teasing the girls if they're boys, or complaining about the boys if they're girls. Afterwards they can, if they so wish, go shop-lifting.

Danny, that life is not for you. However and wherever you grow up, I hope you will spend your time more productively, like dissecting rats, or politicians or something. Or is that tautology?

The other thing I know about Hammersmith is that there's a flyover around here somewhere. I've never driven over it, but whenever I listen to local radio in the morning it seems to get a mention, along with the words 'traffic jam'.

A flyover is a road over part of town, and is high.

The kids in the mall are having a ball.

Ergo, Hammersmith's stational drink is: a high-ball.

Easy when you get the knack, Danny.

Let me have some latte to celebrate.

Cheers.

Now then.

Back to the chase.

The thing is, I'd negotiated two travelators at speed by then so perhaps I hit the next one with a little less concentration than I should have. To be blunt I almost saw my arse. Basically, I leapt on with my weight leaning backwards, the travelator was going a lot faster than I expected, so for a few precious seconds I was desperately trying not to fall on my backside. Somehow I slowly forced myself upright, all the while looking at an oncoming pram in the middle section, the little baby in it gazing back in fascination. I remember it quite clearly. It was wrapped in a pink blanket with its arms above the blanket, it had these huge little wide eyes, hands held towards its mouth, the mouth in a circle, a pink bobble hat falling slowly off its head.

I had this urge to lean over the railing and put it back on straight. Which would have been completely physically impossible given my then stance, not to mention the distance between us.

I don't know who was pushing the pram. A man, a woman, haven't a clue. Mother, father, maid, grandparent, sibling. Could have been any of those. Could have been an orangutan for all I knew.

As I gained my balance and stood upright the pram came nearer, and I turned to watch the baby pass. The baby leaned out of the pram and looked at me, craning its head to look back as the travelator took me away. I took a few steps after it, which was fucking daft. Walking against the flow of a travelator? Lucky I didn't do myself an injury.

And then the baby was gone, lost in the legs of the crowds.

I turned back towards Terminal 3, shaking my head to clear it. As I did so a young woman on the other travelator passed me, headed for the Underground. She was quite pretty, but that wasn't what caught my attention. It was the six foot dragon she had stopped to put down. It was a huge furry toy. It had a bright blue back and face, and a gleaming white front, with huge marble eyes and a broad grin on its face. It was the happiest, friendliest, softest dragon I have ever seen. It would have invited stares almost anywhere. But what was it doing on a travelator in an airport? Coming presumably from a flight that had recently landed? Was she bringing it as a present for some favoured niece or nephew? Why hadn't they been here to meet her?

It's amazing how many questions your mind can ask in a split second. And fail to answer in a lifetime.

And why do we have weird dreams, and why do we have weird thoughts like wondering about somebody else's dragon?

Why a dragon?

I suppose I'll never know now.

Then I snapped out of it. There was still a good deal of travelator to get behind me, and I still didn't know how many more miles of corridor I had to get through. All I knew was that there were too many people in front of me, too many people in the way. In my way.

Ninety-nine percent of the time people on travelators are probably well behaved and polite. Actually, it's probably somewhere around sixty percent, but you just need one complete arsehole blocking things up to set off everyone in a hurry. Having got past the sight of dragon-woman I came up against any number. First there was the hen party. Four young women in their early twenties wearing various outfits indicative of wedding dresses, all about two sizes too small. Or perhaps the other way around: the wearers were two sizes too large. And obviously tipsy, to put it politely.

They were standing two by two, chatting to each other, their scattered suitcases completely blocking the travelator.

'Excuse me,' I said as I came up, 'must get through, in a bit of a hurry.'

'Hey, up, chucks, what's the rush,' said one plump little one.

'Why don't you spend a little time with me?' sang another, just as little, but weighing about twice as much, but with a nice smile.

'No, seriously, excuse me, I must get through,' I insisted.

'I'm single,' said the third, 'want my number?'

'I'm not single,' I said, 'now if you'll just let me through.'

'I'm free,' sang the fourth.

'And easy,' said the first and they cackled.

'Right, fuck this for a joke,' I said. I lifted up two of their suitcases and dropped them over the rail into the central aisle. Then I shot through the resultant gap as the suitcases careered along on their wheels.

Behind me I could hear initial exclamations of surprise followed by a great deal of swearing and threats about what would happen once their boyfriends got to hear about this.

Which is when I saw the next pair of police officers coming towards me, two men, one about six foot five, the other half a foot taller, wearing combat uniforms with caps, revolvers strapped to their legs, body armour, automatic rifles strapped to their chests, etc, etc. One looked curiously at one of the suitcases as it skittered towards him. He nonchalantly put out a booted foot to stop it. The other put his radio to his mouth.

'Bravo One coming your way,' he said as I passed them. 'And the bastard's coming through in one hell of a hurry.'

At any other time I might have connected the dots and realised that I was the Bravo One referred to, not to mention bastard, but just then I checked my watch again.

13h26.

Four minutes to go.

I risked a glance backward. It struck me that the hen party might be coming after me to remonstrate. Instead one was hung over the rail trying to catch her suitcase as it slowed down, two others were chatting up the officers up as they passed each other.

The officers looked back at me inscrutably. The taller one scratched his head. And then I turned back and carried on towards Terminal 3.

Coming into Barons Court.

Only nineteen stops left.

Cockfosters
Oakwood
Southgate
Arnos Grove
Bounds Green
Wood Green
Turnpike Lane
Manor House
Finsbury Park
Arsenal
Holloway Road
Caledonian Road
King's Cross St. Pancras
Russell Square
Holborn
Covent Garden
Leicester Square
Piccadilly Circus
Green Park
Hyde Park Corner
Knightsbridge
South Kensington
Gloucester Road
Earl's Court
Barons Court
Hammersmith
Turnham Green
Acton Town

Ealing Common — South Ealing
North Ealing — Northfields
Park Royal — Boston Manor
Alperton — Osterley
Sudbury Town — Hounslow East
Sudbury Hill — Hounslow Central
South Harrow — Hounslow West
Rayners Lane — Hatton Cross ←
Eastcote — Heathrow T 1-2-3 → Heathrow T4
Ruislip Manor — Heathrow T5
Ruislip
Ickenham
Hillingdon
Uxbridge

# Barons Court

*Estimated time to Earl's Court 3 minutes*

*Estimated time to Bounds Green 41 minutes*

16h05

We should be getting to the start of crush hour around about now. It's still relatively empty. Or at least it's not yet squashing room only. Some schools go on half term next week, so I guess plenty of families will be getting away for a summer break. And it's Friday, so half of office workers will have left early for the weekend, the other half will be in the pubs until the rush hour is over, enjoying the weather.

Not inside the pubs, of course, weather like this they'll be standing outside with a pint in their hands, being very cheerful, blocking the pavements, and pissing off other people who are in a hurry and have no time to spare standing outside a pub with a pint in their hand though they'd dearly love to.

Me, I've got everything I need right here.

Cheers.

A stational drink for Baron's Court. Danny, let's make this a little more difficult.

Barons.

Baron von Richthofen. And his flying circus.

In World War I. In the days some people still believed there was something chivalrous about killing each other. At least in the air, anyway. The ground troops had realised that all the fun had gone out of things by that time. Nothing like mud, blood, death, destruction and having to live with lice to take the fun out of things.

Von Richthofen was given an order to have his aircraft painted in camouflage as the British and French were learning to do. Instead his squadron painted each aircraft a bright colour. His was a red Fokker triplane. He used to have a special cup made up for each of his victories. Up until someone killed him. Either a Canadian in the air or an Australian on the ground.

Schnapps. That was his celebratory drink. So, Barons Court, you get Schnapps.

Cheers. Scheers, even. Gruss Gott or whatever it is they say.

13h26

Finally. I had the end of the travelator in sight. Just one person standing in the way, a portly looking old gent in a fawn suit and homburg hat, suitcase at his side blocking the travelator, walking stick in hand tapping a tune of some sort or other. I was coming up as fast as I could, he was in the way, I was debating whether to be polite and request he make way, or just blast through. Blast through, I decided. His fault for not leaving space when a young man on a desperate and urgent mission was coming up behind him and closing fast.

Just then he either heard something or a sixth sense made him turn. His face registered interested surprise above a bushy moustache. Quick as anything he pulled his suitcase out of the way. Then he doffed his hat.

'You look like you're in a hurry, young man,' he said in a very 1950s Home County accent, as I passed. 'Good luck and God speed.'

'Thank you,' I called back. 'Very kind of you.'

Then I was off the travelator, sliding along to slow down as I approached a bend in the tunnel. As I came around it I found I was faced with what looked like an even longer travelator going towards Terminal 3. And it was busy. And there was a matching one on the right coming towards me on the right. And that was busy. And there was a wide aisle between them. And that was busy.

I checked my watch.

13h27

Three minutes left. If the travelator was the last part I could just about make it. It appeared to dip down and then quite steeply up again.

We're at Earl's Court.

Earl's Court is one of only two stations on the Piccadilly Line to have an apostrophe.

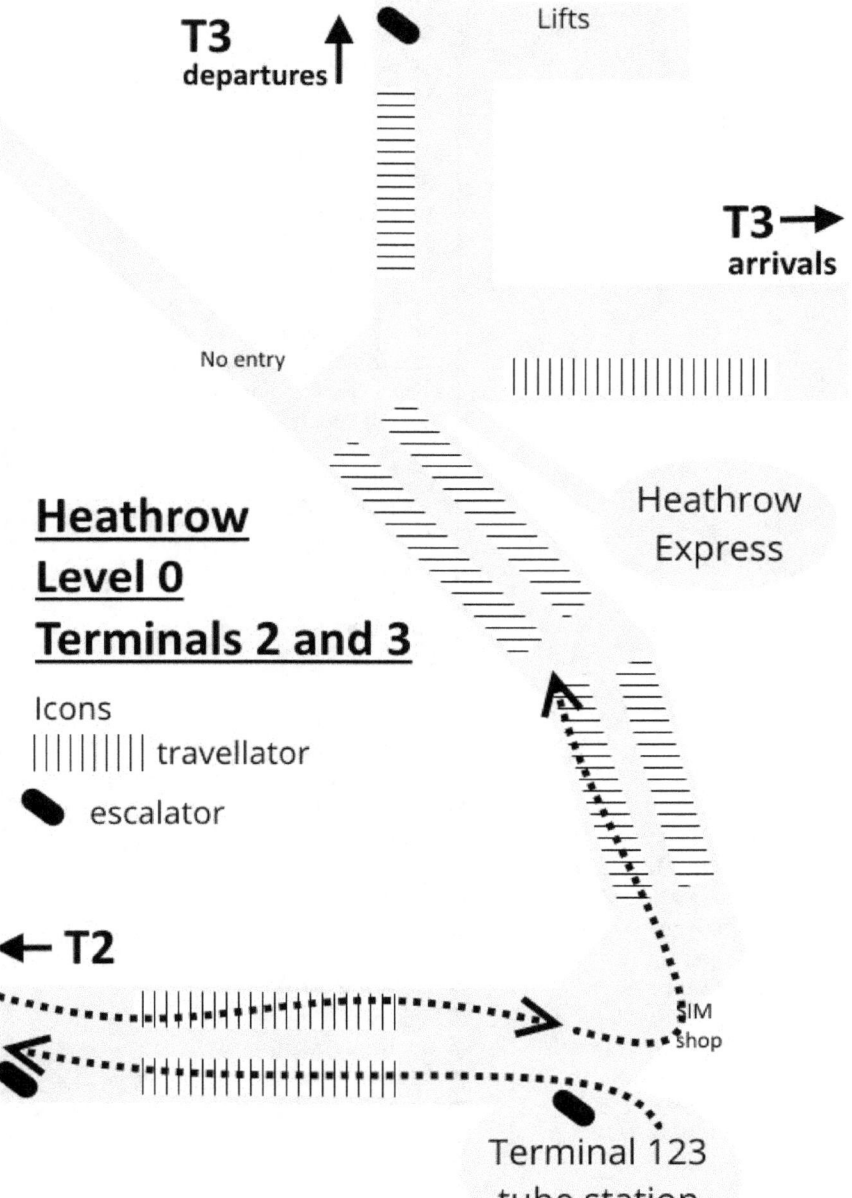

**T3**
departures

Lifts

**T3** →
arrivals

No entry

# Heathrow
# Level 0
# Terminals 2 and 3

Heathrow
Express

Icons

|||||||||| travellator

escalator

← **T2**

SIM
shop

Terminal 123
tube station

Cockfosters
Oakwood
Southgate
Arnos Grove
Bounds Green
Wood Green
Turnpike Lane
Manor House
Finsbury Park
Arsenal
Holloway Road
Caledonian Road
King's Cross St. Pancras
Russell Square
Holborn
Covent Garden
Leicester Square
Piccadilly Circus
Green Park
Hyde Park Corner
Knightsbridge
South Kensington
Gloucester Road
Earl's Court
Barons Court
Hammersmith
Turnham Green
Acton Town

Ealing Common — South Ealing
North Ealing — Northfields
Park Royal — Boston Manor
Alperton — Osterley
Sudbury Town — Hounslow East
Sudbury Hill — Hounslow Central
South Harrow — Hounslow West
Rayners Lane — Hatton Cross ←
Eastcote — Heathrow T 1-2-3 → Heathrow T4
Ruislip Manor — Heathrow T5
Ruislip
Ickenham
Hillingdon
Uxbridge

## Earl's Court

*Estimated time to Gloucester Road 2 minutes*

*Estimated time to Bounds Green 38 minutes*

16h09

I remember visiting a pub here once, quite a few years ago. Can't remember the name. I'm pretty sure the rugby world cup was on, or just about to start. Pub was full of Aussies, Kiwis and South Africans. And some locals. There was a lot of good natured banter and insults flying around. I didn't get any stick, more sympathy than anything, because England weren't expected to get to the semi-finals, let alone be a serious contender. I did point out that I was of Irish descent but they weren't having any of that.

There were some stairs at the end where we were standing, with a balustrade. I think perhaps the loos were up there, or perhaps another drinking room.

Danny, when you've visited as many pubs as I have sometimes you tend to confuse them.

George Orwell once wrote an essay about a pub called The Moon Under Water. It didn't exist. What he was describing was his idea of the perfect pub. It was based on four pubs he often visited around Highbury. Each was good in its own way, but lacked something one of the others had, so he combined them into the fictional perfect pub, The Moon Under Water. Needless to say there are now pubs called The Moon Under Water. I've never visited one, but I'm prepared to bet they're mostly shite.

For Orwell the perfect pub had a family friendly garden. You would have loved it, Danny.

The pub in Earl's Court – let's call it the Rugby Pub, I can't remember the real name, if I ever knew it – would probably have failed all or at least most of Orwell's criteria. It was loud and rambunctious. Almost everyone was drinking lager, some pints, others from stubbies or cans, mostly Fosters.

A stubby is what many people from Down Under call a little bottle of beer, so small as to be a waste of time. As I told one of the Australians

405

there, it's very amusing to hear some of these quaint words the colonials come up with. He offered to take me upstairs and throw me out a window, describing me as a Pommy bastard. As you do.

Danny, if your mother threatens to throw you out a window, well, don't stick around to find out whether women understand the rudiments of banter.

It was actually a woman who caused the trouble in that pub. Your typical, long-legged blonde beauty, young, slim, fit, her clothes showing a lot more flesh than they should, the sort they use to advertise beach holidays. She was coming down the stairs. She stopped halfway down and turned to face the pub, holding something behind her back. I doubt if any of the mostly male crowd would have paid her much attention under normal circumstances.

Okay, she was an advertiser's idea of Aphrodite, but there were more important things to consider at the time. We had beers in our hands, and it was the rugby world cup, after all.

'Hey, boys!' she called, and most of us did glance up.

'Catch!' she shouted and brought out the thing behind her back, pitching it perfectly into the centre of the pub. It was a rugby ball, mostly white, quite possible a replica of a world cup rugby ball. It sailed gently, almost in slow motion, over the heads of the drinkers. And then one man jumped up to catch it, as if in a line-out. He missed. And the room went wild. Half the men were hell-bent on getting the ball, the other half wanted to get out of the way before tables, beer and glass began to fly.

My Aussie friend and I stayed well clear of the action. To protect our drinks.

The reason I've remembered that is because of what happened on the travelator going towards Terminal 3. I was still running. Beginning to breathe quite heavily, but still moving faster than a walk. I leapt onto the next travelator, taking in the people already on. Just in front were two women standing on the right, facing each other, a little gap between them. In front of them were other people, also standing on the right. There were people walking on the left, quite fast. All in all it looked straightforward: run down the left, when catching up people on the left walking, look for a gap on the right, dodge into that and get past the slowcoaches. And so I started.

I got just up to the two women when I realised why they were standing slightly apart. There was a little boy there, about eight years old. And he had a football in his hands.

And as I came up he began bouncing it off the other side of the travelator right in front of my path. I carried on. I assumed his mother would give him a clip and tell him to stop. If not I presumed the woman facing me would restrain the child, seeing me coming up at a rate of knots.

Ever encountered parents who don't seem to think anything their brats do can be wrong? Like banging a football against the side of a travelator that other people are using?

I passed them just as brat-boy tried another bounce. The ball caught my shin and ricocheted at an angle toward my right.

There's a reason footballers wear shin pads. Because it's fucking painful when you aren't expecting it, even with the light balls they use these days.

Behind me I heard the boy shout, 'Oi, that's my ball!'

The ball struck someone's Armalite suitcase on the top corner and bounced back at me at chest height. I vaguely registered that the suitcase owner was a young blonde woman looking at me in a great deal of surprise.

'That's his football,' from one of the women I'd just passed. I took 'his' to refer to brat-boy.

Now the thing is, I coach football. And one of the things you teach the kids is how to control a ball with your chest before dropping it onto your foot. What you do then depends on the situation. If you're a defender controlling a long ball from the opposition, you normally play it forwards a few yards until the opposition strikers get in range, whereupon you pass it up the field to one of your fellow players.

If you're a striker you turn and fire it into the other side's goal. I used to be a striker.

But there was no way on god's earth I was going to turn around while running on a fast-moving travelator and fire a football back to the boy.

In fact it's pretty impossible to control a football when you're trying to run on a moving surface, especially when all you're interested in is getting rid of it. And you've got an irritating little ten-year-old brat-boy tugging on your trousers, insisting, 'Oi! That's my ball.'

So I hoicked it into the air off the travelator. Or that's what I tried to do.

Instead it went straight at the head of a tall, elderly gent just ahead. Give him his due, he didn't hesitate at all. Just headed it straight back at my head. So I headed it out of the way. Straight forward. Right into the path of a helpful young lad who was thoroughly enjoying the sight, and evidently an aspiring footballer, who flicked a leg out and kicked it straight back at me. But this time I was ready. There was just enough of a gap in the right to duck into and let the blasted ball fly past. Straight into brat-boy's face. There was an ironic cheer from those who could see what was happening.

I gave myself a second to enjoy the sight. Then I was off again. I checked my watch.

13h28.

Two minutes to go.

Coming into Gloucester Road.

You know what, Danny? In the end the bloke who got the ball in the pub was a Welshman. There was a huge mound of burly Aussies, Kiwis and South Africans piled up on each other, all asking where the ball was, and there's this little bloke wearing a Wales shirt crawling out from the side with the ball. Then he goes back to the bar, puts the ball on the counter, gets on his stool and calmly resumes drinking his pint while looking at the mound of bodies with nary an expression on his face.

Cockfosters
Oakwood
Southgate
Arnos Grove
Bounds Green
Wood Green
Turnpike Lane
Manor House
Finsbury Park
Arsenal
Holloway Road
Caledonian Road
King's Cross St. Pancras
Russell Square
Holborn
Covent Garden
Leicester Square
Piccadilly Circus
Green Park
Hyde Park Corner
Knightsbridge
South Kensington
Gloucester Road
Earl's Court
Barons Court
Hammersmith
Turnham Green
Acton Town

| | |
|---|---|
| Ealing Common | South Ealing |
| North Ealing | Northfields |
| Park Royal | Boston Manor |
| Alperton | Osterley |
| Sudbury Town | Hounslow East |
| Sudbury Hill | Hounslow Central |
| South Harrow | Hounslow West |
| Rayners Lane | Hatton Cross ← |
| Eastcote | Heathrow T 1-2-3 → Heathrow T4 |
| Ruislip Manor | Heathrow T5 |
| Ruislip | |
| Ickenham | |
| Hillingdon | |
| Uxbridge | |

## Gloucester Road

*Estimated time to South Kensington 2 minutes*

*Estimated time to Bounds Green 36 minutes*

16h15

Danny, there is a type of cheese known as Gloucester. It's produced in the county of Gloucestershire. It comes in two varieties, Single and Double. There is some debate as to whether it goes better with real ale, a Rioja or a Riesling.

There is also something called The Cooper's Hill Cheese-Rolling and Wake which takes place on Cooper's Hill near the town of Gloucester each Spring Bank Holiday. The event is quite simple: someone sends a four kilogram round of Double Gloucester cheese rolling down the very steep Cooper's Hill, and people chase after it. The first one across the winning line wins the cheese.

They don't try to catch the cheese: it can get up speeds of over a hundred kilometres an hour, and you'd need to be seriously insane to think you can beat that speed on foot down a hill. Though to be fair most of the people who take part are a bit off their rockers. The hill is concave so you can't see the bottom; the terrain is rough, uneven and contains potholes; they have paramedics and ambulances at the bottom to take the survivors to hospital; and the "route" is patrolled by "catchers" from the local rugby club and farmer's institution to carry down the ones who have fallen over and can't get up again.

So, Gloucester Road, I'll take the middle option: your stational drink will have to be a Rioja. With some Gloucester cheese.

Isn't that nice of me.

You can even have some crackers.

I think the travelators were a safer bet. Not by much, though.

Danny, you are not going to do any cheese chasing, it's far too dangerous.

The next section of the travelator looked straight-forward. A clear run up to two small people walking side by side, holding hands. I decided I would loudly request passing permission as I came up behind them,

410

expecting them to step aside, I would whizz past, exclaim my thanks and then race onwards. No need to slow down.

As I came haring up I noticed a few things about them. Firstly they were Muslim. She was wearing a full-length formless brown dress, and a veil over her hair. He wore a kufi, a Muslim skull cap, a long baggy shirt two sizes too large, and even baggier trousers called paijamas. They seemed to be chatting away to each other, very quietly. They kept looking in each other's eyes and making little movements with their free hands. As they looked at each other I realised they were probably in their eighties or even nineties. They were diminutive.

They looked, from the back, like a couple of teenagers in love.

As I came closer I began calling,

'Excuse me!'

'Excuse me!'

Nothing.

'Excuse me!'

'Excuse me!'

Still nothing.

Which is when I realised.

They were deaf. They must have been lip-reading and signing. I was coming up behind two Octogenarian teenage deaf lovers. And I couldn't stop. I was about to mow them down like two insignificant leaves in a gale.

I couldn't do it.

But I couldn't stop.

And I couldn't pass.

But I could.

Danny, never, ever try what I did then. Never. Absolutely never, ever. It gives me the shits just thinking about it.

I grabbed hold of the handrail. And swung myself into the non-moving middle aisle.

Landed running.

Kept running.

Faster and faster.

Kept running past the loving couple.

Cleared them by a couple of yards.

Looked up.

Saw two armed coppers coming directly towards me. Wearing the sort of manner that explicitly announces that you aren't going any further.

So I grabbed the handrail now on my left and swung myself back onto the travelator. And carried on running. Past the coppers.

Who had stopped and were regarding me with a kind of professional interest, as if I had cleverly slipped out of their hands this time, but the day was long, they weren't in a hurry, and they knew something I didn't.

I could sense them turn and begin to stroll in the same direction I was headed.

I should have wondered why all these coppers seemed so interested in me.

Cockfosters
Oakwood
Southgate
Arnos Grove
Bounds Green
Wood Green
Turnpike Lane
Manor House
Finsbury Park
Arsenal
Holloway Road
Caledonian Road
King's Cross St. Pancras
Russell Square
Holborn
Covent Garden
Leicester Square
Piccadilly Circus
Green Park
Hyde Park Corner
Knightsbridge
South Kensington
Gloucester Road
Earl's Court
Barons Court
Hammersmith
Turnham Green
Acton Town

Ealing Common
North Ealing
Park Royal
Alperton
Sudbury Town
Sudbury Hill
South Harrow
Rayners Lane
Eastcote
Ruislip Manor
Ruislip
Ickenham
Hillingdon
Uxbridge

South Ealing
Northfields
Boston Manor
Osterley
Hounslow East
Hounslow Central
Hounslow West
Hatton Cross
Heathrow T 1-2-3 ⟶ Heathrow T4
Heathrow T5

# South Kensington

*Estimated time to Knightsbridge 2 minutes*

*Estimated time to Bounds Green 34 minutes*

16h18

We are now definitely underground. Have been since Earl's Court, but it takes me a while to get used to the idea. You can tell the difference between experienced tube users and tourists. The tourists are all pointing out the station signs and taking great interest and loads of photographs, whereas the experienced passenger has given up hope of getting a phone signal and is now either reading something, playing a game on their tablet or mobile, trying to catch up on their sleep or just keep breathing. There's a young lady repairing her make-up, presumably getting ready to meet someone for a night out.

Must say, I wouldn't mind curling up with the young lady next to me and going to sleep. I'm completely exhausted.

To sleep, perchance to dream.

Nope, too knackered for dreams.

I need some latte to wake me up. There we go.

Right.

South Ken. Have to have a stational drink for South Ken. Can't let the side down and miss out a station. Wouldn't be fair.

South Kensington.

Kensington.

Supposedly a very posh area. Very establishment. In reality?

It's certainly very establishment. A favourite haunt of spies, too. There's a restaurant somewhere around here where Christine Keeler had lunch with Eugene Ivanov, the Soviet embassy attaché at the nearby Soviet Embassy. She was a call girl who was also having an affair with John Profumo, a government minister, aka 5th Baron Profumo, the Secretary of State for War. He probably wouldn't have survived the scandal, but made sure of that by denying absolutely everything before having to admit that it was true. These days he would just declare, 'I did not have sex with that woman. Define sex.'

Is that American sex or British sex?

Quite a few other embassies around here.

So, a drink for the establishment.

There used to be a magazine called Punch. It took the mick out of the establishment. And, of course, there's a drink called punch. It's basically booze with fruit in. So, South Kensington, you get punch.

With prunes in. For the hell of it.

And raspberries. All the raspberries you like.

So, Danny, it was the final third of the second travelator. Well, actually the fourth travelator, but the first two were a mistake, so they don't count.

There was a Mummy and a little girl directly ahead, the little girl dancing around excitedly at being on a moving floor in an airport going to a plane, holding Mummy's hand and asking Mummy a hundred and one questions. And Mummy is smiling and looking down at her little angel and answering her as patiently as she can. And then she hears something or sees something out of the side of her eye, notably a madman charging up at full speed and about to take her little darling out. So she puts a hand on the girl's head and draws her to her, saying, 'Let the gentleman past, darling, he seems to be in a hurry.'

And the little girls hugs Mummy's leg, smiles up at her, and then smiles up at me.

'Much obliged, ma'am,' I gasp as I trundle past, trying not to wheeze. 'Have a good trip.'

'You too,' she calls after me. I waved a tired hand in acknowledgement.

Next were a young couple in love. Or lust, possibly. Their limbs were so intertwined they'd have a problem separating them at check-in. Their lips were locked so tight they would have made a good advert for super-glue. There was only one suitcase, so I guessed one of them was leaving, the other would be waving tearfully goodbye. The suitcase was a bright pink, so I presumed it was the girl leaving on a jet plane. Though somehow, my cynical side suggested, such a passionate embrace was more suggestive of a sudden and physical relationship which wouldn't survive the bloke's short journey home. Or maybe they were just Italian.

Then past a nun sailing serenely along in her grey and white habit. It crossed my mind that it was unusual for a nun to be travelling alone.

Maybe she was actually on her way to a hen party, in disguise?

Probably not.

Then there was a clear bit for a while. Which is when I noticed the man coming down the central aisle. He was riding a scooter.

Well, it was a push-type scooter with a bag attached to it. Sort of like a wheelie bag, but with three wheels, a foot-plate built into the suitcase.

The man with one foot on it and the other pushing was wearing a three-piece suit and looked extremely elegant, apart from also looking like an eleven-year-old pushing a scooter.

Twenty feet behind him was a young man, looked about eighteen years old. He had obviously seen the scooter and had an idea. Because he was riding down the incline, standing on his wheelie-case, using it as a skateboard. A very weird, unbalanced skateboard.

I checked my watch.

13h29

One minute left. If Terminal 3 was at the end of the travelator I was going to make it. Otherwise ...

Knightsbridge. Nous avez arrivons au Knightsbridge.

I really should brush up on my French.

Seventeen stops to go.

Cockfosters
Oakwood
Southgate
Arnos Grove
Bounds Green
Wood Green
Turnpike Lane
Manor House
Finsbury Park
Arsenal
Holloway Road
Caledonian Road
King's Cross St. Pancras
Russell Square
Holborn
Covent Garden
Leicester Square
Piccadilly Circus
Green Park
Hyde Park Corner
Knightsbridge
South Kensington
Gloucester Road
Earl's Court
Barons Court
Hammersmith
Turnham Green

Ealing Common          Acton Town
North Ealing           South Ealing
Park Royal             Northfields
Alperton               Boston Manor
Sudbury Town           Osterley
Sudbury Hill           Hounslow East
South Harrow           Hounslow Central
Rayners Lane           Hounslow West
Eastcote               Hatton Cross   ←
Ruislip Manor          Heathrow T 1-2-3 ——→ Heathrow T4
Ruislip                Heathrow T5
Ickenham
Hillingdon
Uxbridge

# Knightsbridge

*Estimated time to Hyde Park Corner 2 minutes*

*Estimated time to Bounds Green 32 minutes*

16h23

A drink, Danny.

Knightsbridge.

Knights.

Bridge.

Knights Templar.

They were a religious order. Arrested by the king of France of the day because they had a lot of money he needed. Disbanded by the pope of the day because king Frenchy told him to.

Religious orders have always been behind brewing alcoholic drinks likely to kill you. Normally green.

What's that green drink that's been banned in most civilised countries? Absinthe? Made from worms. Or with worms. Or to kill worms. No, that's Tequila, the worms one.

No, it is absinthe I'm thinking of. And it was banned in France, where it was known as the Green Fairy, or Green Devil. Liked by madmen like Vincent Van Gogh and poseurs like Ernest Hemingway. It was banned in France and some other countries in 1915. The eagle-eyed might notice that that was in the middle of WWI. It's surprising how many lost battles have been blamed on the poor bloody infantry having too much easy access to cheap alcohol. If that was true all you'd need to do would be to bomb the enemy with booze to win a war.

A few years back the French realised that they were the only country to still have it banned, someone said, 'But it's a French custom, it was the national drink of France!', someone else said, 'We can tax it', and the ban was lifted and the Green Fairy was taxed.

So, Knightsbridge, absinthe is all yours. It's a tenuous link, I grant you, but after a couple of Green Fairies you won't notice. Sláinte.

Danny, there was this chap named Dean Kamen. He invented something called the Segway. Basically it's something to stand on with wheels on

418

either side and a handle to hold on as you let it propel you staidly forward. Like almost any other machine it was born out of the eternal 12-year-old boy's urge to build something that would move faster or fly higher before then crashing spectacularly. It wasn't a huge success because (a) it wasn't that fast, and (b) it didn't crash properly.

Then, not so long ago they started selling hover-boards, named after the items in the film Back To The Future part five hundred and fifty-four. Except they weren't hover-boards, they were 'self-balancing scooters'. Real hover-boards are supposed to hover, or at least levitate a little bit, these just rolled along on wheels. They contained a Lithium battery which tended to burst into flames, they endangered pedestrians, and in terms of something to get about on they were useless. They became an instant hit with schoolboys. So why I had never before seen someone using a wheelie-case as a skate-board is a mystery. Put a boy and wheels together and it's like putting a boy next to a puddle. They mix far too well, and the result is invariably not pretty.

He was a tall, string-bean fellow. And the ceiling was quite low, not to mention the signs hanging from it, especially the ones warning, 'Restricted headway'. So he sailed down the middle aisle, hunched, with his arms out to keep his balance, gathering pace as he came down the incline, describing a series of S turns as he dodged people walking along. He was getting a lot of attention, most of it disapproving.

I couldn't stop to watch. He was going south at speed and I was going north at speed. We passed each other like any normal demented runner and a wheelie-case rider tend to do.

Which is when I came up to the Jehovah's Witnesses. Or born-again Christians. Or something like that. Young, fresh-faced and unbearably cheerful. The boys wore blazers or formal jackets and shirts and ties, with small leather satchels strapped over their shoulders. The girls wore sensible shoes, sensible dresses and had their own sensible bags. They were standing either side of the travelator looking at each other, leaving just enough space for someone to get through the middle. They were clapping their hands quietly and singing softly so as not to disturb the horses, or quite possibly to emphasize just how thoughtful and holy they were being by not disturbing other people any more than was necessary to prove how carefully they were not disturbing other people. I paused to get my breath and my amazement back.

'Oh who will drive the chariot when she comes?' they were singing.

'Oh who will drive the chariot when she comes?

who will drive the chariot?

who will drive the chariot?

oh who will drive the chariot when she comes?'

There was a pause as they beamingly took a breath before the chorus:

'Singing Aye Aye Yippee Yippee Aye

Singing Aye Aye Yippee Yippee Aye

Singing Aye Aye Yippee

Aye Aye Yippee

Aye Aye Yippee Yippee Aye ...'

The only thing missing was the ubiquitous pamphlets. Those were presumably in the sensible leather satchels.

I looked at them and gritted my teeth. Before they could start with the second verse, 'King Jesus, he'll be driver, when she comes', I decided to butt in with the version my dad had sung to me when I was a kid, before mum stopped him.

'She's got a lovely titillating smile' I began. The ones nearest me looked at me with some interest, as if they thought I was about to join their sing-along.

'She's got a lovely titillating smile' I carried on, starting to walk between them. Some of them tried earnestly to join in.

'She's got a lovely titti

a lovely, lovely, titti

She's got a lovely titillating smile'

I paused before the chorus:

'Singing I will if you will, so will I...'

And again they joined in:

'Singing I will if you will, so will I

I will if you will

I will if you will

I will if you will, so will I ...'

As I got towards the end of their line I dropped my voice further and went into my second verse:

'She'll be wearing silk pyjamas when she comes ...'

They picked it up eagerly, but not, I suspect quite realising the import of the words.

'She'll be wearing silk pyjamas when she comes

She'll be wearing silk pyjamas

She'll be wearing silk pyjamas

She'll be wearing silk pyjamas when she comes ...'

And then I nodded politely and began jogging again. Behind me I could hear them continuing:

'Singing I will if you will, so will I

I will if you will

I will if you will

I will if you will, so will I ...'

Danny, if I get a chance I'll sing that to you as it's supposed to be, a children's rhyme. Although the version the religious weirdoes were singing comes from a Negro spiritual, I think. The verses mum used to sing to me were:

She'll be coming round the mountain when she comes

She'll be driving six white horses

We will all go out to meet her when she comes

We will kill the old red rooster

and

Then we'll all have chicken and dumplings.

One of dad's was:

She'll be all wet and sticky when she comes ...

He got into a lot of trouble with mum about that one.

Anyway, back at Heathrow and my run to find your mum.

After the Singing Fruitcakes I was coming up to the end of the travelator. And just ahead was something I really didn't need to find. Four young men blocking the travelator in the sort of relaxed poses that tell you they're nicely bevvied up and looking for a little amusement. Or a fight.

Dressed for a stag do. And of course they didn't notice someone in a rush to get past them. Pure coincidence.

I looked at my watch.

13h30

No minutes left.

'Excuse me,' I said. Suddenly they noticed me and grudgingly made just enough space for me to squeeze through. As I did so one of the bastards slapped me on the back.

'Hey yup lad, what's the rush,' he asked in an accent I recognised immediately.

'Fuck off you Mancunian cunt,' I said, 'I'm in a hurry, tosser.' And then I carried on running.

'And you can keep your fucking canal,' I added over my shoulder.

'It's a Scouse git,' exclaimed one of them with slightly faster thought processes than the other.

'Get him,' cried another.

'You are nearing the end of the travelator' warned a mechanical voice.

As they grabbed their suitcases and began to chase after me in a fruitless quest I jumped off the end of the travelator.

Just then a desperate shout came from somewhere:

'IS ANYONE HERE MICHAEL?'

Immediately after there was a crash from further down as wheelie-case-boy came to his inevitable end. I paused to look back that way. So did the Mancunian lads. Not a good move when you're half pissed and about to come to the end of a travelator. The front two fell over, with the others fell on top of them. Initially they looked at each other in confused surprise. After a couple of seconds they burst into laughter.

And then the next wave arrived, a twin phalanx of surprised-looking Christian singers not expecting to have to negotiate four giggling bodies as they came off the travelator. Give them their due, they didn't hesitate, just used the Manc bastards as stepping stones and walked on.

I turned and lumbered on. I was racing against the clock, and the clock had won.

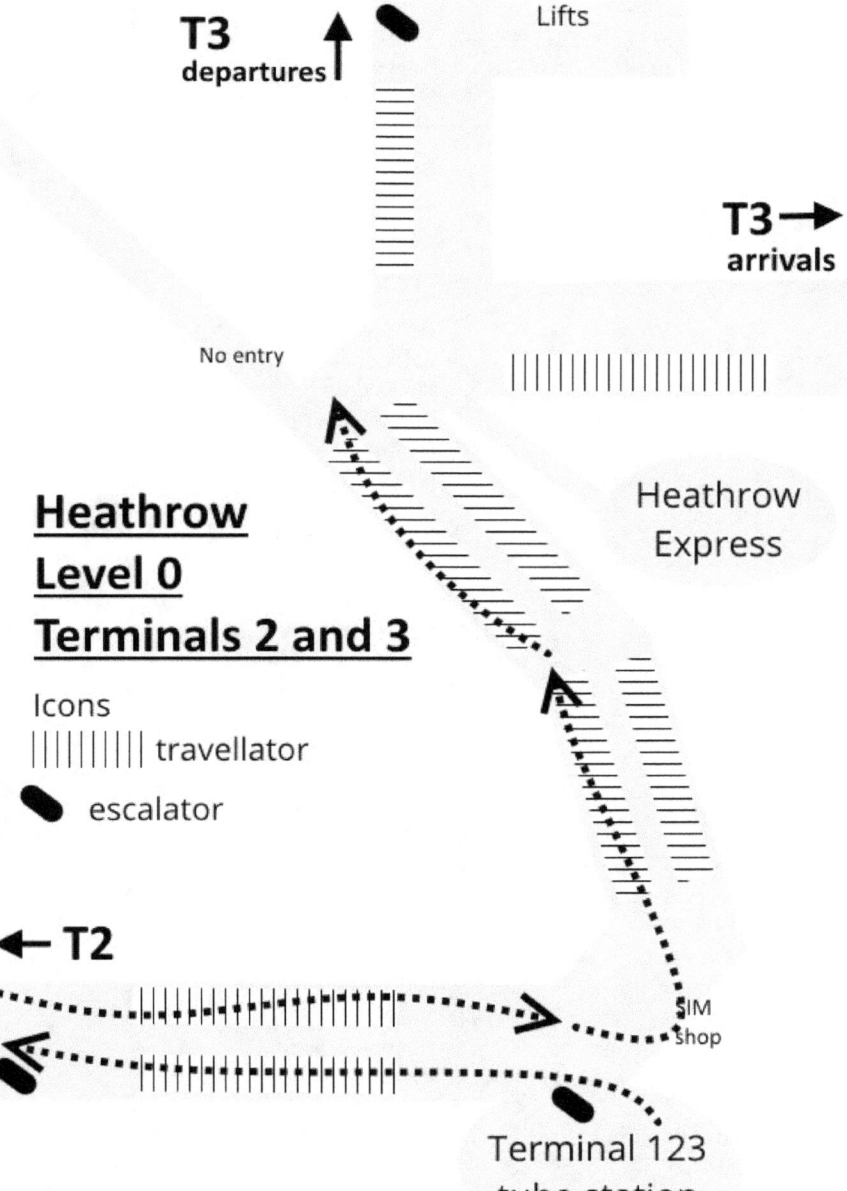

**T3**
departures

Lifts

**T3 →**
arrivals

No entry

# Heathrow
# Level 0
# Terminals 2 and 3

Icons

|||||||||| travellator

escalator

Heathrow
Express

← **T2**

SIM
shop

Terminal 123
tube station

Cockfosters
Oakwood
Southgate
Arnos Grove
Bounds Green
Wood Green
Turnpike Lane
Manor House
Finsbury Park
Arsenal
Holloway Road
Caledonian Road
King's Cross St. Pancras
Russell Square
Holborn
Covent Garden
Leicester Square
Piccadilly Circus
Green Park
Hyde Park Corner
Knightsbridge
South Kensington
Gloucester Road
Earl's Court
Barons Court
Hammersmith
Turnham Green
Acton Town

Ealing Common
North Ealing
Park Royal
Alperton
Sudbury Town
Sudbury Hill
South Harrow
Rayners Lane
Eastcote
Ruislip Manor
Ruislip
Ickenham
Hillingdon
Uxbridge

South Ealing
Northfields
Boston Manor
Osterley
Hounslow East
Hounslow Central
Hounslow West
Hatton Cross
Heathrow T 1-2-3 ⟶ Heathrow T4
Heathrow T5

# Hyde Park Corner

*Estimated time to Green Park 2 minutes*

*Estimated time to Bounds Green 30 minutes*

16h28

Perception, Danny, is everything. For me Hyde Park Corner is synonymous with weirdos ranting. That's because I first encountered a picture of it as a ten year-old, up in Liverpool where my folks stay, your gran and grandad. They had a book about the history of protest in Britain from the days of Roman invasion to the late Twentieth century. It also contrasted movements in the UK with others around the world, partially I think because it provided context, partially because the colour photographs from the Hippy movement in the States were better and prettier than the grainier and more hard-bitten pictures of NUM coalmen being trampled by police horses – or indeed grainy shots of coppers being hit in the head by bricks thrown by NUM coalmen. And there's nothing like dropping in a mention of *Mai 68* to add a frisson of French sophistication and oh-la-la to even out the more pragmatic British 'Oh fuck here comes a rock'.

As often happens when children view adult objects, I became fascinated with a photograph my parents probably flipped over without a thought: a black-and-white picture of some religious crank with a bible in hand, on a podium in Speakers' Corner, dressed in an ill-fitting raincoat and suit, beard all awry, shaking his fist, and apparently condemning all the evils of the day. The burning look in his eyes was enough to give any sane person nightmares, never mind a ten-year-old child. Later I found out that Marx and Lenin and Orwell also used it as a stage to air their views, and I presume they were more staid and logical in their approach, but I've never quite got rid of the image of the area being shrouded in an old and ill-fitting raincoat with large eyebrows and gas-fired eyes.

That was, of course, Hyde Park Corner, rather than Hyde Park, which is a rather large park. I overheard two teenage girls talking about Hyde Park not so long ago, and for them it was "massive" and "awesome" and "wicked" because of some concert they'd been to there. And these days they often put up a huge screen to show some event, a world cup, or the Proms or something.

The suffragettes used to hold meetings in Hyde Park. The police banned their meetings in 1913 for some reason. So the women turned up anyway and said, 'So? What are you going to do?' Apparently the answer was, 'Nothing at all, ma'am, carry on please. If you have a problem the guvnor's over there.' In 2003 thousands of people came out to vote against the Iraq war. The government ignored them.

Danny, I promised I'd take your mother to the Proms this year. Either at Albert Hall or somewhere like Hyde Park Corner.

Bugger.

We're just pulling off, so let me come up with a stational drink for HPC as it's known. Let's go back to the ranting weirdo. By the time you read this you will have mastered that English word, "funny", and will be used to asking someone who describes something as "funny", 'Do you mean funny as in funny-ha-ha, or funny-peculiar?' Well that old bible-bashing-beardie was definitely funny-peculiar. So, HPC, your stational drink will have to be ... Theakston's Old Peculier.

When we were students, long before I met your mum, a group of us went up to Yorkshire for a holiday. We happened to pop into a pub one evening where they served Old Peculier on tap, not a common occurrence – Old P being on tap, not our popping into a pub. One of our number had heard of this marvellous concoction, so we decided to try a pint. We agreed that it was good stuff. We couldn't agree whether the colour was more chocolate-brown or black or ruby. We agreed that it had a fruity taste with a hint of caramel and wood smoke. We had another. We agreed some more. So we had another. And then we returned to lodgings in full agreement about absolutely everything. And when we woke up next morning we felt very relaxed. We had slept well.

Powerful stuff.

When I said I lumbered on into the next section back at Terminal 3, well, for a few yards or so, I soon slowed down. It appeared that I was entering a kink in the tunnel, a jink to the right and then what appeared to be another jink to the left. I decided that I needed to be careful and not take another wrong turn, I couldn't afford to waste a second more. So, confident that I was hidden from the Manc stag and hen parties by the crush of passengers coming and going, I slowed down to a walk so that I could carefully check any available signage, just in case I was accidentally headed towards somewhere out of the way, like Edinburgh or Redruth or Argentina.

Okay, it also admittedly allowed me to get my breath back. It wasn't that I was unfit, just that I wasn't used to dodging and diving for hundreds of yards. Professional footballers train for that sort of thing, and they spend most of the actual match strolling around doing nothing more than committing the occasional foul.

Besides which, that little section was definitely walking room only. It wasn't that there were more people than previously, just that they seemed to be walking across each other. If you've ever watched the Edinburgh Tattoo you'll probably have seen two bands or drum majorette squads march across each other's path to create a sort of hatched design. The US marines do it while twirling WWI rifles with bayonets attached, just to prove they can't afford newer equipment, or razors.

Anyway, that's what was happening. I only realised when I saw a group of teenage schoolkids came into the kink from ahead. They were all wearing a uniform of white trainers, black tracksuit trousers and grey tracksuit jumpers. Initially their discipline was good as they followed the leader. The leader was trying to lead them in a line straight along the wall, but they automatically started turning as soon as they entered the kink and saw the way opening to their right. The crowd moving towards them was doing the same thing in reverse. Without the demarcation lines of travelators and a central reservation they were crossing over each other. For that small section there was nothing I could do but go with the flow. It was like being caught between two currents.

I felt something small and soft take hold of my hand. I looked down and found a little girl of about four or five looking tremulously in front of her, little mouth sucking little fingers in trepidation at the mounting crush coming towards her. She must have taken my hand in the erroneous belief that it was her father's. Or maybe her mother's or uncle's or someone she desperately needed just then. I looked around just as desperately for the relevant adult to hand her over to, but there was no-one paying any attention. She whimpered, her eyes fixed on the crush, and reached up my right arm with one hand and towards my left arm with her other, in the universal child's plea, 'Carry me!'

You know, Danny, I didn't hesitate. I picked the little thing up and held her to my chest, where she put her arms around my neck and buried her face. I held her firmly with my right hand, my left arm out to send a message to all oncoming traffic, 'Keep clear of my little one or die'.

Well, that's probably an exaggeration, but people did seem to see this poor frightened little child being carried towards them and they parted to leave the way clear.

It is also, it has to be said, in hindsight, that I may have been a little wild-eyed, and possibly looked slightly deranged by that stage.

As I got to the corner of the kink, where the tunnel turned to the left, there was an empty gap in the corner leading to soft-drink machines and lifts, I noticed a man and a woman trying to look through the legs of the crowd while having an argument which looked incredibly like 'I thought you had her', 'I thought you were looking after her', 'I left her with you', 'You're her bloody mother', 'I knew I should never have married you', etc. etc. As I came up to them they ignored my top half and tried to look through my legs.

'Anyone missing a little princess?' I asked.

They looked up.

'Emmy-Lou!' exclaimed the mother with a strong American accent, and immediately took the child from me. Emmy-Lou did not demur, presumably being used to being taken from her father by her mother. She unhooked her little arms from around my neck and transferred them to her mother in one easy move.

'You look after her, now,' I said for no other reason but to fill the gap in conversation. 'You'll have to excuse me, I'm in a hurry.'

And then I was on my way again, to Terminal 3 departures and Maddy.

Behind me I heard the man say, straight out of the upper end of Manhattan, 'Hey, what was that guy, some kind of pervert?'

Thanks. mate, next time I meet you I'll give you a lecture on being a responsible father. And then I'll thump the shit out of you.

Son of a bitch was wearing a Proms t-shirt. No, worse than that, it was a Proms polo-shirt. It had 'Albert Hall' and the year printed on it. 1992. What sort of a middle-aged arse buys and wears a Proms polo shirt?

The kind that loses his four-year-old daughter in an international airport, that's who.

At least David Cameron only forgot his daughter in his local pub where everyone knew him and her.

I'll bet that Yank wank doesn't even know the words to Jerusalem. I know them off by heart.

Danny, I might not get to take your mum to the Proms this year but I did make good on one promise I made outside Turnpike Lane tube station. We had just come out of the station, Maddy glanced around and saw adverts tied to the park railings across the road. It was for a funfair at Ducketts Park, the park was a hundred or so yards down the road, and indeed there were the huge travelling vehicles they used, taller and wider and longer than a bus. And Maddy gripped me by the arm and said, 'Mark, promise me you'll take me to the circus.' And I pointed out that it wasn't quite a circus, it was more of a funfair. And she said, 'I don't care, just promise me we'll go.'

It has to be said that there are many different type of feminists and feminisms. Your mother's brand is, 'I am going to do x and so will you, please. No, that wasn't a request.'

So I promised her we'd go. And we did. Not to the one at Ducketts Park, that had closed up and moved on by the time we got a chance to go. But a larger one had appeared at the bottom of Ally Pally as it did every year. Part of the attraction being, not only that it was larger, but that it was in walking distance of the house. And it had dodgems.

Well, it did before your mother got behind the wheel of one of them. They're probably all broken now. All, I can say, Danny, is that I've never experienced your mother driving a car, and if her approach is similar to the dodgems, god help the rest of the traffic.

First we wandered into the area occupied by the funfair, strolled around and around, and then we came across the dodgems and she claps her hand in delight. And, of course, if Maddy's delighted, so am I, I'm in love with her for god's sake. And she grabs my arm and squeals, 'Oh, Mark, dodgems! Can we have a go? Pretty please, can we?' And I kiss her and say, of course my darling, if you want a go on the dodgems we will have a go on the dodgems.

Thinking that I will sit next to her as she drives around bouncing off everyone else. But, no, we had to each have a dodgem. Well, okay, it's not my sort of thing, but for Maddy I'll put up with pretty much anything. And they clear the area for our go, check that everyone has tickets, the power comes on, and I gently press the accelerator to get a feeling of what this dodgem can do, and the next moment, Pow!, I'm hit in the rear end. Like an idiot I turn around to remonstrate with whoever it is, and then, Pow!, another shot up my backside. Out of the corner of my eye I can see a grinning face and recognise it. Your bloody mother taking great delight in ramming me.

Well, I wasn't going to put up with that. I slammed the accelerator down, took off, and immediately ploughed into a mother with her ten-year-old daughter doing the driving. The mother was aghast, but the child squealed in delight and swung the steering wheel around to try to catch me broadsides. Instead she clipped Maddy who was coming up for another go at me. Which gave me enough time to swing to the left violently in order to turn around and come at Maddy from the side. Maddy spotted what I was trying to do and swung right, straight into the side of two boys struggling to control their dodgem, leaving her blocked and right in my path. I pushed the accelerator down full and rammed her, leaving me with two seconds of satisfaction before the young girl and her mother clobbered me from the side.

Fortunately a man and his young son then knocked Maddy out of the way which gave me just enough space to clear the jumble and zoom over to the end of the platform, swinging around expertly and ready to head straight back at anyone not paying attention, Maddy preferably. Only she had had the same idea and was idling on the opposite side. As soon as she spotted me she began circling round the edge, avoiding the others, like a tiger which has seen its prey and has no interest in anything else. Prey? Me? Hah! That'll be the day.

I swung my dodgem around until it was headed towards hers and slammed down on the accelerator down flat, going full blast around the edge of the dodgeming area. It was time to play Chicken.

I caught the glint of resolution in Maddy's eyes. I suspect that she didn't want a direct frontal collision, but she was prepared to brave it out if that was what it took. I didn't waver. If you can't play Chicken in a dodgem car, when can you play Chicken?

We approached each other at top speed, which, admittedly, isn't that fast in dodgems. They don't like the customers killing each other. Closer. And closer. And closer ...

Just before we collided I was clobbered in the rear side by the woman and her daughter, and Maddy copped a collision from the man and his son in her rear end. The next thing we knew Maddy and I were running parallel alongside, directly towards the centre of the arena, unable to do what we wanted most, i.e. crash into each other. With Maddy in the way on the left, all I could do was peel off to the right; I presume she peeled off to her left, because the next thing I knew was that I had rammed the man and his son, while over on the other side Maddy had driven into the woman and her daughter. And then it just collapsed into a complete melee. The two boys popped out of nowhere and clobbered the man and his son.

And all too soon our time was up and the power was switched off as our go came to an end.

Bliss was it then to be young, alive, and in control of a dodgem.

Maddy got out of her dodgem and came over to me as I was getting out of mine. She had a huge grin across her face.

'God, that was fun,' she said, taking my arm.

'Fancy another go?'

'Not right now. Next time we come to the funfair again.'

'Okay. What next?'

'Let's have another wander. Will they have a shooting range?'

'Of sorts. Probably one of those ones where you fire misshaped corks out of pop-guns which have had their barrels just slightly bent, just not enough to be obvious unless you know how to look.'

'Sounds like you have the same sort of crooks we have in Australia.'

So we wandered around and I learnt something new about her: she didn't like candyfloss. But there was an ice-cream van there, so that kept us happy.

There was a shooting range, or whatever you want to call it. Pellet guns or air rifles with dodgy sights and little moving targets that looked easy enough to hit. So we had a go at that. I did pretty well – well enough to win a reasonably large stuffed teddy bear which probably cost a third of the amount I had paid for the privilege. Miss Annie Oakley was extremely miffed at not beating me hands down, and even more miffed at being far worse than me. Naturally I presented her with my prize as any decent hunter-man would on returning from the chase. She hugged it, declared it gorgeous, said she'd love it forever, and then asked me to carry it for her. And, because I could never say no to your mother, I did.

Shortly after we came to a coconut shy. It was a lonely looking sort of thing. A row of poles with cups on top, with coconuts forced into them so solidly only a direct hit from an 88 millimetre could dislodge them, an invitation to young men to prove their stupidity. A grooved counter holding groups of balls, worn old balls that weren't dissimilar to cricket balls, but which had seen service for too many years. The coconuts didn't look that appealing, but when did coconuts ever look appealing? I dare say there was an age when a coconut was some mysterious fruit from far-distant lagoons, and Victorian families would ooh and aah over their young gentlemen showing their prowess in knocking one off its cup-holder before presenting it to his admiring young lady, who would then discreetly hand it over to her maid in waiting as soon as possible, but these days? You can buy them in supermarkets pretty much all year round, and I've yet to see any recipe that required a whole, hairy, uncut coconut.

The stall holder was sitting on a stool perusing a worn old newspaper.

'Fancy a go?' I asked Maddy. She gave the coconuts a dubious look.

'If I win, can they keep the coconut?' she asked. 'Mark, I don't like to make comparisons with Oz, but I'm sure the coconuts I've seen there are a lot bigger and a lot fresher than this lot.'

'They do look a bit minging,' I agreed. 'Shall we seek refreshment instead?'

And so we did, but, Danny, I can still see those coconuts on their poles. I'm sure I could have knocked a couple out. What we would have done with them afterward, well, I suspect they would have lain on the sideboard for a few weeks or months before being quietly recycled somehow. Or, as we say in the vernacular, binned. Or maybe we'd declare war on someone just so we could throw them at the enemy and get rid of them.

And there was a beer tent, with outdoor pub tables outside the tent so that the adults could order some drinks and enjoy them with the kids who would be drinking lemon squash or Coke or whatever. We got a couple of beers – pint for me, bottle of lager for Maddy – and went and sat outside. And there were our foes from the dodgems, mother and daughter, father and son and the two boys, all apparently the same family. We waved and they waved back and we sat down a few tables away, friendly, but not too so. It is England, after all.

'They look like a happy family,' Maddy noted.

'They do, don't they.'

She looked at me.

'So, Mark, how many kids do you want?'

I looked back into her eyes.

'I haven't a clue, sweetness. I haven't really ever thought about it. How many do you want?'

She looked at me.

'You're a teacher, you work with youngsters every day, and you've never thought about how many kids you want?'

'I work with obstreperous balls of slime, Maddy, my sweet. They're enough to put anyone off having kids forever. So, answer the question. How many do you want?'

She looked vaguely somewhere else and took a sip of her lager.

'I don't know. Three maybe. I reckon.'

'Well, there you go, that's that sorted,' I said. 'We'll start with one, work our way up to two if you want, go on to three if you're still happy, and then see how we feel.'

She looked at me.

'Hmmm,' she said, and looked away again.

Danny, there are some things about women I will never understand.

It was exactly the same 'Hmmm' my mum makes when she doesn't believe me, but can't prove I'm lying.

But with your mother I wasn't lying in the slightest. I really hadn't ever thought about how many kids I wanted. Men don't, in general, Danny. And speaking personally I'd always been having too much fun with the undress rehearsal to worry about the opening night.

Cockfosters
Oakwood
Southgate
Arnos Grove
Bounds Green
Wood Green
Turnpike Lane
Manor House
Finsbury Park
Arsenal
Holloway Road
Caledonian Road
King's Cross St. Pancras
Russell Square
Holborn
Covent Garden
Leicester Square
Piccadilly Circus
Green Park
Hyde Park Corner
Knightsbridge
South Kensington
Gloucester Road
Earl's Court
Barons Court
Hammersmith
Turnham Green
Acton Town

Ealing Common          South Ealing
North Ealing           Northfields
Park Royal             Boston Manor
Alperton              Osterley
Sudbury Town          Hounslow East
Sudbury Hill          Hounslow Central
South Harrow          Hounslow West
Rayners Lane          Hatton Cross
Eastcote              Heathrow T 1-2-3 ⟶ Heathrow T4
Ruislip Manor         Heathrow T5
Ruislip
Ickenham
Hillingdon
Uxbridge

## Green Park

*Estimated time to Piccadilly Circus 2 minutes*

*Estimated time to Bounds Green 28 minutes*

16h32

Green Park. One of those sort-of milestone stations, because there's an awful lot of getting on and getting off and changing lines goes on here. I always get the feeling that the driver is sitting there patiently wanting to say, 'Okay, are we quite finished, have you sorted yourselves out, sure you're on the right service? Got all your bags? All the little kiddies on? Nan and grandad on okay? Ready? Sitting comfortably? Well, let's be off, shall we? We've got a lot of stations to see and a lot of people to pick up and let off, so we'll have to get move if we want to be on time, won't we?'

In reality what the driver normally says, if he or she says anything, is 'STAND CLEAR OF THE DOORS' ... doors beep, close, train starts, shudders, stops ... 'STAND CLEAR OF THE DOORS' ... doors beep, open, close, train starts, shudders, stops ... 'STAND CLEAR OF THE DOORS. IF YOU DO NOT STAND CLEAR OF THE DOORS THIS TRAIN WILL BE TAKEN OUT OF SERVICE' doors beep, open, close, passengers are pushing back away from doors, staring at them in fascinated terror, holding their breath in case their tummies come into contact ... train shudders ... passengers hold breath ... train moves slowly ... train departs.

So, Danny, by now, by the time you read this, you will have realised that life is not one happy adventure, fairy tales do not normally come true, and, possibly, that choo-choo journeys do not always have a happy ending.

I had a wooden choo-choo set when I was five. I used to run it off the dining room table and watch it fly off the side and crash down into the floor. I hope that wasn't an omen. An augury of things to come, crashing off.

But, before I continue with the story of my struggle towards terminal 3 departures and you and your mother, let us pause for a little latte – cheers

– and a stational drink for Green Park. There's far too much hustle and bustle in the tunnels at Green Park. I think people should learn to chill. I think they should put up little bistro tables along the platforms so that people can sit and idle the time away, watching other people while enjoying a refreshing aperitif. It would be so much more civilised.

I think an Art Deco theme would be appropriate.

And, as a stational drink, something green. Green Park. Arguably the crown in the jewels as far as London parks go. Possibly a mint julep. Though, as the saying goes, you can take the man out of the puddle, but you can't take the school-boy out of the man. So I would be tempted to go for something like Frog In A Blender

Alternatively something revolting with an avocado. Typical of some species of the human race to take a perfect fruit like the avocado and mash it up into something that resembles toad-sick.

Danny, I'm feeling very positive towards the human race at the moment. Don't know why, the bastards don't deserve it. Quite possible latte-induced. So for the adults, I'll go with my original choice: their stational drink will be – mint julep. Just so long as I don't have to drink the shite.

And for the kids, they can have Frog In A Blender if they want. They'll like that. And they can force their parents to drink some if they wish.

Here's to latte.

Cheers.

Danny, that short section, the kink in the tunnel, was a bit like a timeless interval, a kind of floating through a time-frozen dream, because when I woke up again after having handed over the little tot I checked my watch to find that it was still 13h30. Still out of time, but at least no more out of time than when I had previously checked. So I pulled myself together and prepared to battle on to the very end, wherever that might be.

I turned left with the tunnel and came to a fork with a choice of two further tunnels. There was a single travelator in the left tunnel heading, I guess, North, with people walking south toward me on the walkway next to it on the right. To the right of that there was a tunnel with a single travelator coming towards me on the right, with a walkway alongside on the left with people heading away. At the intersection to the two tunnels stood a group of tourists, being kept in a gaggle by their holiday representative. Some of them moved just sufficiently for me to see the sign saying "Terminal 3" and an arrow pointing down the way to the right tunnel. That was enough for me. I took to my heels and began jogging.

Initially it wasn't too much of a problem. The re-appearance of travelators, or at least one travelator, largely installed a discipline into people, and the confusion of the kink was gone. You walked on the left and travellated the other way on the right. There was enough space for me to slip past the travellers in front of me pushing trolleys or dragging their suitcases for a walk. There were one or two old-fashioned youngsters with backpacks, but it was mostly re-enforced nuclear-capable steel wheelie-bags painted in a variety of garish colours.

And then I saw them.

Everybody else moving in our direction, towards the Underground, was using the travelator as god intended. These two, however, were on our side, coming towards us. An elderly couple who didn't trust metal moving beneath them. And they were pushing trolleys stacked with luggage, huge suitcase on the bottom, slightly less huge one above, normal size above that, topped off with something the size of a front step and looking as solid.

And they were side by side, almost entirely blocking the aisle.

Why? Were they fucking blind? Why couldn't they move in single file to let others past?

As I came racing up there was a young woman with a pram going in my direction trying to pass them. The three of them stopped as the two trolleys and pram got jammed. I didn't slow down. I didn't know what I was going to do. But I didn't slow down. I couldn't slow down. I was coming for you and YBM.

As I got nearer I could hear the old couple tutting at the thoughtlessness of the young woman.

'You could have waited,' the old woman said in a nasal drawl.

'Not enough space for a pram here,' said the man with an echo of the drawl.

'We don't like moving steps,' said the woman.

Moving steps?

Steps?

I was ten paces away when I realised.

Their suitcases were stacked just like steps.

Steps. The things you walk up. And over.

The old woman looked up as I hit my stride. Her mouth dropped open.

'Wilbur –' she started.

'Yes, Mildred –' The old man had just looked up and his mouth dropped open.

I took the suitcase-steps two at a time and bounded over the woman's head as she ducked down. And then I hit the ground. And looked slightly to my right, as I moved, where the travelator was moving in the opposite direction. With two armed police officers on it, leaning back nonchalantly and looking at me with just a hint of surprised admiration.

I suppose it's not every day you see someone launch themselves over the top of a luggage trolley.

And then I was off again. Vaguely I heard one of them say something like, 'That's a negative, Mother Hen, repeat, that's a negative.'

Mother Hen? WTF?

I was half way down that section of tunnel. From what I could see it turned to the left at the end, because that's where people seemed to be going to and coming from. I checked my watch.

13h31.

M-minute plus one.

Cockfosters
Oakwood
Southgate
Arnos Grove
Bounds Green
Wood Green
Turnpike Lane
Manor House
Finsbury Park
Arsenal
Holloway Road
Caledonian Road
King's Cross St. Pancras
Russell Square
Holborn
Covent Garden
Leicester Square
Piccadilly Circus
Green Park
Hyde Park Corner
Knightsbridge
South Kensington
Gloucester Road
Earl's Court
Barons Court
Hammersmith
Turnham Green

Ealing Common
North Ealing
Park Royal
Alperton
Sudbury Town
Sudbury Hill
South Harrow
Rayners Lane
Eastcote
Ruislip Manor
Ruislip
Ickenham
Hillingdon
Uxbridge

Acton Town
South Ealing
Northfields
Boston Manor
Osterley
Hounslow East
Hounslow Central
Hounslow West
Hatton Cross  ←
Heathrow T 1-2-3  ——→  Heathrow T4
Heathrow T5

# Piccadilly Circus

*Estimated time to Leicester Square 1 minutes*

*Estimated time to Bounds Green 26 minutes*

16h36

Danny, they say that hope springs eternal, or at least Alexander Pope did, and he was a poet. They used to be important people once, poets. It was the last thing out of Pandora's box – hope, that is, not poets. Our friend Friedrich Nietzsche described it as the most evil of evils as it forces men to continue enduring the slings and arrows of outrageous fortune long after the logical thing to do would be to top yourself or, preferably, the people giving the orders and making your life a misery. And we live with hope for many things that will never become true; that we will win the lottery and never again have to worry about poverty; that there is a God and a life hereafter where the drudgery and pain will end; that one day we will find that special someone and fall in love for evermore. In the movies, and musicals like Les Mis, this comes with deep pulsating music and quite a bit of swooning. If you want to know what it's like in real life, get a friend to kick you just beneath the ribcage when you're least expecting it.

You will notice, my dear Danny, that the last thing in Pandora's box was hope, not love.

One of the things Piccadilly Circus is famous for, of course, is the statue of Eros, god of love, allegedly. People like to get drunk at New Year and climb it for luck in love, which is why the authorities tend to cordon it off at that time of year; drunks may or may not be lucky in love, but repairs are guaranteed to be bloody expensive. Plus it's a right bastard having to arrange for an ambulance on New Year's Eve to ferry away arseholes with broken limbs, and also to clean the bloodstains off the pavement on the morning after.

But now I've started I suppose I'll have to give it a stational drink which reflects the highs and lows, the sheer ecstasy and desperation, the deep joy and deeper sadness of love. And trust me, Danny, I've been in lust many a time, in love only once, and I know which hurt the most.

441

A drink to love.

A drink to something illogical, irrational, inexplicable, infuriating, exhilarating and, quite frankly, completely and utterly fucking bonkers.

So that'll be a Banana Banshee then.

With nuts in.

Here's a little latte to love

It's what drove me on when I had no hope left.

Not that I was being chased by a huge Banana Banshee.

But it might have helped.

Fortunately I am over that nonsense now.

I have survived.

And, Danny, speaking of hope and Pandora's box, you know something? Just between us, it wasn't a box. That was a mistranslation somewhere along the way. What Pandora actually had was a jar. And we know what's in the jar, don't we.

Yes, Danny, my sweet, there's whiskey in the jar.

Musha ring dumb a do dumb a da.

Cheers.

It was probably only another sixty yards or so to the end of the corridor and a sharp turn to the left. I would estimate that there was one person or group of people for every five yards in my way. The real problem was that, yet again, they were scattered all over the place with varying amounts of luggage. I went left to overtake a young woman dragging a normal-sized suitcase, only to come up behind the elderly gent she was overtaking. Manage to slip through the gap, dodging to the right. Past a heavily pregnant woman struggling to push a trolley, why wasn't anyone helping her? Left again to overtake a family in a row, like ducklings with their parents, father leading, little girl and little boy in the middle behind each other, mother bringing up the rear. Duckle, duckle, duckle, daddy duck beaming, little ducklings grinning and slipstreaming, mummy duck all smug and preening.

It's crap because I was in a hurry.

But mummy duck didn't half look chuffed with her little brood. Daddy duck looked like a happy dork. They could have quacked happily.

Jump right to nip past a young couple holding hands. Past a thin, bearded man with a limp, stomping along, wearing a black suit, dark glasses and a hat. And then the corner is only twenty yards away and there's just a young woman pushing a trolley ahead. I kick in a gear, add a spurt of speed, and I'm past her and at the corner.

I skidded left around the corner, almost taking out an old bloke hobbling along on two walking sticks coming the other way

'Ere, lad, thy wants looking where thy's going,' he said.

'Sorry, bit of a dash. I'm late,' I gasped, dodging past him.

There was no time for polite frivolities. I had seen the sign I'd been looking for. Blazoned across the sky. Or hanging from the low ceiling, anyway.

Terminal 3 Arrivals.

Now there was no stopping me.

Late I might be but I had arrived.

Just an extra spurt of speed and –

What?

WTF?

WTF on poppers?

I slammed on brakes.

Terminal 3 Arrivals?

I didn't want fucking Arrivals.

I wanted fucking Departures.

I bent over, put my hands on my knees, groaned and tried to get my breath back.

'That's what happens, lad, rush around, get nowhere,' said the old bloke behind me, having stopped to watch.

I checked my watch.

13h32

Why I bothered I don't know. I was out of time. I knew it. Time knew it. Shit, the cat in the cradle knew it.

'It's not worth it, lad,' the old duffer carried on. 'When you get to my age you realise that nothing is worth getting into a lather for.'

I looked around at him.

Danny, before I met your mother I would have agreed with every word.

I thought about it for a few seconds as I tried to get my breath back.

'You know something,' I said once I'd regained the power of speech. 'Ninety-nine point nine percent of the time you'd be right.' I stood upright. 'This, I am afraid, is the other half. Now if you'll excuse me, I have a fate to meet.'

Then I walked with all the dignity I could muster back to the travelator going back in the direction I'd just come. Trudged, I think is the word.

'You aren't in love, are you?' called the old man.

'That,' I said, 'is precisely the problem.'

'Ah, should have said, lad, should have said. Good luck to you, you'll need it.'

'Thank you,' I said. I stepped onto the travelator.

'Just don't marry her, lad. I did. Forty-seven years I've regretted it.'

Forty-seven years?

Christ.

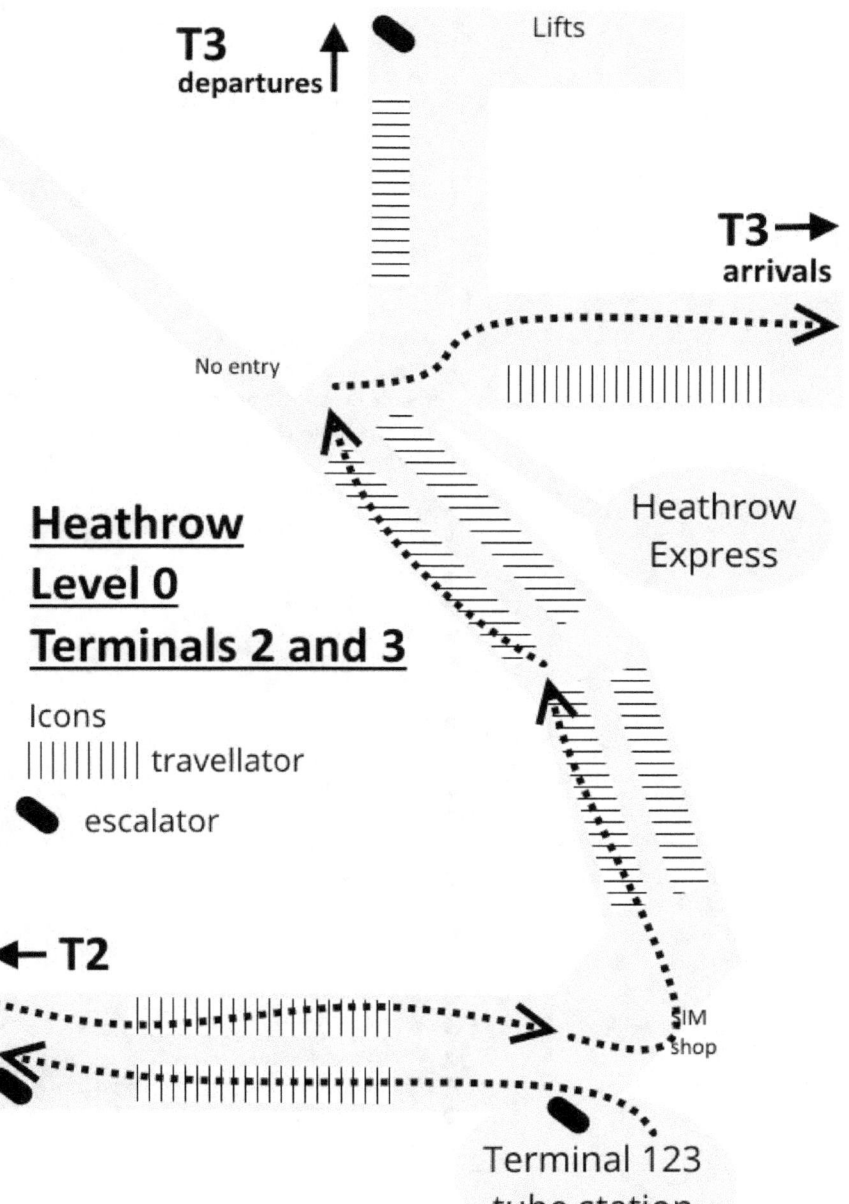

**T3**
**departures**

Lifts

**T3** ➡
**arrivals**

No entry

**Heathrow**
**Level 0**
**Terminals 2 and 3**

Heathrow
Express

Icons
|||||||||| travellator

escalator

← **T2**

SIM
shop

Terminal 123
tube station

Cockfosters
Oakwood
Southgate
Arnos Grove
Bounds Green
Wood Green
Turnpike Lane
Manor House
Finsbury Park
Arsenal
Holloway Road
Caledonian Road
King's Cross St. Pancras
Russell Square
Holborn
Covent Garden
Leicester Square
Piccadilly Circus
Green Park
Hyde Park Corner
Knightsbridge
South Kensington
Gloucester Road
Earl's Court
Barons Court
Hammersmith
Turnham Green
Acton Town

Ealing Common South Ealing
North Ealing Northfields
Park Royal Boston Manor
Alperton Osterley
Sudbury Town Hounslow East
Sudbury Hill Hounslow Central
South Harrow Hounslow West
Rayners Lane Hatton Cross ◄
Eastcote Heathrow T 1-2-3 ⟶ Heathrow T4
Ruislip Manor Heathrow T5
Ruislip
Ickenham
Hillingdon
Uxbridge

## Leicester Square

*Estimated time to Covent Garden 2 minutes*

*Estimated time to Bounds Green 25 minutes*

16h41

Danny, there are loads of things that go on around Leicester Square. But one has a deep place in your mother's heart. It's called the lure of lights, camera, action and the red carpet. A red carpet for a premiere. Movie land. Dream world. So there's really only one stational drink we can award it. One drink that is immediately associated with a movie series. A dry Martini. Shaken, not stirred. With two olives in it.

Strange, that. Movies are full of booze. There's always at least one bar in a Western. Rick's in Casablanca was a bar. Friar Tuck in Robin Hood made beer or mead or ale or something. Yet the one drink that comes through is a revolting tasting concoction which nobody normal drinks.

I wonder what the actors playing James Bond were really drinking when they were pretending to enjoy that shite.

If you have to mix it or add vegetables to it, it isn't a real drink.

As I stepped on to the travelator to head back in the right direction for Terminal 3 departures I looked at my watch.

13h33.

Three minutes too late.

I thought of George Mallory.

Danny, George Mallory was a mountaineer. He was asked once by a reporter why he was so determined to climb Mount Everest. His answer was, 'Because it's there'. If anyone asked me why I was still moving my answer would be, because Maddy might still be there.

The only slight problem is that Everest killed Mallory. In 1924. His body wasn't found until 1999.

It was 13h33.

I set off with a firm stride preparing to break into a run as soon as the various bits of my body agreed. But before I got five paces I found my first problem. There were two young girls in front of me, one about eleven, the other about sixteen. The eleven year-old was pushing a trolley loaded almost to the ceiling with suitcases, bags, parcels, everything bar a couple of pets in cages and a kitchen sink or two. The older girl was walking on ahead complaining into her mobile phone. She wore full face paint, a bright, tight yellow top and jeans that would have needed oiling to get in. I couldn't understand what she was saying, but her body language was universal. Younger sis had been a pain ever since they had left for the airport. She had been a pain when they had got on the flight together. She'd been a pain on the flight. She'd been a pain landing. Having arrived younger sis had insisted that she was going to push the trolley. Older sis had finally flipped, dumped absolutely everything they had brought onto one trolley, quite possibly along with someone else's luggage to make up the weight, and said, 'There you go, push that.' Now she was bitching to someone – the boyfriend, I guessed, her mother wouldn't have had put up with that – about what a pain the younger sis had been ever since they left for the airport. She had been a pain when they got on the plane. She'd been a pain on the flight. She'd been a pain landing. And she was being a pain now. Etc.

The thing is younger sis now had a determined look on her face. She had said she was going to push the trolley, and push the trolley was what she was going to do. She even had the tip of her tongue out of her mouth as she concentrated on her self-allotted task. And she was actually moving it. Not a lot. But unfortunately just enough so that it kept veering from left to right like a drunken sailor in a storm-tossed yacht, preventing me from getting past. I tried saying 'Excuse me' a few times, but the girl's concentration was fully one hundred percent on that overloaded trolley. Her sister's attention was similarly dedicated to her mobile phone, and to ignoring her younger sibling.

It only occurred to me later when I had the time to reflect, that there was no mobile signal in that section.

And I think I was flagging too. I'd already scaled one trolley, now the Everest of luggage in front of me was a mountain too far. I'd been on the go since about four in the morning, I'd had no breakfast or lunch, just half a cup of tea. For a brief moment the lyrics from Tainted Love came to mind. 'Once I ran to you, then I ran from you, then I ran to you, then I ran from you, now I'm running to you again, and bloody exhausting it is too.'

And I'd run out of time. If the aircraft wasn't on the runway waiting to take off, it had already taken off.

Yes, I was going to get to Terminal 3 check in or security or whatever it was, but it wasn't going to be in the sprint that I'd planned, just in the nick of time, it was going to be in the grim and bloodied 'I said I'd get here, I might be late, but here I bloody am, bloody I am, and bloody here. Can I die now, please.'

So I sighed, gently took the left-hand side of the trolley handle from the young girl, steered it to the right, paused, noticed her sister still bitching into her mobile, then gave it a good shove to help it on, right into her jean-tight backside. She yelped, dropped her mobile, bent over to pick it up, got another whack from the front of the trolley and went over. The young girl didn't say a word, but there was a broad smile on her face.

I walked past the now stationary trolley nonchalantly.

I kept walking until I'd got past the luggage mountain and back into the open. I was about to break into a stumble approaching a run when I saw the Jehovah's Witnesses coming my way. They were walking two abreast on the right, still singing,

'Singing I will if you will, so will I

I will if you will

I will if you will

I will if you will, so will I ...'

I presumed they were on their way to meet some poor bastard arriving. If I'd come out of arrivals to find that lot waiting for me I would have been on the next plane out. Their cheerful innocence and youthfulness was positively repelling.

And that's where I saw the two coppers I'd last seen lounging on the travelator going the other way. Now they were walking towards Terminal 3 arrivals and I was on the travelator going away from Terminal 3 arrivals. They were just behind the Christian Youth, almost camouflaged into them. Apart from the fact that the Christian Youth weren't tooled up to the eyebrows. This wasn't JFK, after all.

The airport, not the president.

And they weren't singing. But they looked as if they found it perfectly normal to be strolling up behind a crocodile of singing do-gooders at an international airport.

I could see they were looking for someone or something. Idly scanning the crowds, but scanning them nonetheless. And then the one on the left, closest me, caught sight of me. He nudged his colleague with his elbow and they both stopped and looked at me. And I decided there and then that it was time I was moving again. The time to have a chat with the busies was after Terminal 3 departures.

As I began what could optimistically be called a run I heard one of them say,

'He's on his way now, Mother Hen, coming home to you.'

If I still had half a brain cell in functioning mode I might have worked out that I was headed straight into the arms of Mother Hen, whoever or whatever that was. But even had I made the connection it probably wouldn't have made any difference. There was only one path left to me and I was going to take it.

It was 13h34.

Cockfosters
Oakwood
Southgate
Arnos Grove
Bounds Green
Wood Green
Turnpike Lane
Manor House
Finsbury Park
Arsenal
Holloway Road
Caledonian Road
King's Cross St. Pancras
Russell Square
Holborn
Covent Garden
Leicester Square
Piccadilly Circus
Green Park
Hyde Park Corner
Knightsbridge
South Kensington
Gloucester Road
Earl's Court
Barons Court
Hammersmith
Turnham Green
Acton Town

Ealing Common
North Ealing
Park Royal
Alperton
Sudbury Town
Sudbury Hill
South Harrow
Rayners Lane
Eastcote
Ruislip Manor
Ruislip
Ickenham
Hillingdon
Uxbridge

South Ealing
Northfields
Boston Manor
Osterley
Hounslow East
Hounslow Central
Hounslow West
Hatton Cross  ◄———
Heathrow T 1-2-3 ———► Heathrow T4
Heathrow T5

# Covent Garden

*Estimated time to Holborn 1 minutes*

*Estimated time to Bounds Green 23 minutes*

16h44

Danny, by the time you read this you will know all about Einstein and his theory of relativity. At least you will if I have anything to do with it. If it's up to me – or if I get the slightest half-chance – you will not only have a thorough grounding in science, but also in fallacy. Such as the idea that the shortest distance between two points is the fastest way to get there. For example: the distance between Leicester Square and Covent garden is relatively short, as is that between Covent Garden and Holborn. You would think it would take only minutes to get there. But when you get there you find that pretty much every tourist in the world has arrived at Covent Garden at the same time, and it can take twenty minutes just getting out of the station. Similarly, the distances I was trying to run to get to Terminal 3 departures were also relatively short. I don't think I faced getting past every tourist in the world on my race to T3 departures, just that the ones I did encounter were bloody efficient in getting in the way. It would probably have taken the same amount of time and been far less tiring just to accept the inevitable and go at everybody else's speed.

But, Danny, lest we forget, first a slaking of the thirst with some weak latte.

Tastes pretty good to me.

And then a salute to Covent Garden by way of a stational drink.

Now when I first came to stay with my Aunt Marigold in London I was about ten, and I was convinced that it was called Convent Garden.

Convents are run by an Abbess.

I don't know of any drinks made or titled Abbess.

But they would have had a priest visit for Mass.

Or possibly an Abbot.

So, especially for Covent Garden, I give you Abbot Ale.

Cheers

Actually I cheated on that one because I knew that Covent Garden was originally the site of an Abbey, and indeed a garden or orchard or something. Henry VIII nicked it for one of his drinking buddies. Somewhere along the way it became a market filled with pubs and whorehouses, along with good old coffee-houses, taverns and brothels, though quite what the difference between a whorehouse and a brothel is I'm not quite sure. I suppose the one sounds like more like fun and the other more like business.

Then they moved Covent Garden and gentrified it. Today it's tourist central. Amazing what a few cobblestones will do.

You can also find the London Transport Museum here. It doesn't contain any ancient Piccadilly Line stock. They're still using them on the Piccadilly Line.

Where were we, Danny? Coming back from Terminal 3 arrivals, that's it. Halfway along the travelator, I'd just got past the mountain trolley, spotted the busies, been spotted by the busies, and was trying to convince my legs that this was it, the final run. They didn't believe me.

But I lumbered into what might be considered a stagger. The first person I passed was what appeared to be a sleeping Oriental. East Asian bloke, suit, no tie, suitcase, standing on the right, eyes closed. I have no idea why. Then I had to squeeze past a Home Counties type woman, pearls and twinset, one enormous suitcase, chocolate brown, side on. I had to move her suitcase to get past because she was too fucking lazy to do it herself. She sighed and tutted at my temerity in touching her property which tempted me to pick her up, toss her overboard, and follow that up by throwing the suitcase after her. Unfortunately I could feel the busies not too far away, and the last thing I wanted was to be delayed by them by having to explain why I'd thrown the old cow over the side. I made a mental note to come back after the failure of my mission, find her, and chuck her into a sewer.

Up ahead were two young women pushing trolleys side by side, very efficiently blocking the travelator, discussing a concert they'd been to.

'His Gotterdammerung is so much better than Scholtz, don't you think?' asked the blonde one.

I was about to say 'Excuse me' when I realised that the blonde was actually slowing down.

And the Brunette was speeding up.

I slipped in behind the Brunette.

'Scholtz does Bach well, but his Wagner is a bit weak,' the Brunette agreed. By then we were almost past the Blonde's trolley.

'I think his Strauss is lovely,' said the blonde, 'I've always liked his waltzes.'

And then the Brunette was past the Blonde's trolley, and she moved right, segueing neatly in front of her friend. I've never seen a pas de deux executed with trolleys full of luggage, but they seemed quite comfortable with it, and it allowed me to pass.

'Many thanks,' I said, nipping past with a bit of a spring. 'I'm in a bit of a hurry.'

'No shit, Sherlock,' said the Brunette. 'Good luck.'

'Thank you,' I said.

As I began to make some headway I heard them continue their conversation. I risked a quick look back. The blonde had moved right and speeded up, the Brunette had slowed down, and once again they were sailing serenely alongside each other.

I turned back to face front. There were now only two people ahead of me, a woman on the left standing with a huge bunch of roses blocking the right, and further ahead what looked like a small gentleman wearing a pork pie hat and leaving plenty of space on the right for me to clear. I could see the junction where I had mistakenly taken the arrivals route.

I could also see something unbelievable.

Something I had given up hope of seeing.

My heart stood still for a second.

I could see the black dress that Maddy loved wearing.

She was heading towards the Underground.

I checked my watch again.

It was 13h35.

But that didn't matter anymore.

The target was acquired.

Not quite where I'd expected her to be.
But, full speed ahead.
I thought I had lost all chance.
But now I was going to make it.
I didn't know how.
But I was going to make it after all.
All engines go, including the broken ones.

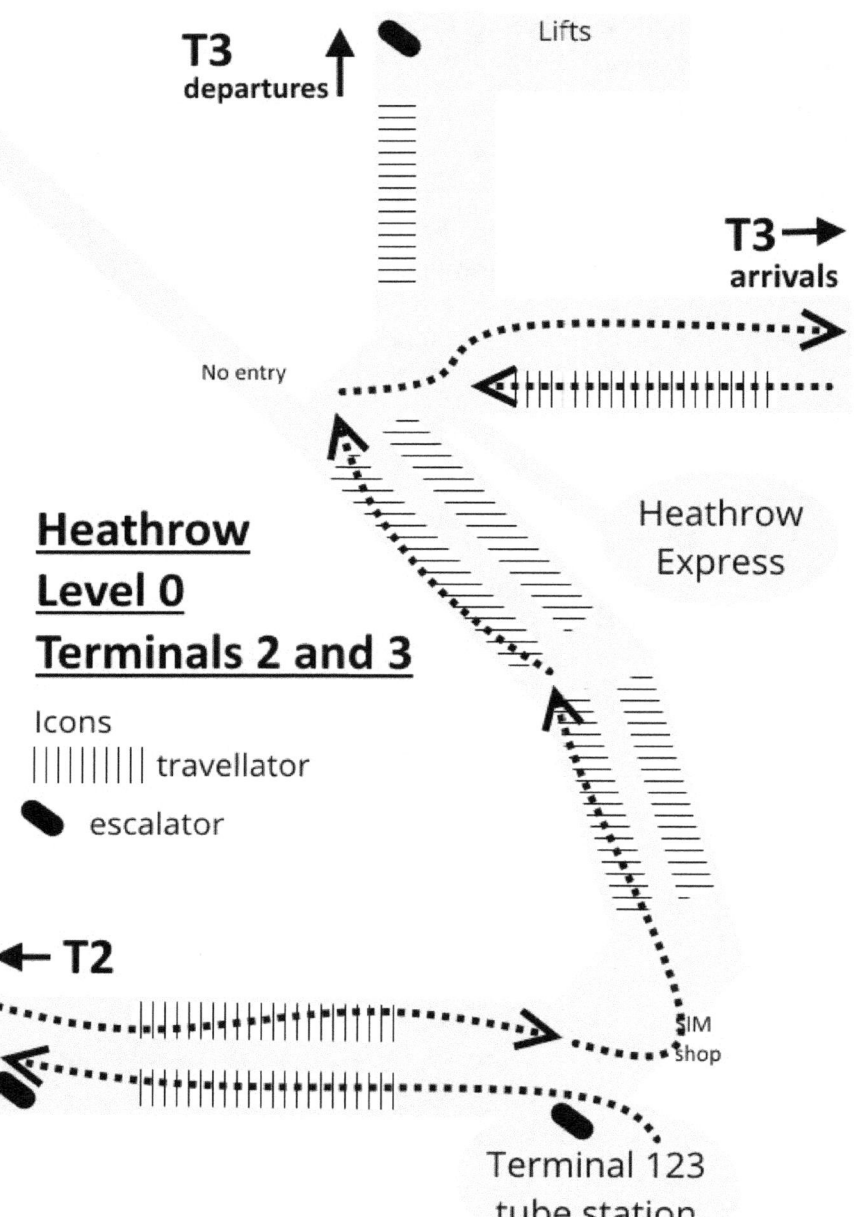

T3
departures

Lifts

T3 →
arrivals

No entry

Heathrow
Express

Heathrow
Level 0
Terminals 2 and 3

Icons

|||||||||| travellator

escalator

← T2

SIM
shop

Terminal 123
tube station

Cockfosters
Oakwood
Southgate
Arnos Grove
Bounds Green
Wood Green
Turnpike Lane
Manor House
Finsbury Park
Arsenal
Holloway Road
Caledonian Road
King's Cross St. Pancras
Russell Square
Holborn
Covent Garden
Leicester Square
Piccadilly Circus
Green Park
Hyde Park Corner
Knightsbridge
South Kensington
Gloucester Road
Earl's Court
Barons Court
Hammersmith
Turnham Green
Acton Town

Ealing Common          South Ealing
North Ealing           Northfields
Park Royal             Boston Manor
Alperton               Osterley
Sudbury Town           Hounslow East
Sudbury Hill           Hounslow Central
South Harrow           Hounslow West
Rayners Lane           Hatton Cross  ←
Eastcote               Heathrow T 1-2-3  ——→ Heathrow T4
Ruislip Manor          Heathrow T5
Ruislip
Ickenham
Hillingdon
Uxbridge

# Holborn

*Estimated time to Russell Square 2 minutes*

*Estimated time to Bounds Green 22 minutes*

16h50

I've always thought of Holborn as being a bit stuck-up. 'It's pronounced How-burn, darling.' Well, maybe and maybe not. There seems to be a bit of contention about that. Some people think it should be pronounced 'Holl-born'. Or 'Ho-born', or 'Ho-burn'. But, because I'm feeling gracious, and the buggers need a bit of whoof in their lives, let's give it something to warm the cockles of everyone's hearts. A bit of burn.

Brandy. Which is, of course, a corruption of "brande wyn", with a j in it somewhere, or "burnt wine", the process through which wine becomes brandy. Like so many things it began as an attempt to avoid taxes, in this case reducing the volume by turning wine into a concentrate. And a wonderful drink it is if you don't have any whiskey to hand.

So, Danny, let's award Holborn the stational drink of brandy, with or without mixers, warmed or not as you like, cinnamon sticks an optional extra.

With a clove stuck up it for anyone who pronounces it Ho-bun.

I remember Holborn from a couple of years back when I did a short course at the LSE in Aldwych. Now the Americans talk of going to college when they mean university. Well, the LSE is the London School of Economics. The LSE is not a school, it's a college. It's one of the colleges that make up the University of London. Another college in the university is University College London. Imperial College London used to belong to the University of London but ceased its membership, so presumably it's a university in its own right. This sort of thing is why people tend to say things like 'I went to Aberystwyth', or 'I studied at King's' rather than 'I got my degree from the London School of Economics and Political Science, part of the University of London'.

I remember it was a gorgeous summer. The trees were green, the parks were blooming. Every day was sunny. Being away from teaching duties was like being on holiday. Being amongst eighteen and nineteen-year-old students was like being back in my university days, beer was cheap, the girls were pretty and adventuresome. And fortunately none of them were my former pupils.

Unfortunately the course only lasted a fortnight, so it was a brief interlude of hope and happiness before returning to the dire reality of teaching at an inner-city comprehensive where hope was an archaeological corpse at best.

Where are you going to go to university, Danny? You'll have to go, you know, because after that you'll be going for a Masters and a doctorate and all the rest. We can't have you slacking.

A woman has just sat down next to me. She's carrying about fifteen bags from different shops, all of them the pointy cardboard type from high-fashion boutiques. She almost took the eyes out of three people getting to her seat, and I'm fending off two bags with my left arm, and since that's in a brace you'd think she'd have the good manners to keep her bloody bags to herself. If I wasn't in such a good mood due to the excellent latte I've been drinking I might throw them down the carriage.

She's finally managed to sit down and get her packages on her lap in such a way that my face is no longer in any danger. She very politely apologised to me, unaware that one of her packages was carving up the face of the bloke on her other side.

Some women should not be allowed to carry any accoutrements or impedimenta, ever.

Like the woman on the travelator with the bunch of roses. I have never seen such a huge bunch. Nor so long stalked. Where did she get them? Did someone meet her at arrivals, hand them over and say, 'I've bought you this enormous bunch of huge roses which you'll struggle to carry and will get in your way and everyone else's way until you get home because I hate you and the rest of the world and be careful or you'll take someone's eye out with them if I'm lucky'?

And she replied, 'Oh, darling, that's so thoughtful of you, they're lovely.' Instead of, 'What the fuck am I supposed to do with this, open up my own fucking flower shop?'

Anyway, by some miracle I'd just seen Maddy, and I don't waste miracles. Tired as I was I broke into something approaching a sprint. I had to get to Maddy before she disappeared into the crowds. I still didn't know what I was going to say to her when I got hold of her, but that wouldn't be relevant if I lost her again.

And the question was, what was I going to do to those roses? Knock them out of the way? Grab them and give them to Maddy as a peace offering?

That would have produced interesting results.

In the end I just ducked under them. Fortunately she didn't drop them in surprise otherwise I really would have ended up with a crown of thorns. As I did so she exclaimed, 'Look where you're going!'

I didn't bother replying. I had neither the time nor breath and I was also concentrating on the little chap in the pork pie hat. He was standing perfectly still, leaving plenty of room to let others pass. The end of the travelator was coming up. It just looked too easy. I was sure he would suddenly bend down, pick up his suitcase and start waving it around, or accidentally put out a walking stick for me to trip over, or do something unexpected that would slow me down.

And of course nothing happened. I whizzed passed him, gave him a suspicious look, noticed that he had his hands tightly folded and his eyes squeezed closed, wondered, 'WTF?' and then shot off the travelator and into the junction of the three channels, one from T3 arrivals, one towards T3 departures, and on towards the Underground, Heathrow Express and Terminal 2 on the left, where Maddy had just disappeared.

I think I vaguely noticed a sign pointing towards the left for Terminals 2, 4, 5, but my concentration wasn't on that. I was back at the kink and straight into a maelstrom of travellers, trolleys and wheelie-bags.

But no Maddy.

I jumped up for a better view.

Nothing.

I turned left and jogged down towards the Underground for a few yards, muttering 'Maddy! Maddy!' like some deranged madman. The channel towards the Heathrow Express came into view on my left.

And there she was, walking towards the Heathrow Express.

'Maddy!' I called.

She didn't turn around. I started to run again.

I only had enough breath to run or to shout. So running it would have to be. I couldn't stand there shouting while Maddy walked away from me, not when she was this close

Coming into Russell Square.

Cockfosters
Oakwood
Southgate
Arnos Grove
Bounds Green
Wood Green
Turnpike Lane
Manor House
Finsbury Park
Arsenal
Holloway Road
Caledonian Road
King's Cross St. Pancras
Russell Square
Holborn
Covent Garden
Leicester Square
Piccadilly Circus
Green Park
Hyde Park Corner
Knightsbridge
South Kensington
Gloucester Road
Earl's Court
Barons Court
Hammersmith
Turnham Green
Acton Town

Ealing Common      South Ealing
North Ealing       Northfields
Park Royal         Boston Manor
Alperton           Osterley
Sudbury Town       Hounslow East
Sudbury Hill       Hounslow Central
South Harrow       Hounslow West
Rayners Lane       Hatton Cross      ←
Eastcote           Heathrow T 1-2-3  →  Heathrow T4
Ruislip Manor      Heathrow T5
Ruislip
Ickenham
Hillingdon
Uxbridge

# Russell Square

*Estimated time to King's Cross St. Pancras 2 minutes*

*Estimated time to Bounds Green 20 minutes*

16h54

I once asked my pupils why the British Museum shouldn't return the Parthenon sculptures to Greece. The answer, of course, is 'Because then they'll have lost their marbles'. That joke would have worked in my previous school, eventually. But my current lot didn't know that the Parthenon sculptures are more commonly referred to as the Elgin Marbles, they didn't know that the Elgin Marbles are kept in the British Museum, and most of them didn't know the phrase 'losing your marbles'.

Still, I repeated it in the staff room later that day and got a groan or two.

I suppose if my lot knew that the Elgin Marbles had been nicked they might have been more interested. Trouble is it's alleged that they were nicked from Greece, and it's the Greeks doing the alleging, the British Museum deny all charges. So for my pupils it's just a lot of political argy-bargy over some rocks.

To my mind Russell Square is synonymous with the British Museum. Technically speaking Holborn is three hundred metres closer – someone told me that once and like many entirely irrelevant facts the figure has irritatingly stuck in my mind ever since – but my first visit to the museum was with my Aunt Marigold, and she had decided that one got off at Russell Square for the British Museum, and that was that. I suspect that she just didn't like Holborn for some reason. She was a woman of strong likes and dislikes and if she suspected a tube station of being impertinent it would suffer disdain for the rest of its life.

So, Danny, what stational drink can we confer on Russel Square? Something to do with Greece? A sort of apology for nicking their rocks.

Ouzo.

Has to be. People dancing in circles while singing and breaking plates.

Doesn't sound very Greek, mind you, Russell Square.

Still, I'm sure they'll manage. The Greeks are very good at having a party.

Danny, marbles. No childhood is complete without marbles. I must make a note to get you some. You'll be the champion marble player of your generation.

Back at Heathrow.

It was 13h37. I'd just spotted Maddy on her way to the Heathrow Express. It was a chance in billions, it would only have taken her about ten seconds to cross over from the tunnel leading to T3 departures to that for the Heathrow Express. For me to be coming down the tunnel towards T3 arrivals during those precise ten seconds in a position to actually see her, the chances must have been awesome. That day I should have bought a lottery ticket.

But I wasn't going to throw away such a chance. Despite being almost out of breath I leapt into action. She hadn't heard me call so I raced up behind her, still without a clue as to what I was going to say to her.

'Maddy!' I called as I came up to a couple of paces behind her. She had on these huge earphones which meant she couldn't hear me. I got close enough to grab her arm.

'Maddy!' I said as she turned around. She pushed her earphones back.

'Oh bugger,' I said, 'you aren't Maddy, are you?'

A very attractive young woman who had looked enough like Maddy for me to jump to desperate conclusions smiled back.

'No, I'm Mary. Is that close enough?'

'No, sorry,' I puffed, 'it's my girlfriend I'm looking for, Madeleine. She wears almost exactly the same sort of outfit. And you look just like her.'

'Pity, I thought maybe I'd scored there.'

'Sorry about that.'

'Not to worry.'

'Well, I'd better get on.'

'Indeed, I've got a train to catch.'

'And I've a plane to stop. Enjoy your journey.'

'You too.'

We looked at each other for a few seconds. Reluctantly I turned and began walking back towards Terminal 3 departures. I think I had so convinced myself it was Maddy I had also convinced myself I was in love with her at the same time.

'Good luck,' she called.

I waved without looking back. I didn't have the energy to do other.

'Are you Michael?' asked the same young man in front of me.

'No I am fucking not. Now piss off, prick,' I said, pushing past him.

'There's no need to be rude if you aren't Michael,' he said.

For a brief second my mind tried to work out whether that meant that, if I was Michael, I would be required to be rude. I quickly shut that neuron down

I looked ahead towards T3 departures. I could see a travelator of about a hundred yards on the left going towards the terminal – definitely departures, not arrivals – and a twenty foot wide walkway alongside on the right for people returning from there, or people going there who did not trust the travelator. Beyond that there was an escalator at the end to the left and stairs going up next to that.

Terminal 3 departures had to be somewhere at the end of that escalator. I had to be near the end. This was it. No more mistakes to be made. No more blind alleys to run down. No doubt about it.

That's when I noticed the hen party I'd ambushed earlier, walking up the walkway. They didn't look happy. Ahead of them was the stag group, also on the walkway. They looked even less happy. Fortunately they were walking away from me.

Maybe they didn't trust travelators any more.

I took a breath and stepped on the travelator. There were only about half a million people on it.

I looked at my watch.

It was 13h38.

I began to jog as best I could.

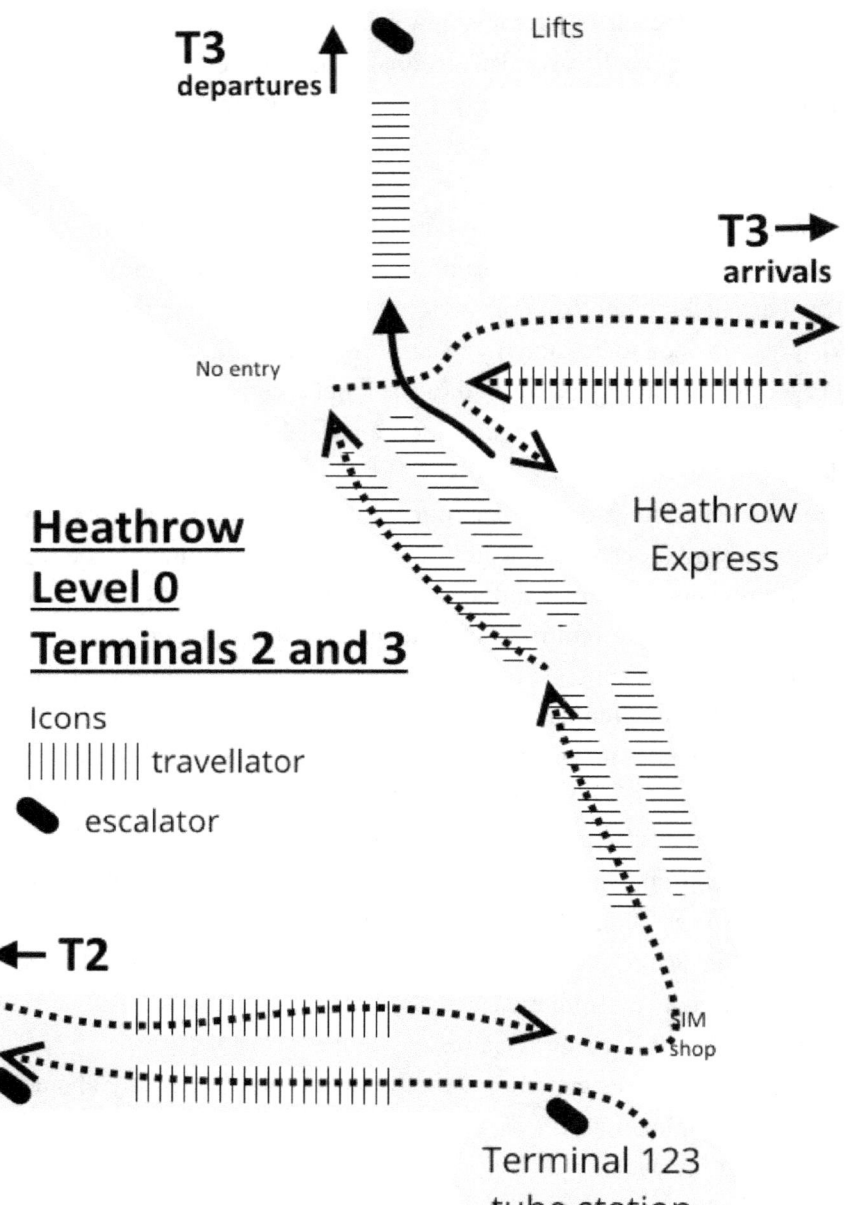

**T3**
departures

Lifts

**T3** → arrivals

No entry

Heathrow
Express

**Heathrow**
**Level 0**
**Terminals 2 and 3**

Icons
|||||||||||| travellator

escalator

← **T2**

SIM
shop

Terminal 123
tube station

Cockfosters
Oakwood
Southgate
Arnos Grove
Bounds Green
Wood Green
Turnpike Lane
Manor House
Finsbury Park
Arsenal
Holloway Road
Caledonian Road
King's Cross St. Pancras
Russell Square
Holborn
Covent Garden
Leicester Square
Piccadilly Circus
Green Park
Hyde Park Corner
Knightsbridge
South Kensington
Gloucester Road
Earl's Court
Barons Court
Hammersmith
Turnham Green
Acton Town

Ealing Common          South Ealing
North Ealing           Northfields
Park Royal             Boston Manor
Alperton               Osterley
Sudbury Town           Hounslow East
Sudbury Hill           Hounslow Central
South Harrow           Hounslow West
Rayners Lane           Hatton Cross ←
Eastcote               Heathrow T 1-2-3 → Heathrow T4
Ruislip Manor          Heathrow T5
Ruislip
Ickenham
Hillingdon
Uxbridge

# King's Cross St. Pancras

*Estimated time to Caledonian Road 4 minutes*

*Estimated time to Bounds Green 18 minutes*

17h00

Quick, Danny, without cheating, without checking the Internet or whatever it is you have in twenty years' time, what's the drink of Kings? Crosses? Saints? Pancrases?

I'll bet you've cheated. I'll bet you've had a chip put in your head that allows you to seamlessly connect to massive warehouses of huge computers holding all the data in the world, including future data which hasn't been discovered or invented yet.

What am I saying? Of course the warehouses won't be huge. They'll be the size of a matchbox, contain all the knowns and unknowns, and replicate in nuclear-proof little bunkers across the world. And be updated every nano-nano-second.

This is all presuming we've managed to get through the next twenty years without a thermo-nuclear war between the main players. We could probably survive a minor exchange between Washington and Pyong Nang. The North Korean missiles will probably fall in the ocean or drop on their toes, anyway.

I'll quaff some latte while you think, Danny.

Quaff, quaff.

And an extra quaff for luck.

Right, Danny, time's up. And the answer is?

Well I gave you a bit of a clue: quaff.

The answer is: mead. It's a sort of wine with honey and herbs and spices as far as I understand. I had some one Christmas on the South Bank. It tasted revolting. So I had seconds to confirm. And because that also tasted revolting I had thirds to numb my taste buds.

I'm led to believe that the legend of mead as a drink of kings is confirmed by Beowulf. So that will be Celtic and Anglo-Saxon kings then. What the Egyptian, Chinese, Aztec and other monarchs quaffed I haven't a clue.

I think the Aztecs did chocolate-and-blood-of-your-enemies. Unless that was the Maya.

Added mayo?

No, don't think so.

So, count them, Danny.

My final obstacles:

One travelator.

One short section.

One escalator.

And something out there.

Then Terminal 3 departures.

It was 13h38.

Eight minutes out of time.

But almost at the end.

Probably.

I began to jog along the travelator, trying to keep to the left where the hen and stag parties wouldn't see me. First I passed a young man on the right wearing headphones and trying to walk briskly along while tapping his feet to the music. It wasn't working, and he was likely to do himself an injury.

Then, jig to the right, pass a security woman standing on the left listening to her radio squawk at the world. Carry on straight, past a woman in a fur coat painting her nails dark blue. For a moment I wondered if I hadn't started hallucinating. A fur coat? It was the height of summer. And who the hell paints their nails dark blue?

Dodge left again, pass standing man staring at his mobile phone in complete and utter disbelief. I didn't know what he saw there, but it wasn't pleasant.

By this time I'm coming up to where the stag and hen parties were trudging along on the walkway.

And would you believe it, there's a party of young people, look like university students, standing on the right of the travelator, chatting, leaving the left clear and blocking the view of the stag ad hen parties. So I jog in a tip-toe fashion hoping the stag and hen parties wouldn't notice.

I almost made it. I was just ahead of them when the group of students ended. I had to dodge to the right to get past someone slowly dragging their wheelie-bag along. Behind me I heard a male voice behind me shout, 'Oi! It's im!', followed by a female voice repeating the cry.

Cockfosters
Oakwood
Southgate
Arnos Grove
Bounds Green
Wood Green
Turnpike Lane
Manor House
Finsbury Park
Arsenal
Holloway Road
Caledonian Road
King's Cross St. Pancras
Russell Square
Holborn
Covent Garden
Leicester Square
Piccadilly Circus
Green Park
Hyde Park Corner
Knightsbridge
South Kensington
Gloucester Road
Earl's Court
Barons Court
Hammersmith
Turnham Green
Acton Town

| | |
|---|---|
| Ealing Common | South Ealing |
| North Ealing | Northfields |
| Park Royal | Boston Manor |
| Alperton | Osterley |
| Sudbury Town | Hounslow East |
| Sudbury Hill | Hounslow Central |
| South Harrow | Hounslow West |
| Rayners Lane | Hatton Cross |
| Eastcote | Heathrow T 1-2-3 ⟶ Heathrow T4 |
| Ruislip Manor | Heathrow T5 |
| Ruislip | |
| Ickenham | |
| Hillingdon | |
| Uxbridge | |

# Caledonian Road

*Estimated time to Holloway Road 1 minutes*

*Estimated time to Bounds Green 14 minutes*

17h04

Now, Danny, you'll be thinking, how on earth is he going to make a connection between Caledonian Road and a stational drink.

Well, let me have another sip of latte and I'll tell you.

There, that's better.

It's the Romans, you see. They called Ireland Hibernia. Tacitus, Ptolemy, Pliny the Elder, all of them. And they called Scotland Caledonia. The land of the Picts, the naughty little wee devils. And that well known Australian Scot, whatsisface, the blue one. The Scottish Smurf from Down Under.

And what do Scots love to drink?

Buckfast, of course. But apart from that?

Whisky.

So, Caledonian Road, your stational drink is Scots whisky, Talisker 10 Year Old if you can afford it, Aldi own brand if you prefer.

Actually the Aldi Highland Black 8 Year Old Whisky comes highly recommended and not only by me.

When the day is done, the labour finished, the sweat wiped from the brow – metaphorically – then it's time to sit and bask in the golden taste of a good whiskey. Or even whisky.

Till then I'll lap a latte.

After all, we're almost there. Seven stations to go.

And all will be revealed.

It was so, so close.

13h39.

Danny, I swear I was almost there. I could see the daylight coming down the escalator, about fifty yards ahead. In my imagination there was a beam of sunlight coming down, a golden sign that the escalator was the way to heaven, or ecstasy, or maybe Terminal 3 departures.

There was still part of the travelator to navigate. The hags and oiks from the stag and hen parties were trying to catch up, but they were loaded down with luggage and early morning drinks, plus I would imagine a full English breakfast and undoubtedly several pounds excess flab. They also had some opposition flow to overcome, especially from people with trolleys coming their way.

For a brief few seconds my attention was caught by a woman pushing a trolley next to the travelator while kidnapped by her mobile phone. She was straying to the right, into the path of people coming towards us, some of whom were also engrossed in their mobile phones. There was another strange pas de deux as her trolley clipped the wheel of another oncoming trolley, also driven by a woman on a mobile phone. They circled each other until their trolleys had done 360 degrees and separated and they each continued in their own clouds. The hags and oiks came up against this display of trolley dancing and paused in a kind of bemused fascination, their urge to catch me up replaced by a second thought confusing their brains. I don't think any of them were my ex-pupils, but there was a definite similarity.

Re-assured that my rear was covered, as they say in military circles, I looked to my front. There was still an ebb and flow of travellers to navigate on the travelator. I ducked right of a little old woman in a brown coat pushing a loaded trolley with all her strength. Another time I might have paused to offer assistance, but (a) I didn't have the time to spare, and (b) she had a solid wood walking stick handling from the handlebars, and I suspected it was used on impertinent young men who unwisely offered their help.

There was about fifty feet of travelator left when I came up behind the three black blokes. They were moving at quite a lick of speed, but too slow for me. The one in front was medium height and seemed perfectly normal, which suggested to me he was the brains of the group. The one immediately behind him was about six foot five, carrying a large travel bag, and had a bag on his back with a skateboard tied securely into it with the wheels outermost, facing backwards. He had an aggressive stance, and I couldn't help but feel that he was prepared to skate away on his back should the necessity arise, legs tucked in on top of his chest.

But the big problem was their friend behind them. He was about eight feet tall, built like a basketball player, wearing a red sleeveless t-shirt, black tracksuit trousers, black shoes, no socks, no headgear, and had huge do-not-disturb earphones over his ears. He was also dragging two wheelie cases along, one either side, completely blocking the travelator.

I tried saying 'Excuse me?' politely. It was a waste of time. I could have used half a dozen giant megaphones and it wouldn't have made a difference.

I looked at the two suitcases. I could have jumped them if he wasn't moving, otherwise, no. I tried tapping him on the shoulder. The suitcases were in the way and I couldn't get close.

Which is when his friend with the skateboard turned around and saw me. He leaned backwards and said, 'Yo man wants to get through.'

To which giant basketball man replied, 'Yo mother too.'

'No, Julius, yo man wants to get past.'

'Yo mother too,' repeated basketball player.

Skateboard man sighed, leaned forward, pulled one earphone away from basketball player's head, shouted 'Yo man behind wants to get past you, you idiot!'

Then he let the earphone go and it slammed back into basketball player's ear, who exclaimed in pain, stopped, and dropped his suitcases to allow him to massage his ear.

'Why yo do that?' he asked plaintively as I jumped over the now stationary suitcases.

'Many thanks,' I said to skateboard man as I passed, 'I'm in a little hurry.'

'You go with god, friend,' he said, winking, 'and if you doan find god, go with the devil.'

'Thank you,' I said and carried on running. Apart from being out of breath and out of things to say I wasn't quite sure how to reply to it. Apart from crying 'Hallelujah!', not in response to his best wishes, but rather because the way was now clear to the escalator. I was now off the travelator. The way was open. Clear open-field running. I could see the metal uprights in front of the escalators to prevent people taking their trolleys on and doing themselves a mischief. The escalator led up to the sunshine. Stairs to the right of the escalator for people without luggage to come down. Lifts to the right of the steps for those with luggage going up or coming down the one level that separated us and outside. All that separated me from Terminal 3 check-in was the escalator, I was sure of it.

As I got close to the escalator I half noticed a group of Dutch tourists standing to the right. I could tell they were Dutch not only by their accents, but by their height. I don't know what they put in the water over there, but they grow some fine rugby wingers. Pity they don't play rugby. Their luggage was all on trolleys, and I had a vague thought that they had concluded they couldn't get the trolleys on the escalator, so now they were debating: should they take the luggage off and abandon the trolleys to their fate or be lazy and take a lift?

I wasn't about to stop and offer them advice. I just felt hugely relieved. The escalator was the last hurdle, and once up and out Terminal 3 departures would be right in front of me, Maddy would be there. The busies had disappeared, the stag and hen party oiks were too far behind and too unfit to make a difference.

I slipped between the steel uprights and was just about to step on the first escalator tread when one of the Dutch party at the back peeled away and stepped onto the escalator in front of me. I paused, swore under my breath, got on the escalator and prepared to push my way past.

The Dutch person turned and faced me.

'Good afternoon, sir,' she said, pulling on her police cap.

I looked at the hardware she was carrying. She wasn't Dutch. It was the policewoman who had first clocked me at Terminal 2 arrivals. She was very politely and very firmly blocking my way.

Instinctively I looked behind me. Her partner, the young Clint Eastwood with the huge Adam's apple, had joined us on the escalator and stood there looking at me with an expressionless face and an unconcealed howitzer on his hip. He was standing on one leg, the other nonchalantly on the tread above, and just coincidentally in my way should I think of doing something silly like make a run for it the wrong way down the escalator.

'I wonder if you can spare a moment to help us with our enquiries,' the police woman said. It didn't sound like a request.

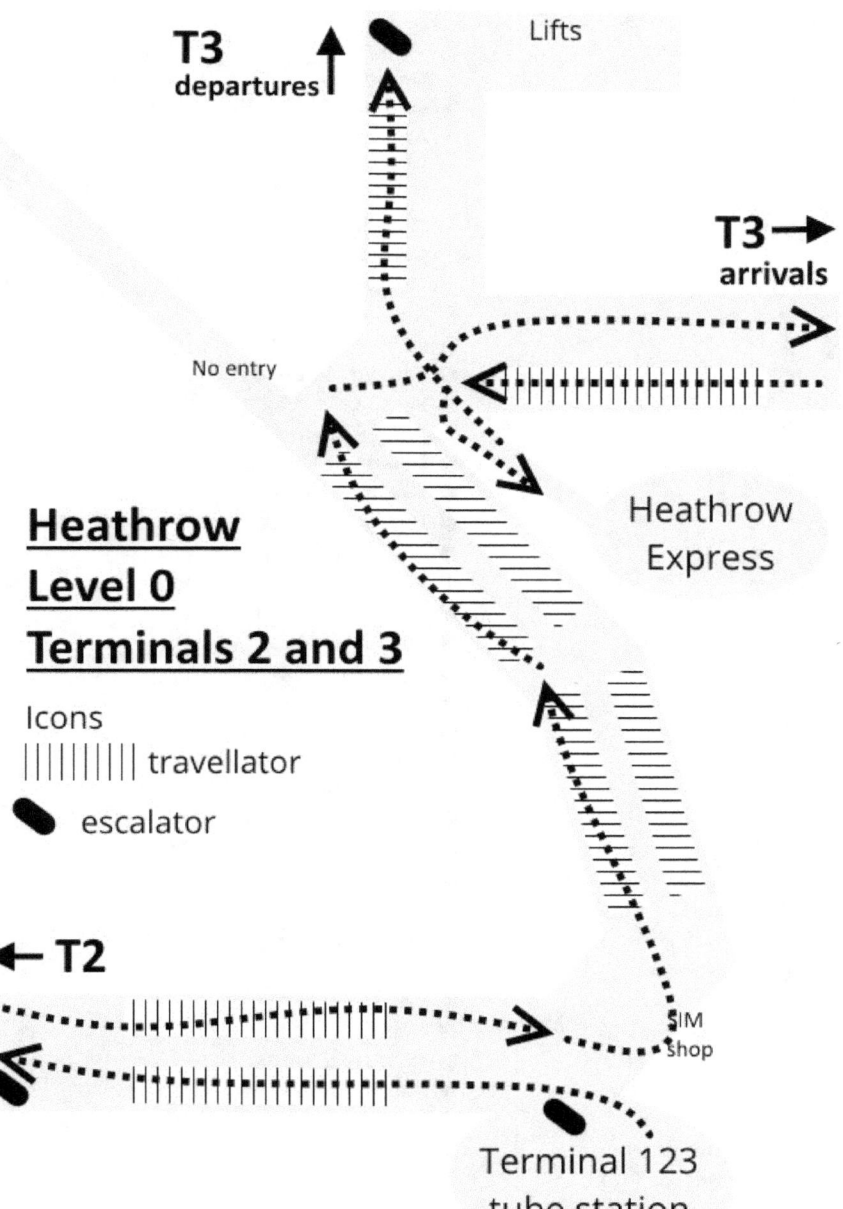

T3
departures

Lifts

T3 →
arrivals

No entry

Heathrow
Express

# Heathrow
# Level 0
# Terminals 2 and 3

Icons

|||||||||| travellator

escalator

← T2

SIM
Shop

Terminal 123
tube station

Cockfosters
Oakwood
Southgate
Arnos Grove
Bounds Green
Wood Green
Turnpike Lane
Manor House
Finsbury Park
Arsenal
Holloway Road
Caledonian Road
King's Cross St. Pancras
Russell Square
Holborn
Covent Garden
Leicester Square
Piccadilly Circus
Green Park
Hyde Park Corner
Knightsbridge
South Kensington
Gloucester Road
Earl's Court
Barons Court
Hammersmith
Turnham Green
Acton Town

Ealing Common          South Ealing
North Ealing           Northfields
Park Royal             Boston Manor
Alperton               Osterley
Sudbury Town           Hounslow East
Sudbury Hill           Hounslow Central
South Harrow           Hounslow West
Rayners Lane           Hatton Cross  ←
Eastcote               Heathrow T 1-2-3  ⟶  Heathrow T4
Ruislip Manor          Heathrow T5
Ruislip
Ickenham
Hillingdon
Uxbridge

# Holloway Road

*Estimated time to Arsenal 2 minutes*

*Estimated time to Bounds Green 13 minutes*

17h07

Danny, here in the UK in the second decade of the twenty-first century people don't tend to think much about the judicial or police apparatus. Not until you get mugged and discover there isn't a police officer for miles, or park slightly the wrong way and find yourself surrounded by parking wardens. The closest most normal, upstanding citizens get to the court system is when they hear that a friend of a friend was called up for jury service, and how they managed to avoid it. Prison is somewhere where either ne'er-do-wells need to be sent for the rest of their life, or terrible Victorian hell-holes from which poor down-trodden victims of society need to be rescued, depending on which newspaper you take. Most of it is hidden behind innocent-looking thick doors and tall anonymous walls, but if you look you'll find you're never far from somewhere where people used to be locked up or strung up.

Holloway Road. Holloway prison used to be around here, the famous women's prison. Or, to be more accurate, the famous prison designed to hold female convicts, the women didn't actually own it. The next station is Arsenal, where many Arsenal football fans would get off if their club was playing at home. It is rumoured that there was a time that some of those supporters on their way to see a match might have had one or two bevvies, or beverages of an alcoholic nature. And on the odd occasion such supporters might have called after young ladies getting off at Holloway Road, 'Oi, luv, give me regards to your mum.'

So, Danny, a stational drink for Holloway Road.

An easy one, that. There was a well-known English artist and satirist called William Hogarth, lived in the mid-1700s. He created two prints designed to be viewed alongside each other, "Beer Street" and "Gin Lane". "Gin Lane" showed examples of the rabble in intoxicated states after having consumed too much gin. The central figure is that of a woman sitting on some steps falling back unconscious as she unwitting

479

drops her baby into the street below. On the surface it's a call to ban alcohol.

But "Beer Street" shows the stolid British Burgher consuming stolid British Ale, and much better he and she is for it too. So it wasn't anti-alcohol, it was anti-that cheap Dutch import, gin. The authorities became so concerned about peasants enjoying their foreign muck that they put a tax on gin. Which encouraged boot-legging and smuggling and not paying taxes and general illegality, which the Yanks were later to rediscover to their cost after bringing in the Volstead Act, otherwise known as Prohibition.

Gin eventually became known by the two nicknames, Mother's Delight and Mother's Ruin.

So, Holloway Road, with your memories of Holloway Prison, what other stational drink can we give you but gin?

The good news is that, add enough tonic and you'll be part-way protected from malaria. The bad news is that it tastes bloody revolting and makes you so depressed malaria will sound like a party.

I think I'll have some more latte instead.

Cheers.

13h40

Danny, you're probably wondering what the busies wanted with me. And I think that's why I hadn't really wondered why they kept popping up and showing such an interest in me: there was absolutely no reason for them to do so. So my brain kind of shut down that question. I hadn't done anything wrong, ergo they couldn't be interested in me, ergo they weren't interested in me, ergo they weren't looking at me all the time the way they were looking at me all the time. I know there isn't any logic in that, but I had one aim only, that was to find your mum before she could leave, and the world could go hang until I'd accomplished that goal.

Unfortunately coppers in general, and women coppers in particular, don't subscribe to that sort of point of view.

'If you don't mind, I'm in a bit of a hurry,' I said. I could have sworn the copper behind me muttered 'You don't say, buddy.' I briefly glanced behind me, but his face was completely blank and innocent. I turned back to Madame Firepower standing on the escalator step above me. 'So if I could please get past?'

'Just as soon as we've asked you some questions, sir. Firstly, is there any specific reason for your hurry?' she asked.

I was tempted to say 'None of your bloody business', but, while that's a perfectly valid response, and the coppers can't insist on you divulging anything you don't want to, it's the sort of response you give when you (a) know your rights, (b) have a lot of time to waste, and (c) are a lawyer.

'Because I'm extremely late,' I finally replied. 'Haven't you seen people running around an airport before? People do find themselves running late on the odd occasion, you know. I'm sure I've already seen ten and I haven't been actively looking.'

'Quite so, sir, quite so. There's just one thing unusual about your haste, if I may say, sir.'

My immediate reply would have been something along the lines of, 'Well say it then, spit it out, and get out of my way.'

Not a good idea. It doesn't even work on my pupils.

'Officer,' I said instead, taking a deep breath and gritting my teeth, 'have I told you that I'm a teacher?'

'Indeed, sir? A teacher. Well, well.'

'Yes, and I'm rapidly approaching supersonic sarcastic mode, so please get whatever it is out of your system and let me get on my way.'

She paused while giving me an incurious look. They train them to do that.

'You haven't asked, sir.'

'Asked? Asked what?'

Another incurious look and pause.

'What's unusual about your haste, sir.'

I closed my eyes and sighed. Then I re-opened them. We were almost at the top of the escalator, but I somehow knew there wasn't likely to be an escape until I'd humoured these two wooden-tops.

'Okay, officer, what is unusual about my haste, then?'

She gave me a 'well, it's perfectly obvious to everyone else' look.

'You don't have any luggage, sir,' she said.

'Very unusual, that,' noted young Clint behind me to no-one in particular.

'The reason for that is that I am not here to catch a plane,' I said through gritted teeth, 'I'm here to stop someone catching a plane.'

'To stop someone catching a plane,' repeated Madame Firepower.

'See, that is unusual,' young Clint mused. 'Like not having luggage. That's unusual, too.'

'And who would this person be?' asked Madam F, deftly stepping backwards off the escalator as we reached the top.

'It's my girlfriend,' I admitted. 'We had a misunderstanding.'

'Me too,' said young Clint. 'We often have those. My girlfriend and me, that is. My ex as well. All my exes. I have more exes than girlfriends.'

'I see,' said Madame F as we came out into an open piazza type area, the sun shining brilliantly overhead in a bright blue sky with a generous scattering of Constable-like cumulus drifting across. She was side on to me, and I could feel the presence of Clint very close behind. They were making it quite clear that I wasn't going anywhere until they were satisfied. Despite that I managed to get a look at an electronic display board which showed where the various airlines' check-in desks could be found. Qantas were located at entrance C. I tried to look around for entrance C without making it obvious. As soon as I identified it I would do a two-step tap-dance to disrupt the coppers' concentration and, the second they blinked, would be off faster than the road-runner. They could follow me at their leisure. It wouldn't matter then.

'What's she look like?' asked young Clint as if comparing notes on girlfriends' looks was quite normal under the circumstances. 'Your missus, like.'

I think my mouth opened and shut a few times. What business of his was it what Maddy looked like?

What did Maddy look like?

She looked like the most beautiful girl in the world. She was the most beautiful woman in the world. She was perfect. She was Aphrodite. She was the original Virgin Mary with a wicked smile and Cupid's sense of humour. She was Cleopatra. She was the Moon Princess. She was the sun goddess of the night and day. She was a child. She was an angel. She was a devil. She was perfection. Of course she was.

Perfection. That's what she bloody looked like.

Of course she was, I was in fucking love with her, what else would she look like? Arseholes.

Which for me was the undeniable truth, though, in hindsight, not of much use to the coppers.

'She almost always wears black,' I finally said, lamely.

'That's what my ex used to wear,' noted young Clint as if in confirmation of his worst fears. 'My last ex. My latest wears yellow. I checked before I started going out with her. Can't be too careful.'

Coming into Arsenal, aka Gillespie Road. Bloody hell, that was quick. Only – five stations to go.

Danny, almost there. This is the secret I mentioned earlier.

Dear old Gillespie Road. Poor thing. Poor, poor thing.

Cockfosters
Oakwood
Southgate
Arnos Grove
Bounds Green
Wood Green
Turnpike Lane
Manor House
Finsbury Park
Arsenal
Holloway Road
Caledonian Road
King's Cross St. Pancras
Russell Square
Holborn
Covent Garden
Leicester Square
Piccadilly Circus
Green Park
Hyde Park Corner
Knightsbridge
South Kensington
Gloucester Road
Earl's Court
Barons Court
Hammersmith
Turnham Green
Acton Town

Ealing Common      South Ealing
North Ealing       Northfields
Park Royal         Boston Manor
Alperton           Osterley
Sudbury Town       Hounslow East
Sudbury Hill       Hounslow Central
South Harrow       Hounslow West
Rayners Lane       Hatton Cross  ←
Eastcote           Heathrow T 1-2-3  →  Heathrow T4
Ruislip Manor      Heathrow T5
Ruislip
Ickenham
Hillingdon
Uxbridge

# Arsenal

*Estimated time to Finsbury Park 1 minutes*

*Estimated time to Bounds Green 11 minutes*

17h10

Arsenal. Where dreams come to die. Or they do if you're an Arsenal fan. Ironically that's the sort of view you only get if you support a good football club that should be in the top four in the league table. Support a useless club that sits permanently at the bottom and you're grateful for any crumbs that come your way.

Danny, never set your sights too low. Professional footballer, you could do that if you don't fancy rugger. Then manager when you retire from top league playing, when you're about thirty-five, maybe forty in the future. It'll take a lot of training, but you'll be able to do it, I'm sure. First thing I'm going to buy you for your birthday is a football. I'll keep it safe somewhere until you're ready for it. I might take it out to make sure it's still kickable every so often.

It's funny what humans can get passionate about, and how. You have the music groupies who shriek and wail when they see their band. Then there are the quiet fanatics who used to inhabit record shops when record shops still existed. You have football fans who cry buckets when their team lose. And you have someone called Arsene Wenger who once lost his temper so badly while manager of Arsenal that he aimed a kick at a bottle of water in frustration during a game. Unbelievably he got sent to the stands for that.

Arsene Wenger was in charge of Arsenal for so long that there are some fans who had never known Arsenal under a different manager. He was known as the Professor because he was intellectual and extremely well learned. That was okay since he was a Foreigner. It's acceptable for Foreigners to be sophisticated intellectuals and also successful football managers. British managers are expected to be more down to earth and stupid. If they really insist on being successful football managers, that's probably okay, but preferably somewhere else, like Japan or Thailand. Germany, at a pinch.

485

Thing is, Wenger was passionate about football, and passionate about Arsenal. But his lip was stiffer than any Englishman's could ever be. Somehow I just can't ever imagine him singing. Certainly not with passion.

Making love?

No, I do not want to think about that.

You'll be a professor too, Danny, I know.

But it does make it quite easy to come up with a stational drink for Arsenal. You see, there was this other long time legend manager of a football club, Alec Ferguson, or Fergie, or SAF: Sir Alec Ferguson. He was also extremely passionate, but in a Scottish way. He used to look after Manchester United, and very successful they were, almost every other football fan hated them. Then he retired and they went downhill.

Thing about Alec Ferguson and Arsene Wenger, though, is that the media portrayed them as arch enemies. Which apparently wasn't true, not after Alec Ferguson retired, anyway. Apparently he'd be very happy sharing a bottle of Bordeaux red with Wenger, even though, as a Scot, he was a definite whisky man himself.

So, Arsenal, as your stational drink you get a whole bottle of Bordeaux red. Don't drink it all at once, and don't use straws.

Actually I have very fond recent memories of Arsenal tube station. It was a Tuesday evening a couple of weeks ago mum phoned me.

'How is everything, Mark?' she asked.

'It was going pretty well until you phoned, mum. What's wrong?'

'Nothing's wrong, Mark. Why should anything be wrong? Aren't I allowed to phone my one and only son?'

'You only phone me when something's wrong, mum,' I pointed out.

'Nonsense, Mark, I often phone just for a chat.'

'You often phone Maddy for a chat,' I corrected. 'You never phone me for a chat because you know I don't do chatting.'

'I hope you're looking after her, Mark.'

'Of course I am. She's the jewel in my life. The reason I keep breathing. I exist only to –'

'Good. Now listen, Mark, your father has four tickets for the match this Saturday.'

'Match? Football? Liverpool?'

'Of course, Liverpool. He wants to know if you and Maddy want to come.'

I couldn't much say that I was that interested in a Liverpool game, but Maddy supports them. Dad had promised to take her to a match. And if Maddy wants to go to a Liverpool match, I want to go to that Liverpool match with her. Privately I may want them to lose, badly, but some things are best left unsaid.

'Mum, we'd love to come up, but I've got soccer on Saturday morning and Maddy's off to Cardiff for a couple of weeks on Sunday afternoon.'

Mum sighed.

Mum sighing at me? It was my job to sigh at her.

'Mark, I thought you were an Arsenal fan.'

'Well, yeah, mum, sort of.'

'And who are they playing this Saturday?'

'Haven't a clue, mum. I didn't even know the season had started.'

'You've got soccer on Saturday and you didn't know the season had started?'

'Well, I knew the school season had started. We aren't exactly the premier league. So, tell me, who are Arsenal playing this Saturday. Man City, by any chance?'

'Have a guess.'

'Um, Chelsea? Spurs?'

'No, Mark, they're playing Liverpool. At the Emirates. Your father and I are coming down for the match, then we're coming back up afterward. Kick-off is at one-thirty.'

'You're coming down? Why don't you stay for the weekend?'

'Because your cousin Fiona is having a baby.'

'Cousin Fiona?'

'I think she's your second cousin once removed. She used to have a crush on you, remember? When you were about six. She had a lisp back then.'

'Vaguely.'

Mum sighed again.

'At some stage you are going to have to introduce Maddy to your cousins and uncles and aunts however removed they might be. If both you and they can remember who you and they are.'

'Of course I can remember who they are, I saw them at Aunt Marigold's funeral.'

'No comment. Anyway, she's due Tuesday, her parents are in the States and can't get back in time, so we promised to be there for them. So what about the game?'

'Game?'

'The football match. Between Liverpool and Arsenal.'

'Oh. Well, yes, I don't see why not. Maddy isn't home yet. I'll have a word and ask her to give you a call.'

Maddy was very much up for it, though I suspected that she wasn't so much interested because it was Liverpool as because she'd never been to a big match before, and even more because mum and dad would be there. I was quite certain that the only reason mum was coming down was to see Maddy. I wouldn't have been surprised if that was the reason dad had got the tickets. He had been an avid fan once upon a time, but that had waned. I think he preferred to remember an era before commercialisation took its grip, a time when players were home-grown, and you might bump into them at their local. And the tickets didn't cost close to half the average annual wage.

For some reason etiquette demanded that I had to phone mum to confirm that we'd be going, after which I handed the phone to Maddy so that she and mum could indulge in their usual half-an-hour natter. Dad and I had never been much on the conversation front, so mum had to make the initial call. Football is a man's thing, so she had to speak to me rather than Maddy. Once that nonsense was out the way she and Maddy were free to talk to each other. The weird thing was that both mum and Maddy thought it perfectly normal.

Saturday comes and Maddy and I go to Euston to meet mum and dad. I get a perfunctory kiss from mum and then she can ignore me in favour of concentrating all her affection on Maddy. Dad looks me up and down with surprise in his face.

'Going like that?' he asks.

I check my clothes. They look perfectly normal.

'Yes. Why?'

'You do realise we'll be in the Liverpool end?'

'And?'

'Well, Mark, it's not for me to say, but don't you think it might be a touch dangerous wearing an Arsenal scarf amongst Liverpool supporters?'

I hadn't thought about that. I'd automatically put on the Arsenal scarf I hardly ever wear these days. Maddy had bought a Liverpool scarf for the occasion. Dad and mum were also wearing Liverpool scarves.

'Too late now,' I said. 'I'll try not to wave it about too much when Arsenal score.

Dad shook his head in disbelief. Mum and Maddy thought it quite funny, but then they hadn't seen the sort of violence that can break out if you find yourself in the wrong place at the wrong time at a football match.

But in the end it was fine. Firstly because it was Arsenal and Liverpool rather than, say, Arsenal and Spurs, in which case my life would have been in danger. Or had I turned up in the Liverpool seats wearing an Everton scarf.

It did almost start off once we were seated and waiting for the game to start with a tap on my shoulder. I turned to find this huge bruiser with a shaven head wearing a Liverpool shirt staring at my scarf.

'Here, lad, think you've come to the wrong side of town,' he said. The five or so blokes with him also gave me the kind of amused smirks normally reserved for someone out-numbered who is about to get a thumping.

'This is me mum and da,' I began, nodding towards mum and dad.

'My mum and dad,' mum automatically corrected me without turning around.

'Sorry, my mum and dad. They're Liverpool supporters. This is my girlfriend, she's also a Liverpool supporter. She's also an O'Connor, by the way. So I was outnumbered and overwhelmed.'

'An O'Connor?' he said, quite impressed at the notion of someone looking like Maddy being an O'Connor.

'Aye.'

'I see they really meant it,' he said, noticing and nodding at the brace on my arm. 'Ah, well then we'll better forgive youse,' he said. He nodded towards mum and dad. 'Mr, Mrs,' he said politely and the others joined in. I pretended not to hear the one who muttered, 'Jesus, them O'Connors is much better looking these days,' but I'm pretty sure Maddy heard.

I think Scousers, like almost all groups with a strong sense of identity, have a deep respect for elders and parents. And the way mum absent-mindedly corrected me as if I were a five year old would have impressed them greatly. Though that was a game mum and I had developed over time. She would correct me when I was about ten years old, and I would dutifully obey. Then as a teenager I would do it to be obnoxious and mum pretty much gave up on it. Then when I became a teacher I did it to tease her, and she responded automatically, pretending I was a tiresome brat not worth getting too excited about, but with a little smile on her lips.

And it was a relatively good natured match. Arsenal almost scored early on but just clipped the top bar to send it flying over, which was met with many jeers and cat-calls from the Liverpool supporters around us. Liverpool immediately counter-attacked and just missed scoring by clipping one of the side bars and sending it wide, prompting jeers and cat-calls from the Arsenal supporters. And that was the template for the rest of the game: attack, just miss, counter-attack, just miss and so on. Each time the supporters hopes were raised and dashed, they jumped up and then sank down, jumped up and sank down, until I think pretty much everyone was drained, except for mum and Maddy and a few others who didn't understand the crucial importance of the game. The crucial importance being that we had to win and they had to lose, of course.

Eventually, after what felt like hours of torture the final whistle went, and a game which should have had a score-line of about 15-14 ended up as a nil-all draw. As the players began leaving the field some Liverpool supporters tried to stir the others into a rendition of You'll Never Walk Alone, but they were struggling to get the crowd going. It was then I noticed mum look at Maddy and give her a wink. Then she stood up and began to sing:

'When you walk through a storm'

And Maddy stood up next to her and took the second line:

'Hold your head up high'

And then they combined:

'And don't be afraid of the dark

At the end of a storm

There's a golden sky

And the sweet silver song of a lark'

By which time dad and I and the others had stood up and were supporting them with our bass tones, dad and I reluctantly, the others with deep feeling

'Walk on

through the wind

Walk on

through the rain

Though your dreams

be tossed and blown

Walk on

walk on'

By then almost everyone had joined in, including the Arsenal fans. And mum and Maddy's voices were being picked up by a directional mike somewhere, and the display screen was showing some daft looking supporters singing, and we were completely ignoring it because the daft looking supporters shown happened to be us.

A mass of Liverpool supporters fronted by two women singing in beautiful harmony, supported by their menfolk either side. One of them looking like a very lonely Arsenal supporter wearing his scarf all on his tod amidst the Scouser thugs.

'With hope in your heart

And you'll never

walk alone

You'll never

walk alone

Walk on

walk on

With hope in your heart

And you'll never

walk

alone

You'll never

walk

aalllooone'

We certainly didn't walk alone back to the tube station. Football supporters wearing their club colours often tend to stick together after a football match, especially if it's an away game and they're in hostile territory. The Scouser fans who had been sitting behind us appeared to have decided that it was their duty to look after mum and dad and Miss O'Connor and make sure they were safe, and they were supported by others who either felt the same need or felt safety in numbers. The end result was that we were escorted by a phalanx of Scouser guards back to Arsenal tube station, some in front, some behind. There was a pretty festive air about it; no shortage of shaven-headed bruisers with tattoos, but also girlfriends – some shaven headed with tattoos, admittedly – and just ordinary folk enjoying a day out.

They graciously allowed us to board the tube first – mum and dad out of respect, Maddy because she was Maddy, myself because I was obviously one of god's special children, to be wearing an Arsenal scarf to a Liverpool match – and at Euston gave us space to say our goodbyes before the train left.

'So when will we be seeing you again in Liverpool, young Madeleine?' asked dad. Maddy looked up at me as if I were some holy authority who could grant or deny such permission.

'Probably not for a couple of weeks,' she said. 'I may be able to get the weekend free in a fortnight. Not next Saturday, the one after. Is that okay, Mark?'

'Sounds good to me,' I replied. 'If I've got any work over that weekend I'll get someone to sub it for me.'

'That's settled, then,' said mum, happy as Larry and able to ignore such words as "if" and "may" and "possibly" in preference to deciding they were now concrete fact.

Then when mum and dad boarded the train the Scouser guardian angels shepherded them to the best window seats where they could wave us goodbye. The last we saw mum and dad was them waving, backed up by red-clad Liverpool fans also waving us goodbye, though in good Scouser fashion there were one or two behind mum and dad making what could be termed impolite gestures at my scarf.

"Not next Saturday," Maddy had said, "the one after."

Things have been so hectic I completely forgot about one salient little fact.

That Saturday is, of course, tomorrow.

Cockfosters
Oakwood
Southgate
Arnos Grove
Bounds Green
Wood Green
Turnpike Lane
Manor House
Finsbury Park
Arsenal
Holloway Road
Caledonian Road
King's Cross St. Pancras
Russell Square
Holborn
Covent Garden
Leicester Square
Piccadilly Circus
Green Park
Hyde Park Corner
Knightsbridge
South Kensington
Gloucester Road
Earl's Court
Barons Court
Hammersmith
Turnham Green
Acton Town

Ealing Common | South Ealing
North Ealing | Northfields
Park Royal | Boston Manor
Alperton | Osterley
Sudbury Town | Hounslow East
Sudbury Hill | Hounslow Central
South Harrow | Hounslow West
Rayners Lane | Hatton Cross
Eastcote | Heathrow T 1-2-3 → Heathrow T4
Ruislip Manor | Heathrow T5
Ruislip
Ickenham
Hillingdon
Uxbridge

# Finsbury Park

*Estimated time to Manor House 2 minutes*

*Estimated time to Bounds Green 10 minutes*

17h15

Back at Terminal 3 it was 13h42.

Ten minutes left to finish this off, Danny. It's now or never, I'm not coming back to it.

Maybe when we're all old and grey you can ask questions. I'll probably make up the answers, but there you go, that's life.

But first, a stational drink for Finsbury Park.

I've never been sure about this place. I know it's got a mosque, and there's been trouble here and the one time they had some problem at King's Cross so they started all of the relevant trains at Finsbury Park which was a complete disaster because it wasn't designed to take all the people who descended on it. Trains stop here before going on to any number of exciting destinations. But it's never had a place in memory or myth, like Clapham Junction in Up The Junction. It's a crossover place, people move from one platform to another, they cross from the Victoria Line to the Piccadilly Line, or to overland trains. They never stop and stare, never just while away the time watching the world go by.

So, I think the poor little over-worked place needs a special stational drink. I think it needs a special little area for special people to enjoy that special stational drink.

Danny, there's a special word that all children should be able to enjoy. And that is, "snug". Somewhere warm and cosy and safe. Once upon a time it was also the name for a special part of a pub, the snug – some pubs anyway. Even today, I read somewhere, you can still find the occasional snug in a pub. A private place, far from the public and prying eyes, the sort of place women could have a quiet drink and feel safe, or illicit lovers could meet for a stiff one and holding hands. And the local copper after hours or parish priest outside of confessional times could pop in for a quiet one out of sight.

Now there's an idea, Danny, maybe one day you and I set out and go find all the snugs still left in the world. We'd sit and enjoy a warming drink while listening to the stories of the ladies and the coppers and the parish priests who didn't want to be seen. And the lovers, if they'd give us a moment.

Anyway, a few years back there was a little Welsh fellow at the school I teach in – taught in. His parents had come to London looking for, I don't know, a better life, more money, better prospects, a career progression, something that they never found. Late one afternoon I came across the little boy sitting behind the bush looking miserable as sin – there's only one bush amongst the concrete – and, though he was too young to be in one of my classes, asked him what the problem was. He was waiting for his mum to pick him up. We had a little chat. Turned out to be the usual thing. He's called Alun, he's a little lad in a strange place, missing his old friends, surrounded by all these new and exotic and unfamiliar and frightening faces – and trust me some of the little buggers' faces scare the shits out of me – all he wants is to go home to the little village he knows and the friends he knows and his nans and grandads and the hills and fields and valleys and so on.

Not much I could do about that. But it was winter, getting dark, wet, all the rest, so I took him back to the staff room where at least he'd be in the warm. Taking pupils into the staff room is a huge no-no, it's the teachers' inner sanctum, somewhere to escape from the little brats, but everyone's gone home and I'm too tired to bother with things like that.

Alun is fascinated. He carefully and dutifully places his bag and winter coat on a seat close to the door before wandering around and gazing at things with awe. This is, to him, forbidden territory. It's an adventure. To me it's trying to find my bloody stuff and pack it away before heading home as soon as his mum has collected him.

At some point he peeked his head over the back of a chair – children, like cats, have the good sense to snuffle under and behind things in strange rooms to get a sense of where they are – and said, 'It's your den, like. The teachers' den.'

'In a way, I suppose.'

He paused and watched me for a while.

'We have a word in Welsh,' he said.

'What's that?'

'Kutch. It means a safe place. Somewhere snug and warm and safe, like your nan's bed under the eiderdown on a cold Sunday before your folks are awake.'

'Sounds nice,' I said, trying to avoid an image of all the teachers snuggled under nan's eiderdown on a cold Sunday morning.

'It's not quite kutch,' he decided, looking around.

'No, I suppose not,' I agreed. 'Not quite kutch.'

So the days go by and I see him maybe once a week as he travels in crocodiles from class to class, and I nod or give a wave and he smiles shyly and gives a little wave back. And then comes December and it's the last day before the Christmas break, and all the little ones are creating a racket and getting ready to go home to annoy their parents because once they've achieved their aim and left school they'll be immediately bored. I'm standing outside taking a break from my class who are also demob-happy, but show it by adopting a superior aloofness in contrast to the little ones excited chatter. Suddenly Alun is in front of me with a plastic carrier bag.

'We're going home,' he announced. 'For good.'

'Home?'

'Wales.'

'Happy?'

'Yes. Sort of.'

He handed me the bag.

'Kutch beer,' he said. 'I asked dad to get me some for you before we leave.'

I could see the label through the plastic: Cwytch. And it clicks. Cwytch, the untranslatable Welsh word for the security and warmth of a happy and dream-filled childhood. And more than that.

'Good luck,' he said, and scampered away towards the gate where his parents were waiting.

'Good luck,' I called. 'In Welsh,' I added to myself.

So, Finsbury Park, may you have a little Cwytch on every platform.

And through latte may I find and celebrate Cwytch.

We all deserve a bit of Cwytch in our lives.

Cheers.

We're almost there, Danny. Hold on.

This is the first part of the secret.

It's not much of a secret.

You've probably guessed it anyway.

I've never been good at keeping secrets.

Anyway.

So, there I am, being delayed by the blasted busies.

It's 13h42.

There's that movie about the Jamaican bob-sleigh team, Cool Runnings. They're completely useless. They haven't got a chance. But they have to take part in the Winter Olympics. Despite never having seen snow. They go through all sorts of heartbreak and humiliation, but make it through to the run-offs. Then, just when it looks like they might just avoid total scorn by actually reaching the finish line in their final heat, a nut comes loose and their bob-sleigh crashes and that's it, they're finished. But because they're there, because a man's got to do what a man's got to do, they suck in a final breath, struggle out from underneath the wreck, and carry the broken sleigh across the finish line on their shoulders. That was me then, Danny. I'd lost. A nut had come loose. But I had to cross the finish line. That was the only fucking reason I was still moving.

In Cool Runnings the Jamaicans get applauded by the people who had previously sneered at them, the Germans or Austrians, I think.

My audience was a couple of coppers tooled up to the eyebrows.

Out in the sunshine.

Terminal 3 check in almost in touching distance.

There's a stainless steel metal tube that goes around the buildings that house check-ins for Terminal 3. It's a couple of inches or so thick and raised to about a foot high. I think it's there to stop careless objects like runaway wheelie-bags crashing into the glass windows that go from the ground to the roof. People, being people, see it as an ideal place to park their backsides, stretch their legs, and enjoy the sunshine as so many were doing then.

I had my eyes on Check In C.

That's where Maddy would be.

That's where Maddy would have been before she checked in, went through security and flew out.

I could almost feel her.

Or the memory of her.

'If you'll just step this way for a few moments,' said Miss-I'm-In-Charge-you-aren't, shepherding me to the left.

'If you don't mind ...' I started.

'Just this way, sir,' she repeated.

I turned and glanced to where she was directing me. There were three police officers about thirty yards away with their backs to us, close to a long line of stacked trolleys.

'The bastard has landed,' said Young Clint behind me into his radio or whatever it was.

The three coppers turned and looked towards us. They too had an awesome amount of firepower strapped to their bodies.

Then they stepped back and to one side as if getting ready to greet us – or me in particular, for some reason.

And there was another fully armed copper sitting on her haunches looking at a black bag.

She turned to look at me.

She stood up and stepped aside.

And I realised it wasn't a black bag.

It was a young woman in black with her legs tucked up towards her chest and her face in her hands as if she were sobbing into them.

I took a deep breath.

I took a really, really fucking deep breath.

'Maddy!' I screamed and began to run towards her.

Fuck.

We're already at Manor House.

17h17

That was quick.

Good timing.

I've almost finished diluting the latte.

One last good strong dose left.

Manor House to Turnpike Lane is quite a stretch.

I might just be able to squeeze the rest of the story in.

Because, Danny, I'm sure you're asking yourself just one question.

At least one question.

Was your mum alive?

And if so, what did she do?

Did she welcome me with open arms?

Or did she grab one of the automatic rifles and try to drill me new oxygen pathways?

And did it leave any life changing scars?

Danny, I promise you, you'll never walk alone.

Cockfosters
Oakwood
Southgate
Arnos Grove
Bounds Green
Wood Green
Turnpike Lane
Manor House
Finsbury Park
Arsenal
Holloway Road
Caledonian Road
King's Cross St. Pancras
Russell Square
Holborn
Covent Garden
Leicester Square
Piccadilly Circus
Green Park
Hyde Park Corner
Knightsbridge
South Kensington
Gloucester Road
Earl's Court
Barons Court
Hammersmith
Turnham Green
Acton Town

Ealing Common          South Ealing
North Ealing           Northfields
Park Royal             Boston Manor
Alperton               Osterley
Sudbury Town           Hounslow East
Sudbury Hill           Hounslow Central
South Harrow           Hounslow West
Rayners Lane           Hatton Cross ←
Eastcote               Heathrow T 1-2-3 → Heathrow T4
Ruislip Manor          Heathrow T5
Ruislip
Ickenham
Hillingdon
Uxbridge

# Manor House

*Estimated time to Turnpike Lane 4 minutes*

*Estimated time to Bounds Green 8 minutes*

17h17

I once asked my pupils if they knew what a manor house was. They looked puzzled for a while until one of them piped up with, 'It's a tube station, innit?' I explained that, yes, there was a tube station named Manor House, and it would have been named after a manor house in the area. It was part of my long-term plan to turn the little shits into class warriors: a manor house is a medieval remnant left over from European feudal systems. It was the residence of the lord of the manor, to whom the peasants would have to pay homage and taxes. There would have been a pecking order, from the lord through the gentry down to the common vassal or villein, from which we get the word villain, or thief. Which, in those days, would have been my pupils. Their status would have lain somewhere below that of the hunting dogs of the manor. Actually it would have been below that of the shadow of the droppings of the toy dogs of the lady of the manor. Sadly my kids were always up for a revolution against their teachers, trying to turn them into enemies of the establishment was a lost cause.

I had thought that maybe taking them to see the manor house after which the station was named might help them imagine what it would have been like. When I made enquiries as to whether the building still existed I was told it no longer did, but it had originally been a public house, i.e. a pub. So I quietly dropped the notion. I don't doubt there's no shortage of revolutions hatched in pubs, I very much doubt whether any survived the hangovers.

Speaking of which, Danny, here's the most important question of all: what stational celebrationally drink are we going to come up with for dear old Manor House?

We've only got a few minutes left.

I feel sorry for Manor House.

It looks lonely, poor thing.

There's a song from World War I that goes something like,
'There's a long, long road a-winding, into the land of my dreams, where
the nightingales are singing, and a white moon beams.'
Something, something, something.
Something about, 'until I end up with you'.
Your basic love-lament. Young boy-men torn from their loved ones, off
to fight a war. They get there and just want to come home instead.
You know what I think, Danny?
I think we invent a whole new drink just for Manor House.
I feel like it.
We'll call it the Moon Beam.
It consists of equal parts Love and Hope.
And Despair.
And Darkness.
You know why, Danny?
No, nor do I.
Just because.
That's life.
So here's to you. Manor House, you get to invent your own stational
drink.
And everyone who drinks it is followed by a moon shadow.
A moon shadow.
You just have to explain why it's called a Moon beam.
Danny, once I got over-excited about your mum. I picked her up around
the waist and swung her around a few times. I was lost in the delirium of
love. It was when we were in Liverpool one time. I remember, because
mum was there. She put her hand on my arm as I put your mum down
and said,
'Be careful, Mark, Madeleine's not a toy doll.'
And your mum said,
'It's okay, mum. I enjoyed that. He's actually quite gentle when he
remembers.'
When I remember?
I'm always gentle with Maddy.

Anyway, back at Terminal 3.

So, there we are.

Outside in the sun. Outside the check-in to Terminal 3.

I've just recognised your mum and I'm running towards her.

She's sitting hunched up on this steel pole thing.

She looks up through tear-filled eyes.

She wipes them with the back of her hand.

Then she recognises me.

She jumps up.

'Mark!' she screams.

And then she's running toward me her arms wide open.

And I'm running towards her, my arms wide open.

And we're fucking lucky it was only about twenty or thirty yards, so we didn't get a chance to pick up speed. We would have crashed when we collided. It would have caused an earthquake or something.

Instead she jumps up at me, I catch her around the waist, lift her off the ground and swing her around, she locks her legs around my waist this time to make sure I wasn't going anywhere, and she's got her arms around my neck while we both try to kiss each other.

'Mark!'

'Maddy!'

Look, Danny, I know it's embarrassing, but we were young and in love.

I'm not sure how long we were completely wrapped up in each other, both figuratively and literally, but at some point I realised that there were only four coppers left, Madame Firepower, Young Clint and two others. They were looking around, scanning the area, checking for potential threats, only occasionally glancing at us with almost blank looks, but with a hint of smiles on their faces. With a little bit of encouragement I managed to convince Maddy to release my waist from her legs and stand on them, but her arms still held me like a limpet, her face squashed into my chest, her eyes crying and closed. One of the coppers noticed that I was slowly joining the rest of the world again.

'We found her here sobbing her heart out, so we asked her what the problem was,' he said. 'She said she was waiting for her boyfriend but he hadn't turned up. When we asked her what her boyfriend looked like she said you were a complete bastard. So we radioed to all our colleagues asking them to keep an eye out for someone in a hurry who looked like a complete bastard.'

'When we saw you running towards Terminal 2 I turned to my colleague and asked, does that look like a complete bastard?' said Young Clint. 'And she replied, if you mean in a metaphorical sense, then yes, you could be right.'

He gave me the biggest, slowest wink I have ever seen. And then added,

'She also dropped mention that you were wearing a wrist brace and had lumps of your head taken out. That made identification a little easier.'

'We just couldn't understand why you were running towards Terminal 2 when she was here at Terminal 3,' said Madame Firepower.

'I thought I saw a sign pointing towards Terminal 3 that way,' I explained. 'I think it was actually a sign to Terminal 2 but I misread it because it was partly obscured by a kid's balloon.'

'Ah, that explains it,' said Young Clint, 'I told my colleague there'd be a good reason.'

'Up until our other colleagues reported you running towards Terminal 3 arrivals. We thought you might be going through there to departures for some reason. Until they saw you running back.'

'Yes, I saw a sign to Terminal 3 and was in such a hurry I didn't realise it was for arrivals until I was almost there.'

'Well, it gave us time to saunter back and be waiting for you before you got here and began charging around Terminal 3 like a bull in a China shop upsetting everyone and wasting your time.'

'Thank you officers,' I said, trying to get Maddy to disentangle. 'It was very kind of you. She's rather precious to me.'

'Oh, Mark I'm so sorry,' said Maddy, still clinging tight.

'It's okay, my sweet, I'm here now,' I said in what, in other circumstances would have sounded like the worst news ever.

'There's a restaurant cum pub over there in arrivals,' said the woman copper. 'The Market Gardener. It's on the left, ground floor. You might want to get out of the limelight.'

I looked around. There were a fair number of people not only enjoying the sunshine, but also this melodrama of two lovers reunited, and every single one of the sons of bitches had a camera. And the lenses were pointed straight at us.

'Good point, officer, and thank you very much again.'

'Our pleasure, sir, it helps brighten up the long hours of boredom. Now we'd better carry on doing what we're paid for. Can't spend all day playing Cupid, now can we? People might complain.'

The four coppers lifted fingers to their caps in salute and wandered off with their lethal cargo ready for action. Just by chance the stag and hen party people had staggered out from the exit and were trundling towards us with menace in their eyes. Their direction was impeded by the four very polite and well-armed officers. There appeared to be a short exchange of pleasant advice from the police officers and the disgruntled groups carried on their way towards check-in X and away from us.

I sighed with relief. It had been a long day, I had, against the odds, found Maddy, and the last thing I needed was a punch up with a stag and hen party.

'Come on, Maddy,' I said, 'where's your luggage?'

'Oh, Mark, I am sorry. I really am,' she said, still clutching me.

I managed to disengage one arm to pick up her suitcase, a small travelling one I recognised, the one she had taken to Cardiff. And then I took her and the suitcase across the piazza to arrivals and inside, where we found the Market Gardener.

'Oh, Mark, I really, really am sorry,' repeated Maddy as I placed her in a chair.

'Now, Brat, enough of that,' I said sternly. 'I'm going to get us some drinks. Here's a handkerchief. You wait here and blow your nose.'

I think it was the "Brat" that did it. She knows I only call her Brat when I'm confident that god's in his heaven, the sun is shining in the sky, and all's well.

I came back with the drinks, a lager for me and a red wine for her. Her eyes were still sparkling from the tears, but she was smiling once again. Or trying to smile, anyway.

'Cheers,' I said, sitting down next to her, very closely next to her, just in case. I put an arm around her to make sure. 'I need this to rehydrate. You won't believe what a day I've had.'

'Oh, Mark, I said I'm sorry.'

'I know, sweetness, about a million times. Just promise me you will never leave me again.'

She looked at me in her most serious little-girl-being-honest way.

'I promise I will never, ever leave you again, Mark. No matter what you do. I realised that as I sat outside. I couldn't go through and board the plane. I couldn't leave you. I just couldn't.'

I stroked her hair away from her eyes. I hadn't missed that "No matter what you do". Translation: I don't like you screwing your students but I suppose I will have to learn to tolerate it, just like other women down the ages.

'I didn't do anything, pet,' I said. 'I did not screw around with that Sharon Runny-nose. I have never slept with any of my pupils.'

A passing waitress dropped some cutlery.

'And in case you're wondering, no, I haven't slept with anyone else since we started going out. And I never will. Not ever. I love you too much.'

Maddy looked into my eyes as if searching for something.

'Promise?' she asked.

How many different ways can you promise something? "Cross my heart and hope to die"? "Scout's honour"?

'On the life of our little one,' I said.

She looked at me and gasped.

'I'd forgotten about that,' she said. 'I was so terrified that you'd decided to dump me. Nothing else seemed to matter.'

'So you are ... you know?'

'Yes,' she said, looking down at her glass. 'I'm sorry, Mark, I never meant to be, it's just that – look, you know what I think of women who deliberately get pregnant to keep their man – Mark, it was an accident, really it was.'

'I'm sure it was, sweetness.'

'I need to powder my nose,' she said, getting up. 'Back in a minute.'

Translation: I need some me-time to think.

But I was going to keep my eyes on every single possible exit just in case.

While she was gone I ordered another round. I needed some drink time in order not to think. I knew what I wanted. I didn't need to think about it.

When she came back I took the chance to visit the gents myself. When I returned she had definitely got her colour back, and her chin was set in a determined sort of a way, the look I identified with her having made a Decision. And so it was.

'Mark, I've been thinking,' she said, taking my hand. 'You remember, I said the lowest thing a woman can do is to get pregnant to force a man to marry her, and I stand by that. I don't expect you to do anything you don't want to. I went into this with my eyes open, and I'm not blaming anyone but myself. There's this girl called Sheila, we used to know each other back in Oz. She lives in London now, in Hounslow West. She said I could stay at her place for a while if I needed it. So I've just phoned her and she said it's fine. So I'll stay there for a week or two. You and I can talk each day while we work out where we are and where we want to go.'

Coming into Turnpike Lane.

17h22.

Be at Bounds Green by half-five.

And then a short bus ride home.

Cockfosters
Oakwood
Southgate
Arnos Grove
Bounds Green
Wood Green
Turnpike Lane
Manor House
Finsbury Park
Arsenal
Holloway Road
Caledonian Road
King's Cross St. Pancras
Russell Square
Holborn
Covent Garden
Leicester Square
Piccadilly Circus
Green Park
Hyde Park Corner
Knightsbridge
South Kensington
Gloucester Road
Earl's Court
Barons Court
Hammersmith
Turnham Green
Acton Town

Ealing Common        South Ealing
North Ealing         Northfields
Park Royal           Boston Manor
Alperton             Osterley
Sudbury Town         Hounslow East
Sudbury Hill         Hounslow Central
South Harrow         Hounslow West
Rayners Lane         Hatton Cross  ←
Eastcote             Heathrow T 1-2-3 ⟶ Heathrow T4
Ruislip Manor        Heathrow T5
Ruislip
Ickenham
Hillingdon
Uxbridge

# Turnpike Lane

*Estimated time to Wood Green 2 minutes*

*Estimated time to Bounds Green 4 minutes*

17h22

Danny, I have never before had a problem with unfinished business. As far as I'm concerned things that need finishing will get finished at some stage, and if they don't they never did. Life moves on, time moves on, pupils move on, lovers move on. We will now, for instance, after Turnpike Lane, get to Wood Green station and then to Bounds Green Station, where I get off to go back to the house in Muswell Hill. I dare say they might reverse the train out at Wood Green, but there'll be another shortly after. The point is that, no matter what happens, I can't just freeze time. There's a metaphor in there somewhere.

This train, for example, is now moving on. Au revoir, Turnpike Lane.

I almost forgot. A stational drink for Turnpike Lane.

I think we should make it blue, in honour of the great British Bobby, even if they are tooled up to the eyes with sub-machine guns.

A Blue Lagoon. That's what we'll give Turnpike Lane. Not only in grateful thanks to the busies, the boys and girls in blue, but because that's probably where they dream of being during the long cold nights of winter.

While they're on duty, that is. I presume they go home to their spouses or lovers or partners or whatever when off duty. I don't know whether it's the uniform or the job or what, but somehow when I see a copper I don't tend to think of their social or private lives, especially not when they're carrying lethal hardware.

Still, they'd make brilliant personalised Christmas cards. "Have a Cool Yule from Clint and Sharon", showing them smiling at the camera, wearing their uniforms and tooled up to the eyebrows, with a note at the bottom saying, 'or else.' And a sprig of mistletoe in Sharon's cap. I'd kiss her.

Getting into Wood Green. That was quick.

Cockfosters
Oakwood
Southgate
Arnos Grove
Bounds Green
Wood Green
Turnpike Lane
Manor House
Finsbury Park
Arsenal
Holloway Road
Caledonian Road
King's Cross St. Pancras
Russell Square
Holborn
Covent Garden
Leicester Square
Piccadilly Circus
Green Park
Hyde Park Corner
Knightsbridge
South Kensington
Gloucester Road
Earl's Court
Barons Court
Hammersmith
Turnham Green
Acton Town

Ealing Common
North Ealing
Park Royal
Alperton
Sudbury Town
Sudbury Hill
South Harrow
Rayners Lane
Eastcote
Ruislip Manor
Ruislip
Ickenham
Hillingdon
Uxbridge

South Ealing
Northfields
Boston Manor
Osterley
Hounslow East
Hounslow Central
Hounslow West
Hatton Cross ←
Heathrow T 1-2-3 → Heathrow T4
Heathrow T5

512

# Wood Green

*Estimated time to Bounds Green 2 minutes*

17h25

Good old Wood Green, eh, Danny. Seems like it's years since we left it this morning. What time was that, six o'clock in the morning or something ridiculous.

I'm tempted to give Wood Green a special yellow stational drink to match the colour of the tiles. Advocaat mixed with gin or something equally revolting. But so many other Piccadilly Line stations have similar matching tiles. I think they got them as a job lot from We-saw-you-coming Incorporated.

But, no, Danny, I've been drinking so much diluted latte I need some strong coffee to sober up. So my gift to all who work at or pass through Wood Green tube station is that well-known cure for feeling down.

Irish Coffee.

Lovely.

I'll have a double.

Cheers.

If you're happy and you know it clap your hands.

Clap clap clap.

You know, Danny, I've been thinking about the kids and Cabaret. Maybe, just maybe, we should give it another go. They put their hearts and souls into it, bless them. They deserve a decent shot.

I'll think about it. There are other things to deal with before then.

Doors are closing.

Bye-bye Wood Green.

We'll be at Bounds Green in about two or three minutes, which is a pity.

You want to know why it's a pity, Danny?

Danny, I'll tell you why it's a pity.

That sounds like a song.

I'm sure I could write a song like that.

It's a real pity.

Okay, Danny, I'll leave the song till later.

I don't think I've ever regretted arriving at my destination so much before.

It's a real pity.

It's a real pity, Danny, because it means I'm going to have to wake your mum.

Poor thing. She's been fast asleep on my shoulder since Terminal 3. She's exhausted. Probably hasn't had a decent night's kip for ages.

Stay with Sheila for a week or two?

She's fucking nuts.

Maddy, I said, back in The Market Gardener, if you even suggest not coming back with me to Muswell Hill, first I will find the nearest lake and dunk you in it. Then I will tie you up and take you to Liverpool and hand you over to the care of mum. And the only person who can get around mum is me. And even then I think I might be fooling myself. So, are we going home or are we going lake hunting?

She gave me her determined little girl face. On anything else I probably would have given in to get some peace. On anything else she probably would have stood her ground. I'll give her that. When she's made up her mind she doesn't change it easily.

She can be a right pain in the arse that way.

'You wouldn't dare,' she said.

'What, dunk you in a lake or take you to mum? 'I asked.

She glared at me.

'Dunk me in a lake.'

'Yes, I would.'

'Wouldn't.'

Pause.

'Okay, I'll just take you up to Liverpool then.'

She folded her arms.

'I don't want to go.'

'I'll tell mum on you.'

She scowled.

And then she stuck her tongue out at me, and I knew I'd won.

So we said goodbye to the Market Gardener and made our way back to the Underground station. We followed the signs down a ramp, around a corner, along a bit, and onto a travelator, which is where I realised that that was the point where I'd turned away from Terminal 3 Arrivals to go back to Terminal 3 Departures. I could have carried on to Arrivals and crossed the piazza to Departures. But them I would have missed my guardian angel, Madame Firepower.

So we got on the travelator. Stood with our arms around each other as young lovers do, blocking the way and irritating the shit out of people in a hurry. Got off, wandered arm in arm to the next one, ditto. Then the last one, ditto. And into the Underground ticket area.

Through ticket barriers like the ones I had briefly thought of vaulting just a short while before – glad I didn't, I don't think even an Olympian hurdler would relish the challenge.

Then a spot of canoodling while we waited for the train.

You know what, Danny?

I ended up carrying her suitcase the whole bloody way.

Some things never change.

Time to wake Sleeping Beauty.

17h30

Stopped in the tunnel.

Danny, how's this for a conversation: I kissed your mum on the forehead and she opened her eyes and looked at me. Then she smiled, closed her eyes again, snuggled even closer into my shoulder, and asked,

'Are we there yet?'

'Almost, my sweet.'

'Mmmm.'

'Maddy?'

'Yes?'

'Will you marry me?'

'Okay.'

'Good.'

Okay?

Okay?

What sort a response is that to a marriage proposal?

Just fucking okay?

We've just agreed to spend the rest of our lives together.

Well, thinking about it, that does sound pretty sort of okay, I suppose.

'Mark?'

'Yes, my sweet?'

'Shall we go up to mum and dad this weekend to break the news?'

'That'll be tomorrow then? Tomorrow being Saturday?'

'Yes.'

'Good thinking, sweetness. It'll give us just enough time to choose an engagement ring. We can do that on our way home. Or even pop up to that middle-class shithole called Brent Cross shopping mall if you really want.'

She opened her eyes again and smiled up at me.

'Let's not tell them right away, Mark. Let's see how long it takes them to guess.'

'With you wearing an engagement ring? Mum will spot it from a hundred yards. Actually, she's got a sixth sense. She probably knows already, somehow.'

'Well, let's see how long it takes dad to work it out.'

'Hokay. His eyesight isn't as good as mum's. I reckon he'll only spot it at the fifty yard mark. Then he'll go all misty-eyed and get his handkerchief out. He's soppy that way.'

'Mmmmm. So are you.'

'No I'm not.'

'Yes you are, darling.'

'Okay.'

Danny, another special stational drink, this time for Bounds Green.

Champagne.

I can't stand the fucking stuff.

I'll put some whiskey in a flute and give it bubbles. We'll call it Champagne.

Sorted.

See you in a few months or so, pumpkin.

**Author's Notes**

The 13h30 Qantas flight to Melbourne Mark was chasing now departs at 13h15.

In the original edition Mark and Maddy went for restorative drinks in a pub-restaurant in the departures section of Terminal 3. But they changed the name of that shortly after, so in this addition it became The Market Gardener in the arrivals section, which was still there the last time I visited.

**Other novels by Bill Dughaille:**

**The FFSG series (aka the Wellbury Chronics)**

*Summers*
The first in the FFSG series.
Detective Sergeant Frank Summers is a man on a mission: to keep his head down, stay out of trouble and enjoy the relaxed atmosphere of the easy-going, genteel town of Wellbury, his new posting. It's a town just made for him, where, he believes, even the criminals take bank holidays off. But, while perceptive in his professional life, he tends to miss the subtleties in his private life. In this case he fails to realise that his own tranquillity is being threatened by three women and a philanderer. The fact that the women in question are his boss, his constable and the local pathologist adds just the touch of danger to his life that he had hoped to avoid. The philanderer has been dead several decades. The women are very much alive. And ticking.

*The Eighty-five-percenters*
The second in the FFSG series.
Detective Sergeant Frank Summers is faced with an unexpected crisis as the staid citizens of the genteel town of Wellbury rapidly descend into disorganised anarchy after a sociology professor announces on radio that eighty-five percent of the population will die in a coming cull. The prediction appears to be coming true as apparently total strangers are felled one by one according to a list of the ten-most-disliked Wellburians, from nagging neighbours to estate agents ... and the police, at a poorly performing number ten. But Frank fails to realise that there is a graver danger closer to home. Three women have decided that he is their responsibility: his boss, his constable and the local pathologist have agreed to become best of enemies. Now they intend to re-arrange his fate the way it should be. And they aren't asking anyone's permission.

*Fakes, Fraud and Deception*
The third in the FFSG series.

Detective Sergeant Frank Summers is in the doghouse, despite having recently arrested an internationally sought con-artist. And since he is in the doghouse he has no intention of pointing out that there is something very strange about the attractive French police woman who has come to interview the arrested man, not to mention the two detectives claiming to be from Scotland Yard. Oh, no, he is going to stay well out of the way this time. Definitely.

### Jokers
The fourth in the FFSG series.

The doctors have pronounced Detective Sergeant Frank Summers physically fit following recovery after his shooting, but his colleagues fear that his sense of humour was extracted along with the bullet. They are, as always, more than willing to interfere in his life in the pursuit of a good cause. If that wasn't enough, a bunch of criminals calling themselves the Joker Gang are laughing at him, the university students are creating mayhem during their rag week, and someone called The Shocker is trying to kill him. The only advantage is that it take his mind off of the ultimatum the three women in his life have given him, one that he has only until the Sunday to resolve. Or leave town.

### Prophecies
The fifth in the FFSG series.

Detective Sergeant Summers is under a hex, otherwise known as his colleagues. First they don't want him to get married, then it is imperative it must happen. Then they decide that a prophecy has been made which threatens the wedding. They don't believe in prophecies, but aren't sure that prophecies understand that. So they'll have to Do Something About It. And if their bumbling efforts aren't enough to ensure he never makes it to the altar, he has to cope with visiting aliens and resident ghosts. He does have tiny Squishy to protect him, but what match can even this plucky little kitten be against a prospective mother-in-law?

### Loonymoon

The sixth in the FFSG series.

The Inspectors Summers have tied the knot and embarked on their honeymoon in a small family-run hotel in Normandy. She has very definite ideas of what she wants out of a honeymoon: to set a seal on their love, and to form a foundation for life-long devotion. He just wants to nick a French police officer's kepi. He had a Bobby's helmet nicked from him once by a French girl while he was on crowd duty one New Year's Eve in London, and now he intends to return the favour. Neither is about to achieve their aim unless they can solve the mystery of the woman in the bath and the missing heroin. Which means pitting their minds against the French Inspectors Simenon. That's Mr and Mrs Simenon, whose marriage has gone beyond the rocks and is now beating itself to death against humdrum reality. One or either or both or neither could be the guilty crumpet. More importantly, is their marriage a portent of what could become of the Loonymooners? Ultimately the decisive question could well be: which side do the peas go?

### Hordes

The seventh in the FFSG series.

Detective Inspector Frank Summers has been booked off work following a near fatal anaphylactic shock. His wife is determined that he should obey his doctor's orders. As she is also his boss that should be simple. But he is determined to identify the perpetrator or perpetrators behind a series of attacks on little old ladies. Both their efforts are impeded by various movements becoming increasingly militant. The police station appears to have gone feminist. The Old Birds army (TOBs, Women Only) is planning a pre-emptive defence of helpless little old ladies. The Cult of The Clueless (TCoTC, Men Only) are demanding their right to ignorance. The Religious Once are threatening outright violence if their tolerant beliefs are not respected. Various New Age and Old Hippy believers, followers and troublemakers are descending on Wellbury in search of ley lines. Frank is embroiled in an e-mail game of double-chess with an anonymous person calling himself A Mason who sends messages which might make some sense if anybody could work out what they meant, but whatever they are they sound distinctly threatening. Frank and Frieda are running out of time as they approach Demonstration Day, when TOBs and TCoTC plan on settling the Religious Once's hash.

And, being off work, it's Frank's turn to cook dinner.

**Others:**

### The Window

Little does Jim Allbright realise just how much paperwork his letter containing a simple enquiry to his local council is about to produce, nor the strange events he will experience as a result of the 'system'. But if the system cannot be beaten the interchange of letters can be used to have a little fun and get to know some of the people struggling behind it, especially the woman who signs herself as 'Sandi (pp the Administrator)', and perhaps, one day even meet her.

### Diary of a Sane Man

In a cross between 'Last Of The Summer Wine' and 'One Flew Over The Cuckoo's Nest', set against a backdrop of the brave new world of New Labour's end of honeymoon, Fred is the Last Cynical Optimistic Realist.

Believing that he's found the perfect niche – three square meals a day plus all the newspapers he can read just for occasionally pretending to be mad – he's not going to be the one to rock the apple cart. Oh, no.

Safe from the wiles of women and the woes of the world, he's not going to rock the boat. Oh, no.

No, he's just going to sit and observe, and comment quietly on the insanity of life outside.

Well, maybe just little one tug of the loose strand of wool on life's jersey ...

Did you know they elected a monkey as mayor in Hartlepool?

### The Weekend At Longwood

A whodunnit in the classic sense, set against the backdrop of World War II and the trials, tribulations and romances of nine suspects.

A group of friends get together during the last weekend of August 1939 at the rural retreat named Longwood, just a few miles from Portsmouth. They are there to celebrate the last time they will see Georgina Riley, famed American novelist and socialite, for some time, as she is scheduled to leave for her native New York in order to marry her childhood sweetheart. During the afternoon they good-humouredly assign to each other the most suitable names of the nine muses, the daughters of Zeus and Mnemosyne:

Calliope: the muse of epic poetry and rhetoric

Clio: history

Erato: love poems and mimicry

Euterpe: lyric poetry

Melpomene: tragedy

Polymnia: hymns to the gods and heroes

Terpsichore: dance

Thalia: comedy

Urania: astronomy, astrology and prophecy

The following morning Georgina is discovered in her bedroom covered in blood, her throat slit, barely alive. Her American maid is dead. A tiara Georgina had been flaunting the day before has disappeared.

Detective Inspector Rudman arrives to investigate. But with Georgina in a coma and no solid evidence there is little he can do apart from haunt their lives. With Germany's invasion of Poland a week later they disperse across the land, some to the air-force, some to the army, others to reserved civilian jobs.

But Rudman does not give up. Wherever they are he can be found. Whatever other duties he is tasked to, he will find time to keep tabs on them. Whatever the defeats and victories of the Allied cause, he has only one aim: to find the person responsible for the murder done that weekend in Longwood.

The war ends; some of the Muses have survived, some not. Some have prospered, some married, some matured, others have found despair. And then comes invitation to spend another weekend at Longwood. The message is that Rudman has found the evidence he has been looking for.

And so one of the surviving couples motor slowly down to Portsmouth, remembering the original weekend, the trials and the tribulations of the past years, and wonder: what will be revealed during the coming weekend at Longwood?

### *Firelight*

A modern-day tale of an ordinary family gathering at Christmas; the good, the bad, the dysfunctional and the forgotten.

George Browne and his wife Winifred have retired to a large, run-down pile in the country. Rumour has it that it was once the abode of a mad aristocratic family with a penchant for Satanism, and that both they and their victims still haunt the corridors. Other rumours are that it was a lunatic asylum for much of the nineteenth and twentieth century, and bodies of the inhabitants are buried around the large gardens in unmarked graves.

The Brownes are an unremarkable retired couple who, depending on who you might ask, have bought it as an investment, or alternatively as somewhere with enough bedrooms to accommodate their children, grand-children, and the little baby great-grandchildren. Too often in the past excuses have been made at special times, the most common of which has been of the 'I don't want to put you to any trouble' variety. That excuse can no longer hold water.

Now it is approaching Christmas. Winter has set in, but the house is snug with oil heaters and real fires. As the various relations arrive, or don't arrive, it becomes clearer why invitations might have been refused in the past. The men of the family believe in having their way. The women of the family are strong-willed in their own different ways, and have various means of getting what they want.

The guests of the family – friends, boyfriends, girlfriends, wives and husbands – discover that their partners have a totally different side to them as the explosive hatreds of long-nurtured fights and feuds simmer to the surface before quickly boiling over.

One evening Winifred Browne encourages them to each tell a story as they sit in the lounge with the large fire warming them, the television off, no access to broadband, computers or mobile connections. Reluctantly at first they begin. As each evening passes: with different members taking turns, they announce in stories the feelings and hopes they cannot voice in public.

Finally it's the turn of Winifred Browne. Her story will be the one that tells them who they are, where they come from, and maybe why they have turned out the way they have.

### ... *13* ...

This is a story about a trial that never took place. The prosecuting counsel wasn't a nine-foot high vulture wearing what looked like a budgie as a wig; the defence counsel wasn't short and roly-poly and didn't wear a huge bright-blue-rinse wig. The defendant wasn't called Norah the Nose, the litigant wasn't known as Edgar The Ears. The judge wasn't called Judge Beak. The jury did not include a Quiet American, Miss Strawberry Mousse, The Major, Hugo The Accountant, Miss F, Miss F's Mother, Mr Sleepy, Vicar Preachy, Mrs Baggs, Mrs Plum, a Prim Maiden Aunt, Clowns named Clyde and Bonnie, or a Nun With Guitar who didn't speak in a deep Russian accent and didn't wear Goth make-up and tight-fitting sequinned habits which didn't shimmer with thousands of blinking, winking dots. The narrator did not fall in love with the Nun With Guitar who wasn't and hadn't. And it's only ever ... 11 ... 12 ... ... 14 ... 15 ... There never is a ... 13 ...

For further details on these visit:

www. dughaille. info